This book belongs to

Peggy Shields

231 N. Hazel St. La Habra, Calif.

The SHIRLEY TEMPLE TREASURY

The SHIRLEY

Illustrated with drawings by ROBERT PATTERSON

and with photographs from motion pictures featuring Shirley Temple

RANDOM HOUSE, NEW YORK

TEMPLE

Treasury

FOREWORD

"Is Shirley Temple a little girl or a mother?"

Many children ask this question nowadays, I am told. It's little wonder. One day they see me on television as a grownup, acting in some of my favorite fairy tales on the Shirley Temple Storybook program. The next day—or often even the same day—they see on that same television screen a re-run of the motion pictures in which I appeared as a curly-haired child.

It was in my role as a mother that I put together my favorite stories for the *Storybook* which was published last year. The warmth and appreciation with which that book was received was a thrilling experience for me.

One recent day, as some friends and I were looking through my scrapbook of old movie photographs, it occurred to me that readers might welcome a collection of the stories in which I played the leading roles for motion pictures when I was a little girl.

There were too many, of course, to put into one book, but the four you will find here—*Heidi, Rebecca of Sunnybrook Farm, Captain January,* and *The Little Colonel*—are all dearly loved stories with which every child is familiar. They are cherished because they are perfect examples of the art of good storytelling, tug at the heartstrings as few modern stories do, and provide enduring satisfaction to young and old alike. Each reader seems eager to establish a sense of identification with the captivating heroines, whose honesty, loyalty, and friendliness cannot fail to win admiration. The underlying theme in all four stories is that one should make the best of one's surroundings whether good or bad, and adopt a cheerful, optimistic attitude despite hardship and disappointment. Such tales will always appeal to boys and girls, whose noblest instincts and aspirations are awakened and strengthened through such classic reading as this.

To all the young in heart, therefore, I fondly dedicate this *Treasury.*

Shirley Temple.

HEIDI

One clear sunny morning in June two figures could be seen climbing a narrow mountain path in the Swiss Alps. One was a tall, strong-looking girl named Dete, the other a five-year-old child whom she was leading by the hand and whose little cheeks glowed bright red through her sunburnt skin.

And this was hardly to be wondered at, for in spite of the hot June sun, the child was bundled up as if to keep off the bitterest frost.

After an hour's climb they came to the hamlet of Dorfli, halfway up the mountain, which had once been Dete's home. Heads popped out from all of the doors.

"Hello, Dete! Where are you going?" her old friends wanted to know.

Dete did not pause to reply. She held tight to the child's hand and hurried on. But when her friend Barbel called, "Wait a minute, Dete. If you're going up the mountain, I'll walk with you," Dete stopped. The child immediately let go her hand and sat down on the ground.

"Are you tired, Heidi?" asked her companion.

"No, I'm hot," answered the child.

"We shall soon get to the top now. You must walk bravely on a little longer, and take good long steps, and in another hour we shall be there," said Dete.

Now Barbel joined them and walked on ahead with Dete, while Heidi wandered behind them.

"Where are you off to with the little girl? It's your sister's child, isn't it?" asked Barbel.

"Yes. I'm taking her to live with her grandfather," Dete answered.

"With the Alm-Uncle? Dete!" exclaimed Barbel. "Have you lost your senses? You know what he's like. Everybody's afraid of him. He'll make you take her home again."

Dete tossed her head. "He can't do that! He's her grandfather! I've taken care of the child since her mother died, and I'm not going to give up the good position I've been offered, just for her sake. And I certainly can't take her with me."

"Why, where are you going?"

"To Frankfurt," answered Dete.

"Well, I'm glad I am not that child!" exclaimed Barbel. "The old man up there looks wild, with his bushy brows and his great beard. He never sets foot in church; and when he comes down to the village, everybody keeps out of his way."

"He's her grandfather, and he's got to take care of her," Dete insisted.

"Why does he live as he does?" asked Barbel.

"They say when he was a young man he got in with evil company and lost his farm and everything he had," Dete answered. "His parents died of grief. Then he himself disappeared and nobody heard from him until, years later, he came back with a young son, Tobias. When he found all doors closed to him, he moved to Dorfli."

"Why is he called the Alm-Uncle?" Barbel wanted to know.

"Our family called him Uncle because his son was married to my sister Adelheid, and soon the whole village called him Uncle. When Tobias was killed in an accident, leaving my sister and Heidi alone, people said it was a judgment upon the Uncle. He grew bitter and moved to the top of Alm Mountain, vowing he would never come down. That's why people call him the Alm-Uncle."

"Well!" exclaimed Barbel when she heard this. "How you can take the child to live with him, I don't know!" At this she turned toward a little hut in a hollow and said, "I have to stop here to see about some spinning. Good luck!"

Trailing behind Dete and Barbel while they talked, Heidi had made friends with a young goatherd, Peter, who lived in a hut halfway up the Alm. Peter was eleven years old. He knew many places where there were good shrubs for his goats to nibble, and he was in the habit of leading his flock aside from the beaten path. At first Heidi had watched Peter as he sprang nimbly here and there on his bare feet. Then she tried to follow him.

It was hot, though, and her clothes were too heavy. All at once she sat down on the ground, and as fast as her little fingers could move, began pulling off her red, woolen scarf and her shoes and stockings. Then the dresses came off, all the dresses Dete had put on her to save the trouble of carrying them.

Now Heidi stood up, clad only in a light petticoat, and stretched out her little bare arms with glee. She put all her clothes together in a tidy heap, and went jumping and climbing after Peter and the goats.

Dete was very cross when she saw what Heidi had done, and scolded her. She made Peter go back and pick up the clothes.

At the end of another hour's climb, Heidi and Dete and Peter reached the Alm-Uncle's hut on the top of the mountain. On a bench before the hut sat the old man. Heidi went straight to him and said, "Good evening, Grandfather!"

"What's the meaning of this?" he asked

"Good evening, Uncle," said Dete, stepping forward. "I've brought Tobias' little girl to you. I've done my duty by her. Now you must do yours."

"So!" said the old man. "What can a child do with me up here?

"That's your affair," retorted Dete. "If harm comes to her, you will be answerable."

At that the old man rose, his eyes flashing. "Be off with you," he thundered.

"Good-bye, then," said Dete quickly. "And good-bye to you, too, Heidi."

While the Alm-Uncle sat down to think, Heidi ran off to investigate her new surroundings. She peeped into the shed where the goats were kept. She went behind the hut to the tall fir trees and listened to the wind blowing through their branches. When she came back, her grandfather was still sitting on his bench, puffing at his pipe. She walked up to him.

"What is it you want?" he asked.

"I want to see what you have inside the house," answered Heidi.

"Bring your bundle of clothes in with you," he said, rising and opening the door.

"I shan't want them any more," was her

prompt answer.

The old man turned and looked at her. "And why shall you not want them any more?" he asked.

"Because I want to go about like the goats with their thin light legs."

"Well, you can do so if you like," said her grandfather, "but bring the things in, we must put them in the cupboard."

The hut had only one large room. Heidi took it in at a glance: the table, the chair, the old man's bed, the kettle hanging over the fireplace. A door in the wall opened onto a cupboard.

On one shelf were dishes; on another, bread, cheese, and dried meat; on the third, the Uncle's clothes. Heidi pushed her bundle to the back of this shelf.

She looked carefully round the room and asked, "Where am I to sleep, Grandfather?"

"Wherever you like," he answered.

She saw a ladder that reached to the floor above, and quickly climbed up. There was a hayloft with a large round window overlooking the valley. "Oh, it's lovely! I shall sleep up here, Grandfather," she called down, "but I'll need a sheet," and she began to gather the sweet-scented hay.

Together they arranged a bed, with hay for a mattress and two thick sacks for a sheet and a cover. "I wish it were night so I could get into this lovely bed now," Heidi said.

"Hadn't we better eat first?" Grandfather asked.

Heidi followed him down the ladder and watched him go to the hearth and swing the kettle over the fire. Then he put some cheese on a long fork and held it over the flame, turning it until it was toasted a nice golden yellow. Heidi set the table.

"What will you do for a seat?" Grandfather asked.

Heidi ran to the hearth and fetched a small three-legged stool. But it was so low she could not reach the table. Grandfather filled a bowl with warm milk, set in on the chair, and drew it up before Heidi where she sat on her low stool. Then he laid the toasted cheese on some bread and told her to eat. After which he sat down on the corner of the table and began his own meal.

Heidi soon emptied her bowl. "It's the best milk I ever drank," she said. Grandfather filled her bowl again. When they had finished eating, Heidi followed him out to a shed where he began working with his tools. Soon she saw he had made a three-legged stool like his, only with longer legs. "It's for me, I know," she said, delighted to have something of her own.

Evening came, and the wind sang through the fir trees louder than ever. Soon Heidi heard a shrill whistle, and down from the heights came Peter and his goats. Heidi ran outside to see two of them come up to her grandfather and lick the salt he held in his hands, as Peter and the others disappeared down the mountain side.

"Are these two ours?" Heidi asked excitedly.

"Yes," said Grandfather, "their names are White Swan and Little Bear. Go get your bowl and some bread." And when he had milked White Swan he filled the bowl, and told Heidi to eat and run off to bed.

"Good night, Grandfather," Heidi called, as he took his goats to the shed. A few minutes later she climbed the ladder and hurried into her bed.

Before you could spell her name, she was sleeping as happily as a princess on a silken couch.

The next morning a loud whistle woke Heidi. Hearing her grandfather's voice, she jumped up, dressed, and hurried down the ladder. There stood Peter with his goats, waiting for the Uncle to bring his to join them.

"Do you want to go up the mountain with Peter?" asked Grandfather. Heidi was delighted. "Then wash and tidy yourself," he said, "or the sun will laugh at you." He put a large piece of bread and cheese for Heidi into Peter's lunch box, handed him a bowl and said, "Milk two bowlfuls for her at noon. And take care she does not fall over the rocks."

As they started up the mountain, Heidi dashed this way and that to look at the beautiful flowers. Sometimes she would run ahead and sit down in a field of blossoms and Peter would have to call to know where she was. "She's as bad as the goats," he grumbled.

"Now I must watch them and her too."

When they came to the place where he usually halted his goats to pasture, Peter laid his lunch box in a hollow so the wind wouldn't blow it away, and threw himself down for a nap. Heidi filled her apron with flowers, then sat down beside him. How beautiful was the snow on the peaks! How beautiful the green valley! And she had never seen so many flowers in her life!

Peter's stomach soon told him it was time to eat, so he sat up and opened his lunch box. He laid Heidi's bread and cheese to one side, and his to the other. Then he filled the bowl with White Swan's milk and called Heidi. She drank two bowls of milk, but she broke off only a small piece of bread.

The rest and the cheese she handed to Peter, saying, "You may have it." He thought at first she must be joking. When he saw that she meant it, he set to on the biggest lunch he had had in a long time.

Much later Heidi saw that the sun was casting a reddish glow over the peaks, the snow, and the flowers. "Peter! Isn't it beautiful!" she cried. But Peter had no eye for sunsets. He had seen too many.

"It's time to go," he said.

Just then he caught sight of one of the goats taking leaps in the direction of the cliff, and, dashing up to it, lifted his stick to give it a good beating as punishment.

Heidi cried out. "You have no right to touch her; it will hurt her. Let her alone!"

"I'll let her off if you will give me some more of your cheese tomorrow," said Peter.

"You shall have it all, tomorrow and every day; but you must promise never to beat any of the goats," Heidi said.

"All right," Peter promised. "I don't care."

Day after day Heidi went up the mountain with Peter and his herd. She grew healthy and brown in the sun, and as carefree as the birds.

At last autumn came, and with it, heavier and stronger winds. Grandfather would say, "You must stay at home today, Heidi, or the wind will blow you over the rocks."

Peter did not like this. He hated to miss that extra lunch. Besides, the goats had grown so used to Heidi that they would refuse to go unless she was with them. But she did not mind staying at home. She liked following Grandfather about, watching him making cheese, or working with his tools.

Finally it grew so cold that she had to put on the shoes and stockings she had hidden in the cupboard. Then one morning a blanket of snow lay over the mountain.

Now Peter and his goats stopped coming altogether, for there was not a green thing to be seen. It snowed until Heidi thought the hut would be buried in it. Then one day it stopped, and Grandfather went out to shovel paths.

That afternoon there came a thump at the door, and in walked Peter. The Alm-Uncle invited him to stay for supper.

How Peter's eyes popped when the old man handed him some bread with a big piece of meat on it!

When he had finished eating, Peter said, "I must go now. Grandmother sent word that she would like Heidi to come and see her one day."

Almost as soon as Heidi was up the next morning, she announced, "I must go to see Peter's grandmother today. She will be expecting me."

Grandfather told her to wait until the snow was not so deep. But each day she said the same thing. On the fourth morning the snow was hard as ice.

"All right then," Grandfather said this time. "Come along."

He wrapped Heidi in the heavy sack from her bed, and dragged the sled out of the shed. Then he sat on the low seat, took Heidi on his lap, and pushed off with his foot.

They shot down the mountain so fast that Heidi thought they were flying.

When they reached Peter's hut, Grandfather said, "As soon as it begins to grow dark, you must come home." And he went back up the mountain.

In the hut, Peter's mother was mending his coat; the old grandmother sat in the corner, spinning.

Heidi walked up to her and said, "Good morning, Grandmother. I've come at last."

"It's the child who lives with the Alm-Uncle, isn't it?" the grandmother asked, pleased that she had come. As they talked,

one of the shutters flapped against the window.

"See that! It will break the window," Heidi said. "Grandfather must fix it."

The grandmother said she could hear it slap and feel the old house shake, but she could not see anything, for she was blind. That made Heidi very sad. "Who can make it light for you again? Can no one do it?" she cried. It took the grandmother a long time to quiet her.

Heidi stayed at the hut until Peter came home from school.

"How is the reading getting on?" asked the grandmother.

"Not very well," was Peter's answer.

The old woman sighed. "Ah well," she said, "I hoped you would have something different to tell me. Up there on the shelf is an old prayer book, with beautiful songs in it which I have not heard for a long time. I hoped that you would soon learn enough to be able to read one of them to me sometimes."

When it grew dark, Heidi said, "I must go now, but I'll come tomorrow."

Grandfather met her outside, wrapped the sack around her, and carried her up the mountain.

Heidi told him about the flapping shutter and the shaky house. "We must go tomorrow with the hammer and fix it," she said.

"Who says so?" Grandfather wanted to know.

Heidi told him that nobody had said so. She knew it herself. "The grandmother lies awake when the wind blows because she is afraid the house will fall down. She is blind, too. You could help her, couldn't you?"

"At least we can fix the rattling," Grandfather said.

And the next day when he and Heidi went down to the hut, he took along his hammer and nails. In fact, every time he went down he took his tools along and spent many hours making the cottage sound and tight. He would never go inside, though, even to be thanked for his work, for he did not believe people ever meant to be kind. When he was finished, the hut no longer groaned and rattled the whole night through, and the grandmother said she would never forget what the Alm-

Uncle had done for her.

The winter passed, summer had gone its way, and now another winter was almost over. Heidi was nearly eight, yet she had never been to school. The teacher at Dorfli sent word by Peter that she must come to school at once. Grandfather sent word back that she was not coming, now or ever. Then the pastor from the village came up to see the Alm-Uncle. He, too, said that Heidi must go to school and that the Alm-Uncle should move to the village so she need not miss a day. Grandfather shook his head. "The people of Dorfli despise me, and I them. It's better we live apart."

"My friend, if you will make your peace with God, you will see how quickly people will be friendly," the pastor replied. But the Alm-Uncle said he would never move to the village. And for the next few days, he did not even take Heidi down to see Peter's grandmother.

Then suddenly one afternoon, Dete walked into the hut, in a feathered hat and a long trailing dress. She praised Heidi's appearance, saying, "I can see she's had good care, Uncle, but I know she must be in your way so I've come to take her with me." The Alm-Uncle just stared at her. "Some wealthy relatives of the people I serve are looking for a companion for their young invalid daughter," she went on. "No one can say what might happen. They might even adopt—"

"Have you finished?" snapped the old man.

Dete was angry. "I'm responsible for my sister's child," she retorted, "and she must go to school. Everybody in Dorfli agrees with me. I advise you to think it over before letting the matter go to court."

The Alm-Uncle's eyes flashed. "Be gone, with your hat and feathers, and such words on your tongue," he shouted, and strode out of the hut.

Dete told Heidi to get her clothes quickly.

"But I'm not going to leave Grandfather," said the little girl.

"Nonsense!" said Dete. "In Frankfurt you will have all sorts of nice things."

When Heidi did not move, Dete found her clothes, and, taking the girl by the hand, almost dragged her down the mountain. "If you don't like it, you can come back whenever you wish," she said as Heidi began to cry.

When they reached the grandmother's hut, Heidi wanted to stop to say good-bye, but Dete would not let her. "You can bring her something nice when you come home, maybe some soft white rolls. She's too old to eat hard bread."

Pleased at the thought of doing something for the grandmother, Heidi said no more and went with Dete.

It was the evening of the next day when Heidi and Dete reached the home of Herr Sesemann in Frankfurt and were shown to the study where Clara, the invalid daughter, lay waiting on her couch. At a small table, embroidering, sat Fraulein Rottenmeier, the housekeeper, with a queer-looking cap on her head. Fraulein looked Heidi over, and did not seem pleased with her appearance.

"Can you read?" she asked. Heidi said that she could not. Fraulein was shocked. "How old are you?" she went on. Dete answered quickly that she must be about ten. Heidi said she was eight. "Eight!" exclaimed Fraulein. "You know Clara is twelve. I asked for a companion her own age. This child cannot even read. How could you think of bringing her to me!"

"I thought she seemed made for the place," said Dete. Then, fearing there was to be trouble, she added, "I must be going now. My mistress expects me," and backed out of the room before the surprised Fraulein could try to stop her. Fraulein did not like Heidi's name, either, and declared, "You were baptized Adelheid and that is what I shall call you."

But Clara smiled, and said, "If your name is Heidi, I will call you Heidi." She said it would be fun to have her as a companion, and was sure she would soon learn to read under her kind tutor.

In spite of her unhappiness, the first thing Heidi noticed as she sat at the big table at dinner that evening, was a soft white roll by her plate. She asked Sebastian, the butler, if she might have it, and when he nodded his head she tucked it into her pocket to take to the grandmother.

Fraulein said, with a sigh: "I see I shall have to teach you some table manners," and she went on with a long list. But Clara laughed and said that the little girl had not heard a word. She was so tired from her long journey that she had fallen fast asleep!

The next morning when Heidi awoke she wondered where she was. Then she remembered the big house Dete had brought her to, and jumping out of bed, ran from window to window trying to see grass and mountains. She saw nothing but walls. It was as though she were shut in a cage. She was dressing to run outdoors, as she did at home, when the maid Tinette knocked and said breakfast was ready. And as soon as she and Clara finished eating, they went straight to the study to wait for the tutor. Clara told Heidi how kind he was, and Heidi told Clara about her grandfather and his hut and Peter.

The moment the tutor arrived, Fraulein took him aside and told him that Heidi could not read. She hoped he would say that she must be sent home. But instead he said patience was all that was needed. That did not please Fraulein, but she did not dare send the little girl away of her own accord.

And so Heidi began her schooling. An hour later Fraulein heard the sound of a frightful crash in the study. She rushed into the room. On the floor lay books, inkstand, and other articles, while from beneath them a dark stream of ink was flowing all across the floor. Heidi was nowhere to be seen. She had disappeared.

Fraulein ran down the stairs. There, at the bottom, standing in the open doorway, was Heidi, looking in amazement up and down the street.

"What are you doing? What are you thinking of to run away like that?" cried Fraulein.

"I heard the sound of fir trees, but I can't see where they are, and now I can't hear them any more," answered Heidi.

"Fir trees!" repeated Fraulein scornfully. "Do you suppose we are in a wood? What a silly idea! The sound you heard came from the passing carriages. Come upstairs and see the mischief you have done!" Heidi followed Fraulein Rottenmeier upstairs; she was quite surprised when she saw the damage, for in her hurry she had not realized what she was doing.

"I'll excuse you this time, but don't let it happen again," said Fraulein, pointing to the floor. "During your lesson time you are to sit still and pay attention. If you don't, I shall have to tie you to the chair. Do you understand?":

"Yes," replied Heidi. She had learned an-

other rule.

But for some reason, for all the tutor's patience, Heidi did not learn easily. She grew more and more unhappy, and whenever she talked with Clara, she would say, "Tomorrow I must go home to Grandfather." Clara said she must wait until Herr Sesemann came home. So each day Heidi put two more rolls in her closet to take to the old blind grandmother.

In the afternoons, when Clara was resting, Heidi was left to amuse herself. One day she slipped out into the street and, with the kindly assistance of an organ grinder, set off in the direction of a tower with a golden dome which she had often seen from her window. It was a church. Heidi went in. When she came out, she was carrying a little kitten in each of her pockets! The tower-keeper, whose cat had just had a new litter of kittens, had given them to her. Heidi was late for dinner that night; the others were already seated at the table.

Fraulein was very cross. "You behaved very badly," she scolded, "running out of the house as you did, without asking permission, without anyone's knowing where you went, and then coming back here at such an hour."

"Miau!" came the answer.

Fraulein became very angry. "How dare you make a joke of it!"

"I did not"—began Heidi—"Miau, miau!"

"That will do," said Fraulein. "Get up and leave the room!"

"But Heidi," put in Clara, "when you see that it makes Fraulein angry, why do you keep on saying 'miau'?"

"It's not I, it's the kittens in my pocket," Heidi was at last given time to say.

"Kittens!" shrieked Fraulein. "Take them away!"

And she rushed out of the room, while Heidi and Clara quickly arranged with Sebastian to hide the kittens in a place where Fraulein was not likely to find them.

Often, when she was not playing with the kittens, Heidi would sit in her room by herself, thinking of the time when she would return to her mountains. One day she felt she could stand it no longer. She must run away. She wrapped all the rolls in her red shawl, put on her old straw hat, and got as far as the front door, when Fraulein caught her. How she scolded! Heidi cried and said that she just had to go home. But Fraulein called Sebastian, and Heidi went back to her room. That night, as usual, she put a roll in her pocket. But she did not touch her dinner.

A few days later Fraulein went through Heidi's clothes closet to see what she would need before Herr Sesemann came home, and she discovered the rolls! "Tinette! Throw this stale bread away. And that old straw hat, too!" she ordered.

"No!" screamed Heidi, trying to stop her. "I must keep the hat, and the rolls are for the grandmother." But Fraulein pulled her away and Tinette went off with the things. Heidi threw herself onto Clara's couch and wept.

"Don't cry," Clara said, trying to comfort her. "You'll have fresh rolls to take to the grandmother when you go."

Heidi dried her tears. That night when she went to bed, she found her old straw hat where Sebastian had hidden it under her bedspread. Happily she hid it in a corner of her closet.

Then one day there was much excitement in the house. Herr Sesemann, Clara's father, had come home, and everyone was bustling about, carrying boxes from his carriage. But no sooner had he entered the house than Fraulein began to tell him about Heidi and how unfit she was to be a companion for Clara. Herr Sesemann listened, asked questions, and said he would see what Clara had to say. Of course, Clara wanted Heidi to stay. That was all Herr Sesemann needed to know. If Clara liked her, she must stay. Fraulein was not pleased at his decision. But Herr Sesemann told her that if she could not manage, she must remember that his mother was coming soon, and *she* could get along with anybody!

In a few days Herr Sesemann returned to Paris. Soon a letter came from his mother, telling just when she would arrive. There was so much talk about "Grandmamma," as Clara called her, that Heidi began calling her Grandmamma, too. At this Fraulein frowned and said, "Remember, you are always to address Frau Sesemann as 'Madam!' Do you understand?" Heidi did not, but would ask no questions.

She liked Clara's grandmamma the moment she saw her. She liked her kind voice and her beautiful white hair. But when Heidi called her "Madam" Grandmamma laughed and said, "You may call me Grandmamma, as Clara does."

That afternoon while Clara was resting, Grandmamma looked for Heidi. She was shocked to find that the little girl was alone in her room. "Bring her to me at once," she said to Fraulein. "I have some books for her."

"Oh, she doesn't read!" said Fraulein. "She can't even learn her ABC's."

"That's strange! She doesn't look to me like a stupid child," said Grandmamma. "Well, she can look at the pictures."

Fraulein was about to say more, but Grandmamma had turned away and gone quickly towards her own room. Heidi was delighted with the books. She liked especially the picture of a shepherd leaning on his staff, watching his flocks.

But as she looked at it, she burst into tears.

"Don't cry, dear child. The picture has reminded you of something," Grandmamma said kindly. But for a long time Heidi could not control her tears. When she was quiet again, Grandmamma said, "How are you getting along with your lessons? Have you learned to read?"

"No," answered Heidi. "But I knew before I started that it was impossible. Peter told me so. He tried and couldn't learn."

"How odd Peter must be!" Grandmamma said. "Of course you can learn. And when you can read the story that goes with that picture, I will give you the book." She gave Heidi her first lesson that day.

Grandmamma knew that the little girl was unhappy, but she did not know why. Heidi would not tell her for fear she and Clara would think her ungrateful for their kindness. Grandmamma told her that she must tell God about it in her prayers. He would surely help her.

A sudden gleam of joy came into Heidi's eyes. "May I tell Him everything, everything?"

"Yes, Heidi, everything," Grandmamma said.

Heidi drew away her hand, which Grandmamma had been holding affectionately between her own, and said, "May I go?"

"Yes, of course," was the answer, and Heidi ran off at once to her own room and, kneeling on the floor, told God that she wanted to return to her grandfather.

One morning, a week or so later, the tutor asked if he might speak to Frau Sesemann.

"I have surprising news," he said. "Heidi can read!"

But if the tutor was surprised, Grandmamma was not. She had found that Heidi learned easily. But she went down to the study to see for herself. There sat Heidi, reading aloud to Clara! That evening at dinner Heidi found the book at her plate.

Nothing pleased the little girl more than to be asked to read aloud. But the story that she liked best always made her the saddest—the story of the shepherd Joseph. "The Prodigal Son," Grandmamma called it. One picture showed him at home tending the sheep; the next, in a strange land, lonely and forsaken; the third, returning to his native land, ragged but happy to be back home again. Heidi never tired of hearing Grandmamma tell this story.

Every day she learned something new—to sew and make dolls' clothes, to read ever so many new stories. Still Grandmamma knew that she was not happy. One day she asked, "Have you told God about the thing that makes you unhappy?" Heidi said she had. "And do you still pray to Him?" Heidi said she did not. Grandmamma asked why.

"It's no use," sighed Heidi. "For weeks I've prayed for the same thing, and He does not give it to me. But I can understand that. There must be hundreds in Frankfurt asking for things."

"You must not stop praying," Grandmamma said. "God will think you have forsaken Him."

Heidi went at once to ask God to forgive her and promised she would not forget Him again.

Soon it was time for Grandmamma to be returning home. And when she left, how big and silent the house seemed! One afternoon Heidi was reading aloud to Clara to pass the time when she happened upon a story about a grandmother dying.

"Oh!" she cried out, "then the grandmother is dead!" and burst into tears.

Clara explained that it was only a story and had nothing to do with the grandmother on the mountain. But Heidi, now more homesick than ever, felt that she would never see her friends again. When Fraulein heard her crying, she came and scolded her, saying: "Now, that's enough of all this nonsense. If you start crying again while you are reading, I shall take the book away from you and shall not let you have it again." Heidi at once dried her tears. She could not bear to lose her dearest possession. But though she never cried again when she read, it did not mean that she was less homesick. She grew pale and lost her appetite and became so thin that Sebastian noticed it and tried his hardest to make her eat.

But it was of no use. Heidi scarcely ate anything at all, and when she went to bed at night she buried her face in her pillow and wept.

Weeks passed. At last autumn came, then the winter, then another spring. It made no difference to Heidi. The walls and windows she looked upon showed no change, and she never went out-of-doors except when Clara was well enough to be taken for a drive.

Even then they went only a little way, and though they saw fine streets and large houses and crowds of people, they never saw grass and flowers or fir trees and mountains.

It was these things that Heidi longed for more and more.

In her lonely room she would think of Grandfather's hut, of the grandmother, of Peter and the goats, the golden flowers in the sunlight, and the bright colors of the rocks at sunset.

And each time she thought of them she grew a little sadder. They seemed so far away. For days there had been mysterious happenings in the Sesemann household. No matter how fast the door was barred at night, when the servants went downstairs in the morning it was always open. It could not be a thief; nothing was ever missing. Could it be a ghost? This thought made Fraulein so nervous that she would not go into any of the empty rooms without Tinette. Tinette would not go upstairs or down unless Sebastian went along. Sebastian never peeped into a dark corner unless John the footman were at his heels, nor would John go anywhere without Sebastian.

All day long the cook would say, "That I should live to hear of such a thing!" Of course no one spoke of these things before the children.

Fraulein finally persuaded Sebastian and John to sit up all night and find out who was doing the mischief. One evening they armed themselves with several weapons and took up their watch. They ate and talked and dozed. Around midnight Sebastian tried to rouse John, but could not. Then at one o'clock John sat up and said, as though he were a man of courage, "Come, Sebastian. We must see what's going on."

But as he stepped into the hall a gust of

wind blew out the candle, and he fell back against Sebastian, nearly upsetting him.

When Sebastian lighted the candle again, John was as white as a ghost.

"What did you see?" Sebastian asked.

"It's open," gasped John, "and there's a white figure on the stairs."

Shivering, they sat down and did not stir from their seats until daybreak. Then they went out and closed and barred the door, and hastened to tell Fraulein of their experience.

Fraulein could stand the strain of this mystery no longer. She wrote that very day to Herr Sesemann about it, asking him to come at once. But Herr Sesemann had his own ideas about ghosts. "You and the servants should be able to solve this mystery," he replied. "If not, write for my mother to come. *She* is not afraid of anything." So Fraulein wrote to Frau Sesemann. Frau Sesemann answered that she had no intention of returning to look for a ghost. "If there's one in the house, it must be alive, and you ought to be able to deal with it, Rottenmeier," she wrote.

Now Fraulein was angry. Herr Sesemann must come home, and she knew a way to bring him. She wrote him that the ghost was making Clara more and more nervous and that she might become very ill unless something were done about it.

He came on the next train.

Herr Sesemann suspected Sebastian of playing tricks on Fraulein and began at once to question him. But he soon saw that Sebastian was as frightened as Fraulein.

So he sent for his friend, the doctor who attended Clara, and that night they took up their watch in the same room in which Sebastian and John had waited.

They lighted a candle and laid their loaded revolvers between them.

Then they talked and waited until the clock struck twelve.

Then one.

And then—they heard the bar of the outer door being lifted!

"Who's there?" roared the doctor, opening the door.

A little white figure turned. It was Heidi—barefooted and shivering.

"What are you doing here, child?" asked the kindly doctor.

Heidi did not know. The doctor lifted her in his arms, carried her upstairs, and put her in her bed. When she stopped trembling, he asked if she had been dreaming.

"Yes," she said, "I dream every night of being at home with Grandfather. But when I wake in the morning, I am always in my bed in Frankfurt."

When the doctor heard this, he said, "Go to sleep now, Heidi. Everything will be all right tomorrow."

He went downstairs and told Herr Sesemann, "She must go back at once to her mountains. She's sick and thin as a skeleton." Herr Sesemann was shocked that this should have happened in his house without anyone's noticing it. "But first we must make her sound and strong," he protested.

"Her illness cannot be cured by pills," the doctor said, adding that if she were sent home at once, she might recover in the mountain air. Herr Sesemann understood and agreed.

At daybreak he went upstairs and awakened Fraulein and the servants. "Come down at once," he ordered. "We must prepare for a journey."

Frightened, they jumped out of their beds. Had the ghost attacked the master, and were they being called to his assistance? With pale faces, they crept into the dining room. John was sent for the carriage; Sebastian to bring Dete to the house; Tinette to wake Heidi and dress her. Just then Fraulein came into the room, so befuddled that she had put her cap on backwards. Herr Sesemann told her to get out a trunk and pack all Heidi's things in it and a good part of Clara's, too. Meanwhile he would go up to wake his daughter and break the news to her.

Clara was distressed at losing her companion, but when her father explained that Heidi was homesick, she understood. "Just let Heidi's trunk be brought in here so that I may put in some things for her," she said.

Sebastian returned with Dete at his heels in a great state of excitement. Why was Heidi being sent home? As for herself, she was sorry, but she could not get away just now. Her mistress needed her. She was thinking of Uncle's last words to her, and did not want

to see him again.

So Sebastian was put in charge of the little girl on her journey. "When you stop at the hotel tonight," Herr Sesemann warned him, "be sure her windows are fastened, so that they cannot be easily opened. After Heidi is in bed, lock the door of her room on the outside, for she walks in her sleep and might hurt herself if she went wandering downstairs and tried to open the front door. Do you understand?"

"So that was it!" Sebastian exclaimed, remembering the open door.

"Yes," said Herr Sesemann, "and you are all idiots for not finding it out for yourselves."

And with that Herr Sesemann went off to his study to write a letter to the Alm-Uncle.

Perhaps Heidi was the most surprised of all at being called so early in the morning. Tinette put on her best dress without telling her why. When Herr Sesemann explained that she was going back to her grandfather, she was too excited to eat. She ran up to Clara's room to wait for the carriage.

"See what I have put in the trunk for you!" cried Clara, pointing to it in the middle of the room. Then she showed her dresses and

aprons and handkerchiefs, and other lovely things. "And look here," she added, as she held up a basket. Inside were twelve soft, white rolls for the grandmother.

Heidi had never been happier.

Someone announced that the carriage was ready, and Heidi ran to her room to get her book from under her pillow. Then she took her shawl from the closet, put her old hat in it, and placed the two on top of her basket. Fraulein tried to take the shawl from her, but Herr Sesemann said she might keep it.

Soon Heidi was on her way to the train, the basket of rolls on her knees. "Are you sure the grandmother is not dead?" she kept asking Sebastian.

"I don't see why she should be," he would answer. And Heidi would be comforted for a while.

When they reached Mayenfeld, Sebastian found a man with a cart who agreed to take Heidi to Dorfli. "I can go by myself from there," Heidi said. Sebastian paid the man well for his trouble, then handed the little girl a package for herself and a letter for her grandfather from Herr Sesemann, and told her to take good care not to lose them. She

put them in her basket under the rolls.

The peaks looked down on Heidi like old friends, and the trees seemed to wave a welcome home. She thought the cart would never reach Dorfli. But at last it stopped and she jumped out, still holding her basket.

"Thank you," she said to the man. "Grandfather will come for the trunk tomorrow."

Would she find the grandmother by the spinning wheel? She kept asking herself that question as she hurried up the steep path. At last she saw the little hut in the hollow, and ran in, calling, "Grandmother! Grandmother! I'm back."

The grandmother was too surprised to speak. But when she put her hand on Heidi's hair, she said, "It is indeed the little girl. God has granted my prayer."

Heidi laid the rolls in the old woman's lap. "There, Grandmother!" she said. "Now you won't have to eat hard bread for days."

Peter's mother was as surprised and happy as the grandmother was to see Heidi. "What a pretty hat you have on!" she said.

"You shall have it, for I do not need it any more," said Heidi. She put on the old hat that she had worn when she went away. She re-

membered what Grandfather had said about Dete and her feathers! Then she took off her pretty dress and put on her old shawl.

"I want Grandfather to see me as I used to be so he will surely know me," she said, and hurried up the mountain.

How good it was to be home again! Everything was even more beautiful than she had remembered it. At last she saw the tops of the fir trees, then the roof of her grandfather's hut, then the whole of it. There, before it, as in the old days, sat Grandfather puffing away at his pipe. Heidi dropped her basket and rushed to him, flinging her arms round his neck.

"Grandfather! Grandfather!" was all she could say.

The old man took Heidi on his knees and looked at her. "Did they send you away?" he asked.

"Oh, no, Grandfather. They were very kind. I just wanted to come back to you. I think it's all in the letter," she said, handing it and the package to him. But he gave the package back, saying "That's yours." The letter he read and put in his pocket.

"Now you must have some milk," Grandfather said, rising to go inside. "Bring the package with you. There is money in it for you. You can buy a nice bed and bedclothes and dresses for a couple of years with it."

"I don't want the money. I have a bed and Clara gave me plenty of dresses," Heidi said.

"Take it and put it in the cupboard; you will want it some day, I have no doubt."

Heidi obeyed and skipped happily after her grandfather into the house; she looked into every corner of the room, then she ran up the ladder to the loft above. "Oh Grandfather! My bed's gone," she said. Grandfather said they would make another.

Later, as they sat at the table eating, Heidi said, "Grandfather, this is the best milk in the world." The old man smiled.

"So you're back again!" exclaimed Peter when he came with the goats. "Will you go up the mountain tomorrow?"

"Not tomorrow, but the day after, perhaps," said Heidi, "for tomorrow I must go down to see the grandmother."

That night Grandfather went up the ladder a dozen times to make sure Heidi was not going to walk in her sleep, as Herr Sesemann wrote she had done in Frankfurt. But Heidi was resting well. She was in her own mountains again with her grandfather, happier than she had been since she left.

The next morning Grandfather went to Dorfli for the trunk, while Heidi stopped at Peter's hut to see how the grandmother liked her rolls.

"I believe they have made me stronger already," the old woman told her, with a grateful smile.

"I shall write Clara to send you more when these are gone," Heidi promised. Then she thought of the money Herr Sesemann had given her.

She would use that to buy more rolls!

"No, no, I cannot let you. It's your money," the grandmother said; but Heidi was determined. She was sure if the grandmother grew strong she would be able to see again.

"Shall I read you one of the hymns from your book?" Heidi asked a moment later.

The grandmother could hardly believe a child so young could read when Peter did not know one word from another.

But Heidi got the book off the shelf and read until the old woman's face was alight with joy. Then Grandfather knocked at the window. Heidi left, promising to come back the next day.

When she told her grandfather that she wanted to use her money to buy rolls for the grandmother, he asked, "But what about your bed? It would be nice to have a proper bed." Heidi replied that she slept better on hay than on her fine bed in Frankfurt. "The money is yours. Do what you like with it," he agreed then.

For a while they walked along in silence. Suddenly Heidi said, "Everything has turned out as Grandmamma said it would. If I had come home when I wanted to, the grandmother would have had only a few rolls, and I would not have been able to read to her. I'm glad God did not let me have what I asked for at once. Now I shall always pray to God, and when He does not do anything I ask for I shall think to myself, 'Perhaps He is going to do something better still.' We will pray every day now, won't we, and never forget Him again."

"What if one has forgotten God?" asked Grandfather.

"Then everything goes wrong. Grandmamma told me so," Heidi answered. "And people say you ran away from God, when He would have helped you if you had let Him."

"But if we have forgotten God, we cannot go back," Grandfather murmured.

"Oh, yes we can. There's a story in my book that explains it." When they reached home she got down her book and read the story aloud. It was of the prodigal son, who when he had wasted his life and money, went back to his father and was forgiven. "You see?" said Heidi. "We can go back."

That night as she lay asleep, Grandfather stood looking at her a long time. Then he prayed, "Father, I have sinned against God and man. I am not worthy to be called Thy son."

Early the next morning Grandfather called up to Heidi, "Put on your best dress and come down. We're going to church."

She was too surprised to ask any questions. But it did not take her long to get ready.

When she came down the ladder, there stood Grandfather in a coat with shining silver buttons.

"Grandfather!" she cried. "I've never seen you look so nice."

As they walked down the mountain the church bells rang out from the valley below, and the nearer they walked, the sweeter was the music. By the time they reached the church, the congregation had gathered and was singing. Women turned to look and lost their places in their books. "See that!" they whispered. "The Alm-Uncle has come to church!" The pastor was happy indeed.

When the services were over, Grandfather took Heidi to the pastor's home. Then how the people talked! "Maybe he's not so bad after all!" some said. "See how he takes the little one by the hand!"

The Alm-Uncle announced he was going to follow the pastor's advice and move to Dorfli the next winter so that Heidi could go to school. The pastor was pleased, and shook his hand warmly. Now the congregation, too, went up to shake hands, each trying to be first. And when the Alm-Uncle told them he was going to move to Dorfli for the winter, they walked halfway up the mountain with him.

"Grandfather, you just look nicer and nicer

today," Heidi said when they were alone.

He smiled. "It is good to be at peace with God and man," he said. "God was good when He sent you to my hut." This time when they reached Peter's house, the two walked in together. "Good morning, Grandmother!" said Uncle.

"That I should live to see such a thing!" exclaimed the surprised old woman. "May God reward you for all you have done for me. And if I have ever injured you, do not punish me by sending the child away again while I live."

"Have no fear," said Uncle.

Just then Peter rushed in with a letter for Heidi, the first she had ever had. It was from Clara. She told her how they missed her in Frankfurt, and promised that next summer she and Grandmamma would come to visit her. "Grandmamma," she wrote, "is sending some coffee to go with the rolls."

There was such excitement at all this news that no one noticed how the time was passing, until Uncle reminded Heidi they must be going home. "Come again soon," the grandmother said. And Uncle promised they would, the very next day. As he and Heidi climbed up the mountain toward home, the evening chimes rang out like a lovely song. Heidi was happier than she had been in all her life. And so, I think, was her grandfather.

THE LITTLE COLONEL

CHAPTER I.

It was one of the prettiest places in all Kentucky where the Little Colonel stood that morning. She was reaching up on tiptoes, her eager little face pressed close against the iron bars of the great entrance gate that led to a fine old estate known as "Locust."

A ragged little Scotch and Skye terrier stood on its hind feet beside her.

They were looking down a long avenue that stretched for nearly a quarter of a mile between rows of stately old locust trees.

At the far end they could see the white pillars of a large stone house gleaming through the Virginia creeper that nearly covered it. But they could not see the old Colonel in his big chair on the porch behind the cool screen of vines.

At that very moment he had caught the rattle of wheels along the road, and had picked up his field glass to see who was passing. It was only a colored man jogging along in the heat and dust with a cart full of chicken-coops. The Colonel watched him drive up a lane that led to the back of the new hotel that had just been opened in this quiet country place. Then his glance fell on the two small strangers coming through his gate down the avenue toward him. One was the friskiest dog he had ever seen in his life. The other was a child he judged to be about five years old.

Her shoes were covered with dust, and her white sunbonnet had slipped off and was hanging over her shoulders. A bunch of wild flowers she had gathered on the way hung limp and faded in her little warm hand. Her soft, light hair was cut as short as a boy's.

There was something strangely familiar about the child, especially in the erect, graceful way she walked.

Old Colonel Lloyd was puzzled. He had lived all his life in Lloydsborough, and this was the first time he had ever failed to recognize one of the neighbors' children.

"I ought to know that child as well as I know my own name," he said to himself. "But the dog is a stranger in these parts. Liveliest thing I ever set eyes on! They must have come from the hotel. Wonder what they want."

He carefully wiped the lens for a better view. When he looked again he saw that they evidently had not come to visit him.

They had stopped halfway down the avenue, and climbed up on a rustic seat to rest.

The dog sat motionless about two minutes, his red tongue hanging out as if he were completely exhausted.

Suddenly he gave a spring, and bounded away through the tall blue grass. He was back again in a moment, with a stick in his mouth. Standing up with his forepaws in the lap of his little mistress, he looked so wistfully into her face that she could not refuse this invitation for a romp.

The Colonel chuckled as they went tumbling about in the grass to find the stick which the child repeatedly tossed away.

He hitched his chair along to the other end of the porch as they kept getting farther away from the avenue.

It had been many a long year since those old locust trees had seen a sight like that. Children never played any more under their dignified shadows.

Time had been (but they only whispered this among themselves on rare spring days

23

like this) when the little feet chased each other up and down the long walk, as much at home as the pewees in the beeches.

Suddenly the little maid stood up straight, and began to sniff the air, as if some delicious odor had blown across the lawn.

"Fritz," she exclaimed, in delight, "I 'mell 'trawberries!"

The Colonel, who could not hear the remark, wondered at the abrupt pause in the game. He understood it, however, when he saw them wading through the tall grass, straight to his strawberry bed. It was the pride of his heart, and the finest for miles around. The first berries of the season had been picked only the day before. Those that now hung temptingly red on the vines he intended to send to his next neighbor, to prove his boasted claim of always raising the finest and earliest fruit.

He did not propose to have his plans spoiled by these stray guests. Laying the field glass in its accustomed place on the little table beside his chair, he picked up his hat and strode down the walk.

Colonel Lloyd's friends all said he looked like Napoleon, or rather like Napoleon might have looked had he been born and bred a Kentuckian.

He made an imposing figure in his suit of white duck.

The Colonel always wore white from May till October.

There was a military precision about him, from his erect carriage to the cut of the little white goatee on his determined chin.

No one looking into the firm lines of his resolute face could imagine him ever abandoning a purpose or being turned aside when he once formed an opinion.

Most children were afraid of him. The darkies about the place shook in their shoes when he frowned. They had learned from experience that "ole Marse Lloyd had a tigah of a tempah in him."

As he passed down the walk there were two mute witnesses to his old soldier life. A spur gleamed on his boot heel, for he had just returned from his morning ride, and his right sleeve hung empty.

He had won his title bravely. He had given

his only son and his strong right arm to the Southern cause. That had been nearly thirty years ago.

He did not charge down on the enemy with his usual force this time. The little head, gleaming like sunshine in the strawberry patch, reminded him so strongly of a little fellow who used to follow him everywhere, —Tom, the sturdiest, handsomest boy in the county,—Tom, whom he had been so proud of, whom he had so nearly worshipped.

Looking at this fair head bent over the vines, he could almost forget that Tom had ever outgrown his babyhood, that he had shouldered a rifle and followed him to camp, a mere boy, to be shot down by a Yankee bullet in his first battle.

The old Colonel could almost believe he had him back again, and that he stood in the midst of those old days the locusts sometimes whispered about.

He could not hear the happiest of little voices that was just then saying, "Oh, Fritz, isn't you glad we came? An' isn't you glad we've got a gran'fathah with such good 'trawberries?"

It was hard for her to put the "s" before her consonants.

As the Colonel came nearer she tossed another berry into the dog's mouth. A twig snapped, and she raised a startled face toward him.

"Suh?" she said, timidly, for it seemed to her that the stern, piercing eyes had spoken.

"What are you doing here, child?" he asked, in a voice so much kinder than his eyes that she regained her usual self-possession at once.

"Eatin' 'trawberries," she answered, coolly.

"Who are you, anyway?" he exclaimed, much puzzled. As he asked the question his gaze happened to rest on the dog, who was peering at him through the ragged, elfish wisps of hair nearly covering its face, with eyes that were startlingly human.

" 'Peak when yo'ah 'poken to, Fritz," she said, severely, at the same time popping another luscious berry into her mouth.

Fritz obediently gave a long yelp. The Colonel smiled grimly.

"What's your name?" he asked, this time

looking directly at her.

"Mothah calls me her baby," was the soft-spoken reply, "but papa an' Mom Beck they calls me the Little Cun'l."

"What under the sun do they call you that for?" he roared.

"'Cause I'm so much like you," was the startling answer.

"Like me!" fairly gasped the Colonel. "How are you like me?"

"Oh, I'm got such a vile tempah, an' I stamps my foot when I gets mad, an' gets all red in the face. An' I hollahs at folks, an' looks jus' zis way."

She drew her face down and puckered her lips into such a sullen pout that it looked as if a thunderstorm had passed over it. The next instant she smiled up at him serenely.

The Colonel laughed. "What makes you think I am like that?" he said. "You never saw me before."

"Yes, I have too," she persisted. "You's a-hangin' in a gold frame over ou' mantel."

Just then a clear, high voice was heard calling out in the road.

The child started up in alarm. "Oh, deah," she exclaimed in dismay, at sight of the stains on her white dress, where she had been kneeling on the fruit, "that's Mom Beck. Now I'll be tied up, and maybe put to bed for runnin' away again. But the berries is mighty nice," she added, politely. "Good mawnin', suh. Fritz, we mus' be goin' now."

The voice was coming nearer.

"I'll walk down to the gate with you," said the Colonel, anxious to learn something more about his little guest.

"Oh, you'd bettah not, suh!" she cried in alarm. "Mom Beck doesn't like you a bit. She just hates you! She's goin' to give you a piece of her mind the next time she sees you. I heard her tell Aunt Nervy so."

There was as much real distress in the child's voice as if she were telling him of a promised flogging.

"Lloyd! Aw, Lloy-eed!" the call came again.

A neat-looking colored woman glanced in at the gate as she was passing by, and then stood still in amazement. She had often found her little charge playing along the roadside or hiding behind trees, but she had never before known her to pass through anyone's gate.

As the name came floating down to him through the clear air, a change came over the Colonel's stern face. He stooped over the child. His hand trembled as he put it under her soft chin and raised her eyes to his.

"Lloyd, Lloyd!" he repeated, in a puzzled way. "Can it be possible? There certainly is a wonderful resemblance. You have my little Tom's hair, and only my baby Elizabeth ever had such hazel eyes."

He caught her up in his one arm, and strode on to the gate, where the colored woman stood.

"Why, Becky, is that you?" he cried, recognizing an old, trusted servant who had lived at Locust in his wife's lifetime.

Her only answer was a sullen nod.

"Whose child is this?" he asked, eagerly, without seeming to notice her defiant looks. "Tell me if you can."

"How can I tell you, suh," she demanded, indignantly, "when you have fo'bidden even her name to be spoken befo' you?"

A harsh look came into the Colonel's eyes. He put the child hastily down, and pressed his lips together.

"Don't tie my sunbonnet, Mom Beck," she begged. Then she waved her hand with an engaging smile.

"Good-bye, suh," she said, graciously. "We've had a mighty nice time!"

The Colonel took off his hat with his usual courtly bow, but he spoke no word in reply.

When the last flutter of her dress had disappeared around the bend of the road, he walked slowly back toward the house.

Halfway down the long avenue where she had stopped to rest, he sat down on the same rustic seat. He could feel her soft little fingers resting on his neck, where they had lain when he carried her to the gate.

A very un-Napoleonlike mist blurred his sight for a moment. It had been so long since such a touch had thrilled him, so long since any caress had been given him.

More than a score of years had gone by since Tom had been laid in a soldier's grave, and the years that Elizabeth had been lost to him seemed almost a lifetime.

And this was Elizabeth's little daughter. Something very warm and sweet seemed to surge across his heart as he thought of the Little Colonel. He was glad, for a moment, that they called her that; glad that his only grandchild looked enough like himself for others to see the resemblance.

But the feeling passed as he remembered that his daughter had married against his wishes, and he had closed his doors for ever against her.

The old bitterness came back redoubled in its force.

The next instant he was stamping down the avenue, roaring for Walker, his body-servant, in such a tone that the cook's advice was speedily taken: "Bettah hump yo'self outen dis heah kitchen befo' de ole tigah gits to lashin' roun' any pearter."

CHAPTER II.

Mom Beck carried the ironing board out of the hot kitchen, set the irons off the stove, and then tiptoed out to the side porch of the little cottage.

"Is yo' head feelin' any bettah, honey?" she said to the pretty, girlish-looking woman lying in the hammock. "I promised to step up to the hotel this evenin' to see one of the chambahmaids. I thought I'd take the Little Cun'l along with me if you was willin'. She's always wild to play with Mrs. Wyford's children up there."

"Yes, I'm better, Becky," was the languid reply. "Put a clean dress on Lloyd if you are going to take her out."

Mrs. Sherman closed her eyes again, thinking gratefully, "Dear, faithful old Becky! What a comfort she has been all my life, first as my nurse, and now as Lloyd's! She is worth her weight in gold!"

The afternoon shadows were stretching long across the grass when Mom Beck led the child up the green slope in front of the hotel.

The Little Colonel had danced along so gaily with Fritz that her cheeks glowed like wild roses. She made a quaint little picture with such short sunny hair and dark eyes shining out from under the broad-brimmed white hat she wore.

Several ladies who were sitting on the shady piazza, busy with their embroidery, noticed her admiringly.

"It's Elizabeth Lloyd's little daughter," one of them explained. "Don't you remember what a scene there was some years ago when she married a New York man? Sherman, I believe, his name was, Jack Sherman. He was a splendid fellow, and enormously wealthy. Nobody could say a word against him, except that he was a Northerner. That was enough for the old Colonel, though. He hates Yankees like poison. He stormed and

swore, and forbade Elizabeth ever coming in his sight again. He had her room locked up, and not a soul on the place ever dares mention her name in his hearing."

The Little Colonel sat down demurely on the piazza steps to wait for the children. The nurse had not finished dressing them.

She amused herself by showing Fritz the pictures in an illustrated weekly. It was not long until she began to feel that the ladies were talking about her. She had lived among older people so entirely that her thoughts were much deeper than her baby speeches would lead one to suppose.

She understood dimly, from what she had heard the servants say, that there was some trouble between her mother and grandfather. Now she heard it rehearsed from beginning to end. She could not understand what they meant by "bank failures" and "unfortunate investments," but she understood enough to know that her father had lost nearly all his money, and had gone West to make more.

Mrs. Sherman had moved from their elegant New York home two weeks ago to this little cottage in Lloydsborough that her mother had left her. Instead of the houseful of servants they used to have, there was only faithful Mom Beck to do everything.

There was something magnetic in the child's eyes.

Mrs. Wyford shrugged her shoulders uneasily as she caught their piercing gaze fixed on her.

"I do believe that little witch understood every word I said," she exclaimed.

"Oh, certainly not," was the reassuring answer. "She's such a little thing."

But she had heard it all, and understood enough to make her vaguely unhappy. Going home she did not frisk along with Fritz, but walked soberly by Mom Beck's side, holding tight to the friendly black hand.

"We'll go through the woods," said Mom Beck, lifting her over the fence. "It's not so long that way."

As they followed the narrow, straggling path into the cool dusk of the woods, she began to sing. The crooning chant was as mournful as a funeral dirge.

"The clouds hang heavy, an' it's gwine to
    rain.
    Fa'well, my dyin' friends.
 I'm gwine to lie in the silent tomb.
    Fa'well, my dyin' friends."

A muffled little sob made her stop and look down in surprise.

"Why, what's the mattah, honey?" she exclaimed. "Did Emma Louise make you mad? Or is you cryin' 'cause you're so ti'ed? Come! Ole Becky'll tote her baby the rest of the way."

She picked the light form up in her arms, and, pressing the troubled little face against her shoulder, resumed her walk and her song.

"It's a world of trouble we're travellin'
    through.
    Fa'well, my dyin' friends."

"Oh, don't, Mom Beck," sobbed the child, throwing her arms around the woman's neck, and crying as though her heart would break.

"Land sakes, what is the mattah?" she asked, in alarm. She sat down on a mossy log, took off the white hat, and looked into the flushed, tearful face.

"Oh, it makes me so lonesome when you sing that way," wailed the Little Colonel. "I just can't 'tand it! Mom Beck, is my moth-ah's heart all broken? Is that why she is sick so much, and will it kill her suah 'nuff?"

"Who's been tellin' you such nonsense?" asked the woman, sharply.

"Some ladies at the hotel were talkin' about it. They said that gran'fathah didn't love her any moah, an' it was just a-killin' her." Mom Beck frowned fiercely.

The child's grief was so deep and intense that she did not know just how to quiet her. Then she said, decidedly, "Well, if that's all that's a-troublin' you, you can jus' get down an' walk home on yo' own laigs. Yo' mamma's a-grievin' 'cause yo' papa has to be away all the time. She's all wo'n out, too, with the work of movin', when she's nevah been used to doin' anything. But her heart isn't broke any moah'n my neck is."

The positive words and the decided toss

Mom Beck gave her head settled the matter for the Little Colonel. She wiped her eyes and stood up much relieved.

"Don't you nevah go to worryin' 'bout what you heahs," continued the woman. "I tell you p'intedly you can't nevah b'lieve what you heahs."

"Why doesn't gran'fathah love my moth-ah?" asked the child, as they came in sight of the cottage. She had puzzled over the knotty problem all the way home. "How can papas not love their little girls?"

"'Cause he's stubbo'n," was the unsatis-factory answer. "All the Lloyds is. Yo' mam-ma's stubbo'n, an' you's stubbo'n—"

"I'm not!" shrieked the Little Colonel, stamping her foot. "You sha'n't call me names!"

Then she saw a familiar white hand wav-ing to her from the hammock, and she broke away from Mom Beck with very red cheeks and very bright eyes.

Cuddled close in her mother's arms, she had a queer feeling that she had grown a great deal older in that short afternoon.

Maybe she had. For the first time in her little life she kept her troubles to herself, and did not once mention the thought that was uppermost in her mind.

"Yo' great-aunt Sally Tylah is comin' this mawnin'," said Mom Beck, the day after their visit to the hotel. "Do fo' goodness' sake keep yo'self clean. I'se got too many spring chickens to dress to think 'bout dres-sin' you up again."

"Did I evah see her befo'?" questioned the Little Colonel.

"Why, yes, the day we moved heah. Don't you know she came and stayed so long, and the rockah broke off the little white rockin' chair when she sat down in it?"

"Oh, now I know!" laughed the child. "She's the big fat one with curls hangin' round her eahs like shavin's. I don't like her, Mom Beck. She keeps a-kissin' me all the time, an' a-'queezin' me, an' tellin' me to sit on her lap an' be a little lady. Mom Beck, I de'pise to be a little lady."

There was no answer to her last remark. Mom Beck had stepped into the pantry for more eggs for the cake she was making.

"Fritz," said the Little Colonel, "yo' great-aunt Sally Tylah's comin' this mawnin', an' if you don't want to say 'howdy' to her you'll have to come with me."

A few minutes later a resolute little figure squeezed between the palings of the garden fence down by the gooseberry bushes.

"Now walk on your tiptoes, Fritz!" commanded the Little Colonel, "else somebody will call us back."

Mom Beck, busy with her extra baking, supposed she was with her mother on the shady, vine-covered porch.

She would not have been singing quite so gaily if she could have seen half a mile up the road.

The Little Colonel was sitting in the weeds by the railroad track, deliberately taking off her shoes and stockings.

No telling how long she might have sat there enjoying the forbidden pleasure of dragging her rosy toes through the warm dust, if she had not heard a horse's hoof-beats coming rapidly along.

"Fritz, it's gran'fathah," she whispered, in alarm, recognizing the erect figure of the rider in its spotless suit of white duck.

"Sh! Lie down in the weeds, quick! Lie down, I say!"

They both made themselves as flat as possible, and lay there panting with the exertion of keeping still.

Presently the Little Colonel raised her head cautiously.

"Oh, he's gone down that lane!" she exclaimed. "Now you can get up." After a moment's deliberation she asked, "Fritz, would you rathah have some 'trawberries an' be tied up fo' runnin' away, or not be tied up and not have any of those nice tas'en 'trawberries?"

CHAPTER III.

Two hours later, Colonel Lloyd, riding down the avenue under the locusts, was surprised by a novel sight on his stately front steps.

Three little darkies and a big flop-eared hound were crouched on the bottom step, looking up at the Little Colonel, who sat just above them.

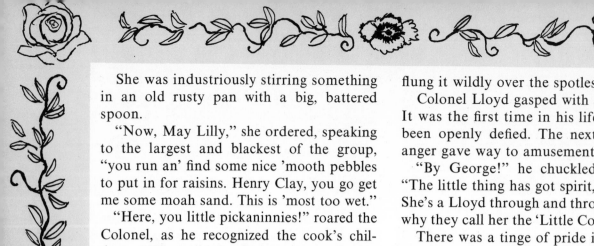

She was industriously stirring something in an old rusty pan with a big, battered spoon.

"Now, May Lilly," she ordered, speaking to the largest and blackest of the group, "you run an' find some nice 'mooth pebbles to put in for raisins. Henry Clay, you go get me some moah sand. This is 'most too wet."

"Here, you little pickaninnies!" roared the Colonel, as he recognized the cook's children. "What did I tell you about playing around here, tracking dirt all over my premises? You just chase back to the cabin where you belong!"

The sudden call startled Lloyd so that she dropped the pan, and the great mud pie turned upside down on the white steps.

"Well, you're a pretty sight!" said the Colonel, as he glanced with disgust from her soiled dress and muddy hands to her bare feet.

He had been in a bad humor all morning. The sight of the steps covered with sand and muddy tracks gave him an excuse to give vent to his cross feelings.

It was one of his theories that a little girl should always be kept as fresh and dainty as a flower. He had never seen his own little daughter in such a plight as this, and she had never been allowed to step outside of her own room without her shoes and stockings.

"What does your mother mean," he cried, savagely, "by letting you run barefooted around the country just like poor white trash? I suppose it's some of your father's miserable Yankee notions."

May Lilly, peeping around the corner of the house, rolled her frightened eyes from one angry face to the other. The same temper that glared from the face of the man, sitting erect in his saddle, seemed to be burning in the eyes of the child, who stood so defiantly before him.

The same kind of scowl drew their eyebrows together darkly.

"Don't you talk that way to me," cried the Little Colonel, trembling with a wrath she did not know how to express.

Suddenly she stooped, and snatching both hands full of mud from the overturned pie,

flung it wildly over the spotless white coat.

Colonel Lloyd gasped with astonishment. It was the first time in his life he had ever been openly defied. The next moment his anger gave way to amusement.

"By George!" he chuckled, admiringly. "The little thing has got spirit, sure enough. She's a Lloyd through and through. So that's why they call her the 'Little Colonel,' is it?"

There was a tinge of pride in the look he gave her haughty little head and flashing eyes.

"There, there, child!" he said, soothingly. "I didn't mean to make you mad, when you were good enough to come and see me. It isn't often I have a little lady like you pay me a visit."

"I didn't come to see you, suh," she answered, indignantly, as she started toward the gate. "I came to see May Lilly. But I nevah would have come inside yo' gate if I'd known you was goin' to hollah at me an' be so cross."

She was walking off with the air of an offended queen, when the Colonel remembered that if he allowed her to go away in that mood she would probably never set foot on his grounds again. Her display of temper had interested him immensely.

Now that he had laughed off his ill humor, he was anxious to see what other traits of character she possessed.

He wheeled his horse across the walk to bar her way, and quickly dismounted.

"Oh, now, wait a minute," he said, in a coaxing tone. "Don't you want a nice big saucer of strawberries and cream before you go? Walker's picking some now. And you haven't seen my hothouse. It's just full of the loveliest flowers you ever saw. You like roses, don't you, and pinks and lilies and pansies?"

He saw he had struck the right chord as soon as he mentioned the flowers. The sullen look vanished as if by magic. Her face changed as suddenly as an April day.

"Oh, yes!" she cried, with a beaming smile. "I loves'm bettah than anything!"

He tied his horse, and led the way to the conservatory. He opened the door for her to pass through, and then watched her closely to see what impression it would make on

her. He had expected a delighted exclamation of surprise, for he had good reason to be proud of his rare plants. They were arranged with a true artist's eye for color and effect.

She did not say a word for a moment, but drew a long breath, while the delicate pink in her cheeks deepened and her eyes lighted up. Then she began going slowly from flower to flower, laying her face against the cool, velvety purple of the pansies, touching the roses with her lips, and tilting the white lily-cups to look into their golden depths.

As she passed from one to another as lightly as a butterfly might have done, she began chanting in a happy undertone.

Ever since she had learned to talk she had a quaint little way of singing to herself. All the names that pleased her fancy she strung together in a crooning melody of her own.

There was no special tune. It sounded happy, although nearly always in a minor key.

"Oh, the jonquils an' the lilies!" she sang. "All white an' gold an' yellow. Oh, they're all a-smilin' at me, an' a-sayin' howdy! howdy!"

She was so absorbed in her intense enjoyment that she forgot all about the old Colonel. She was wholly unconscious that he was watching or listening.

"She really does love them," he thought, complacently. "To see her face one would think she had found a fortune."

It was another bond between them.

After awhile he took a small basket from the wall, and began to fill it with his choicest blooms.

"You shall have these to take home," he said. "Now come into the house and get your strawberries."

She followed him reluctantly, turning back several times for one more long sniff of the delicious fragrance.

She was not at all like the Colonel's ideal of what a little girl should be, as she sat in one of the high, stiff chairs, enjoying her strawberries. Her dusty little toes wriggled around in the curls on Fritz's back, as she used him for a footstool. Her dress was draggled and dirty, and she kept leaning

over to give the dog berries and cream from the spoon she was eating with herself.

He forgot all this, however, when she began to talk to him.

"My great-aunt Sally Tylah is to ou' house this mawnin'," she announced, confidentially. "That's why we came off. Do you know my Aunt Sally Tylah?"

"Well, slightly!" chuckled the Colonel. "She was my wife's half-sister. So you don't like her, eh? Well, I don't like her either."

He threw back his head and laughed heartily. The more the child talked the more entertaining he found her. He did not remember when he had ever been so amused before as he was by this tiny counterpart of himself.

When the last berry had vanished, she slipped down from the tall chair.

"Do you 'pose it's very late?" she asked, in an anxious voice. "Mom Beck will be comin' for me soon."

"Yes, it is nearly noon," he answered. "It didn't do much good to run away from your Aunt Tyler; she'll see you after all."

"Well, she can't 'queeze me an' kiss me, 'cause I've been naughty, an' I'll be put to bed like I was the othah day, just as soon as I get home. I 'most wish I was there now," she sighed. "It's so fa' an' the sun's so hot. I lost my sunbonnet when I was comin' heah, too."

Something in the tired, dirty face prompted the old Colonel to say, "Well, my horse hasn't been put away yet. I'll take you home on Maggie Boy."

The next moment he repented making such an offer, thinking what the neighbors might say if they should meet him on the road with Elizabeth's child in his arm.

But it was too late. He could not unclasp the trusting little hand that was slipped in his. He could not cloud the happiness of the eager little face by retracting his promise.

He swung himself into the saddle, with her in front.

Then he put his one arm around her with a firm clasp, as he reached forward to take the bridle.

"You couldn't take Fritz on behin', could you?" she asked, anxiously. "He's mighty ti'ed too."

"No," said the Colonel, with a laugh. "Maggie Boy might object and throw us all off."

Hugging her basket of flowers close in her arms, she leaned her head against him contentedly as they cantered down the avenue.

"Look!" whispered all the locusts, waving their hands to each other excitedly. "Look! The master has his own again. The dear old times are coming back to us."

"How the trees blow!" exclaimed the child, looking up at the green arch overhead. "See! They's all a-noddin' to each othah."

"We'll have to get my shoes an' 'tockin's," she said, presently, when they were nearly home. "They're in that fence cawnah behin' a log."

The Colonel obediently got down and handed them to her. As he mounted again he saw a carriage coming toward them. He recognized one of his nearest neighbors. Striking the astonished Maggie Boy with his spur, he turned her across the railroad track, down the steep embankment, and into an unfrequented lane.

"This road is just back of your garden," he said. "Can you get through the fence if I take you there?"

"That's the way we came out," was the answer. "See that hole where the palin's are off?"

Just as he was about to lift her down, she put one arm around his neck, and kissed him softly on the cheek.

"Good-bye, gran'fathah'," she said, in her most winning way. "I've had a mighty nice time." Then she added, in a lower tone, " 'Kuse me fo' throwin' mud on yo' coat."

He held her close a moment, thinking nothing had ever before been half so sweet as the way she called him grandfather.

From that moment his heart went out to her as it had to little Tom and Elizabeth. It made no difference if her mother had forfeited his love. It made no difference if Jack Sherman was her father, and that the two men heartily hated each other.

It was his own little grandchild he held in his arms.

She had sealed the relationship with a trusting kiss.

"Child," he said, huskily, "you will come and see me again, won't you, no matter if they do tell you not to? You shall have all the flowers and berries you want, and you can ride Maggie Boy as often as you please."

She looked up into his face. It was very familiar to her. She had looked at his portrait often, unconsciously recognizing a kindred spirit that she longed to know.

Her ideas of grandfathers, gained from stories and observation, led her to class them with fairy godmothers. She had always wished for one.

The day they moved to Lloydsborough, Locust had been pointed out to her as her grandfather's home. From that time on she slipped away with Fritz on every possible occasion to peer through the gate, hoping for a glimpse of him.

"Yes, I'll come suah!" she promised. "I likes you just lots, gran'fathah!"

He watched her scramble through the hole in the fence. Then he turned his horse's head slowly homeward.

A scrap of white lying on the grass attracted his attention as he neared the gate.

"It's the lost sunbonnet," he said, with a

smile. He carried it into the house, and hung it on the hat-rack in the wide front hall.

"Ole marse is crosser'n two sticks," growled Walker to the cook at dinner. "There ain't no livin' with him. What do you s'pose is the mattah?"

CHAPTER IV.

Mom Beck was busy putting lunch on the table when the Little Colonel looked in at the kitchen door.

So she did not see a little tramp, carrying her shoes in one hand, and a basket in the other, who paused there a moment. But when she took up the pan of beaten biscuit she was puzzled to find that several were missing.

"It beats my time," she said, aloud. "The parrot couldn't have reached them, an' Lloyd an' the dog have been in the pa'lah all mawnin'. Somethin' has jus' natch'ly done sperrited 'em away."

Fritz was gravely licking his lips, and the Little Colonel had her mouth full, when they suddenly made their appearance on the front porch.

Aunt Sally Tyler gave a little shriek, and stopped rocking.

"Why, Lloyd Sherman!" gasped her mother, in dismay. "Where have you been? I thought you were with Becky all the time. I was sure I heard you singing out there a little while ago."

"I've been to see my gran'fathah," said the child, speaking very fast. "I made mud pies on his front 'teps, an' we both of us got mad, an' I throwed mud on him, an' he gave me some 'trawberries an' all these flowers, an' brought me home on Maggie Boy."

She stopped out of breath.

Mrs. Tyler and her niece exchanged astonished glances.

"But, baby, how could you disgrace mother so by going up there looking like a dirty little beggar?"

"He didn't care," replied Lloyd, calmly. "He made me promise to come again, no mattah if you all did tell me not to."

Just then Becky announced that lunch was ready, and carried the child away to make her presentable.

To Lloyd's great surprise she was not put to bed, but was allowed to go to the table as soon as she was dressed. It was not long until she had told every detail of the morning's experience.

While she was taking her afternoon nap, the two ladies sat out on the porch, gravely discussing all she had told them.

"It doesn't seem right for me to allow her to go there," said Mrs. Sherman, "after the way papa has treated us. I can never forgive him for all the terrible things he has said about Jack, and I know Jack can never be friends with him on account of what he has said about me. He has been so harsh and unjust that I don't want my little Lloyd to have anything to do with him. I wouldn't for worlds have him think that I encourage her going there."

"Well, yes, I know," answered her aunt, slowly. "But there are some things to consider besides your pride, Elizabeth. There's the child herself, you know. Now that Jack has lost so much, and your prospects are so uncertain, you ought to think of her interests. It would be a pity for Locust to go to strangers when it has been in your family for so many generations. That's what it certainly will do unless something turns up to interfere. Old Judge Woodard told me himself that your father had made a will, leaving everything he owns to some medical institution. Imagine Locust being turned into a sanitarium or a training-school for nurses!"

"Dear old place!" said Mrs. Sherman, with tears in her eyes. "No one ever had a happier childhood than I passed under these old locusts. Every tree seems like a friend. I would be glad for Lloyd to enjoy the place as I did."

"I'd let her go as much as she pleases, Elizabeth. She's so much like the old Colonel that they ought to understand each other, and get along capitally. Who knows, and it might end in you all making up some day."

Mrs. Sherman raised her head haughtily. "No, indeed, Aunt Sally. I can forgive and forget much, but you are greatly mistaken if you think I can go to such lengths as that. He closed his doors against me with a curse, for no reason on earth but that the man I loved was born north of the Mason and Dixon line. There never was a nobler man living than Jack, and papa would have seen it if he hadn't deliberately shut his eyes and refused to look at him. He was just prejudiced and stubborn."

Aunt Sally said nothing, but her thoughts took the shape of Mom Beck's declaration, "The Lloyds is all stubbo'n."

"I wouldn't go through his gate now if he got down on his knees and begged me," continued Elizabeth, hotly.

"It's too bad," exclaimed her aunt; "he was always so perfectly devoted to 'little daughter,' as he used to call you. I don't like him myself. We never could get along together at all, because he is so high-strung and overbearing. But I know it would have made your poor mother mighty unhappy if she could have foreseen all this."

Elizabeth sat with the tears dropping down on her little white hands, as her aunt proceeded to work on her sympathies in every way she could think of.

Presently Lloyd came out all fresh and rosy from her long nap, and went to play in the shade of the great beech trees that guarded the cottage.

"I never saw a child with such influence over animals," said her mother, as Lloyd came around the house with the parrot perched on the broom she was carrying. "She'll walk right up to any strange dog and make friends with it, no matter how savage-looking it is. And there's Polly, so old and cross that she screams and scolds dreadfully if any of us go near her. But Lloyd dresses her up in doll's clothes, puts paper bonnets on her, and makes her just as uncomfortable as she pleases. Look! That is one of her favourite amusements."

The Little Colonel squeezed the parrot into a tiny doll carriage, and began to trundle it back and forth as fast as she could run.

"Ha! Ha!" screamed the bird. "Polly is a lady! Oh, Lordy! I'm so happy!"

"She caught that from the washerwoman," laughed Mrs. Sherman. "I should think the poor thing would be dizzy from whirling around so fast."

"Quit that, chillun; stop yo' fussin'," screamed Polly, as Lloyd grabbed her up and began to pin a shawl around her neck. She clucked angrily, but never once attempted to snap at the dimpled fingers that squeezed her tight. Suddenly, as if her patience was completely exhausted, she uttered a disdainful "Oh, pshaw!" and flew up into an old cedar tree.

"Mothah! Polly won't play with me any moah," shrieked the child, flying into a rage. She stamped and scowled and grew red in the face. Then she began beating the trunk of the tree with the old broom she had been carrying.

"Did you ever see anything so much like the old Colonel?" said Mrs. Tyler, in astonishment. "I wonder if she acted that way this morning."

"I don't doubt it at all," answered Mrs. Sherman. "She'll be over it in just a moment. These little spells never last long."

Mrs. Sherman was right. In a few moments Lloyd came up the walk, singing.

"I wish you'd tell me a pink story," she said, coaxingly, as she leaned against her mother's knee.

"Not now, dear; don't you see that I am busy talking to Aunt Sally? Run and ask Mom Beck for one."

"What on earth does she mean by a pink story?" asked Mrs. Tyler.

"Oh, she is so fond of colors. She is always asking for a pink or a blue or a white story. She wants everything in the story tinged with whatever color she chooses,—dresses, parasols, flowers, sky, even the icing on the cakes and the paper on the walls."

"What an odd little thing she is!" exclaimed Mrs. Tyler. "Isn't she lots of company for you?"

She need not have asked that question if she could have seen them that evening, sitting together in the early twilight.

Lloyd was in her mother's lap, leaning her head against her shoulder as they rocked slowly back and forth on the dark porch.

There was an occasional rattle of wheels along the road, a twitter of sleepy birds, a

distant croaking of frogs.

Mom Beck's voice floated in from the kitchen, where she was stepping briskly around.

"Oh, the clouds hang heavy, an' it's gwine to rain.
 Fa'well, my dyin' friends."

she sang.

Lloyd put her arms closer around her mother's neck.

"Let's talk about Papa Jack," she said. "What you 'pose he's doin' now, 'way out West?"

Elizabeth, feeling like a tired, homesick child herself, held her close, and was comforted as she listened to the sweet little voice talking about the absent father.

The moon came up after awhile, and streamed in through the vines of the porch. The hazel eyes slowly closed as Elizabeth began to hum an old-time negro lullaby.

"Wondah if she'll run away tomorrow," whispered Mom Beck, as she came out to carry her in the house.

"Who'd evah think now, lookin' at her pretty, innocent face, that she could be so naughty? Bless her little soul!"

The kind old black face was laid lovingly a moment against the fair, soft cheek of the Little Colonel. Then she lifted her in her strong arms, and carried her gently away to bed.

CHAPTER V.

Summer lingers long among the Kentucky hills. Each passing day seemed fairer than the last to the Little Colonel, who had never before known anything of country life.

Roses climbed up and almost hid the small white cottage. Red birds sang in the woodbine. Squirrels chattered in the beeches. She was out-of-doors all day long.

Sometimes she spent hours watching the ants carry away the sugar she sprinkled for them. Sometimes she caught flies for an old spider that had his den under the porch steps.

"He is an ogah" (ogre), she explained to Fritz. "He's bewitched me so's I have to kill whole families of flies for him to eat."

She was always busy and always happy.

Before June was half over it got to be a common occurrence for Walker to ride up to the gate on the Colonel's horse. The excuse was always to have a passing word with Mom Beck. But before he rode away, the Little Colonel was generally mounted in front of him. It was not long before she felt almost as much at home at Locust as she did at the cottage.

The neighbors began to comment on it after awhile. "He will surely make up with Elizabeth at this rate," they said. But at the end of the summer the father and daughter had not even had a passing glimpse of each other.

One day, late in September, as the Little Colonel clattered up and down the hall with her grandfather's spur buckled on her tiny foot, she called back over her shoulder: "Papa Jack's comin' home tomorrow."

The Colonel paid no attention.

"I say," she repeated, "Papa Jack's comin' home tomorrow."

"Well," was the gruff response. "Why couldn't he stay where he was? I suppose you won't want to come here any more after he gets back."

"No, I 'pose not," she answered, so carelessly that he was conscious of a very jealous feeling.

"Chilluns always like to stay with their fathahs when they's nice as my Papa Jack is."

The old man growled something behind his newspaper that she did not hear. He would have been glad to choke this man who had come between him and his only child, and he hated him worse than ever when he realized what a large place he held in Lloyd's little heart.

She did not go back to Locust the next day, nor for weeks after that.

She was up almost as soon as Mom Beck next morning, thoroughly enjoying the bustle of preparation.

She had a finger in everything, from polishing the silver to turning the ice cream freezer.

Even Fritz was scrubbed till he came out

of his bath with his curls all white and shining. He was proud of himself, from his silky bangs to the tip of his tasselled tail.

Just before train time, the Little Colonel stuck his collar full of late pink roses, and stood back to admire the effect. Her mother came to the door, dressed for the evening. She wore an airy-looking dress of the palest, softest blue. There was a white rosebud caught in her dark hair. A bright color, as fresh as Lloyd's own, tinged her cheeks, and the glad light in her brown eyes made them unusually brilliant.

Lloyd jumped up and threw her arms about her. "Oh, mothah," she cried, "you an' Fritz is so bu'ful!"

The engine whistled up the road at the crossing. "Come, we have just time to get to the station," said Mrs. Sherman, holding out her hand.

They went through the gate, down the narrow path that ran beside the dusty road. The train had just stopped in front of the little station when they reached it.

A number of gentlemen, coming out from the city to spend Sunday at the hotel, came down the steps.

They glanced admiringly from the beautiful, girlish face of the mother to the happy child dancing impatiently up and down at her side. They could not help smiling at Fritz as he frisked about in his imposing rose-collar.

"Why, where's Papa Jack?" asked Lloyd, in distress, as passenger after passenger stepped down. "Isn't he goin' to come?"

The tears were beginning to gather in her eyes, when she saw him in the door of the car; not hurrying along to meet them as he always used to come, so full of life and vigor, but leaning heavily on the porter's shoulder, looking very pale and weak.

Lloyd looked up at her mother, from whose face every particle of color had faded. Mrs. Sherman gave a low, frightened cry as she sprang forward to meet him.

"Oh, Jack! What is the matter? What has happened to you?" she exclaimed, as he took her in his arms. The train had gone on, and they were left alone on the platform.

"Just a little sick spell," he answered, with

a smile. "We had a fire out at the mines, and I overtaxed myself some. I've had fever ever since, and it has pulled me down considerably."

"I must send somebody for a carriage," she said, looking around anxiously.

"No, indeed," he protested. "It's only a few steps; I can walk it as well as not. The sight of you and the baby has made me stronger already."

He sent a colored boy on ahead with his valise, and they walked slowly up the path, with Fritz running wildly around them, bark-

ing a glad welcome.

"How sweet and homelike it all looks!" he said, as he stepped into the hall, where Mom Beck was just lighting the lamps. Then he sank down on the couch, completely exhausted, and wearily closed his eyes.

The Little Colonel looked at his white face in alarm. All the gladness seemed to have been taken out of the homecoming.

Her mother was busy trying to make him comfortable, and paid no attention to the disconsolate little figure wandering about the house alone. Mom Beck had gone for the doctor.

The supper was drying up in the warming-oven. The ice cream was melting in the freezer. Nobody seemed to care. There was no one to notice the pretty table with its array of flowers and cut glass and silver.

When Mom Beck came back, Lloyd ate all by herself, and then sat out on the kitchen doorstep while the doctor made his visit.

She was just going mournfully off to bed with an aching lump in her throat, when her mother opened the door.

"Come tell papa good-night," she said. "He's lots better now."

She climbed up on the bed beside him, and buried her face on his shoulder to hide the tears she had been trying to keep back all evening.

"How the child has grown!" he exclaimed. "Do you notice, Beth, how much plainer she talks? She does not seem at all like the baby I left last spring. Well, she'll soon be six years old,—a real little woman. She'll be papa's little comfort."

The ache in her throat was all gone after

that. She romped with Fritz all the time she was undressing.

Papa Jack was worse next morning. It was hard for Lloyd to keep quiet when the late September sunshine was so gloriously yellow and the whole outdoors seemed so wide awake.

She tiptoed out of the darkened room where her father lay, and swung on the front gate until she saw the doctor riding up on his bay horse. It seemed to her that the day never would pass.

Mom Beck, rustling around in her best dress ready for church, that afternoon, took pity on the lonesome child.

"Go get yo' best hat, honey," she said, "an' I'll take you with me."

It was one of the Little Colonel's greatest pleasures to be allowed to go to the colored church.

She loved to listen to the singing, and would sit perfectly motionless while the sweet voices blended like the chords of some mighty organ as they sent the old hymns rolling heavenward.

Service had already commenced by the

time they took their seats. Nearly everybody in the congregation was swaying back and forth in time to the mournful melody of "Sinnah, sinnah, where's you boun'?"

One old woman across the aisle began clapping her hands together, and repeated in a singsong tone, "Oh, Lordy! I'm so happy!"

"Why, that's just what our parrot says," exclaimed Lloyd, so much surprised that she spoke right out loud.

Mom Beck put her handkerchief over her mouth, and a general smile went around.

After that the child was very quiet until the time came to take the collection. She always enjoyed this part of the service more than anything else. Instead of passing baskets around, each person was invited to come forward and lay his offering on the table.

Woolly heads wagged, and many feet kept time to the tune:

> "Oh! I'se boun' to git to glory.
> Hallelujah! Le' me go!"

The Little Colonel proudly marched up with Mom Beck's contribution, and then watched the others pass down the aisle. One young girl in a gorgeously trimmed dress paraded up to the table several times, singing at the top of her voice.

"Look at that good-fo'-nothin' Lize Rich-a'ds," whispered Mom Beck's nearest neighbour, with a sniff. "She done got a nickel changed into pennies so she could ma'ch up an' show herself five times."

It was nearly sundown when they started home. A tall colored man, wearing a high silk hat and carrying a gold-headed cane, joined them on the way out.

"Howdy, Sistah Po'tah," he said, gravely shaking hands. "That was a fine disco'se we had the pleasuah of listenin' to this evenin'."

" 'Deed it was, Brothah Fostah," she answered. "How's all up yo' way?"

The Little Colonel, running on after a couple of white butterflies, paid no attention to the conversation until she heard her own name mentioned.

"Mistah Sherman came home last night, I heah."

"Yes, but not to stay long, I'm afraid. He's a mighty sick man, if I'm any judge. He's down with fevah,—regulah typhoid. He doesn't look to me like he's long for this world. What's to become of poah Miss 'Lizabeth if that's the case, is moah'n I know."

"We mustn't cross the bridge till we come to it, Sistah Po'tah," he suggested.

"I know that; but a lookin' glass broke yeste'day mawnin' when nobody had put a fingah on it. An' his picture fell down off the wall while I was sweepin' the pa'lah. Pete said his dawg done howl all night last night, an' I've dremp three times hand runnin' 'bout muddy watah."

Mom Beck felt a little hand clutch her skirts, and turned to see a frightened little face looking anxiously up at her.

"Now, what's the mattah with you, honey?" she asked. "I'm only a-tellin' Mistah Fostah about some silly old signs my mammy used to believe in. But they don't mean nothin' at all."

Lloyd couldn't have told why she was unhappy. She had not understood all that Mom Beck had said, but her sensitive little mind was shadowed by a foreboding of trouble.

The shadow deepened as the days passed. Papa Jack got worse instead of better. There were times when he did not recognize any one, and talked wildly of things that had happened out at the mines.

All the long, beautiful October went by, and still he lay in the darkened room. Lloyd wandered listlessly from place to place, trying to keep out of the way, and to make as little trouble as possible.

"I'm a real little woman now," she repeated, proudly, whenever she was allowed to pound ice or carry fresh water. "I'm papa's little comfort."

One cold, frosty evening she was standing in the hall, when the doctor came out of the room and began to put on his overcoat.

Her mother followed him to take his directions for the night.

He was an old friend of the family's. Elizabeth had climbed on his knees many a time when she was a child. She loved this faithful, white-haired old doctor almost as dearly as she had her father.

"My daughter," he said, kindly, laying his

hand on her shoulder, "you are wearing yourself out, and will be down yourself if you are not careful. You must have a professional nurse. No telling how long this is going to last. As soon as Jack is able to travel you must have a change of climate."

Her lips trembled. "We can't afford it, doctor," she said. "Jack has been too sick from the very first to talk about business. He always said a woman should not be worried with such matters, anyway. I don't know what arrangements he has made out West. For all I know, the little I have in my purse now may be all that stands between us and the poorhouse."

The doctor drew on his gloves.

"Why don't you tell your father how matters are?" he asked.

Then he saw he had ventured a step too far.

"I believe Jack would rather die than take help from his hands," she answered, drawing herself up proudly. Her eyes flashed. "I would, too, as far as I am concerned myself."

Then a tender look came over her pale, tired face, as she added, gently, "But I'd do anything on earth to help Jack get well."

The doctor cleared his throat vigorously, and bolted out with a gruff good-night. As he rode past Locust, he took solid satisfaction in shaking his fist at the light in an upper window.

CHAPTER VI.

The Little Colonel followed her mother to the dining room, but paused on the threshold as she saw her throw herself into Mom Beck's arms and burst out crying.

"Oh, Becky!" she sobbed, "what is going to become of us? The doctor says we must have a professional nurse, and we must go away from here soon. There are only a few dollars left in my purse, and I don't know what we'll do when they are gone. I just know Jack is going to die, and then I'll die, too, and then what will become of the baby?"

Mom Beck sat down, and took the trembling form in her arms.

"There, there!" she said, soothingly, "have

yo' cry out. It will do you good. Poah chile! All wo'n out with watchin' an' worry. Ne'm min', ole Becky is as good as a dozen nuhses yet. I'll get Judy to come up an' look aftah the kitchen. An' nobody ain' gwine to die, honey. Don't you go to slayin' all you's got befo' you's called on to do it. The good Lawd is goin' to pahvide fo' us same as Abraham."

The last Sabbath's sermon was still fresh in her mind.

"If we only hold out faithful, there's boun' to be a ram caught by the hawns some place, even if we haven't got eyes to see through the thickets. The Lawd will pahvide whethah it's a burnt offerin' or a meal's vittles. He sho'ly will."

Lloyd crept away frightened. It seemed such an awful thing to see her mother cry.

All at once her bright, happy world had changed to such a strange, uncertain place. She felt as if all sorts of terrible things were about to happen.

She went into the parlor, and crawled into a dark corner under the piano, feeling that there was no place to go for comfort, since the one who had always kissed away her little troubles was so heartbroken herself.

There was a patter of soft feet across the carpet, and Fritz poked his sympathetic nose into her face. She put her arms around him, and laid her head against his curly back with a desolate sob.

It is pitiful to think how much imaginative children suffer through their wrong conception of things.

She had seen the little roll of bills in her mother's pocketbook. She had seen how much smaller it grew every time it was taken out to pay for the expensive medicines that had to be bought so often. She had heard her mother tell the doctor that was all that stood between them and the poorhouse.

There was no word known to the Little Colonel that brought such thoughts of horror as the word poorhouse.

Her most vivid recollection of her life in New York was something that happened a few weeks before they left there.

One day in the park she ran away from the

maid, who, instead of Mom Beck, had taken charge of her that afternoon.

When the angry woman found her, she frightened her almost into a spasm by telling her what always happened to naughty children who ran away.

"They take all their pretty clothes off," she said, "and dress them up in old things made of bed-ticking. Then they take 'm to the poorhouse, where nobody but beggars live. They don't have anything to eat but cabbage and corn-dodger, and they have to eat that out of tin pans. And they just have a pile of straw to sleep in."

On their way home she had pointed out to the frightened child a poor woman who was grubbing in an ash-barrel.

"That's the way people get to look who live in poorhouses," she said.

It was this memory that was troubling the Little Colonel now.

"Oh, Fritz!" she whispered, with the tears running down her cheeks, "I can't beah to think of my pretty mothah goin' there. That woman's eyes were all red, an' her hair was jus' awful. She was so bony an' stahved-lookin'. It would jus' kill poah Papa Jack to lie on straw an' eat out of a tin pan. I know it would!"

When Mom Beck opened the door, hunting her, the room was so dark that she would have gone away if the dog had not come running out from under the piano.

"You heah, too, chile?" she asked, in surprise. "I have to go down now an' see if I can get Judy to come help tomorrow. Do you think you can undress yo'self tonight?"

"Of co'se," answered the Little Colonel. Mom Beck was in such a hurry to be off that she did not notice the tremble in the voice that answered her.

"Well, the can'le is lit in yo' room. So run along now like a nice little lady, an' don't bothah yo' mamma. She got her hands full already."

"All right," answered the child.

A quarter of an hour later she stood in her little white nightgown with her hands on the doorknob.

She opened the door just a crack and peeped in. Her mother laid her finger on her

lips, and beckoned silently. In another instant Lloyd was in her lap. She had cried herself quiet in the dark corner under the piano; but there was something more pathetic in her eyes than tears. It was the expression of one who understood and sympathized.

"Oh, mothah," she whispered, "we does have such lots of troubles."

"Yes, chickabiddy, but I hope they will soon be over now," was the answer, as the anxious face tried to smile bravely for the child's sake. "Papa is sleeping so nicely now he is sure to be better in the morning."

That comforted the Little Colonel some, but for days she was haunted by the fear of the poorhouse.

Every time her mother paid out any money she looked anxiously to see how much was still left. She wandered about the place, touching the trees and vines with caressing hands, feeling that she might soon have to leave them.

She loved them all so dearly,—every stick and stone, and even the stubby old snowball bushes that never bloomed.

Her dresses were outgrown and faded, but no one had any time or thought to spend on getting her new ones. A little hole began to come in the toe of each shoe.

She was still wearing her summer sunbonnet, although the days were getting frosty.

She was a proud little thing. It mortified her for any one to see her looking so shabby. Still she uttered no word of complaint, for fear of lessening the little amount in the pocketbook that her mother had said stood between them and the poorhouse.

She sat with her feet tucked under her when any one called.

"I wouldn't mind bein' a little beggah so much myself," she thought, "but I jus' can't have my bu'ful sweet mothah lookin' like that awful red-eyed woman."

One day the doctor called Mrs. Sherman out into the hall. "I have just come from your father's," he said. "He is suffering from a severe attack of rheumatism. He is confined to his room, and is positively starving for company. He told me he would give anything in the world to have his little grandchild with him. There were tears in his eyes when he said

it, and that means a good deal from him. He fairly idolizes her. The servants have told him she mopes around and is getting thin and pale. He is afraid she will come down with the fever, too. He told me to use any stratagem I liked to get her there. But I think it's better to tell you frankly how matters stand. It will do the child good to have a change, Elizabeth, and I solemnly think you ought to let her go, for a week at least."

"But, doctor, she has never been away from me a single night in her life. She'd die of homesickness, and I know she'll never consent to leave me. Then suppose Jack should get worse—"

"We'll suppose nothing of the kind," he interrupted, brusquely. "Tell Becky to pack up her things. Leave Lloyd to me. I'll get her consent without any trouble."

"Come, Colonel," he called, as he left the house. "I'm going to take you for a little ride."

No one ever knew what the kind old fellow said to her to induce her to go to her grandfather's.

She came back from her ride looking brighter than she had in a long time. She felt that in some way, although in what way she could not understand, her going would help them to escape the dreaded poorhouse.

"Don't send Mom Beck with me," she pleaded, when the time came to start. "You come with me, mothah."

Mrs. Sherman had not been past the gate for weeks, but she could not refuse the coaxing hands that clung to hers.

It was a dull, dreary day. There was a chilling hint of snow in the damp air. The leaves whirled past them with a mournful rustling.

Mrs. Sherman turned up the collar of Lloyd's cloak.

"You must have a new one soon," she said, with a sigh. "Maybe one of mine could be made over for you. And those poor little shoes! I must think to send to town for a new pair."

The walk was over so soon. The Little Colonel's heart beat fast as they came in sight of the gate. She winked bravely to keep back the tears; for she had promised the doctor not to let her mother see her cry.

A week seemed such a long time to look forward to.

She clung to her mother's neck, feeling that she could never give her up so long.

"Tell me good-bye, baby dear," said Mrs. Sherman, feeling that she could not trust herself to stay much longer. "It is too cold for you to stand here. Run on, and I'll watch you till you get inside the door."

The Little Colonel started bravely down the avenue, with Fritz at her heels. Every few steps she turned to look back and kiss her hand.

Mrs. Sherman watched her through a blur of tears. It had been nearly seven years since she had last stood at that old gate. Such a crowd of memories came rushing up!

She looked again. There was a flutter of a white handkerchief as the Little Colonel and Fritz went up the steps. Then the great front door closed behind them.

CHAPTER VII.

That early twilight hour just before the lamps were lit was the lonesomest one the Little Colonel had ever spent.

Her grandfather was asleep upstairs. There was a cheery wood fire crackling on the hearth of the big fireplace in the hall, but the great house was so still. The corners were full of shadows.

She opened the front door with a wild longing to run away.

"Come, Fritz," she said, closing the door softly behind her, "let's go down to the gate."

The air was cold. She shivered as they raced along under the bare branches of the locusts. She leaned against the gate, peering out through the bars. The road stretched white through the gathering darkness in the direction of the little cottage.

"Oh, I want to go home so bad!" she sobbed. "I want to see my mothah."

She laid her hand irresolutely on the latch, pushed the gate ajar, and then hesitated.

"No, I promised the doctah I'd stay," she thought. "He said I could help mothah and Papa Jack, both of 'em, by stayin' heah, an' I'll do it."

Fritz, who had pushed himself through the partly opened gate to rustle around among

the dead leaves outside, came bounding back with something in his mouth.

"Heah, suh!" she called. "Give it to me!" He dropped a small gray kid glove in her outstretched hand. "Oh, it's mothah's!" she cried. "I reckon she dropped it when she was tellin' me good-bye. Oh, you deah old dog fo' findin' it."

She laid the glove against her cheek as fondly as if it had been her mother's soft hand. There was something wonderfully comforting in the touch.

As they walked slowly back toward the house she rolled it up and put it lovingly away in her tiny apron pocket.

All that week it was a talisman whose touch helped the homesick little soul to be brave and womanly.

When Maria, the colored housekeeper, went into the hall to light the lamps, the Little Colonel was sitting on the big fur rug in front of the fire, talking contentedly to Fritz, who lay with his curly head in her lap.

"You all's goin' to have tea in the Cun'l's room tonight," said Maria. "He tole me to tote it up soon as he rung the bell."

"There it goes now," cried the child, jumping up from the rug.

She followed Maria up the wide stairs. The Colonel was sitting in a large easy chair, wrapped in a gaily flowered dressing-gown, that made his hair look unusually white by contrast.

His dark eyes were intently watching the door. As it opened to let the Little Colonel pass through, a very tender smile lighted up his stern face.

"So you did come to see grandpa after all," he cried, triumphantly. "Come here and give me a kiss. Seems to me you've been staying away a mighty long time."

As she stood beside him with his arm around her, Walker came in with a tray full of dishes.

"We're going to have a regular little tea-party," said the Colonel.

Lloyd watched with sparkling eyes as Walker set out the rare old-fashioned dishes. There was a fat little silver sugar bowl with a butterfly perched on each side to form the handles, and there was a slim, graceful cream pitcher shaped like a lily.

"They belonged to your great-great-grandmother," said the Colonel, "and they're going to be yours some day if you grow up and have a house of your own."

The expression on her beaming face was worth a fortune to the Colonel.

When Walker pushed her chair up to the table, she turned to her grandfather with shining eyes.

"Oh, it's just like a pink story," she cried, clapping her hands. "The shades on the can'les, the icin' on the cake, an' the posies in the bowl,—why, even the jelly is that colah, too. Oh, my darlin' little teacup! It's jus' like a pink rosebud. I'm so glad I came!"

The Colonel smiled at the success of his plan. In the depths of his satisfaction he even had a plate of quail and toast set down on the hearth for Fritz.

"This is the nicest pahty I evah was at," remarked the Little Colonel, as Walker helped her to jam the third time.

Her grandfather chuckled.

"Blackberry jam always makes me think of Tom," he said. "Did you ever hear what your Uncle Tom did when he was a little fellow in dresses?"

She shook her head gravely.

"Well, the children were all playing hide-and-seek one day. They hunted high and they hunted low after everybody else had been caught, but they couldn't find Tom. At last they began to call, 'Home free! You can come home free!' but he did not come. When he had been hidden so long they were frightened about him, they went to their mother and told her he wasn't to be found anywhere. She looked down the well and behind the fire-boards in the fireplaces. They called and called till they were out of breath. Finally she thought of looking in the big dark pantry where she kept her fruit. There stood Mister Tom. He had opened a jar of blackberry jam, and was just going for it with both hands. The jam was all over his face and hair and little gingham apron, and even up his wrists. He was the funniest sight I ever saw."

The Little Colonel laughed heartily at his description, and begged for more stories. Before he knew it he was back in the past with

his little Tom and Elizabeth.

Nothing could have entertained the child more than these scenes he recalled of her mother's childhood.

"All her old playthings are up in the garret," he said, as they rose from the table. "I'll have them brought down tomorrow. There's a doll I brought her from New Orleans once when she was about your size. No telling what it looks like now, but it was a beauty when it was new."

Lloyd clapped her hands and spun around the room like a top.

"Oh, I'm so glad I came!" she exclaimed for the third time. "What did she call the doll, gran'fathah, do you remembah?"

"I never paid much attention to such things," he answered, "but I do remember the name of this one, because she named it for her mother,—Amanthis."

"Amanthis," repeated the child, dreamily, as she leaned against his knee. "I think that is a lovely name, gran'fathah. I wish they had called me that." She repeated it softly several times. "It sounds like the wind a-blowin' through white clovah, doesn't it?"

"It is a beautiful name to me, my child," answered the old man, laying his hand tenderly on her soft hair, "but not so beautiful as the woman who bore it. She was the fairest flower of all Kentucky. There never was another lived as sweet and gentle as your Grandmother Amanthis."

He stroked her hair absently, and gazed into the fire. He scarcely noticed when she slipped away from him.

She buried her face a moment in the bowl of pink roses. Then she went to the window and drew back the curtain. Leaning her head against the window sill, she began stringing on the thread of a tune the things that just then thrilled her with a sense of their beauty.

"Oh, the locus' trees a-blowin'," she sang, softly. "An' the moon a-shinin' through them. An' the starlight an' pink roses; an' Amanthis—an' Amanthis!"

She hummed it over and over until Walker had finished carrying the dishes away.

It was a strange thing that the Colonel's unfrequent moods of tenderness were like those warm days that they call weather-breeders.

They were sure to be followed by a change of atmosphere. This time as the fierce rheumatic pain came back he stormed at Walker, and scolded him for everything he did and everything he left undone.

When Maria came up to put Lloyd to bed, Fritz was tearing around the room barking at his shadow.

"Put that dog out, M'ria!" roared the Colonel, almost crazy with its antics. "Take it downstairs, and put it out of the house, I say! Nobody but a heathen would let a dog sleep in the house, anyway."

The homesick feeling began to creep over Lloyd again. She had expected to keep Fritz in her room at night for company. But for the touch of the little glove in her pocket, she would have said something ugly to her grandfather when he spoke so harshly.

His own ill humor was reflected in her scowl as she followed Maria down the stairs to drive Fritz out into the dark.

They stood a moment in the open door, after Maria had slapped him with her apron to make him go off the porch.

"Oh, look at the new moon!" cried Lloyd, pointing to the slender crescent in the autumn sky.

"I'se feared to, honey," answered Maria, "less I should see it through the trees. That 'ud bring me bad luck for a month, suah. I'll go out on the lawn where it's open, an' look at it ovah my right shouldah."

While they were walking backward down the path, intent on reaching a place where they could have an uninterrupted view of the moon, Fritz sneaked around to the other end of the porch.

No one was watching. He slipped into the house as noiselessly as his four soft feet could carry him.

Maria, going through the dark upper hall, with a candle held high above her head and Lloyd clinging to her skirts, did not see a tasselled tail swinging along in front of her. It disappeared under the big bed when she led Lloyd into the room next the old Colonel's.

The child felt very sober while she was being put to bed.

The furniture was heavy and dark. An ugly portrait of a cross old man in a wig frowned

at her from over the mantel. The dancing fire-light made his eyes frightfully lifelike.

The bed was so high she had to climb on a chair to get in. She heard Maria's heavy feet go shuffling down the stairs. A door banged. Then it was so still she could hear the clock tick in the next room.

It was the first time in all her life that her mother had not come to kiss her good night.

Her lips quivered, and a big tear rolled down on the pillow.

She reached out to the chair beside her bed, where her clothes were hanging, and felt in her apron pocket for the little glove. She sat up in bed, and looked at it in the dim fire-light. Then she held it against her face. "Oh, I want my mothah! I want my mothah!" she sobbed, in a heartbroken whisper.

Laying her head on her knees, she began to cry quietly, but with great sobs that nearly choked her.

There was a rustling under the bed. She lifted her wet face in alarm. Then she smiled through her tears, for there was Fritz, her own dear dog, and not an unknown horror wait-ing to grab her.

He stood on his hind legs, eagerly trying to lap away her tears with his friendly red tongue.

She clasped him in her arms with an ec-static hug. "Oh, you're such a comfort!" she whispered. "I can go to sleep now."

She spread her apron on the bed, and mo-tioned him to jump. With one spring he was beside her.

It was nearly midnight when the door from the Colonel's room was noiselessly opened.

The old man stirred the fire gently until it burst into a bright flame. Then he turned to the bed. "You rascal!" he whispered, looking at Fritz, who raised his head quickly with a threatening look in his wicked eyes.

Lloyd lay with one hand stretched out, holding the dog's protecting paw. The other held something against her tear-stained cheek.

"What under the sun!" he thought, as he drew it gently from her fingers. The little glove lay across his hand, slim and aristocratic-looking. He knew instinctively whose it was. "Poor little thing's been crying," he thought. "She wants Elizabeth. And so do I! And so

do I!" his heart cried out with bitter longing. "It's never been like home since she left."

He laid the glove back on her pillow, and went to his room.

"If Jack Sherman should die," he said to himself many times that night, "then she would come home again. Oh, little daughter, little daughter! Why did you ever leave me?"

CHAPTER VIII.

The first thing that greeted the Little Colo-nel's eyes when she opened them next morn-ing was her mother's old doll. Maria had laid it on the pillow beside her.

It was beautifully dressed, although in a queer, old-fashioned style that seemed very strange to the child.

She took it up with careful fingers, remem-bering its great age. Maria had warned her not to waken her grandfather, so she admired it in whispers.

"Jus' think, Fritz," she exclaimed, "this doll has seen my Gran'mothah Amanthis, an' it's named for her. My mothah wasn't any bigger'n me when she played with it. I think it is the loveliest doll I evah saw in my whole life."

Fritz gave a jealous bark.

"Sh!" commanded his little mistress. "Didn't you heah M'ria say, 'Fo' de Lawd's sake don't wake up ole Marse?' Why don't you mind?"

The Colonel was not in the best of hu-mors after such a wakeful night, but the sight of her happiness made him smile in spite of himself, when she danced into his room with the doll.

She had eaten an early breakfast and gone back upstairs to examine the other toys that were spread out in her room.

The door between the two rooms was ajar. All the time he was dressing and taking his coffee he could hear her talking to someone. He supposed it was Maria. But as he glanced over his mail he heard the Little Colonel say-ing, "May Lilly, do you know about Billy Goat Gruff? Do you want me to tell you that story?"

He leaned forward until he could look

through the narrow opening of the door. Two heads were all he could see,—Lloyd's, soft-haired and golden, May Lilly's, covered with dozens of tightly braided little black tails.

He was about to order May Lilly back to the cabin, when he remembered the scene that followed the last time he had done so. He concluded to keep quiet and listen.

"Billy Goat Gruff was so fat," the story went on, "jus' as fat as gran'fathah."

The Colonel glanced up with an amused smile at the fine figure reflected in an opposite mirror.

"Trip-trap, trip-trap, went Billy Goat Gruff's little feet ovah the bridge to the giant's house."

Just at this point Walker, who was putting things in order, closed the door between the rooms.

"Open that door!" called the Colonel, furious at the interruption.

In his haste to obey, Walker knocked over a pitcher of water that had been left on the floor beside the washstand.

Then the Colonel yelled at him to be quick about mopping it up, so that by the time the door was finally opened, Lloyd was finishing her story.

The Colonel looked in just in time to see her put her hands to her temples, with her forefingers protruding from her forehead like horns. She said in a deep voice, as she brandished them at May Lilly, "With my two long speahs I'll poke yo' eyeballs through yo'

eahs."

The little darky fell back giggling. "That sut'n'y was like a billy goat. We had one once that 'ud make a body step around mighty peart. It slip up behine me one mawnin' on the poach, an' fo' awhile I thought my haid was buss open suah. I got up toreckly, though, an' I cotch him, and when I done got through, Mistah billy goat feel po'ly moah'n a week. He sut'n'y did."

Walker grinned, for he had witnessed the scene.

Just then Maria put her head in at the door to say, "May Lilly, yo' mammy's callin' you."

Lloyd and Fritz followed her noisily downstairs. Then for nearly an hour it was very quiet in the great house.

The Colonel, looking out of the window, could see Lloyd playing hide-and-seek with Fritz under the bare locust trees.

When she came in her cheeks were glowing from her run in the frosty air. Her eyes shone like stars, and her face was radiant.

"See what I've found down in the dead leaves," she cried. "A little blue violet, bloomin' all by itself."

She brought a tiny cup from the next room, that belonged to the set of doll dishes, and put the violet in it.

"There!" she said, setting it on the table at her grandfather's elbow. "Now I'll put Aman-this in this chair, where you can look at her, an' you won't get lonesome while I'm playing outdoors."

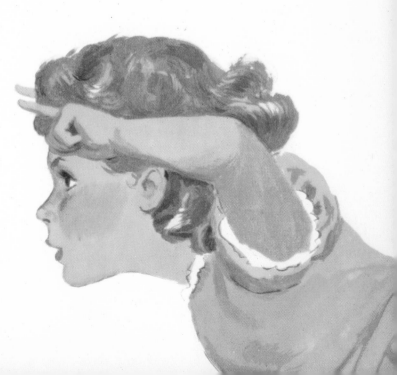

He drew her toward him and kissed her.

"Why, how cold your hands are!" he exclaimed. "Staying in this warm room all the time makes me forget it is so wintry outdoors. I don't believe you are dressed warmly enough. You ought not to wear sunbonnets this time of year."

Then for the first time he noticed her outgrown cloak and shabby shoes.

"What are you wearing these old clothes for?" he said, impatiently. "Why didn't they dress you up when you were going visiting? It isn't showing proper respect to send you off in the oldest things you've got."

It was a sore point with the Little Colonel. It hurt her pride enough to have to wear old clothes without being scolded for it. Besides, she felt that in some way her mother was being blamed for what could not be helped.

"They's the best I've got," she answered, proudly choking back the tears. "I don't need any new ones, 'cause maybe we'll be goin' away pretty soon."

"Going away!" he echoed, blankly. "Where?"

She did not answer until he repeated the question. Then she turned her back on him, and started toward the door. The tears she was too proud to let him see were running down her face.

"We's goin' to the poah-house," she exclaimed, defiantly, "jus' as soon as the money in the pocketbook is used up. It was nearly gone when I came away."

Here she began to sob, as she fumbled at the door she could not see to open.

"I'm goin' home to my mothah right now. She loves me if my clothes are old and ugly."

"Why, Lloyd," called the Colonel, amazed and distressed by her sudden burst of grief. "Come here to grandpa. Why didn't you tell me so before?"

The face, the tone, the outstretched arm, all drew her irresistibly to him. It was a relief to lay her head on his shoulder, and unburden herself of the fear that had haunted her so many days.

With her arms around his neck, and the precious little head held close to his heart, the old Colonel was in such a softened mood that he would have promised anything to comfort her.

"There, there," he said, soothingly, stroking her hair with a gentle hand, when she had told him all her troubles. "Don't you worry about that, my dear. Nobody is going to eat out of tin pans and sleep on straw. Grandpa just won't let them."

She sat up and wiped her eyes on her apron. "But Papa Jack would die befo' he'd take help from you," she wailed. "An' so would mothah. I heard her tell the doctah so."

The tender expression on the Colonel's face changed to one like flint, but he kept on stroking her hair.

"People sometimes change their minds," he said, grimly. "I wouldn't worry over a little thing like that if I were you. Don't you want to run downstairs and tell M'ria to give you a piece of cake?"

"Oh, yes," she exclaimed, smiling up at him. "I'll bring you some, too."

When the first train went into Louisville that afternoon, Walker was on board with an order in his pocket to one of the largest dry goods establishments in the city. When he came out again that evening, he carried a large box into the Colonel's room.

Lloyd's eyes shone as she looked into it. There was an elegant fur-trimmed cloak, a pair of dainty shoes, and a muff that she caught up with a shriek of delight.

"What kind of a thing is this?" grumbled the Colonel, as he took out a hat that had been carefully packed in one corner of the box. "I told them to send the most stylish thing they had. It looks like a scarecrow," he continued, as he set it askew on the child's head.

She snatched it off to look at it herself. "Oh, it's jus' like Emma Louise Wyfo'd's!" she exclaimed. "You didn't put it on straight. See! This is the way it goes."

She climbed up in front of the mirror, and put it on as she had seen Emma Louise wear hers.

"Well, it's a regular Napoleon hat," exclaimed the Colonel, much pleased. "So little girls nowadays have taken to wearing soldier's caps, have they? It's right becoming to you with your short hair. Grandpa is real proud of his 'little Colonel.' "

She gave him the military salute he had taught her, and then ran to throw her arms around him. "Oh, gran'fathah!" she exclaimed, between her kisses, "you'se jus' as good as Santa Claus, every bit."

The Colonel's rheumatism was better next day; so much better that toward evening he walked downstairs into the long drawing-room. The room had not been illuminated in years as it was that night.

Every wax taper was lighted in the silver candelabra, and the dim old mirrors multiplied their lights on every side. A great wood fire threw a cheerful glow over the portraits and the frescoed ceiling. All the linen covers had been taken from the furniture.

Lloyd, who had never seen this room except with the chairs shrouded and the blinds down, came running in presently. She was bewildered at first by the change. Then she began walking softly around the room, examining everything.

In one corner stood a tall, gilded harp that her grandmother had played in her girlhood. The heavy cover had kept it fair and untarnished through all the years it had stood un-

used. To the child's beauty-loving eyes it seemed the loveliest thing she had ever seen.

She stood with her hands clasped behind her as her gaze wandered from its pedals to the graceful curves of its tall frame. It shone like burnished gold in the soft firelight.

"Oh, gran'fathah!" she asked at last in a low, reverent tone, "where did you get it? Did an angel leave it heah fo' you?"

He did not answer for a moment. Then he said, huskily, as he looked up at a portrait over the mantel, "Yes, my darling, an angel did leave it here. She always was one. Come here to grandpa."

He took her on his knee, and pointed up to the portrait. The same harp was in the picture. Standing beside it, with one hand resting on its shining strings, was a young girl all in white.

"That's the way she looked the first time I ever saw her," said the Colonel, dreamily. "A June rose in her hair, and another at her throat; and her soul looked right out through those great, dark eyes—the purest, sweetest soul God ever made! My beautiful Amanthis!"

"My bu'ful Amanthis!" repeated the child, in an awed whisper.

She sat gazing into the lovely young face for a long time, while the old man seemed lost in dreams.

"Gran'fathah," she said at length, patting his cheek to attract his attention, and then nodding toward the portrait, "did she love my mothah like my mothah loves me?"

"Certainly, my dear," was the gentle reply.

It was the twilight hour, when the home-sick feeling always came back strongest to Lloyd.

"Then I jus' know that if my bu'ful gran'-mothah Amanthis could come down out of that frame, she'd go straight and put her arms around my mothah an' kiss away all her sorry feelin's."

The Colonel fidgeted uncomfortably in his chair a moment. Then to his great relief the tea bell rang.

CHAPTER IX.

Every evening after that during Lloyd's visit the fire burned on the hearth of the long drawing-room. All the wax candles were lighted, and the vases were kept full of flowers, fresh from the conservatory.

She loved to steal into the room before her grandfather came down, and carry on imaginary conversations with the old portraits.

Tom's handsome, boyish face had the greatest attraction for her. His eyes looked down so smilingly into hers that she felt he surely understood every word she said to him.

Once Walker overheard her saying, "Uncle Tom, I'm goin' to tell you a story 'bout Billy Goat Gruff."

Peeping into the room, he saw the child looking earnestly up at the picture, with her hands clasped behind her, as she began to repeat her favorite story. "It do beat all," he said to himself, "how one little chile like that can wake up a whole house. She's the life of the place."

The last evening of her visit, as the Colonel was coming downstairs he heard the faint vibration of a harp-string. It was the first time Lloyd had ever ventured to touch one. He paused on the steps opposite the door, and looked in.

"Heah, Fritz," she was saying, "you get up on the sofa, an' be the company, an' I'll sing fo' you."

Fritz, on the rug before the fire, opened one sleepy eye and closed it again. She stamped her foot and repeated her order. He paid no attention. Then she picked him up bodily, and, with much puffing and pulling, lifted him into a chair.

He waited until she had gone back to the harp, and then, with one spring, disappeared under the sofa.

"N'm min'," she said, in a disgusted tone. "I'll pay you back, mistah." Then she looked up at the portrait. "Uncle Tom," she said, "you be the company, an' I'll play fo' you."

Her fingers touched the strings so lightly that there was no discord in the random tones. Her voice carried the air clear and true, and the faint trembling of the harp strings interfered with the harmony no more than if a wandering breeze had been tangled in them as it passed.

"Sing me the songs that to me were so deah
    Long, long ago, long ago.
Tell me the tales I delighted to heah
    Long, long ago, long ago."

The sweet little voice sang it to the end without missing a word. It was the lullaby her mother oftenest sang to her.

The Colonel, who had sat down on the steps to listen, wiped his eyes.

"My 'long ago' is all that I have left to me," he thought, bitterly, "for tomorrow this little one, who brings back my past with every word and gesture, will leave me, too. Why can't that Jack Sherman die while he's about it, and let me have my own back again?"

That question recurred to him many times during the week after Lloyd's departure. He missed her happy voice at every turn. He missed her bright face at the table. The house seemed so big and desolate without her. He ordered all the covers put back on the drawing-room furniture, and the door locked as before.

It was a happy moment for the Little Colo-

nel when she was lifted down from Maggie Boy at the cottage gate.

She went dancing into the house, so glad to find herself in her mother's arms that she forgot all about the new cloak and muff that had made her so proud and happy.

She found her father propped up among the pillows, his fever all gone, and the old mischievous twinkle in his eyes.

He admired her new clothes extravagantly, paying her joking compliments until her face beamed; but when she had danced off to find Mom Beck, he turned to his wife. "Elizabeth," he said, wonderingly, "what do you suppose the old fellow gave her clothes for? I don't like it. I'm no beggar if I have lost lots of money. After all that's passed between us I don't feel like taking anything from his hands, or letting my child do it, either."

To his great surprise she laid her head down on his pillow beside his and burst into tears.

"Oh, Jack," she sobbed, "I spent the last dollar this morning. I wasn't going to tell you, but I don't know what is to become of us. He gave Lloyd those things because she was just in rags, and I couldn't afford to get anything new."

He looked perplexed. "Why, I brought home so much," he said, in a distressed tone. "I knew I was in for a long siege of sickness, but I was sure there was enough to tide us over that."

She raised her head. "You brought money home!" she replied, in surprise. "I hoped you had, and looked through all your things, but there was only a little change in one of your pockets. You must have imagined it when you were delirious."

"What!" he cried, sitting bolt upright, and then sinking weakly back among the pillows. "You poor child! You don't mean to tell me you have been skimping along all these weeks on just that check I sent you before starting home?"

"Yes," she sobbed, her face still buried in the pillow. She had borne the strain of continued anxiety so long that she could not stop her tears, now they had once started.

It was with a very thankful heart she watched him take a pack of letters from the coat she brought to his bedside, and draw out a sealed envelope.

"Well, I never once thought of looking among those letters for money," she exclaimed, as he held it up with a smile.

His investments of the summer before had prospered beyond his greatest hopes, he told her. "Brother Rob is looking after my interests out West, as well as his own," he explained, "and as his father-in-law is the grand mogul of the place, I have the inside track. Then that firm I went security for in New York is nearly on its feet again, and I'll have back every dollar I ever paid out for them. Nobody ever lost anything by those men in the long run. We'll be on top again by this time next year, little wife; so don't borrow any more trouble on that score."

The doctor made his last visit that afternoon. It really seemed as if there would never be any more dark days at the little cottage.

"The clouds have all blown away and left us their silver linings," said Mrs. Sherman the day her husband was able to go out-of-doors for the first time. He walked down to the post office, and brought back a letter from the West. It had such encouraging reports of his business that he was impatient to get back to it. He wrote a reply early in the afternoon, and insisted on going to mail it himself.

"I'll never get my strength back," he protested, "unless I have more exercise."

It was a cold, gray November day. A few flakes of snow were falling when he started.

"I'll stop and rest at the Tylers'," he called back, "so don't be uneasy if I'm out some time."

After he left the post office the fresh air tempted him to go farther than he had intended. At a long distance from his home his strength seemed suddenly to desert him. The snow began to fall in earnest. Numb with cold, he groped his way back to the house, almost fainting from exhaustion.

Lloyd was blowing soap-bubbles when she saw him come in and fall heavily across the couch. The ghastly pallor of his face and his closed eyes frightened her so that she dropped the little clay pipe she was using. As she stooped to pick up the broken pieces, her mother's cry startled her still more. "Lloyd, run call Becky, quick, quick! Oh, he's dying!"

Lloyd gave one more terrified look and ran to the kitchen, screaming for Mom Beck. No one was there.

The next instant she was running bareheaded as fast as she could go, up the road to Locust. She was confident of finding help there.

The snowflakes clung to her hair and blew against her soft cheeks. All she could see was her mother wringing her hands, and her father's white face. When she burst into the house where the Colonel sat reading by the fire, she was so breathless at first that she could only gasp when she tried to speak.

"Come quick!" she cried. "Papa Jack's a-dyin'! Come stop him!"

At her first impetuous words the Colonel was on his feet. She caught him by the hand and led him to the door before he fully realized what she wanted. Then he drew back. She was impatient at the slightest delay, and only half answered his questions.

"Oh, come, gran'fathah!" she pleaded. "Don't wait to talk!" But he held her until he had learned all the circumstances. He was convinced by what she told him that both Lloyd and her mother were unduly alarmed. When he found that no one had sent for him, but that the child had come of her own accord, he refused to go.

He did not believe that the man was dying, and he did not intend to step aside one inch from the position he had taken. For

seven years he had kept the vow he made when he swore to be a stranger to his daughter. He would keep it for seventy times seven years if need be.

She looked at him perfectly bewildered. She had been so accustomed to his humoring her slightest whims, that it had never occurred to her he would fail to help in a time of such distress.

"Why, gran'fathah," she began, her lips trembling piteously. Then her whole expression changed. Her face grew startlingly white, and her eyes seemed so big and black. The Colonel looked at her in surprise. He had never seen a child in such a passion before. "I hate you! I hate you!" she exclaimed, all in a tremble. "You's a cruel, wicked man. I'll nevah come heah again, nevah! nevah!

The tears rolled down her cheeks as she banged the door behind her and ran down the avenue, her little heart so full of grief and disappointment that she felt she could not possibly bear it.

For more than an hour the Colonel walked up and down the room, unable to shut out the anger and disappointment of that little face.

He knew she was too much like himself ever to retract her words. She would never come back. He never knew until that hour how much he loved her, or how much she had come to mean in his life. She was gone hopelessly beyond recall, unless—

He unlocked the door of the drawing-room and went in. A faint breath of dried rose-leaves greeted him. He walked over to the empty fireplace and looked up at the sweet face of the portrait a long time. Then he leaned his arm on the mantel and bowed his head on it. "Oh, Amanthis," he groaned, "tell me what to do."

Lloyd's own words came back to him. "She'd go right straight an' put her arms around my mothah an' kiss away all the sorry feelin's."

It was a long time he stood there. The battle between his love and pride was a hard one. At last he raised his head and saw that the short winter day was almost over. Without waiting to order his horse he started off in the falling snow toward the cottage.

CHAPTER X.

A good many forebodings crowded into the Colonel's mind as he walked hurriedly on. He wondered how he would be received. What if Jack Sherman had died after all? What if Elizabeth should refuse to see him? A dozen times before he reached the gate he pictured to himself the probable scene of their meeting.

He was out of breath and decidedly disturbed in mind when he walked up the path. As he paused on the porch steps, Lloyd came running around the house carrying her parrot on a broom.

Her hair was blowing around her rosy face under the Napoleon hat she wore, and she was singing.

The last two hours had made a vast change in her feelings. Her father had only fainted from exhaustion.

When she came running back from Locust, she was afraid to go in the house, lest what she dreaded most had happened while she was gone. She opened the door timidly and peeped in. Her father's eyes were open. Then she heard him speak. She ran into the room, and, burying her head in her mother's lap, sobbed out the story of her visit to Locust.

To her great surprise her father began to laugh, and laughed so heartily as she repeated her saucy speech to her grandfather, that it took the worst sting out of her disappointment.

All the time the Colonel had been fighting his pride among the memories of the dim old drawing-room, Lloyd had been playing with Fritz and Polly.

Now as she came suddenly face to face with her grandfather, she dropped the disgusted bird in the snow, and stood staring at him with startled eyes. If he had fallen out of the sky she could not have been more astonished.

"Where is your mother, child?" he asked, trying to speak calmly. With a backward look, as if she could not believe the evidence of her own sight, she led the way.

"Mothah! Mothah!" she called, pushing open the parlor door. "Come heah, quick!"

The Colonel, taking the hat from his white head, and dropping it on the floor, took an expectant step forward. There was a slight rustle, and Elizabeth stood in the doorway. For just a moment they looked into each other's faces. Then the Colonel held out his arm.

"Little daughter," he said, in a tremulous voice. The love of a lifetime seemed to tremble in those two words.

In an instant her arms were around his neck, and he was "kissing away the sorry feelin's" as tenderly as the lost Amanthis could have done.

As soon as Lloyd began to realize what was happening, her face grew radiant. She danced around in such excitement that Fritz barked wildly.

"Come an' see Papa Jack, too," she cried leading him into the next room.

Whatever deep-rooted prejudices Jack Sherman may have had, they were unselfishly put aside after one look into his wife's happy face.

He raised himself on his elbow as the dignified old soldier crossed the room. The white hair, the empty sleeve, the remembrance of all the old man had lost, and the thought that after all he was Elizabeth's father, sent a very tender feeling through the younger man's heart.

"Will you take my hand, sir?" he asked, sitting up and offering it in his straightforward way.

"Of co'se he will!" exclaimed Lloyd, who still clung to her grandfather's arm. "Of co'se he will!"

"I have been too near death to harbor ill will any longer," said the younger man, as their hands met in a strong, forgiving clasp.

The old Colonel smiled grimly.

"I had thought that even death itself could not make me give in," he said, "but I've had to make a complete surrender to the Little Colonel."

That Christmas there was such a celebration at Locust that May Lilly and Henry Clay nearly went wild in the general excitement of the preparation. Walker hung up cedar and holly and mistletoe till the big house looked like a bower. Maria bustled about,

airing rooms and bringing out stores of linen and silver.

The Colonel himself filled the great punch-bowl that his grandfather had brought from Virginia.

"I'm glad we're goin' to stay heah tonight," said Lloyd, as she hung up her stocking Christmas Eve. "It will be so much easiah fo' Santa Claus to get down these big chimneys."

In the morning when she found four tiny stockings hanging beside her own, overflowing with candy for Fritz, her happiness was complete.

That night there was a tree in the drawing-room that reached to the frescoed ceiling. When May Lilly came in to admire it and get her share from its loaded branches, Lloyd came skipping up to her. "Oh, I'm goin' to live heah all wintah," she cried. "Mom Beck's goin' to stay heah with me, too, while mothah an' Papa Jack go down South where the alli-gatahs live. Then when they get well an' come back, Papa Jack is goin' to build a house on

the othah side of the lawn. I'm to live in both places at once; mothah said so."

There were music and light, laughing voices and happy hearts in the old home that night. It seemed as if the old place had awakened from a long dream and found itself young again.

The plan the Little Colonel unfolded to May Lilly was carried out in every detail. It seemed a long winter to the child, but it was a happy one. There were not so many displays of temper now that she was growing older, but the letters that went southward every week were full of her old speeches and mischievous pranks. The old Colonel found it hard to refuse her anything. If it had not been for Mom Beck's decided ways, the child would have been sadly spoiled.

At last spring came again. The pewees sang in the cedars. The dandelions sprinkled the roadsides like stars. The locust trees tossed up the white spray of their fragrant blossoms with every wave of their green boughs.

"They'll soon be heah! They'll soon be heah!" chanted the Little Colonel every day.

The morning they came she had been down the avenue a dozen times to look for them before the carriage had even started to meet them.

"Walkah," she called, "cut me a big locus' bough. I want to wave it fo' a flag!"

Just as he dropped a branch down at her feet, she caught the sound of wheels. "Hurry, gran'fathah," she called; "they's comin'." But the old Colonel had already started on toward the gate to meet them. The carriage stopped, and in a moment more Papa Jack was tossing Lloyd up in his arms, while the old Colonel was helping Elizabeth to alight.

"Isn't this a happy mawnin'?" exclaimed the Little Colonel, as she leaned from her seat on her father's shoulder to kiss his sunburned cheek.

"A very happy morning," echoed her grandfather, as he walked on toward the house with Elizabeth's hand clasped close in his own.

Long after they had passed up the steps the old locusts kept echoing the Little Colonel's words. Years ago they had showered their fragrant blossoms in this same path to make a sweet white way for Amanthis's little feet to tread when the Colonel brought home his bride.

They had dropped their tribute on the coffin lid when Tom was carried home under their drooping branches. The soldier-boy had loved them so, that a little cluster had been laid on the breast of the gray coat he wore.

Night and day they had guarded this old home like silent sentinels that loved it well.

Now, as they looked down on the united family, a thrill passed through them to their remotest bloom-tipped branches.

It sounded only like a faint rustling of leaves, but it was the locusts whispering together. "The children have come home at last," they kept repeating. "What a happy morning! Oh, what a happy morning!"

REBECCA OF SUNNYBROOK FARM

The old stage-coach was rumbling along the dusty road that runs from Maplewood to Riverboro. The day was as warm as midsummer, though it was only the middle of May, and Mr. Jeremiah Cobb was favoring the horses as much as possible, yet never losing sight of the fact that he carried the mail. His brimmed hat of worn felt was well pulled over his eyes, and he revolved a quid of tobacco in his left cheek.

There was one passenger in the coach,—a small dark-haired person in a glossy buff calico dress. Whenever the wheels sank farther than usual into a rut, or jolted suddenly over a stone, she bounded involuntarily into the air, came down again, pushed back her funny little straw hat, and picked up or settled more firmly a small pink sunshade, which seemed to be her chief responsibility,—unless we except a bead purse, into which she looked whenever the condition of the roads would permit, finding great apparent satisfaction in that its precious contents neither disappeared nor grew less. Mr. Cobb guessed nothing of these harassing details of travel. Indeed he had forgotten the very existence of this one unnoteworthy little passenger.

When he was about to leave the post office in Maplewood that morning, a woman had alighted from a wagon, and coming up to him, inquired whether this were the Riverboro stage, and if he were Mr. Cobb. Being answered in the affirmative, she nodded to a child who was eagerly waiting for the answer. The child might have been ten or eleven years old perhaps, but she had an air of being small for her age. Her mother helped her into the stagecoach, deposited a bundle and a bouquet of lilacs beside her, superintended the "roping on" behind of an old hair trunk, and finally paid the fare, counting out the silver with great care.

"I want you should take her to my sisters' in Riverboro," she said. "Do you know Mirandy and Jane Sawyer? They live in the brick house."

Lord bless your soul, he knew 'em as well as if he'd made 'em!

"Well, she's going there, and they're expecting her. Will you keep an eye on her, please? Good-bye, Rebecca; try not to get into any mischief, and sit quiet, so you'll look neat an' nice when you get there. Don't be any trouble to Mr. Cobb."

"Good-bye, mother, don't worry; you know it isn't as if I hadn't traveled before."

The woman gave a short sardonic laugh and said to Mr. Cobb, "She's been to Wareham and stayed overnight."

"It *was traveling*, mother," said the child eagerly and willfully. "It was leaving the farm, and putting up lunch in a basket, and a little riding and a little steam cars, and we carried our nightgowns."

"Don't tell the whole village about it, if we did," said the mother, interrupting the reminiscences of this experienced voyager. "Haven't I told you before, " she whispered, in a last attempt at discipline, "that you shouldn't talk about nightgowns and stockings and—things like that, in a loud tone of voice, and especially when there's men-folks round?"

"I know, mother, I know, and I won't. All I want to say is"—here Mr. Cobb gave a cluck, slapped the reins, and the horses started sedately on their daily task—"all I want to say is that it is a journey when"—the stage was really under way now and Rebecca had to put her head out of the window over the door in order to finish her sentence—"it *is* a journey when you carry a nightgown!"

The objectionable word, uttered in a high treble, floated back to the offended ears of Mrs. Randall, who watched the stage out of sight, gathered up her packages from the bench at the store door, and stepped into the wagon that had been standing at the hitching-post. As she turned the horse's head towards home she rose to her feet for a moment, and shading her eyes with her hand, looked at a cloud of dust in the dim distance.

"Mirandy'll have her hands full, I guess," she said to herself; "but I shouldn't wonder if it would be the making of Rebecca."

All this had been half an hour ago, and the sun, the heat, the dust, the contemplation of errands to be done in the great metropolis of Milltown, had lulled Mr. Cobb's never active mind into complete oblivion as to his promise of keeping an eye on Rebecca.

Suddenly he heard a small voice above the rattle and rumble of the wheels and the creaking of the harness. At first he thought it was a cricket, a tree toad, or a bird, but having determined the direction from which it came, he turned his head over his shoulder and saw a small shape hanging as far out of the window as safety would allow. A long black braid of hair swung with the motion of the coach; the child held her hat in one hand and with the other made ineffectual attempts to stab the driver with her microscopic sunshade.

"Please let me speak!" she called.

Mr. Cobb drew up the horses obediently.

"Does it cost any more to ride up there with you?" she asked. "It's so slippery and shiny down here, and the stage is so much too big for me, that I rattle round in it till I'm 'most black and blue. And the windows are so small I can only see pieces of things, and I've 'most broken my neck stretching round to find out whether my trunk has fallen off the back. It's my mother's trunk, and she's very choice of it."

Mr. Cobb waited until this flow of conversation, or more properly speaking this flood of criticism, had ceased, and then said jocularly:—

"You can come up if you want to; there ain't no extry charge to sit side o' me." Whereupon he helped her out, "boosted" her up to the front seat, and resumed his own place.

Rebecca sat down carefully, smoothing her dress under her with painstaking precision, and putting her sunshade under its extended folds between the driver and herself. This done she pushed back her hat, pulled up her darned white cotton gloves, and said delightedly:—

"Oh! this is better! This is like traveling! I am a real passenger now, and down there I felt like our setting hen when we shut her up in a coop. I hope we have a long, long ways to go?"

"Oh! we've only just started on it," Mr. Cobb responded genially; "it's more'n two hours."

"Only two hours," she sighed. "That will be half-past one; mother will be at Cousin Ann's, the children at home will have had their dinner, and Hannah cleared all away. I have some lunch, because mother said it would be a bad beginning to get to the brick house hungry and have Aunt Mirandy have to get me something to eat the first thing.—It's a good growing day, isn't it?"

"It is, certain; too hot, most. Why don't you put up your parasol?"

She extended her dress still farther over the article in question as she said, "Oh, dear, no!

I never put it up when the sun shines; pink fades awfully, you know, and I only carry it to meetin' cloudy Sundays; sometimes the sun comes out all of a sudden, and I have a dreadful time covering it up; it's the dearest thing in life to me, but it's an awful care."

At this moment the thought gradually permeated Mr. Jeremiah Cobb's slow-moving mind that the bird perched by his side was a bird of very different feather from those to which he was accustomed in his daily drives. He put the whip back in its socket, took his first good look at the passenger, a look which she met with a grave, childlike stare of friendly curiosity.

The buff calico was faded, but scrupulously clean, and starched within an inch of its life. From the little standing ruffle at the neck the child's slender throat rose very brown and thin, and the head looked small to bear the weight of dark hair that hung in a thick braid to her waist. Her face was without color and sharp in outline. As to features, she must have had the usual number, though Mr. Cobb's attention never proceeded so far as nose, fore-

head, or chin, being caught on the way and held fast by the eyes. Rebecca's eyes were like faith,—"the substance of things hoped for, the evidence of things not seen." Under her delicately etched brows they glowed like two stars, their dancing lights half hidden in lustrous darkness. They had never been accounted for, Rebecca's eyes. The schoolteacher and the minister at Temperance had tried and failed; the young artist who came for the summer to sketch the red barn, the ruined mill, and the bridge ended by giving up all these local beauties and devoting herself to the face of a child,—a small, plain face illuminated by a pair of eyes carrying such messages, such suggestions, such hints of sleeping power and insight, that one never tired of looking into their shining depths.

Mr. Cobb made none of these generalizations; his remark to his wife that night was simply to the effect that whenever the child looked at him she knocked him galley-west.

"Miss Ross, a lady that paints, gave me the sunshade," said Rebecca, when she had exchanged looks with Mr. Cobb and learned his

face by heart. "Did you notice the pinked double ruffle and the white tip and handle? They're ivory. The handle is scarred, you see. That's because Fanny sucked and chewed it in meeting when I wasn't looking. I've never felt the same to Fanny since."

"Is Fanny your sister?"

"She's one of them."

"How many are there of you?"

"Seven. There's verses written about seven children:—

"Quick was the little Maid's reply,
O master! we are seven!

I learned it to speak in school, but the scholars were hateful and laughed. Hannah is the oldest, I come next, then John, then Jenny, then Mark, then Fanny, then Mira."

"Well, that *is* a big family!"

"Far too big, everybody says," replied Rebecca with an unexpected and thoroughly grown-up candor that induced Mr. Cobb to murmur, "I swan!" and insert more tobacco in his left cheek.

"They're dear, but such a bother, and cost so much to feed, you see," she rippled on. "Hannah and I haven't done anything but put babies to bed at night and take them up in the morning for years and years. But it's finished, that's one comfort, and we'll have a lovely time when we're all grown up and the mortgage is paid off."

"All finished? Oh, you mean you've come away?"

"No, I mean they're all over and done with; our family's finished. Mother says so, and she always keeps her promises. There has n't been any since Mira, and she's three. She was born the day father died. Aunt Miranda wanted Hannah to come to Riverboro instead of me, but mother couldn't spare her; she takes hold of housework better than I do, Hannah does. I told mother last night if there was likely to be any more children while I was away I'd have to be sent for, for when there's a baby it always takes Hannah and me both, for mother has the cooking and the farm."

"Oh, you live on a farm, do ye? Where is it?—near to where you got on?"

"Near? Why, it must be thousands of miles!

We came from Temperance in the cars. Then we drove a long ways to Cousin Ann's and went to bed. Then we got up and drove ever so far to Maplewood, where the stage was. Our farm is away off from everywheres, but our school and meeting-house is at Temperance, and that's only two miles. Sitting up here with you is most as good as climbing the meeting-house steeple. I know a boy who's been up on our steeple. He said the people and cows looked like flies. We haven't met any people yet, but I'm *kind* of disappointed in the cows;—they don't look so little as I hoped they would; still" (brightening) "they don't look quite as big as if we were down side of them, do they? Boys always do the nice splendid things, and girls can only do the nasty dull ones that get left over. They can't climb so high, or go so far, or stay out so late, or run so fast, or anything."

Mr. Cobb wiped his mouth on the back of his hand and gasped. He had a feeling that he was being hurried from peak to peak of a mountain range without time to take a good breath in between.

"I can't seem to locate your farm," he said, "though I've been to Temperance and used to live up that way. What's your folks' name?"

"Randall. My mother's name is Aurelia Randall; our names are Hannah Lucy Randall, Rebecca Rowena Randall, John Halifax Randall, Jenny Lind Randall, Marquis Randall, Fanny Ellsler Randall, and Miranda Randall. Mother named half of us and father the other half, but we didn't come out even, so they both thought it would be nice to name Mira after Aunt Miranda in Riverboro; they hoped it might do some good, but it didn't, and now we call her Mira. We are all named after somebody in particular. Hannah is 'Hannah at the Window Binding Shoes,' and I am taken out of 'Ivanhoe'; John Halifax was a gentleman in a book; Mark is after his uncle, Marquis de Lafayette, that died a twin. (Twins very often don't live to grow up, and triplets almost never—did you know that, Mr. Cobb?) We don't call him Marquis, only Mark. Jenny is named for a singer and Fanny for a beautiful dancer, but mother says they're both misfits, for Jenny can't carry a tune and Fanny's kind of stiff-legged. Mother would like to call them Jane and Frances and give up their middle names, but she says it wouldn't be fair to father. She says we must always stand up for father, because everything was against him, and he wouldn't have died if he hadn't had such bad luck. I think that's all there is to tell about us," she finished seriously.

"Land o' Liberty! I should think it was enough," ejaculated Mr. Cobb. "There wa'n't many names left when your mother got through choosin'! You've got a powerful good memory! I guess it ain't no trouble for you to learn your lessons, is it?"

"Not much; the trouble is to get the shoes to go and learn 'em. These are spandy new I've got on, and they have to last six months. Mother always says to save my shoes. There don't seem to be any way of saving shoes but taking 'em off and going barefoot; but I can't do that in Riverboro without shaming Aunt Mirandy. I'm going to school right along now when I'm living with Aunt Mirandy, and in two years I'm going to the seminary at Wareham; mother says it ought to be the making of me! I'm going to be a painter like Miss Ross when I get through school. At any rate, that's what *I* think I'm going to be. Mother thinks I'd better teach."

"Your farm ain't the old Hobbs place, is it?"

"No, it's just Randall's Farm. At least that's what mother calls it. I call it Sunnybrook Farm."

"I guess it don't make no difference what you call it so long as you know where it is," remarked Mr. Cobb sententiously.

Rebecca turned the full light of her eyes upon him reproachfully, almost severely, as she answered:—

"Oh! don't say that, and be like all the rest! It does make a difference what you call things. When I say Randall's Farm, do you see how it looks?"

"No, I can't say I do," responded Mr. Cobb uneasily.

"Now when I say Sunnybrook Farm, what does it make you think of?"

Mr. Cobb felt like a fish removed from his native element and left panting on the sand; there was no evading the awful responsibility of a reply, for Rebecca's eyes were search-

lights that pierced the fiction of his brain and perceived the bald spot on the back of his head.

"I s'pose there's a brook somewheres near it," he said timorously.

Rebecca looked disappointed but not quite disheartened. "That's pretty good," she said encouragingly. "You're warm but not hot; there's a brook, but not a common brook. It has young trees and baby bushes on each side of it, and it's a shallow chattering little brook with a white sandy bottom and lots of little shiny pebbles. Whenever there's a bit of sunshine the brook catches it, and it's always full of sparkles the livelong day. Don't your stomach feel hollow? Mine does! I was so 'fraid I'd miss the stage I couldn't eat any breakfast."

"You'd better have your lunch, then. I don't eat nothin' till I get to Milltown; then I get a piece o' pie and cup o' coffee."

"I wish I could see Milltown. I suppose it's bigger and grander even than Wareham; more like Paris? Miss Ross told me about Paris; she bought my pink sunshade there and my bead purse. You see how it opens with a snap? I've twenty cents in it, and it's got to last three months, for stamps and paper and ink. Mother says Aunt Mirandy won't want to buy things like those when she's feeding and clothing me and paying for my school books."

"Paris ain't so great," said Mr. Cobb disparagingly. "It's the dullest place in the State o' Maine. I've druv there many a time."

Again Rebecca was obliged to reprove Mr. Cobb, tacitly and quietly, but none the less surely, though the reproof was dealt with one glance, quickly sent and as quickly withdrawn.

"Paris is the capital of France, and you have to go to it on a boat," she said instructively. "It's in my geography, and it says: 'The French are a gay and polite people, fond of dancing and light wines.' I asked the teacher what light wines were, and he thought it was something like new cider, or maybe ginger pop. *I* can see Paris as plain as day by just shutting my eyes. But you can see Milltown most every day with your eyes wide open," Rebecca said wistfully.

"Milltown ain't so great, neither," replied Mr. Cobb, with the air of having visited all the cities of the earth and found them as naught. "Now you watch me heave this newspaper right onto Mis' Brown's doorstep."

Piff! and the packet landed exactly as it was intended, on the corn-husk mat in front of the screen door.

"Oh, how splendid that was!" cried Rebecca with enthusiasm.

"I might fail on some of 'em, you know," said Mr. Cobb, beaming with modest pride. "If your Aunt Mirandy 'll let you, I'll take you down to Milltown some day this summer when the stage ain't full."

A thrill of delicious excitement ran through Rebecca's frame, from her new shoes, up, up to the leghorn cap and down the black braid. She pressed Mr. Cobb's knee ardently and said in a voice choking with tears of joy and astonishment, "Oh, it can't be true, it can't; to think I should see Milltown. It's like having a fairy godmother who asks you your wish and then gives it to you! Did you ever read 'Cinderella,' or 'The Yellow Dwarf,' or 'The Enchanted Frog,' or 'The Fair One with Golden Locks'?"

"No," said Mr. Cobb cautiously, after a moment's reflection. "I don't seem to think I ever did read jest those partic'lar ones. Where'd you get a chance at so much readin'?"

"Oh, I've read lots of books," answered Rebecca casually. "Father's and Miss Ross's and all the dif'rent school teachers', and all in the Sunday-School library. I've read 'The Lamplighter,' and 'Scottish Chiefs,' and 'Ivanhoe,' and 'The Heir of Redclyffe,' and 'Cora, the Doctor's Wife,' and 'David Copperfield,' and 'The Gold of Chickaree,' and 'Plutarch's Lives,' and 'Thaddeus of Warsaw,' and 'Pilgrim's Progress,' and lots more.—What have you read?"

"I've never happened to read those partic'lar books; but land! I've read a sight in my time! Nowadays I'm so drove I get along with the Almanac, the 'Weekly Argus,' and the 'Maine State Agriculturist.'—There's the river again; this is the last long hill, and when we get to the top of it we'll see the chimbleys of Riverboro in the distance. 'T ain't fur. I live 'bout half a mile beyond the brick house myself."

Rebecca's hand stirred nervously in her lap and she moved in her seat. "I didn't think I was going to be afraid," she said almost under her breath; "but I guess I am, just a little mite —when you say it's coming so near."

"Would you go back?" asked Mr. Cobb curiously.

She flashed him an intrepid look and then said proudly, "I'd never go back—I might be frightened, but I'd be ashamed to run. Going to Aunt Mirandy's is like going down cellar in the dark. There might be ogres and giants under the stairs,—but, as I tell Hannah, there *might* be elves and fairies and enchanted frogs!—Is there a main street in the village, like that in Wareham?"

"I s'pose you might call it a main street, an' your Aunt Sawyer lives on it, but there ain't no stores nor mills, an' it's an awful one-horse village!"

"I'm almost sorry," she sighed, "because it would be so grand to drive down a real main street, sitting high up like this behind two splendid horses, with my pink sunshade up, and everybody in town wondering who the bunch of lilacs and the hair trunk belongs to. It would be just like the beautiful lady in the parade. Last summer the circus came to Temperance, and they had a procession in the morning. And there were lovely horses and animals in cages, and clowns on horseback; and at the very end came a little red and gold chariot drawn by two ponies, and in it, sitting on a velvet cushion, was the snake charmer, all dressed in satin and spangles. She was so beautiful beyond compare, Mr. Cobb, that you had to swallow lumps in your throat when you looked at her, and little cold feelings crept up and down your back. Don't you know how I mean? Didn't you ever see anybody that made you feel like that?"

Mr. Cobb was more distinctly uncomfortable at this moment than he had been at any one time during the eventful morning, but he evaded the point dexterously by saying, "There ain't no harm, as I can see, in our makin' the grand entry in the biggest style we can. I'll take the whip out, set up straight, an' drive fast; you hold your bo'quet in your lap, an' open your little red parasol, an' we'll jest make the natives stare!"

The child's face was radiant for a moment, but the glow faded just as quickly as she said, "I forgot—mother put me inside, and maybe she'd want me to be there when I got to Aunt Mirandy's. Maybe I'd be more genteel inside, and then I wouldn't have to be jumped down and my clothes fly up, but could open the door and step down like a lady passenger. Would you please stop a minute, Mr. Cobb, and let me change?"

The stage-driver good-naturedly pulled up his horses, lifted the excited little creature down, opened the door, and helped her in, putting the lilacs and the pink sunshade beside her.

"We've had a great trip," he said, "and we've got real well acquainted, haven't we?— You won't forget about Milltown?"

"Never!" she exclaimed fervently; "and you're sure you won't either?"

"Never! Cross my heart!" vowed Mr. Cobb solemnly, as he remounted his perch.

And as the stage rumbled down the village street between the green maples, those who looked from their windows saw a little brown elf in buff calico sitting primly on the back seat holding a great bouquet tightly in one hand and a pink parasol in the other. Had they been far-sighted enough they might have seen, when the stage turned into the side dooryard of the old brick house, a calico yoke rising and falling tempestuously over the beating heart beneath, the red color coming and going in two pale cheeks, and a mist of tears swimming in two brilliant dark eyes.

Rebecca's journey had ended.

"There's the stage turnin' into the Sawyer girls' dooryard," said Mrs. Perkins to her husband. "That must be the niece from up Temperance way. It seems they wrote to Aurelia and invited Hannah, the oldest, but Aurelia said she could spare Rebecca better, if 't was all the same to Mirandy an' Jane; so it's Rebecca that's come. She'll be good comp'ny for our Emma Jane, but I don't believe they'll keep her three months! She looks black as an Injun what I can see of her; black and kind of up-an'-comin'. They used to say that one o' the Randalls married a Spanish woman, somebody that was teachin' music and languages at a boardin' school. Lorenzo was

dark complected, you remember, and this child is, too. Well, I don't know as Spanish blood is any real disgrace, not if it's a good ways back and the woman was respectable."

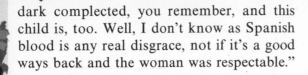

2
REBECCA'S RELATIONS

They had been called the Sawyer girls when Miranda at eighteen, Jane at twelve, and Aurelia at eight participated in the various activities of village life; and when Riverboro fell into a habit of thought or speech, it saw no reason for falling out of it; at any rate, in the same century. So although Miranda and Jane were between fifty and sixty at the time this story opens, Riverboro still called them the Sawyer girls. They were spinsters; but Aurelia, the youngest, had made what she called a romantic marriage and what her sisters termed a mighty poor speculation. "There's worse things than bein' old maids," they said; whether they thought so is quite another matter.

The element of romance in Aurelia's marriage existed chiefly in the fact that Mr. L. D. M. Randall had a soul above farming or trading and was a votary of the Muses. He taught the weekly singing-school (then a feature of village life) in half a dozen neighboring towns, he played the violin and "called off" at dances, or evoked rich harmonies from church melodeons on Sundays. He taught certain uncouth lads, when they were of an age to enter society, the intricacies of contra dances, or the steps of the schottische and mazurka, and he was a marked figure in all social assemblies, though conspicuously absent from town-meetings and the purely masculine gatherings at the store or tavern or bridge.

His hair was a little longer, his hands a little whiter, his shoes a little thinner, his manner a trifle more polished, than that of his soberer mates; indeed the only department of life in which he failed to shine was the making of

sufficient money to live upon. Luckily he had no responsibilities; his father and his twin brother had died when he was yet a boy, and his mother, whose only noteworthy achievement had been the naming of her twin sons Marquis de Lafayette and Lorenzo de Medici Randall, had supported herself and educated her child by making coats up to the very day of her death. She was wont to say plaintively, "I'm afraid the faculties was too much divided up between my twins. L. D. M. is awful talented, but I guess M. D. L. would 'a' been the practical one if he'd 'a' lived."

"L. D. M. was practical enough to get the richest girl in the village," replied Mrs. Robinson.

"Yes," sighed his mother, "there it is again; if the twins could 'a' married Aurelia Sawyer, 't would 'a' been all right. L. D. M. was talented 'nough to *get* Reely's money, but M.D. L. would 'a' ben practical 'nough to have *kep'* it."

Aurelia's share of the modest Sawyer property had been put into one thing after another by the handsome and luckless Lorenzo de Medici. He had a graceful and poetic way of making an investment for each new son and daughter that blessed their union. "A birthday present for our child, Aurelia," he would say,—"a little nest-egg for the future." But Aurelia once remarked in a moment of bitterness that the hen never lived that could sit on those eggs and hatch anything out of them.

Miranda and Jane had virtually washed their hands of Aurelia when she married Lorenzo de Medici Randall. Having exhausted the resources of Riverboro and its immediate vicinity, the unfortunate couple had moved on and on in a steadily decreasing scale of prosperity until they had reached Temperance, where they had settled down and invited fate to do its worst, an invitation which was promptly accepted. The maiden sisters at home wrote to Aurelia two or three times a year, and sent modest but serviceable presents to the children at Christmas, but refused to assist L. D. M. with the regular expenses of his rapidly growing family. His last investment, made shortly before the birth of Miranda (named in a lively hope of favors which never came), was a small farm two miles from Temperance. Aurelia managed this herself, and so it proved a home at least, and a place for the unsuccessful Lorenzo to die and to be buried from, a duty somewhat too long deferred, many thought, which he performed on the day of Mira's birth.

It was in this happy-go-lucky household that Rebecca had grown up. It was just an ordinary family; two or three of the children were handsome and the rest plain, three of them rather clever, two industrious, and two commonplace and dull. Rebecca had her father's facility and had been his aptest pupil. She "carried" the alto by ear, danced without being taught, played the melodeon without knowing the notes. Her love of books she inherited chiefly from her mother, who found it hard to sweep or cook or sew when there was a novel in the house. Fortunately books were scarce, or the children might sometimes have gone ragged and hungry.

But other forces had been at work in Rebecca, and the traits of unknown forbears had been wrought into her fiber. Lorenzo de Medici was flabby and boneless; Rebecca was a thing of fire and spirit: he lacked energy and courage; Rebecca was plucky at two and dauntless at five. Mrs. Randall and Hannah had no sense of humor; Rebecca possessed and showed it as soon as she could walk and talk.

She had not been able, however, to borrow her parents' virtues and those of other generous ancestors and escape all the weaknesses in the calendar. She had not her sister Hannah's patience or her brother John's sturdy staying power. Her will was sometimes willfulness, and the ease with which she did most things led her to be impatient of hard tasks or long ones. But whatever else there was or was not, there was freedom at Randall's farm. The children grew, worked, fought, ate what and slept where they could; loved one another and their parents pretty well, but with no tropical passion; and educated themselves for nine months of the year, each one in his own way.

As a result of this method Hannah, who could only have been developed by forces applied from without, was painstaking, humdrum, and limited; while Rebecca, who apparently needed nothing but space to develop in, and a knowledge of terms in which to express herself, grew and grew and grew, always from within outward. Her forces of one sort and another had seemingly been set in motion when she was born; they needed no daily spur, but moved of their own accord—towards what no one knew, least of all Rebecca herself. The field for the exhibition of her creative instinct was painfully small, and the only use she had made of it as yet was to leave eggs out of the corn bread one day and milk another, to see how it would turn out; to part Fanny's hair sometimes in the middle, sometimes on the right, and sometimes on the left side; and to play all sorts of fantastic pranks with the children, occasionally bringing them to the table as fictitious or historical characters found in her favorite books. Rebecca amused her mother and her family generally, but she never was counted of serious importance, and though considered "smart" and old for her age, she was never thought superior in any way. Aurelia's experience of genius, as exemplified in the deceased Lorenzo de Medici, led her into a greater admiration of plain, every-day common sense, a quality in which Rebecca, it must be confessed, seemed sometimes painfully deficient.

Hannah was her mother's favorite, so far as Aurelia could indulge herself in such recreations as partiality. The parent who is obliged to feed and clothe seven children on an income of fifteen dollars a month seldom has time to discriminate carefully between the various members of her brood, but Hannah at fourteen was at once companion and partner in all her mother's problems. She it was who kept the house while Aurelia busied herself in barn and field. Rebecca was capable of certain set tasks, such as keeping the small children from killing themselves and one another, feeding the poultry, picking up chips, hulling strawberries, wiping dishes; but she was thought irresponsible, and Aurelia, needing somebody to lean on (having never enjoyed that luxury with the gifted Lorenzo), leaned on Hannah. Hannah showed the result of this attitude somewhat, being a trifle careworn in face and sharp in manner; but she was a self-contained, well-behaved, dependable child, and that is the reason her aunts had invited her to Riverboro to be a member of their family and participate in all the advantages of their loftier position in the world. It was several years since Miranda and Jane had seen the children, but they remembered with pleasure that Hannah had not spoken a word during the interview, and it was for this reason that they had asked for the pleasure of her company. Rebecca, on the other hand, had dressed up the dog in John's clothes, and being requested to get the three younger children ready for dinner, she had held them under the pump and then proceeded to "smack" their hair flat to their heads by vigorous brushing, bringing them to the table in such a moist and hideous state of shininess that their mother was ashamed of their appearance. Rebecca's own black locks were commonly pushed smoothly off her forehead, but on this occasion she formed what I must perforce call by its only name, a "spit-curl," directly in the center of her brow, an ornament which she was allowed to wear a very short time, only in fact till Hannah was able to call her mother's attention to it, when she was sent into the next room to remove it and come back looking like a Christian. This command she interpreted somewhat too literally, perhaps, because she contrived in a space of two minutes an extremely pious style of hairdressing, fully as effective if not as startling as the first. These antics were solely the result of nervous irritation, a mood born of Miss Miranda Sawyer's stiff, grim, and martial attitude.

The remembrance of Rebecca was so vivid that their sister Aurelia's letter was something of a shock to the quiet, elderly spinsters of the brick house; for it said that Hannah could not possibly be spared for a few years yet, but that Rebecca would come as soon as she could be made ready; that the offer was most thankfully appreciated, and that the regular schooling and church privileges, as well as the influence of the Sawyer home, would doubtless be "the making of Rebecca."

3
A DIFFERENCE IN HEARTS

"I don' know as I cal'lated to be the makin' of any child," Miranda had said as she folded Aurelia's letter and laid it in the lightstand drawer. "I s'posed, of course, Aurelia would send us the one we asked for, but it's just like her to palm off that wild young one on somebody else."

"You remember we said that Rebecca or even Jenny might come, in case Hannah couldn't," interposed Jane.

"I know we did, but we hadn't any notion it would turn out that way," grumbled Miranda.

"She was a mite of a thing when we saw her three years ago," ventured Jane; "she's had time to improve."

"And time to grow worse!"

"Won't it be kind of a privilege to put her on the right track?" asked Jane timidly.

"I don' know about the privilege part; it'll be considerable of a chore, I guess. If her mother hain't got her on the right track by now, she won't take to it herself all of a sudden."

"If she makes as much work after she comes as she has before, we might as well give up hope of ever gettin' any rest," sighed Miranda as she hung the dish towels on the barberry bushes at the side door.

"But we should have had to clean house, Rebecca or no Rebecca," urged Jane; "and I can't see why you've scrubbed and washed and baked as you have for that one child, nor why you've about bought out Watson's stock of dry goods."

"I know Aurelia if you don't," responded Miranda. "I've seen her house, and I've seen that batch o' children, wearin' one another's clothes and never carin' whether they had 'em on right sid' out or not; I know what they've had to live and dress on, and so do you. That child will like as not come here with a passel o' things borrowed from the rest o' the family. She'll have Hannah's shoes and John's undershirts and Mark's socks most likely. I suppose she never had a thimble on her finger in her life, but she'll know the feelin' o' one before she's ben here many days. I've bought a piece of unbleached muslin and a piece o' brown gingham for her to make up; that'll keep her busy. Of course she won't pick up anything after herself; she probably never saw a duster, and she'll be as hard to train into our ways as if she was a heathen."

"She'll make a dif'rence," acknowledged Jane, "but she may turn out more biddable 'n we think."

"She'll mind when she's spoken to, biddable or not," remarked Miranda with a shake of the last towel.

Miranda Sawyer had a heart, of course, but she had never used it for any other purpose than the pumping and circulating of blood. She was just, conscientious, economical, industrious; a regular attendant at church and Sunday-School, and a member of the State Missionary and Bible Societies, but in the presence of all these chilly virtues you longed for one warm little fault, or lacking that, one likable failing, something to make you sure she was thoroughly alive. She had never had any education other than that of the neighborhood district school, for her desires and ambitions had all pointed to the management of the house, the farm, and the dairy. Jane, on the other hand, had gone to an academy, and also to a boarding-school for young ladies; so had Aurelia; and after all the years that had elapsed there was still a slight difference in language and in manner between the elder and the two younger sisters.

Jane, too, had had the inestimable advantage of a sorrow; not the natural grief at the loss of her aged father and mother, for she had been content to let them go; but something far deeper. She was engaged to marry young Tom Carter, who had nothing to marry on, it is true, but who was sure to have, some time or other. Then the war broke out. Tom enlisted at the first call. Up to that time Jane had loved him with a quiet, friendly sort of affection, and had given her country a mild emotion of the same sort. But the strife, the danger, the anxiety of the time, set new currents of feeling in motion. Life became something other than the three meals a day, the round of cooking, washing, sewing, and church-going. Personal gossip vanished from

the village conversation. Big things took the place of trifling ones,—sacred sorrows of wives and mothers, pangs of fathers and husband's self-denials, sympathies, new desire to bear one another's burdens. Men and women grew fast in those days of the nation's trouble and danger, and Jane awoke from the vague dull dream she had hitherto called life to new hopes, new fears, new purposes. Then after a year's anxiety, a year when one never looked in the newspaper without dread and sickness of suspense, came the telegram saying that Tom was wounded; and without so much as asking Miranda's leave, she packed her trunk and started for the South. She was in time to hold Tom's hand through hours of pain; to show him for once the heart of a prim New England girl when it is ablaze with love and grief; to put her arms about him so that he could have a home to die in, and that was all; —all, but it served.

It carried her through weary months of nursing—nursing of other soldiers for Tom's dear sake; it sent her home a better woman; and though she had never left Riverboro in all the years that lay between. and had grown into the counterfeit presentment of her sister and of all other thin, spare, New England spinsters, it was something of a counterfeit, and underneath was still the faint echo of that wild heartbeat of her girlhood. Having learned the trick of beating and loving and suffering, the poor faithful heart persisted, although it lived on memories and carried on its sentimental operations mostly in secret.

"You're soft, Jane," said Miranda once; "you allers was soft, and you allers will be. If 't wa'n't for me keeping you stiffened up, I b'lieve you'd leak out o' the house into the dooryard."

It was already past the appointed hour for Mr. Cobb and his coach to be lumbering down the street.

"The stage ought to be here," said Miranda, glancing nervously at the tall clock for the twentieth time. "I guess everything's done. I've tacked up two thick towels back of her washstand and put a mat under her slop-jar; but children are awful hard on furniture. I expect we sha'n't know this house a year from now. You wait and see!"

Jane's frame of mind was naturally depressed and timorous, having been affected by Miranda's gloomy presages of evil to come. The only difference between the sisters in this matter was that while Miranda only wondered how they could endure Rebecca, Jane had flashes of inspiration in which she wondered how Rebecca would endure them. It was in one of these flashes that she ran up the back stairs to put a vase of apple blossoms and a red tomato-pincushion on Rebecca's bureau.

The stage rumbled to the side door of the brick house, and Mr. Cobb handed Rebecca out like a real lady passenger. She alighted with great circumspection, put the bunch of faded flowers in her Aunt Miranda's hand, and received her salute; it could hardly be called a kiss without injuring the fair name of that commodity.

"You needn't 'a' bothered to bring flowers," remarked that gracious and tactful lady; "the garden's always full of 'em here when it comes time."

Jane then kissed Rebecca, giving a somewhat better imitation of the real thing than her sister. "Put the trunk in the entry, Jeremiah, and we'll get it carried upstairs this afternoon," she said.

"I'll take it up for ye now, if ye say the word, girls."

"No, no; don't leave the horses; somebody'll be comin' past, and we can call 'em in."

"Well, good-bye, Rebecca; good-day, Mirandy 'n' Jane. You've got a lively little girl there. I guess she'll be a first-rate company keeper."

Miss Sawyer shuddered openly at the adjective "lively" as applied to a child; her belief being that though children might be seen, if absolutely necessary, they certainly should never be heard if she could help it. "We're not much used to noise, Jane and me," she remarked acidly.

Mr. Cobb saw that he had taken the wrong tack, but he was too unused to argument to explain himself readily, so he drove away, trying to think by what safer word than "lively" he might have described his interesting little passenger.

"I'll take you up and show you your room, Rebecca," Miss Miranda said. "Shut the mosquito-nettin' door tight behind you, so's to keep the flies out; it ain't flytime yet, but I want you to start right; take your passel along with ye and then you won't have to come down for it; always make your head save your heels. Rub your feet on that braided rug; hang your hat and cape in the entry there as you go past."

"It's my best hat," said Rebecca.

"Take it upstairs then and put it in the clothes-press; but I shouldn't 'a' thought you'd 'a' worn your best hat on the stage."

"It's my only hat," explained Rebecca. "My everyday hat wasn't good enough to bring. Fanny's going to finish it."

"Lay your parasol in the entry closet."

"Do you mind if I keep it in my room, please? It always seems safer."

"There ain't any thieves hereabouts, and if there was, I guess they wouldn't make for your sunshade; but come along. Remember to always go up the back way; we don't use the front stairs on account o' the carpet; take care o' the turn and don't ketch your foot; look to your right and go in. When you've washed your face and hands and brushed your hair you can come down, and by and by we'll unpack your trunk and get you settled before supper. Ain't you got your dress on hind sid' foremost?"

Rebecca drew her chin down and looked at the row of smoked pearl buttons running up and down the middle of her flat little chest.

"Hind side foremost? Oh, I see! No, that's all right. If you have seven children you can't keep buttonin' and unbuttonin' 'em all the time—they have to do themselves. We're always buttoned up in front at our house. Mira's only three, but she's buttoned up in front, too."

Miranda said nothing as she closed the door, but her looks were at once equivalent to and more eloquent than words.

Rebecca stood perfectly still in the center of the floor and looked about her. There was a square of oilcloth in front of each article of furniture and a drawn-in rug beside the single four poster, which was covered with a fringed white dimity counterpane.

Everything was as neat as wax, but the ceilings were much higher than Rebecca was accustomed to. It was a north room, and the window, which was long and narrow, looked out on the back buildings and the barn.

It was not the room, which was far more comfortable than Rebecca's own at the farm, nor the lack of view, nor yet the long journey, for she was not conscious of weariness; it was not the fear of a strange place, for she loved new places and courted new sensations; it was because of some curious blending of uncomprehended emotions that Rebecca stood her sunshade in the corner, tore off her best hat, flung it on the bureau with the porcupine quills on the underside, and stripping down the dimity spread, precipitated herself into the middle of the bed and pulled the counterpane over her head.

In a moment the door opened quietly. Knocking was a refinement quite unknown in Riverboro, and if it had been heard of would never have been wasted on a child.

Miss Miranda entered, and as her eye wandered about the vacant room, it fell upon a white and tempestuous ocean of counterpane, an ocean breaking into strange movements of wave and crest and billow.

"Rebecca!"

The tone in which the word was voiced gave it all the effect of having been shouted from the housetops.

A dark ruffled head and two frightened eyes appeared above the dimity spread.

"What are you layin' on your good bed in the daytime for, messin' up the feathers, and dirtyin' the pillers with your dusty boots?"

Rebecca rose guiltily. There seemed no excuse to make. Her offense was beyond explanation or apology.

"I'm sorry, Aunt Mirandy—something came over me; I don't know what."

"Well, if it comes over you very soon again we'll have to find out what 't is. Spread your bed up smooth this minute, for 'Bijah Flagg's bringin' your trunk upstairs, and I wouldn't let him see such a cluttered-up room for anything; he'd tell it all over town."

When Mr. Cobb had put up his horses that night he carried a kitchen chair to the side of his wife, who was sitting on the back porch.

"I brought a little Randall girl down on the stage from Maplewood today, mother. She's kin to the Sawyer girls an' is goin' to live with 'em," he said, as he sat down and began to whittle. "She's that Aurelia's child, the one that ran away with Susan Randall's son just before we come here to live."

"How old a child?"

"'Bout ten, or somewhere along there, an' small for her age; but land! she might be a hundred to hear her talk! She kep' me jumpin' tryin' to answer her! Of all the queer children I ever come across she's the queerest. She ain't no beauty—her face is all eyes; but if she ever grows up to them eyes an' fills out a little she'll make folks stare. Land, mother! I wish 't you could 'a' heard her talk."

"I don't see what she had to talk about, a child like that, to a stranger," replied Mrs. Cobb.

"Stranger or no stranger, 't wouldn't make no difference to her. She'd talk to a pump or a grindstun; she'd talk to herself ruther'n keep still."

"What did she talk about?"

"Blamed if I can repeat any of it. She kep' me so surprised I didn't have my wits about me. She had a little pink sunshade—it kind

o' looked like a doll's amberill, 'n' she clung to it like a burr to a woolen stockin'. I advised her to open it up—the sun was so hot; but she said no,'t would fade, an' she tucked it under her dress. 'It's the dearest thing in life to me,' says she, 'but it's a dreadful care.' Them's the very words, an' it's all the words I remember. 'It's the dearest thing in life to me, but it's an awful care!'"—here Mr. Cobb laughed aloud as he tipped his chair back against the side of the house. "There was another thing, but I can't get it right exactly. She was talkin' 'bout the circus parade an' the snake charmer in a gold chariot, an' says she, 'She was so beautiful beyond compare, Mr. Cobb, that it made you have lumps in your throat to look at her.' She'll be comin' over to see you, mother, an' you can size her up for yourself. I don' know how she'll git on with Mirandy Sawyer—poor little soul!"

This doubt was more or less openly expressed in Riverboro, which, however, had two opinions on the subject; one that it was a most generous thing in the Sawyer girls to take one of Aurelia's children to educate, the other that the education would be bought at a price wholly out of proportion to its intrinsic value.

4

WISDOM WAYS

The day of Rebecca's arrival had been Friday, and on the Monday following she began her education at the school which was in Riverboro Center, about a mile distant. Miss Sawyer borrowed a neighbor's horse and wagon and drove to the schoolhouse, interviewing the teacher, Miss Dearborn, arranging for books, and generally starting the child on a path that was to lead to boundless knowledge.

Rebecca walked to school after the first morning. She loved this part of the day's program. When the dew was not too heavy and the weather was fair there was a short cut through the woods. She turned off the main road, crept through Uncle Josh Woodman's bars, waved away Mrs. Carter's cows, trod the short grass of the pasture, with its well-worn path running through gardens of buttercups and whiteweed, and groves of ivory leaves and sweet fern. She descended a little hill, jumped from stone to stone across a woodland brook, startling the drowsy frogs, who were always winking and blinking in the morning sun. Then came the "woodsy bit," with her feet pressing the slippery carpet of brown pine needles; the "woodsy bit" so full of dewy morning surprises. Then she climbed a stile, went through a grassy meadow, slid under another pair of bars, and came out into the road again, having gained nearly half a mile.

How delicious it all was! Rebecca clasped her Quackenbos's Grammar and Greenleaf's Arithmetic with a joyful sense of knowing her lessons. Her dinner pail swung from her right hand, and she had a blissful consciousness of the two soda biscuits spread with butter and syrup, the baked cup-custard, the doughnut, and the square of hard gingerbread. Sometimes she said whatever "piece" she was going to speak on the next Friday afternoon.

A soldier of the Legion lay dying in Algiers,
There was lack of woman's nursing, there was
    dearth of woman's tears.

How she loved the swing and the sentiment of it! How her young voice quivered whenever she came to the refrain:—

But we'll meet no more at Bingen, dear Bingen
    on the Rhine.

It always sounded beautiful in her ears, as she sent her tearful little treble into the clear morning air. Another early favorite (for we must remember that Rebecca's only knowledge of the great world of poetry consisted of the selections in vogue in school readers) was:—

Woodman, spare that tree!
    Touch not a single bough!
In youth it sheltered me,
    And I'll protect it now.

When Emma Jane Perkins walked through the "short cut" with her, the two children used to render this with appropriate dramatic action. Emma Jane always chose to be the woodman because she had nothing to do but raise on high an imaginary axe.

At the last pair of bars the two girls were sometimes met by a detachment of the Simpson children, who lived in a black house with a red door and a red barn behind, on the Blueberry Plains road. Rebecca felt an interest in the Simpsons from the first, because there were so many of them and they were so patched and darned, just like her own brood at the home farm.

The little schoolhouse with its flagpole on top and its two doors in front, one for boys and the other for girls, stood on the crest of a hill, with rolling fields and meadows on one side, a stretch of pine woods on the other, and the river glinting and sparkling in the dis-

tance. It boasted no attractions within. All was as bare and ugly and uncomfortable as it well could be, for the villages along the river expended so much money in repairing and rebuilding bridges that they were obliged to be very economical in school privileges. The teacher's desk and chair stood on a platform in one corner; there was an uncouth stove, never blackened oftener than once a year, a map of the United States, two blackboards, a ten-quart tin pail of water and long-handled dipper on a corner shelf, and wooden desks and benches for the scholars, who only numbered twenty in Rebecca's time. The seats were higher in the back of the room, and the more advanced and longer-legged pupils sat there, the position being greatly to be envied, as they were at once nearer to the windows and farther from the teacher.

There were classes of a sort, although nobody, broadly speaking, studied the same book with anybody else, or had arrived at the same degree of proficiency in any one branch of learning. Rebecca in particular was so difficult to classify that Miss Dearborn at the end of a fortnight gave up the attempt altogether. She read with Dick Carter and Living Perkins, who were fitting for the academy; recited arithmetic with lisping little Thuthan Thimpthon; geography with Emma Jane Perkins, and grammar after school hours to Miss Dearborn alone. Full to the brim as she was of clever thoughts and quaint fancies, she made at first but a poor hand at composition. The labor of writing and spelling, with the added difficulties of punctuation and capitals, interfered sadly with the free expression of ideas. She took history with Alice Robinson's class, which was attacking the subject of the Revolution, while Rebecca was bidden to begin with the discovery of America. In a week she had mastered the course of events up to the Revolution, and in ten days had arrived at Yorktown, where the class had apparently established summer quarters. Then finding that extra effort would only result in her reciting with the oldest Simpson boy, she deliberately held herself back, for wisdom's ways were not those of pleasantness nor her paths those of peace if one were compelled to tread them in the company of "Seesaw" Simpson.

Samuel Simpson was generally called "Seesaw," because of his difficulty in making up his mind. Whether it were a question of fact, of spelling, or of date, of going swimming or fishing, of choosing a book in the Sunday-School library or a stick of candy at the village store, he had no sooner determined on one plan of action than his wish fondly reverted to the opposite one. Seesaw was pale, flaxen-haired, blue-eyed, round-shouldered, and given to stammering when nervous. Perhaps because of his very weakness Rebecca's decision of character had a fascination for him, and although she snubbed him to the verge of madness, he could never keep his eyes away from her. The force with which she tied her shoe when the lacing came undone, the flirt over shoulder she gave her black braid when she was excited or warm, her manner of studying,—book on desk, arms folded, eyes fixed on the opposite wall,—all had an abiding charm for Seesaw Simpson. When, having obtained permission, she walked to the water pail in the corner and drank from the dipper, unseen forces dragged Seesaw from his seat to go and drink after her. It was not only that there was something akin to association and intimacy in drinking next, but there was the fearful joy of meeting her in transit and receiving a cold and disdainful look from her wonderful eyes.

On a certain warm day in summer Rebecca's thirst exceeded the bounds of propriety. When she asked a third time for permission to quench it at the common fountain Miss Dearborn nodded "yes," but lifted her eyebrows unpleasantly as Rebecca neared the desk. As she replaced the dipper Seesaw promptly raised his hand, and Miss Dearborn indicated a weary affirmative.

"What is the matter with you, Rebecca?" she asked.

"I had salt mackerel for breakfast," answered Rebecca.

There seemed nothing humorous about this reply, which was merely the statement of a fact, but an irrepressible titter ran through the school. Miss Dearborn did not enjoy jokes neither made nor understood by herself, and her face flushed.

"I think you had better stand by the pail

for five minutes, Rebecca; it may help you to control your thirst."

Rebecca's heart fluttered. She to stand in the corner by the water pail and be stared at by all the scholars! She unconsciously made a gesture of angry dissent and moved a step nearer her seat, but was arrested by Miss Dearborn's command in a still firmer voice.

"Stand by the pail, Rebecca! Samuel, how many times have you asked for water to-day?"

"This is the f-f-fourth."

"Don't touch the dipper, please. The school has done nothing but drink this afternoon; it has had no time whatever to study. I suppose you had something salt for breakfast, Samuel?" queried Miss Dearborn with sarcasm.

"I had m-m-mackerel, j-just like Reb-b-becca." (Irrepressible giggles by the school.)

"I judged so. Stand by the other side of the pail, Samuel."

Rebecca's head was bowed with shame and wrath. Life looked too black a thing to be endured. The punishment was bad enough, but to be coupled in correction with Seesaw Simpson was beyond human endurance.

Singing was the last exercise in the afternoon, and Minnie Smellie chose "Shall We Gather at the River?" It was a baleful choice and seemed to hold some secret and subtle association with the situation and general progress of events; or at any rate there was apparently some obscure reason for the energy and vim with which the scholars shouted the choral invitation again and again:—

> Shall we gather at the river,
> The beautiful, the beautiful river?

Miss Dearborn stole a look at Rebecca's bent head and was frightened. The child's face was pale save for two red spots glowing on her cheeks. Tears hung on her lashes; her breath came and went quickly, and the hand that held her pocket handkerchief trembled like a leaf.

"You may go to your seat, Rebecca," said Miss Dearborn at the end of the first song. "Samuel, stay where you are till the close of school. And let me tell you, scholars, that I asked Rebecca to stand by the pail only to break up this habit of incessant drinking, which is nothing but empty-mindedness and desire to walk to and fro over the floor. Every time Rebecca has asked for a drink today the whole school has gone to the pail one after another. She is really thirsty, and I dare say I ought to have punished you for following her example, not her for setting it. What shall we sing now, Alice?"

" 'The Old Oaken Bucket,' please."

"Think of something dry, Alice, and change the subject. Yes, 'The Star Spangled Banner' if you like, or anything else."

Rebecca sank into her seat and pulled the singing-book from her desk. Miss Dearborn's public explanation had shifted some of the weight from her heart, and she felt a trifle raised in her self-esteem.

Under cover of the general relaxation of singing, votive offerings of respectful sympathy began to make their appearance at her shrine. Living Perkins, who could not sing, dropped a piece of maple sugar in her lap as he passed her on his way to the blackboard to draw the map of Maine. Alice Robinson rolled a perfectly new slate pencil over the floor with her foot until it reached Rebecca's place, while her seat-mate, Emma Jane, had made up a little mound of paper balls and labeled them "Bullets for you know who."

Altogether existence grew brighter, and when she was left alone with the teacher for her grammar lesson she had nearly recovered her equanimity, which was more than Miss Dearborn had. The last clattering foot had echoed through the hall, Seesaw's backward glance of penitence had been met and answered defiantly by one of cold disdain.

"Rebecca, I am afraid I punished you more than I meant," said Miss Dearborn, who was only eighteen herself, and in her year of teaching country schools had never encountered a child like Rebecca.

"I hadn't missed a question this whole day, nor whispered either," quavered the culprit; "and I don't think I ought to be shamed just for drinking."

"You started all the others, or it seemed as if you did. Whatever you do they all do, whether you laugh, or miss, or write notes, or ask to leave the room, or drink; and it must be stopped."

"Sam Simpson is a copy-cat!" stormed Rebecca. "I wouldn't have minded standing in the corner alone—that is, not so very much, but I couldn't bear standing with him."

"I saw that you couldn't, and that's the reason I told you to take your seat, and left him in the corner. Remember that you are a stranger in the place, and they take more notice of what you do, so you must be careful. Now let's have our conjugations. Give me the verb 'to be,' potential mood, past perfect tense."

I might have been	We might have been
Thou mightst have been	You might have been
He might have been	They might have been.

"Give me an example, please."

> I might have been glad
> Thou mightst have been glad
> He, she, or it might have been glad.

" 'He' or 'she' might have been glad because they are masculine and feminine, but could 'it' have been glad?" asked Miss Dearborn, who was very fond of splitting hairs.

"Why not?" asked Rebecca.

"Because 'it' is neuter gender."

"Couldn't we say, 'The kitten might have been glad if it had known it was not going to be drowned' ?"

"Ye—es," Miss Dearborn answered hesitatingly, never very sure of herself under Rebecca's fire; "but though we often speak of a baby, a chicken, or a kitten as 'it,' they are really masculine or feminine gender, not neuter."

Rebecca reflected a long moment and then asked, "Is a hollyhock neuter?"

"Oh, yes, of course it is, Rebecca."

"Well, couldn't we say, 'The hollyhock might have been glad to see the rain, but there was a weak little hollyhock bud growing out of its stalk and it was afraid that that might be hurt by the storm; so the big hollyhock was kind of afraid, instead of being real glad' ?"

Miss Dearborn looked puzzled as she answered, "Of course, Rebecca, hollyhocks could not be sorry, or glad, or afraid, really."

"We can't tell, I s'pose," replied the child, "but I think they are, anyway. Now, what shall I say?"

"The subjunctive mood, past perfect tense of the verb 'to know.' "

If I had known	If we had known
If thou hadst known	If you had known
If he had known	If they had known.

"Oh, it is the saddest tense," sighed Rebecca with a little break in her voice; "nothing but *ifs, ifs, ifs*! It makes you feel that if they only *had* known, things might have been better!"

Miss Dearborn had not thought of it before but on reflection she believed the subjunctive mood was a "sad" one and "if" rather a sorry "part of speech."

"Give me some more examples of the subjunctive, Rebecca, and that will do for this afternoon," she said.

"If I had not loved mackerel I should not have been thirsty," said Rebecca with an April smile, as she closed her grammar. "If thou hadst loved me truly thou wouldst not have stood me up in the corner. If Samuel had not loved wickedness he would not have followed me to the water pail."

"And if Rebecca had loved the rules of the school she would have controlled her thirst," finished Miss Dearborn with a kiss, and the two parted friends.

5

SUNSHINE IN A SHADY PLACE

The little schoolhouse on the hill had its moments of triumph as well as its scenes of tribulation, but it was fortunate that Rebecca had her books and her new acquaintances to keep her interested and occupied, or life would have gone heavily with her that first summer in Riverboro. She tried to like her Aunt Miranda (the idea of loving her had been given up at the moment of meeting), but failed ignominiously in the attempt. She was a very faulty and passionately human child, with no aspirations toward being an angel of the house, but she had a sense of duty and a desire to be good,—respectably, decently good. Whenever she fell below this self-imposed standard she was miserable. She did not like to be under her aunt's roof, eating bread, wearing clothes, and studying books provided by her, and dislike her so heartily all the time. She felt instinctively that this was wrong and mean, and whenever the feeling of remorse was strong within her she made a desperate effort to please her grim and difficult relative. But how could she succeed when she was never herself in her Aunt Miranda's presence? The searching look of the eyes, the sharp voice, the hard knotty fingers, the thin straight lips, the long silences, the "front-piece" that didn't match her hair, the very obvious "parting" that seemed sewed in with linen thread on black net,—there was not a single item that appealed to Rebecca. There are certain narrow, unimaginative, and autocratic old people who seem to call out the most mischievous, and sometimes the worst traits in children. Miss Miranda, had she lived in a populous neighborhood, would have had her doorbell pulled, her gate tied up, or "dirt traps" set in her garden paths. The Simpson twins stood in such awe of her that they could not be persuaded to come to the side door even when Miss Jane held gingerbread cookies in her outstretched hands.

It is needless to say that Rebecca irritated her aunt with every breath she drew. She continually forgot and started up the front stairs because it was the shortest route to her bedroom; she left the dipper on the kitchen shelf instead of hanging it up over the pail; she sat in the chair the cat liked best; she was willing to go on errands, but often forgot what she was sent for; she left the screen doors ajar, so that flies came in; her tongue was ever in motion; she sang or whistled when she was picking up chips; she was always messing with flowers, putting them in vases, pinning them on her dress, and sticking them in her hat; finally she was an everlasting reminder of her foolish, worthless father, whose handsome face and engaging manner had so deceived Aurelia, and perhaps, if the facts were known, others besides Aurelia. The Randalls were

aliens. They had not been born in Riverboro nor even in York County. Miranda would have allowed, on compulsion, that in the nature of things a large number of persons must necessarily be born outside this sacred precinct; but she had her opinion of them, and it was not a flattering one. Now if Hannah had come—Hannah took after the other side of the house; she was "all Sawyer." (Poor Hannah! That was true!) Hannah spoke only when spoken to, instead of first, last, and all the time; Hannah at fourteen was a member of the church; Hannah liked to knit; Hannah was, probably, or would have been, a pattern of all the smaller virtues; instead of which here was this black-haired gypsy, with eyes as big as cartwheels, installed as a member of the household.

What sunshine in a shady place was Aunt Jane to Rebecca! Aunt Jane with her quiet voice, her understanding eyes, her ready excuses, in these first difficult weeks, when the impulsive little stranger was trying to settle down into the "brick house ways." She did learn them, in part, and by degrees, and the constant fitting of herself to these new and difficult standards of conduct seemed to make her older than ever for her years.

The child took her sewing and sat beside Aunt Jane in the kitchen while Aunt Miranda had the post of observation at the sitting-room window. Sometimes they would work on the side porch where the clematis and woodbine shaded them from the hot sun. To Rebecca the lengths of brown gingham were interminable. She made hard work of sewing, broke the thread, dropped her thimble into the syringa bushes, pricked her finger, wiped the perspiration from her forehead, could not match the checks, puckered the seams. She polished her needles to nothing, pushing them in and out of the emery strawberry, but they always squeaked. Still Aunt Jane's patience held good, and some small measure of skill was creeping into Rebecca's fingers, fingers that held pencil, paint brush, and pen so cleverly and were so clumsy with the dainty little needle.

When the first brown gingham frock was completed, the child seized what she thought an opportune moment and asked her Aunt

Miranda if she might have another color for the next one.

"I bought a whole piece of the brown," said Miranda laconically. "That'll give you two more dresses, with plenty for new sleeves, and to patch and let down with, an' be more economical."

"I know. But Mr. Watson says he'll take back part of it, and let us have pink and blue for the same price."

"Did you ask him?"

"Yes'm."

"It was none o' your business."

"I was helping Emma Jane choose aprons, and didn't think you'd mind which color I had. Pink keeps clean just as nice as brown, and Mr. Watson says it'll boil without fading."

"Mr. Watson's a splendid judge of washing, I guess. I don't approve of children being rigged out in fancy colors, but I'll see what your Aunt Jane thinks."

"I think it would be all right to let Rebecca have one pink and one blue gingham," said Jane. "A child gets tired of sewing on one color. It's only natural she should long for a change; besides she'd look like a charity child always wearing the same brown with a white apron. And it's dreadful unbecoming to her!"

" 'Handsome is as handsome does,' say I. Rebecca never'll come to grief along of her beauty, that's certain, and there's no use in humoring her to think about her looks. I believe she's vain as a peacock now, without anything to be vain of."

"She's young and attracted to bright things —that's all. I remember well enough how I felt at her age."

"You was considerable of a fool at her age, Jane."

"Yes, I was, thank the Lord! I only wish I'd known how to take a little of my foolishness along with me, as some folks do, to brighten my declining years."

There finally was a pink gingham, and when it was nicely finished, Aunt Jane gave Rebecca a delightful surprise. She showed her how to make a pretty trimming of narrow white linen tape, by folding it in pointed shapes and sewing it down very flat with neat little stitches.

"It'll be good fancy work for you, Rebecca;

for your Aunt Miranda won't like to see you always reading in the long winter evenings. Now if you think you can baste two rows of white tape round the bottom of your pink skirt and keep it straight by the checks, I'll stitch them on for you and trim the waist and sleeves with pointed tape-trimming, so the dress'll be real pretty for second-best."

Rebecca's joy knew no bounds. "I'll baste like a house afire!" she exclaimed. "It's a thousand yards round that skirt, as well I know, having hemmed it; but I could sew pretty trimming on if it was from here to Milltown. Oh! Do you think Aunt Mirandy 'll ever let me go to Milltown with Mr. Cobb? He's asked me again, you know; but one Saturday I had to pick strawberries, and another it rained, and I don't think she really approves of my going. It's *twenty-nine* minutes past four, Aunt Jane, and Alice Robinson has been sitting under the currant bushes for a long time waiting for me. Can I go and play?"

"Yes, you may go, and you'd better run as far as you can out behind the barn, so 't your noise won't distract your Aunt Mirandy. I see

Susan Simpson and the twins and Emma Jane Perkins hiding behind the fence."

Rebecca leaped off the porch, snatched Alice Robinson from under the currant bushes, and what was much more difficult, succeeded by means of a complicated system of signals, in getting Emma Jane away from the Simpson party and giving them the slip altogether. They were much too small for certain pleasurable activities planned for that afternoon; but they were not to be despised, for they had the most fascinating dooryard in the village. In it, in bewildering confusion, were old sleighs, pungs, horse rakes, hogsheads, settees without backs, bedsteads without heads, in all stages of disability, and never the same on two consecutive days. Mrs. Simpson was seldom at home, and even when she was, had little concern as to what happened on the premises. A favorite diversion was to make the house into a fort, gallantly held by a handful of American soldiers against a besieging force of the British army. Great care was used in apportioning the parts, for there was no disposition to let anybody win but the Americans. Seesaw Simpson was usually made commander-in-chief of the British army, and a limp and uncertain one he was, capable, with his contradictory orders and his fondness for the extreme rear, of leading any regiment to an inglorious death. Sometimes the long-suffering house was a log hut, and the brave settlers defeated a band of hostile Indians, or occasionally were massacred by them; but in either case the Simpson house looked, to quote a Riverboro expression, "as if the devil had been having an auction in it."

6
COLOR OF ROSE

On the very next Friday there were great doings in the little schoolhouse on the hill. Friday afternoon was always the time chosen for dialogues, songs, and recitations, but it can-

not be stated that it was a gala day in any true sense of the word. Most of the children hated "speaking pieces"; hated the burden of learning them, dreaded the danger of breaking down in them. Miss Dearborn commonly went home with a headache, and never left her bed during the rest of the afternoon or evening; and the casual female parent who attended the exercises sat on a front bench with beads of cold sweat on her forehead, listening to the all-too-familiar halts and stammers. Sometimes a bellowing infant who had clean forgotten his verse would cast himself bodily on the maternal bosom and be borne out into the open air, where he was sometimes kissed and occasionally spanked; but in any case the failure added an extra dash of gloom and dread to the occasion. The advent of Rebecca had somehow infused a new spirit into these hitherto terrible afternoons. She had taught Elijah and Elisha Simpson so that they recited three verses of something with such comical effect that they delighted themselves, the teacher, and the school; while Susan, who lisped, had been provided with a humorous poem in which she impersonated a lisping child. Emma Jane and Rebecca had a dialogue, and the sense of companionship buoyed up Emma Jane and gave her self-reliance. In fact, Miss Dearborn announced on this particular Friday morning that the exercises promised to be so interesting that she had invited the doctor's wife, the minister's wife, two members of the school committee, and a few mothers. Living Perkins was asked to decorate one of the blackboards and Rebecca the other. Living, who was the star artist of the school, chose the map of North America. Rebecca liked better to draw things less realistic, and speedily, before the eyes of the enchanted multitude, there grew under her skillful fingers an American flag done in red, white, and blue chalk, every star in its right place, every stripe fluttering in the breeze. Beside this appeared a figure of Columbia, copied from the top of the cigar box that held the crayons.

Miss Dearborn was delighted. "I propose we give Rebecca a good hand-clapping for such a beautiful picture—one that the whole school may well be proud of!"

The scholars clapped heartily, and Dick Carter, leaping to his feet, waved his hand and gave a rousing cheer.

Rebecca's heart leaped for joy, and to her confusion she felt the tears rising in her eyes. She could hardly see the way back to her seat, for in her ignorant lonely little life she had never been singled out for applause, never lauded, nor crowned, as in this wonderful, dazzling moment. If "nobleness enkindleth nobleness," so does enthusiasm beget enthusiasm, and so do wit and talent enkindle wit and talent. Alice Robinson proposed that the school should sing "Three Cheers for the Red, White, and Blue!" and when they came to the chorus, all point to Rebecca's flag. Dick Carter suggested that Living Perkins and Rebecca Randall should sign their names to their pictures, so that the visitors would know who drew them. Huldah Meserve asked permission to cover the largest holes in the plastered walls with boughs and fill the water pail with wild flowers. Rebecca's mood was above and beyond all practical details. She sat silent, her heart so full of grateful joy that she could hardly remember the words of her dialogue. At recess she bore herself modestly, notwithstanding her great triumph.

Miss Dearborn dismissed the morning session at quarter to twelve, so that those who lived near enough could go home for a change of dress. Emma Jane and Rebecca ran nearly every step of the way, from sheer excitement, only stopping to breathe at the stiles.

"Will your Aunt Mirandy let you wear your best, or only your buff calico?" asked Emma Jane.

"I think I'll ask Aunt Jane," Rebecca replied. "Oh! If my pink was only finished! I left Aunt Jane making the buttonholes!"

"I'm going to ask my mother to let me wear her garnet ring," said Emma Jane. "It would look perfectly elergant flashing in the sun when I point to the flag. Good-bye; don't wait for me going back; I may get a ride."

Rebecca found the side door locked, but she knew that the key was under the step, and so of course did everybody else in Riverboro, for they all did about the same thing with it. She unlocked the door and went into the din-

ing room to find her lunch laid on the table and a note from Aunt Jane saying that they had gone to Moderation with Mrs. Robinson in her carryall. Rebecca swallowed a piece of bread and butter, and flew up the front stairs to her bedroom. On the bed lay the pink gingham dress finished by Aunt Jane's kind hands. Could she, dare she, wear it without asking? Did the occasion justify a new costume, or would her aunts think she ought to keep it for the concert?

"I'll wear it," thought Rebecca. "They're not here to ask, and maybe they wouldn't mind a bit; it's only gingham after all, and wouldn't be so grand if it wasn't new, and hadn't tape trimming on it, and wasn't pink."

She unbraided her two pigtails, combed out the waves of her hair and tied them back with a ribbon, changed her shoes, and then slipped on the pretty frock, managing to fasten all but the three middle buttons, which she reserved for Emma Jane.

Then her eye fell on her cherished pink sunshade, the exact match, and the girls had never seen it. It wasn't quite appropriate for school, but she needn't take it into the room; she would wrap it in a piece of paper, just show it, and carry it coming home. She glanced in the parlor looking-glass downstairs and was electrified at the vision. It seemed almost as if beauty of apparel could go no further than that heavenly pink gingham dress! The sparkle of her eyes, glow of her cheeks, sheen of her falling hair, passed unnoticed in the all-conquering charm of the rose-colored garment. Goodness! It was twenty minutes to one and she would be late. She danced out the side door, pulled a pink rose from a bush at the gate, and covered the mile between the brick house and the seat of learning in an incredibly short time, meeting Emma Jane, also breathless and resplendent, at the entrance.

"Rebecca Randall!" exclaimed Emma Jane, "you're handsome as a picture!"

"I?" laughed Rebecca. "Nonsense! It's only the pink gingham."

"You're not good looking every day," insisted Emma Jane; "but you're different somehow. See my garnet ring; mother scrubbed it in soap and water. How on earth did your Aunt Mirandy let you put on your bran' new dress?"

"They were both away and I didn't ask," Rebecca responded anxiously. "Why? Do you think they'd have said no?"

"Miss Mirandy always says no, doesn't she?" asked Emma Jane.

"Ye—es; but this afternoon is very special —almost like a Sunday-School concert."

"Yes," assented Emma Jane, "it is, of course; with your name on the board, and our pointing to your flag, and our elergant dialogue, and all that."

The afternoon was one succession of solid triumphs for everybody concerned. There were no real failures at all, no tears, no parents ashamed of their offspring. Miss Dearborn heard many admiring remarks passed upon her ability, and wondered whether they belonged to her or partly, at least, to Rebecca. The child had no more to do than several others, but she was somehow in the foreground. It transpired afterwards at various village entertainments that Rebecca couldn't be kept in the background; it positively refused to hold her. Her worst enemy could not have called her pushing. She was ready and willing and never shy; but she sought for no chances of display and was, indeed, remarkably lacking in self-consciousness, as well as eager to bring others into whatever fun or entertainment there was. If wherever the MacGregor sat was the head of the table, so in the same way wherever Rebecca stood was the center of the stage. Her clear high treble soared above all the rest in the choruses, and somehow everybody watched her, took note of her gestures, her whole-souled singing, her irrepressible enthusiasm.

Finally it was all over, and it seemed to Rebecca as if she should never be cool and calm again, as she loitered on the homeward path. There would be no lessons to learn to-night, and the vision of helping with the preserves on the morrow had no terrors for her—fears could not draw breath in the radiance that flooded her soul. There were thick gathering clouds in the sky, but she took no note of them save to be glad that she could raise her sunshade. She did not tread the solid ground at all, or have any sense of belonging to the common human family, until she entered the side

yard of the brick house and saw her Aunt Miranda standing in the open doorway. Then with a rush she came back to earth.

7
ASHES OF ROSES

"There she is, over an hour late; a little more an' she'd 'a' been caught in a thunder shower, but she'd never look ahead," said Miranda to Jane; "and added to all her other iniquities, if she ain't rigged out in that new dress, steppin' along with her father's dancin'-school steps, and swingin' her parasol for all the world as if she was play-actin'. Now I'm the oldest, Jane, an' I intend to have my say out; if you don't like it you can go into the kitchen till it's over. Step right in here, Rebecca; I want to talk to you. What did you put on that good new dress for, on a school day, without permission?"

"I had intended to ask you at noontime, but you weren't at home, so I couldn't," began Rebecca.

"You did no such a thing; you put it on because you was left alone, though you knew well enough I wouldn't have let you."

"If I'd been *certain* you wouldn't have let me I'd never have done it," said Rebecca, trying to be truthful; "but I wasn't *certain,* and it was worth risking. I thought perhaps you might, if you knew it was almost a real exhibition at school."

"Exhibition!" exclaimed Miranda scornfully; "you are exhibition enough by yourself, I should say. Was you exhibitin' your parasol?"

"The parasol *was* silly," confessed Rebecca, hanging her head; "but it's the only time in my whole life when I had anything to match it, and it looked so beautiful with the pink dress! Emma Jane and I spoke a dialogue about a city girl and a country girl, and it came to me just the minute before I started how nice it would come in for the city girl; and it did. I haven't hurt my dress a mite, Aunt Mirandy."

"It's the craftiness and underhandedness of your actions that's the worst," said Miranda coldly. "And look at the other things you've done! It seems as if Satan possessed you! You went up the front stairs to your room, but you didn't hide your tracks, for you dropped your handkerchief on the way up. You left the screen out of your bedroom window for the flies to come in all over the house. You never cleared away your lunch nor set away a dish, *and you left the side door unlocked* from half-past twelve to three o'clock, so 't anybody could 'a' come in and stolen what they liked!"

Rebecca sat down heavily in her chair as she heard the list of her transgressions. How could she have been so careless? The tears began to flow now as she attempted to explain sins that never could be explained or justified.

"Oh, I'm so sorry!" she faltered. "I was trimming the schoolroom, and got belated, and ran all the way home. It was hard getting into my dress alone, and I hadn't time to eat but a mouthful, and just at the last minute, when I honestly—*honestly*—would have thought about clearing away and locking up, I looked at the clock and knew I could hardly get back to school in time to form in the line; and I thought how dreadful it would be to go in late and get my first black mark on a Friday afternoon, with the minister's wife and the doctor's wife and the school committee all there!"

"Don't wail and carry on now; it's no good cryin' over spilt milk," answered Miranda. "An ounce of good behavior is worth a pound of repentance. Instead of tryin' to see how little trouble you can make in a house that ain't your own home, it seems as if you tried to see how much you could put us out. Take that rose out o' your dress and let me see the spot it's made on your yoke, an' the rusty holes where the wet pin went in. No, it ain't; but it's more by luck than forethought. I ain't got any patience with your flowers and frizzled-out hair and furbelows an' airs an' graces, for all the world like your Miss-Nancy father."

Rebecca lifted her head in a flash. "Look here, Aunt Mirandy, I'll be as good as I know how to be. I'll mind quick when I'm spoken to and never leave the door unlocked again, but I won't have my father called names. He was a p-perfectly l-lovely father, that's what he was, and it's *mean* to call him Miss Nancy!"

"Don't you dare answer me back that imperdent way, Rebecca, tellin' me I'm mean; your father was a vain, foolish, shiftless man, an' you might as well hear it from me as anybody else; he spent your mother's money and left her with seven children to provide for."

"It's s-something to leave s-seven nice children," sobbed Rebecca.

"Not when other folks have to help feed, clothe, and educate 'em," responded Miranda. "Now you step upstairs, put on your nightgown, go to bed, and stay there till mornin'. You'll find a bowl o' crackers an' milk on your bureau, an' I don't want to hear a sound from you till breakfast time. Jane, run an' take the dish towels off the line and shut the shed doors; we're goin' to have a turrible shower."

"We've had it, I should think," said Jane quietly, as she went to do her sister's bidding. "I don't often speak my mind, Mirandy; but you ought not to have said what you did about Lorenzo. He was what he was, and can't be made any different; but he was Rebecca's father, and Aurelia always says he was a good

husband."

Miranda had never heard the proverbial phrase about the only "good Indian," but her mind worked in the conventional manner when she said grimly, "Yes, I've noticed that dead husbands are usually good ones; but the truth needs an airin' now and then, and that child will never amount to a hill o' beans till she gets some of her father trounced out of her. I'm glad I said just what I did."

"I dare say you are," remarked Jane, with what might be described as one of her annual bursts of courage; "but all the same, Mirandy, it wasn't good manners, and it wasn't good religion!"

The clap of thunder that shook the house just at that moment made no such peal in Miranda Sawyer's ears as Jane's remark made when it fell with a deafening roar on her conscience.

Perhaps after all it is just as well to speak only once a year and then speak to the purpose.

Rebecca mounted the back stairs wearily, closed the door of her bedroom, and took off the beloved pink gingham with trembling fingers. She smoothed it out carefully, pinched up the white ruffle at the neck, and laid it away in a drawer with an extra little sob at the roughness of life. The withered pink rose fell on the floor. Rebecca looked at it and thought to herself, "Just like my happy day!" Nothing could show more clearly the kind of child she was than the fact that she instantly perceived the symbolism of the rose, and laid it in the drawer with the dress as if she were burying the whole episode with all its sad memories.

She braided her hair in the two accustomed pigtails, took off her best shoes (which had happily escaped notice), with all the while a fixed resolve growing in her mind, that of leaving the brick house and going back to the farm. She would not be received there with open arms,—there was no hope of that,—but she would help her mother about the house and send Hannah to Riverboro in her place. "I hope she'll like it!" she thought in a momentary burst of vindictiveness. She sat by the window trying to make some sort of plan, watching the lightning play over the hilltop and the streams of rain chasing each other down the lightning rod. And this was the day that had dawned so joyfully! It had been a red sunrise, and she had leaned on the window sill studying her lesson and thinking what a lovely world it was. And what a golden morning! The changing of the bare, ugly little school-room into a bower of beauty; the privilege of decorating the blackboard; the intoxicating moment when the school clapped her! And what an afternoon! How it went on from glory to glory, beginning with Emma Jane's telling her, Rebecca Randall, that she was as "handsome as a picture."

She had thought Aunt Miranda might be pleased that the piece invited down from the farm had succeeded so well at school; but no, there was no hope of pleasing her in that or in any other way. She would go to Maplewood on the stage next day with Mr. Cobb and get home somehow from cousin Ann's. On second thought her aunts might not allow it. Very well, she would slip away now and see if she could stay all night with the Cobbs and be off next morning before breakfast.

Rebecca never stopped long to think, more's the pity, so she put on her oldest dress and hat and jacket, then wrapped her nightdress, comb, and toothbrush in a bundle and dropped it softly out of the window. Her room was in the L and her window at no very dangerous distance from the ground, though had it been, nothing could have stopped her at that moment. Somebody who had gone on the roof to clean out the gutters had left a cleat nailed to the side of the house about halfway between the window and the top of the back porch. Rebecca heard the sound of the sewing machine in the dining room and the chopping of meat in the kitchen; so knowing the whereabouts of both her aunts, she scrambled out of the window, caught hold of the lightning rod, slid down to the helpful cleat, jumped to the porch, used the woodbine trellis for a ladder, and was flying up the road in the storm before she had time to arrange any details of her future movements.

Jeremiah Cobb sat at his lonely supper at the table by the kitchen window. "Mother," as he with his old-fashioned habits was in the habit of calling his wife, was nursing a sick neighbor. Mrs. Cobb was mother only to a little headstone in the churchyard, where reposed "Sarah Ann, beloved daughter of Jeremiah and Sarah Cobb, aged seventeen months"; but the name of mother was better than nothing, and served at any rate as a reminder of her woman's crown of blessedness.

The rain still fell, and the heavens were dark, though it was scarcely five o'clock. Looking up from his "dish of tea," the old man saw at the open door a very figure of woe. Rebecca's face was so swollen with tears and so sharp with misery that for a moment he scarcely recognized her. Then when he heard her voice asking, "Please may I come in, Mr. Cobb?" he cried, "Well, I vow! It's my little lady passenger! Come to call on old Uncle Jerry and pass the time o' day, hev ye? Why, you're wet as sops. Draw up to the stove. I made a fire, hot as it was, thinkin' I wanted somethin' warm for my supper, bein' kind o' lonesome without mother. She's settin' up with Seth Strout tonight. There, we'll hang your soppy hat on the nail, put your jacket over the chair rail, an' then you turn your back to the stove an' dry yourself good."

Uncle Jerry had never before said so many words at a time, but he had caught sight of the child's red eyes and tear-stained cheeks, and his big heart went out to her in her trouble, quite regardless of any circumstances that might have caused it.

Rebecca stood still for a moment until Uncle Jerry took his seat again at the table, and then, unable to contain herself longer, cried, "Oh, Mr. Cobb, I've run away from the brick house, and I want to go back to the farm. Will you keep me tonight and take me up to Maplewood in the stage? I haven't got any money for my fare, but I'll earn it somehow afterwards."

"Well, I guess we won't quarrel 'bout money, you and me," said the old man; "and we've never had our ride together, anyway, though we allers meant to go down river, not up."

"I shall never see Milltown now!" sobbed Rebecca.

"Come over here side o' me an' tell me all about it," coaxed Uncle Jerry. "Jest set down on that there wooden cricket an' out with the whole story."

Rebecca leaned her aching head against Mr. Cobb's homespun knee and recounted the history of her trouble. Tragic as that his-

tory seemed to her passionate and undisciplined mind, she told it truthfully and without exaggeration.

8
RAINBOW BRIDGES

Uncle Jerry coughed and stirred in his chair a good deal during Rebecca's recital, but he carefully concealed any undue feeling of sympathy, just muttering, "Poor little soul! We'll see what we can do for her!"

"You will take me to Maplewood, won't you, Mr. Cobb?" begged Rebecca piteously.

"Don't you fret a mite," he answered, with a crafty little notion at the back of his mind; "I'll see the lady passenger through somehow. Now take a bite o' somethin' to eat, child. Spread some o' that tomato preserve on your bread; draw up to the table. How'd you like to set in mother's place an' pour me out another cup o' hot tea?"

Mr. Jeremiah Cobb's mental machinery was simple, and did not move very smoothly save when propelled by his affection or sympathy. In the present case these were both employed to his advantage, and mourning his stupidity and praying for some flash of inspiration to light his path, he blundered along, trusting to Providence.

Rebecca, comforted by the old man's tone, and timidly enjoying the dignity of sitting in Mrs. Cobb's seat and lifting the blue china teapot, smiled faintly, smoothed her hair, and dried her eyes.

"I suppose your mother'll be turrible glad to see you back again?" queried Mr. Cobb.

A tiny fear—just a baby thing—in the bottom of Rebecca's heart stirred and grew larger the moment it was touched with a question.

"She won't like it that I ran away, I s'pose, and she'll be sorry that I couldn't please Aunt Mirandy; but I'll make her understand, just as I did you."

"I s'pose she was thinkin' o' your schoolin',

lettin' you come down here; but land! you can go to school in Temperance, I s'pose?"

"There's only two months' school now in Temperance, and the farm's too far from all the other schools."

"Oh, well! there's other things in the world beside edjercation," responded Uncle Jerry, attacking a piece of apple pie.

"Ye—es; though mother thought that was going to be the making of me," returned Rebecca sadly, giving a dry little sob as she tried to drink her tea.

"It'll be nice for you to be all together again at the farm—such a house full o' children!" remarked the dear old deceiver, who longed for nothing so much as to cuddle and comfort the poor little creature.

"It's too full—that's the trouble. But I'll make Hannah come to Riverboro in my place."

"S'pose Mirandy 'n' Jane'll have her? I should be 'most afraid they wouldn't. They'll be kind o' mad at your goin' home, you know, and you can't hardly blame 'em."

This was quite a new thought,—that the brick house might be closed to Hannah, since she, Rebecca, had turned her back upon its cold hospitality.

"How is this school down here in Riverboro—pretty good?" inquired Uncle Jerry, whose brain was working with an altogether unaccustomed rapidity,—so much so that it almost terrified him.

"Oh, it's a splendid school! And Miss Dearborn is a splendid teacher!"

"You like her, do you? Well, you'd better believe she returns the compliment. Mother was down to the store this afternoon buyin' liniment for Seth Strout, an' she met Miss Dearborn on the bridge. They got to talkin' 'bout school, for mother has summer-boarded a lot o' the schoolmarms, an' likes 'em. 'How does the little Temperance girl git along?' asks mother. 'Oh, she's the best scholar I have!' says Miss Dearborn. 'I could teach school from sunup to sundown if scholars was all like Rebecca Randall,' says she."

"Oh, Mr. Cobb, *did* she say that?" glowed Rebecca, her face sparkling and dimpling in an instant. "I've tried hard all the time, but I'll study the covers right off of the books now."

"You mean you would if you'd ben goin' to stay here," interposed Uncle Jerry. "Now ain't it too bad you've jest got to give it all up on account o' your Aunt Mirandy? Well, I can't hardly blame ye. She's cranky an' she's sour; I should think she'd ben nussed on bonny-clabber an' green apples. She needs bearin' with; an' I guess you ain't much on patience, be ye?"

"Not very much," replied Rebecca dolefully.

"If I'd had this talk with ye yesterday," pursued Mr. Cobb, "I believe I'd have advised ye different. It's too late now, an' I don't feel to say you've ben all in the wrong; but if 't was to do over again, I'd say, well, your Aunt Mirandy gives you clothes and board and schoolin' and is goin' to send you to Wareham at a big expense. She's turrible hard to get along with, an' kind o' heaves benefits at your head, same's she would bricks; but they're benefits jest the same, an' mebbe it's your job to kind o' pay for 'em in good behavior. Jane's a leetle bit more easy goin' than Mirandy, ain't she, or is she jest as hard to please?"

"Oh, Aunt Jane and I get along splendidly," exclaimed Rebecca; "she's just as good and kind as she can be, and I like her better all the time. I think she kind of likes me, too; she smoothed my hair once. I'd let her scold me all day long, for she understands; but she can't stand up for me against Aunt Mirandy; she's about as afraid of her as I am."

"Jane'll be real sorry to-morrow to find you've gone away, I guess; but never mind, it can't be helped. If she has a kind of a dull time with Mirandy, on account o' her bein' so sharp, why of course she'd set great store by your comp'ny. Mother was talkin' with her after prayer meetin' the other night. 'You wouldn't know the brick house, Sarah,' says Jane. 'I'm keepin' a sewin' school, an' my scholar has made three dresses. What do you think o' that,' says she, 'for an old maid's child? I've taken a class in Sunday-School,' says Jane, 'an' think o' renewin' my youth an' goin' to the picnic with Rebecca,' says she; an' mother declares she never see her look so young 'n' happy."

There was a silence that could be felt in the little kitchen; a silence only broken by the ticking of the tall clock and the beating of Rebecca's heart, which, it seemed to her, almost drowned the voice of the clock. The rain ceased, a sudden rosy light filled the room, and through the window a rainbow arch could be seen spanning the heavens like a radiant bridge. Bridges took one across difficult places, thought Rebecca, and Uncle Jerry seemed to have built one over her troubles and given her strength to walk.

"The shower's over," said the old man, filling his pipe; "it's cleared the air, washed the face o' the airth nice an' clean, an' everything tomorrer will shine like a new pin— when you an' I are drivin' up river."

Rebecca pushed her cup away, rose from the table, and put on her hat and jacket quietly. "I'm not going to drive up river, Mr. Cobb," she said. "I'm going to stay here and —catch bricks; catch 'em without throwing 'em back, too. I don't know as Aunt Mirandy will take me in after I've run away, but I'm going back now while I have the courage. You wouldn't be so good as to go with me, would you, Mr. Cobb?"

"You'd better b'lieve your Uncle Jerry don't propose to leave till he gits this thing fixed up," cried the old man delightedly. "Now you've had all you can stan' tonight, poor little soul, without gettin' a fit o' sickness; an' Mirandy'll be sore an' cross an' in no condition for argyment; so my plan is jest this: to drive you over to the brick house in my top buggy; to have you set back in the corner, an' I git out an' go to the side door; an' when I git your Aunt Mirandy 'n' Aunt Jane out int' the shed to plan for a load o' wood I'm goin' to have hauled there this week, you'll slip out o' the buggy and go upstairs to bed. The front door won't be locked, will it?"

"Not this time of night," Rebecca answered; "not till Aunt Mirandy goes to bed; but oh! what if it should be?"

"Well, it won't; an' if 't is, why we'll have to face it out; though in my opinion there's things that won't bear facin' out an' had better be settled comfortable an' quiet. You see you ain't run away yet; you've only come over here to consult me 'bout runnin' away, an' we've concluded it ain't wuth the trouble. The only real sin you've committed, as I figger it out, was in comin' here by the winder when you'd ben sent to bed. That ain't so very black, an' you can tell your Aunt Jane 'bout it Sunday, when she's chock full o' religion, an' she can advise you when you'd better tell your Aunt Mirandy. I don't believe in deceivin' folks, but if you've hed hard thoughts you ain't obleeged to own 'em up; take 'em to the Lord in prayer, as the hymn says, and then don't go on hevin' 'em. Now come on; I'm all hitched up to go over to the post office; don't forget your bundle; 'it's always a journey, mother, when you carry a nightgown'; them's the first words your Uncle Jerry ever heard you say! He didn't think you'd be bringin' your nightgown over to his house. Step in an' curl up in the corner; we ain't goin' to let folks see little runaway gals, 'cause they're goin' back to begin all over ag'in!"

When Rebecca crept upstairs, and undressing in the dark finally found herself in her bed that night, though she was aching and throbbing in every nerve, she felt a kind of peace stealing over her. She had been saved from foolishness and error; kept from troubling her poor mother; prevented from angering and mortifying her aunts.

Her heart was melted now, and she determined to win Aunt Miranda's approval by some desperate means, and to try and forget the one thing that rankled worst, the scornful mention of her father, of whom she thought with the greatest admiration, and whom she had not yet heard criticized; for such sorrows and disappointments as Aurelia Randall had suffered had never been communicated to her children.

It would have been some comfort to the bruised, unhappy little spirit to know that Miranda Sawyer was passing an uncomfortable night, and that she tacitly regretted her harshness, partly because Jane had taken such a lofty and virtuous position in the matter. She could not endure Jane's disapproval, although she would never have confessed to such a weakness.

As Uncle Jerry drove homeward under the stars, well content with his attempts at keeping the peace, he thought wistfully of the touch of Rebecca's head on his knee, and the rain of her tears on his hand; of the sweet reasonableness of her mind when she had the matter put rightly before her; of her quick decision when she had once seen the path of duty: of the touching hunger for love and understanding that were so characteristic in her. "Lord A'mighty!" he ejaculated under his breath, "Lord A'mighty! to hector and abuse a child like that one! 'T ain't *abuse* exactly, I know, or 't wouldn't be to some o' your elephant-hided young ones; but to that little tender will-o'-the-wisp a hard word's like a lash. Mirandy Sawyer would be a heap better woman if she had a little gravestun to remember, same's mother 'n' I have."

"I never see a child improve in her work as Rebecca has today," remarked Miranda Sawyer to Jane on Saturday evening. "That settin' down I gave her was probably just what she needed, and I dare say it'll last for a month."

"I'm glad you're pleased," returned Jane. "A cringing worm is what you want, not a bright, smiling child. Rebecca looks to me as if she'd been through the Seven Years' War. When she came downstairs this morning it seemed to me she'd grown old in the night. If you follow my advice, which you seldom do, you'll let me take her and Emma Jane down beside the river to-morrow afternoon and bring Emma Jane home to a good Sunday supper. Then if you'll let her go to Milltown with the Cobbs on Wednesday, that'll hearten her up a little and coax back her appetite. Wednesday's a holiday on account of Miss Dearborn's going home to her sister's wedding, and the Cobbs and Perkinses want to go down to the Agricultural Fair."

9
"THE STIRRING OF THE POWERS"

Rebecca's visit to Milltown was all that her glowing fancy had painted it, except that recent readings about Rome and Venice disposed her to believe that those cities might have an advantage over Milltown in the matter of mere pictorial beauty. So soon does the soul outgrow its mansions that after once seeing Milltown her fancy ran out to the future sight of Portland; for that, having islands and a harbor and two public monuments, must be far more beautiful than Milltown, which would, she felt, take its proud place among the cities of the earth, by reason of its tremendous business activity rather than by any irresistible appeal to the imagination.

It would be impossible for two children to see more, do more, walk more, talk more, eat more, or ask more questions than Rebecca and Emma Jane did on that eventful Wednesday.

"She's the best company I ever see in all my life," said Mrs. Cobb to her husband that evening. "We ain't had a dull minute this day. She's well-mannered, too; she didn't ask for anything, and was thankful for whatever she got. Did you watch her face when we went into that tent where they was actin' out 'Uncle Tom's Cabin'? And did you take notice of the way she told us about the book when we sat down to have our ice cream? I tell you Harriet Beecher Stowe herself couldn't 'a' done it better justice."

"I took it all in," responded Mr. Cobb, who was pleased that "mother" agreed with him about Rebecca. "I ain't sure but she's goin' to turn out somethin' remarkable,—a singer, or a writer, or a lady doctor like that Miss Parks up to Cornish."

"Lady doctors are always home'paths, ain't they?" asked Mrs. Cobb, who, it is needless to say, was distinctly of the old school in medicine.

"Land, no, mother; there ain't no home'-path 'bout Miss Parks—she drives all over the country."

"I can't see Rebecca as a lady doctor, somehow," mused Mrs. Cobb. "Her gift o' gab is what's goin' to be the makin' of her; mebbe she'll lecture, or recite pieces, like that Portland elocutionist that come out here to the harvest supper."

"I guess she'll be able to write down her own pieces," said Mr. Cobb confidently; "she could make 'em up faster 'n she could read 'em out of a book."

"It's a pity she's so plain looking," remarked Mrs. Cobb, blowing out the candle.

"*Plain looking,* mother?" exclaimed her husband in astonishment. "Look at the eyes of her; look at the hair of her, an' the smile, an' that there dimple! Look at Alice Robinson, that's called the prettiest child on the river, an' see how Rebecca shines her ri' down out o' sight! I hope Mirandy'll favor her comin' over to see us real often, for she'll let off some of her steam here, an' the brick house'll be consid'able safer for everybody concerned. We've known what it was to hev children, even if 't was more'n thirty years ago, an' we can make allowances."

Notwithstanding the encomiums of Mr. and Mrs. Cobb, Rebecca made a poor hand at composition writing at this time. Miss Dearborn gave her every sort of subject that she had ever been given herself; "Cloud Pictures"; "Abraham Lincoln"; "Nature"; Philanthropy"; "Slavery"; "Intemperance"; "Joy and Duty"; "Solitude"; but with none of them did Rebecca seem to grapple satisfactorily.

"Write as you talk, Rebecca," insisted poor Miss Dearborn, who secretly knew that she could never manage a good composition herself.

"But gracious me, Miss Dearborn! I don't talk about nature and slavery. I can't write unless I have something to say, can I?"

"That is what compositions are for," returned Miss Dearborn doubtfully; "to make you have things to say. Now in your last one, on solitude, you haven't said anything very interesting, and you've made it too common and everyday to sound well. There are too many 'yous' and 'yours' in it; you ought to say 'one' now and then, to make it seem more like good writing. 'One opens a favorite book'; 'One's thoughts are a great comfort in solitude'; and so on."

"I don't know any more about solitude this week than I did about joy and duty last week," grumbled Rebecca.

"You tried to be funny about joy and duty," said Miss Dearborn reprovingly; "so of course you didn't succeed."

"I didn't know you were going to make us

94

read the things out loud," said Rebecca with an embarrassed smile of recollection.

"Joy and Duty" had been the inspiring subject given to the older children for a theme to be written in five minutes.

Rebecca had wrestled, struggled, perspired in vain. When her turn came to read she was obliged to confess she had written nothing.

"You have at least two lines, Rebecca," insisted the teacher, "for I see them on your slate."

"I'd rather not read them, please; they are not good," pleaded Rebecca.

"Read what you have, good or bad, little or much; I am excusing nobody."

Rebecca rose, overcome with secret laughter, dread, and mortification; then in a low voice she read the couplet:—

When Joy and Duty clash
Let Duty go to smash.

Dick Carter's head disappeared under the desk, while Living Perkins choked with laughter.

Miss Dearborn laughed too; she was little more than a girl, and the training of the young idea seldom appealed to the sense of humor.

"You must stay after school and try again, Rebecca," she said, but she said it smilingly.

"Your poetry hasn't a very nice idea in it for a good little girl who ought to love duty."

"It wasn't *my* idea," said Rebecca apologetically. "I had only made the first line when I saw you were going to ring the bell and say the time was up. I had 'clash' written, and I couldn't think of anything then but 'hash' or 'rash' or 'smash.' I'll change it to this:—

> When Joy and Duty clash,
> 'T is Joy must go to smash."

"That is better," Miss Dearborn answered, "though I cannot think 'going to smash' is a pretty expression for poetry."

Having been instructed in the use of the indefinite pronoun "one" as giving a refined and elegant touch to literary efforts, Rebecca painstakingly rewrote her composition on solitude, giving it all the benefit of Miss Dearborn's suggestion. It then appeared in the following form, which hardly satisfied either teacher or pupil:—

SOLITUDE

It would be false to say that one could ever be alone when one has one's lovely thoughts to comfort one. One sits by one's self, it is true, but one thinks; one opens one's favorite book and reads one's favorite story; one speaks to one's aunt or one's brother, fondles one's cat, or looks at one's photograph album. There is one's work also: what a joy it is to one, if one happens to like work. All one's little household tasks keep one from being lonely. Does one ever feel bereft when one picks up one's chips to light one's fire for one's evening meal? Or when one washes one's milk pail before milking one's cow? One would fancy not.

R. R. R.

"It is perfectly dreadful," sighed Rebecca when she read it aloud after school. "Putting in 'one' all the time doesn't make it sound any more like a book, and it looks silly besides."

"You say such queer things," objected Miss Dearborn. "I don't see what makes you do it. Why did you put in anything so common as picking up chips?"

"Because I was talking about 'household tasks' in the sentence before, and it *is* one of my household tasks. Don't you think calling supper 'one's evening meal' is pretty? And is n't 'bereft' a nice word?"

"Yes, that part of it does very well. It is the cat, the chips, and the milk pail that I don't like."

"All right!" sighed Rebecca. "Out they go! Does the cow go too?"

"Yes, I don't like a cow in a composition," said the difficult Miss Dearborn.

The Milltown trip had not been without its tragic consequences of a small sort; for the next week Minnie Smellie's mother told Miranda Sawyer that she'd better look after Rebecca, for she was given to "swearing and profane language"; that she had been heard saying something dreadful that very afternoon, saying it before Emma Jane and Living Perkins, who only laughed and got down on all fours and chased her.

Rebecca, on being confronted and charged with the crime, denied it indignantly, and Aunt Jane believed her.

"Search your memory, Rebecca, and try to think what Minnie overheard you say," she pleaded. "Don't be ugly and obstinate, but think real hard. When did they chase you up the road, and what were you doing?"

A sudden light broke upon Rebecca's darkness.

"Oh! I see it now," she exclaimed. "It had rained hard all the morning, you know, and the road was full of puddles. Emma Jane, Living, and I were walking along, and I was ahead. I saw the water streaming over the road towards the ditch, and it reminded me of 'Uncle Tom's Cabin' at Milltown, when Eliza took her baby and ran across the Mississippi on the iceblocks, pursued by the bloodhounds. We couldn't keep from laughing after we came out of the tent because they were acting on such a small platform that Eliza had to run round and round, and part of the time the one dog they had pursued her, and part of the time she had to pursue the dog. I knew Living would remember, too, so I took off my waterproof and wrapped it round my books for a baby; then I shouted, '*My God! the river!*' just like that—the same as Eliza did in the play; then I leaped from puddle to puddle, and Living and Emma Jane pursued me like the bloodhounds. It's just like that stupid Minnie Smellie who doesn't know a game when she sees one. And Eliza wasn't swearing when she said, 'My God! the river!' It was more like praying."

"Well, you've got no call to be prayin', any more than swearin', in the middle of the road," said Miranda; "but I'm thankful it's no worse. You're born to trouble as the sparks fly upward, an' I'm afraid you allers will be till you learn to bridle your unruly tongue."

"I wish sometimes that I could bridle Minnie's," murmured Rebecca, as she went to set the table for supper.

"I declare she *is* the beatin'est child!" said Miranda, taking off her spectacles and laying down her mending. "You don't think she's a leetle mite crazy, do you, Jane?"

"I don't think she's like the rest of us," responded Jane thoughtfully and with some anxiety in her pleasant face; "but whether it's for the better or the worse I can't hardly tell till she grows up. She's got the making of 'most anything in her, Rebecca has; but I feel sometimes as if we were not fitted to cope with her."

"Stuff an' nonsense!" said Miranda. "Speak for yourself. I feel fitted to cope with any child that ever was born int' the world!"

"I know you do, Mirandy; but that don't *make* you so," returned Jane with a smile.

The habit of speaking her mind freely was certainly growing on Jane to an altogether terrifying extent.

10
SNOW-WHITE; ROSE-RED

Just before Thanksgiving the affairs of the Simpsons reached what might have been called a crisis, even in their family, which had been born and reared in a state of adventurous poverty and perilous uncertainty.

Riverboro was doing its best to return the entire tribe of Simpsons to the land of its fathers, so to speak, thinking rightly that the town which had given them birth, rather than the town of their adoption, should feed them and keep a roof over their heads until the children were of an age for self-support. There was little to eat in the household and less to wear, though Mrs. Simpson did, as always, her poor best.

Life was rather dull and dreary, however, and in the chill and gloom of November weather, the young Simpsons groped about for some inexpensive form of excitement, and settled upon the selling of soap for a premium. They had sold enough to their immediate neighbors during the earlier autumn to secure a child's handcart, which, though very weak on its pins, could be trundled over the country roads. With large business sagacity and an executive capacity which must have been inherited from their father, they now proposed to extend their operations to a larger area and distribute soap to contiguous villages, if these villages could be induced to buy. The Excelsior Soap Company paid a very small return of any kind to its infantile agents, who were scattered through the state, but it inflamed their imaginations by the issue of circulars with highly colored pictures of the premiums to be awarded for the sale of a certain number of cakes. It was at this juncture that Clara Belle and Susan Simpson consulted Rebecca, who threw herself solidly and wholeheartedly into the enterprise, promising her help and that of Emma Jane Perkins. The premiums within their possible grasp were three: a bookcase, a plush reclining chair, and a banquet lamp. Of course the Simpsons had no books, and casting aside, without thought or pang, the plush chair, which might have been of some use in a family of seven persons (not counting Mr. Simpson, who ordinarily sat elsewhere at the town's expense), they warmed themselves rapturously in the vision of the banquet lamp, which speedily became to them more desirable than food, drink, or clothing. Neither Emma Jane nor Rebecca perceived anything incongruous in the idea of the Simpsons striving for a banquet lamp. They looked at the picture daily and knew that if they themselves were free agents they would toil, suffer, ay sweat, for the happy privilege of occupying the same room with that lamp through the coming winter evenings. It looked to be about eight feet tall in the catalogue, and Emma Jane advised Clara Belle to measure the height of the Simpson ceilings; but a note in the margin of the circular informed them that it stood two and a half feet high when set up in all its dignity and splendor on a proper table, three dollars extra. It was only of polished brass, continued the circular, though it was invariably mistaken for solid gold, and the shade that accompanied it (at least it accompanied it if the agent sold a hundred extra cakes) was of crinkled crêpe paper printed in a dozen delicious hues, from which the joy-dazzled agent might take his choice.

Seesaw Simpson was not in the syndicate. Clara Belle was rather a successful agent, but Susan, who could only say "thoap," never made large returns, and the twins, who were somewhat young to be thoroughly trustworthy, could be given only a half dozen cakes at a time, and were obliged to carry with them on their business trips a brief document stating the price per cake, dozen, and box. Rebecca and Emma Jane offered to go two or three miles in some one direction and see what they could do in the way of stirring up a popular demand for the Snow-White and Rose-Red brands, the former being devoted to laundry purposes and the latter being intended for the toilet.

There was a great amount of hilarity in the preparation for this event, and a long council in Emma Jane's attic. They had the soap company's circular from which to arrange a proper speech, and they had, what was still better, the remembrance of a certain patent-medicine vender's discourse at the Milltown Fair. His method, when once observed, could never be forgotten; nor his manner, nor his vocabulary. Emma Jane practiced it on Rebecca, and Rebecca on Emma Jane.

"Can I sell you a little soap this afternoon? It is called the Snow-White and Rose-Red Soap, six cakes in an ornamental box, only twenty cents for the white, twenty-five cents for the red. It is made from the purest ingredients, and if desired could be eaten by an invalid with relish and profit."

"Oh, Rebecca, don't let's say that!" interposed Emma Jane hysterically. "It makes me feel like a fool."

"It takes so little to make you feel like a fool, Emma Jane," rebuked Rebecca, "that sometimes I think that you must *be* one. I don't get to feeling like a fool so awfully easy; now leave out that eating part if you don't like it, and go on."

"The Snow-White is probably the most remarkable laundry soap ever manufactured. Immerse the garments in a tub, lightly rubbing the more soiled portions with the soap; leave them submerged in water from sunset to sunrise, and then the youngest baby can

wash them without the slightest effort."

"*Babe,* not baby," corrected Rebecca from the circular.

"It's just the same thing," argued Emma Jane.

"Of course it's just the same *thing;* but a baby has got to be called babe or infant in a circular, the same as it is in poetry! Would you rather say infant?"

"No," grumbled Emma Jane; "infant is worse even than babe. Rebecca, do you think we'd better do as the circular says, and let Elijah or Elisha try the soap before we begin selling?"

"I can't imagine a babe doing a family wash with *any* soap," answered Rebecca; "but it must be true or they would never dare to print it, so don't let's bother. Oh! won't it be the greatest fun, Emma Jane? At some of the houses—where they can't possibly know me —I shan't be frightened, and I shall reel off the whole rigmarole, invalid, babe, and all. Perhaps I shall say even the last sentence, if I can remember it: 'We sound every chord in the great macrocosm of satisfaction.'"

This conversation took place on Friday afternoon at Emma Jane's house, where Rebecca, to her unbounded joy, was to stay over Sunday, her aunts having gone to Portland to the funeral of an old friend. Saturday being a holiday, they were going to have the old white horse, drive to North Riverboro three miles away, eat a twelve o'clock dinner with Emma Jane's cousins, and be back at four o'clock punctually.

When the children asked Mrs. Perkins if they could call at just a few houses coming and going, and sell a little soap for the Simpsons, she at first replied decidedly in the negative. She was an indulgent parent, however, and really had little objection to Emma Jane amusing herself in this unusual way; it was only for Rebecca, as the niece of the difficult Miranda Sawyer, that she raised scruples; but when fully persuaded that the enterprise was a charitable one, she acquiesced.

The girls called at Mr. Watson's store, and arranged for several large boxes of soap to be charged to Clara Belle Simpson's account. These were lifted into the back of the wagon, and a happier couple never drove along the country road than Rebecca and her companion. It was a glorious Indian summer day, which suggested nothing of Thanksgiving, near at hand as it was. It was a rustly day, a scarlet and buff, yellow and carmine, bronze and crimson day. There were still many leaves on the oaks and maples, making a goodly show of red and brown and gold. The air was like sparkling cider, and every field had its heaps of yellow and russet good things to eat, all ready for the barns, the mills, and the markets. The horse forgot his twenty years, sniffed the sweet bright air, and trotted like a colt; Nokomis Mountain looked blue and clear in the distance; Rebecca stood in the wagon, and apostrophized the landscape with sudden joy of living:—

Great, wide, beautiful, wonderful World,
With the wonderful water round you curled,
And the wonderful grass upon your breast,
World, you are beautifully drest!

Dull Emma Jane had never seemed to Rebecca so near, so dear, so tried and true; and Rebecca, to Emma Jane's faithful heart, had never been so brilliant, so bewildering, so fascinating, as in this visit together, with its intimacy, its freedom, and the added delights of an exciting business enterprise.

11

MR. ALADDIN

A single hour's experience of the vicissitudes incident to a business career clouded the children's spirits just the least bit. They did not accompany each other to the doors of their chosen victims, feeling sure that together they could not approach the subject seriously; but they parted at the gate of each house, the one holding the horse while the other took the soap samples and interviewed any one who seemed of a coming-on disposition. Emma Jane had disposed of three single cakes, Rebecca of three small boxes; for a difference

in their ability to persuade the public was clearly defined at the start, though neither of them ascribed either success or defeat to anything but the imperious force of circumstances. Housewives looked at Emma Jane and desired no soap; listened to her description of its merits, and still desired none. Other stars in their courses governed Rebecca's doings. The people whom she interviewed either remembered their present need of soap, or reminded themselves that they would need it in the future; the notable point in the case being that lucky Rebecca accomplished, with almost no effort, results that poor little Emma Jane failed to attain by hard and conscientious labor.

"It's your turn, Rebecca, and I'm glad, too," said Emma Jane, drawing up to a gateway and indicating a house that was set a considerable distance from the road. "I haven't got over trembling from the last place yet." (A lady had put her head out of an upstairs window and called, "Go away, little girl; whatever you have in your box we don't want any.") "I don't know who lives here, and the blinds are all shut in front. If there's nobody at home you mustn't count it, but take the next house as yours."

Rebecca walked up the lane and went to the side door. There was a porch there, and seated in a rocking-chair, husking corn, was a good-looking young man, or was he middle-aged? Rebecca could not make up her mind. At all events he had an air of the city about him,—well-shaven face, well-trimmed mustache, well-fitting clothes. Rebecca was a trifle shy at this unexpected encounter, but there was nothing to be done but explain her presence, so she asked, "Is the lady of the house at home?"

"I am the lady of the house at present," said the stranger, with a whimsical smile. "What can I do for you?"

"Have you ever heard of the—would you like, or I mean—do you need any soap?" queried Rebecca.

"Do I look as if I did?" he responded unexpectedly.

Rebecca dimpled. "I didn't mean *that;* I have some soap to sell; I mean I would like to introduce to you a very remarkable soap, the best now on the market. It is called the—"

"Oh! I must know that soap," said the gentleman genially. "Made out of pure vegetable fats, isn't it?"

"The very purest," corroborated Rebecca.

"No acid in it?"

"Not a trace."

"And yet a child could do the Monday washing with it and use no force."

"A babe," corrected Rebecca.

"Oh! A babe, eh? That child grows younger every year, instead of older—wise child!"

This was great good fortune, to find a customer who knew all the virtues of the article in advance. Rebecca dimpled more and more, and at her new friend's invitation sat down on a stool at his side near the edge of the porch. The beauties of the ornamental box which held the Red-Rose were disclosed, and the prices of both that and the Snow-White were unfolded. Presently she forgot all about her silent partner at the gate and was talking as if she had known this grand personage all her life.

"I'm keeping house today, but I don't live here," explained the delightful gentleman. "I'm just on a visit to my aunt, who has gone to Portland. I used to be here as a boy, and I am very fond of the spot."

"I don't think anything takes the place of the farm where one lived when one was a child," observed Rebecca, nearly bursting with pride at having at last successfully used the indefinite pronoun in general conversation.

The man darted a look at her and put down his ear of corn. "So you consider your childhood a thing of the past, do you, young lady?"

"I can still remember it," answered Rebecca gravely, "though it seems a long time ago."

"I can remember mine well enough, and a particularly unpleasant one it was," said the stranger.

"So was mine," sighed Rebecca. "What was your worst trouble?"

"Lack of food and clothes principally."

"Oh!" exclaimed Rebecca sympathetically, —"mine was no shoes and too many babies and not enough books. But you're all right and happy now, aren't you?" she asked doubtfully, for though he looked handsome, well-fed, and prosperous, any child could see that his eyes were tired and his mouth was sad when he was not speaking.

"I'm doing pretty well, thank you," said the man, with a delightful smile. "Now tell me, how much soap ought I to buy to-day?"

"How much has your aunt on hand now?" suggested the very modest and inexperienced agent; "and how much would she need?"

"Oh, I don't know about that; soap keeps, doesn't it?"

"I'm not certain," said Rebecca conscientiously, "but I'll look in the circular—it's sure to tell"; and she drew the document from her pocket.

"What are you going to do with the magnificent profits you get from this business?"

"We are not selling for our own benefit," said Rebecca confidentially. "My friend who is holding the horse at the gate is the daughter of a very rich blacksmith, and doesn't need any money. I am poor, but I live with my aunts in a brick house, and of course they wouldn't like me to be a peddler. We are try-ing to get a premium for some friends of ours."

Rebecca had never thought of alluding to the circumstances with her previous customers, but unexpectedly she found herself describing Mr. Simpson, Mrs. Simpson, and the Simpson family; their poverty, their joy-less life, and their abject need of a banquet lamp to brighten their existence.

"You needn't argue that point," laughed the man, as he stood up to get a glimpse of the "rich blacksmith's daughter" at the gate. "I can see that they ought to have it if they want it, and especially if you want them to have it. I've known what it was myself to do without a banquet lamp. Now give me the circular, and let's do some figuring. How much do the Simpson's lack at this moment?"

"If they sell two hundred more cakes this month and next, they can have the lamp by Christmas," Rebecca answered, "and they can get a shade by summer time; but I'm afraid I can't help very much after today, because my Aunt Miranda may not like to have me."

"I see. Well, that's all right. I'll take three

hundred cakes, and that will give them shade and all."

Rebecca had been seated on a stool very near to the edge of the porch, and at this remark she made a sudden movement, tipped over, and disappeared into a clump of lilac bushes. It was a very short distance, fortunately, and the amused capitalist picked her up, set her on her feet, and brushed her off. "You should never seem surprised when you have taken a large order," said he; "you ought to have replied, 'Can't you make it three hundred and fifty?' instead of capsizing in that unbusinesslike way."

"Oh, I could never say anything like that!" exclaimed Rebecca, who was blushing crimson at her awkward fall. "But it doesn't seem right for you to buy so much. Are you sure you can afford it?"

"If I can't, I'll save on something else," returned the jocose philanthropist.

"What if your aunt shouldn't like the kind of soap?" queried Rebecca nervously.

"My aunt always likes what I like," he returned.

"Mine doesn't!" exclaimed Rebecca.

"Then there's something wrong with your aunt!"

"Or with me," laughed Rebecca.

"What is your name, young lady?"

"Rebecca Rowena Randall, sir."

"What?" with an amused smile. "*Both?* Your mother was generous."

"She couldn't bear to give up either of the names, she says."

"Do you want to hear my name?"

"I think I know already," answered Rebecca, with a bright glance. "I'm sure you must be Mr. Aladdin in the 'Arabian Nights.' Oh, please, can I run down and tell Emma Jane? She must be so tired waiting, and she will be so glad!"

At the man's nod of assent Rebecca sped down the lane, crying irrepressibly as she neared the wagon, "Oh, Emma Jane! Emma Jane! We are sold out!"

Mr. Aladdin followed smilingly to corroborate this astonishing, unbelievable statement; lifted all their boxes from the back of the wagon, and taking the circular, promised to write to the Excelsior Company that night concerning the premium.

"If you could contrive to keep a secret, you two little girls, it would be rather a nice surprise to have the lamp arrive at the Simpsons' on Thanksgiving Day, wouldn't it?" he asked, as he tucked the old lap-robe cozily over their feet.

They gladly assented, and broke into a chorus of excited thanks, during which tears of joy stood in Rebecca's eyes.

"Oh, don't mention it!" laughed Mr. Aladdin, lifting his hat. "I was a sort of commercial traveler myself once,—years ago,—and I like to see the thing well done. Good-bye, Miss Rebecca Rowena! Just let me know whenever you have anything to sell, for I'm certain beforehand I shall want it."

"Good-bye, Mr. Aladdin! I surely will!" cried Rebecca, tossing back her dark braids delightedly and waving her hand.

"Oh, Rebecca!" said Emma Jane in an awe-struck whisper. "He raised his hat to us, and we not thirteen! It'll be five years before we're ladies."

"Never mind," answered Rebecca, "we are the *beginnings* of ladies, even now."

"He tucked the lap-robe round us, too," continued Emma Jane, in an ecstasy of reminiscence. "Oh! isn't he perfectly elergant? And wasn't it lovely of him to buy us out? And just think of having both the lamp and the shade for one day's work! Aren't you glad you wore your pink gingham now, even if mother did make you put on flannel underneath? You do look so pretty in pink and red, Rebecca, and so homely in drab and brown!"

"I know it," sighed Rebecca. "I wish I was like you—pretty in all colors!" And Rebecca looked longingly at Emma Jane's fat, rosy cheeks; at her blue eyes, which said nothing; at her neat nose, which had no character; at her red lips, from between which no word worth listening to had ever issued.

Never mind!" said Emma Jane comfortingly. "Everybody says you're awful bright and smart, and mother thinks you'll be better looking all the time as you grow older. You wouldn't believe it, but I was a dreadful homely baby, and homely right along till a year or two ago, when my red hair began to grow dark. What was the nice man's name?"

"I never thought to ask!" ejaculated Rebecca. "Aunt Miranda would say that was just like me, and it is. But I called him Mr. Aladdin because he gave us a lamp. You know the story of Aladdin and the wonderful lamp?"

"Oh, Rebecca! how could you call him a nickname the very first time you ever saw him?"

"Aladdin isn't a nickname exactly; anyway, he laughed and seemed to like it."

By dint of superhuman effort, and putting such a seal upon their lips as never mortals put before, the two girls succeeded in keeping their wonderful news to themselves; although it was obvious to all beholders that they were in an extraordinary and abnormal state of mind.

On Thanksgiving the lamp arrived in a large packing-box, and was taken out and set up by Seesaw Simpson, who suddenly began to admire and respect the business ability of his sisters. Rebecca had heard the news of its arrival, but waited until nearly dark before asking permission to go to the Simpsons', so that she might see the gorgeous trophy lighted and sending a blaze of crimson glory through its red crêpe paper shade.

12
THE BANQUET LAMP

There had been company at the brick house to the bountiful Thanksgiving dinner which had been provided at one o'clock,—the Burnham sisters, who lived between North Riverboro and Shaker Village, and who for more than a quarter of a century had come to pass the holiday with the Sawyers every year.

Rebecca sat silent with a book after the dinner dishes were washed, and when it was nearly five asked if she might go to the Simpsons'.

"What do you want to run after those Simpson children for on a Thanksgiving Day?"

queried Miss Miranda. "Can't you set still for once and listen to the improvin' conversation of your elders? You never can let well enough alone, but want to be forever on the move."

"The Simpsons have a new lamp, and Emma Jane and I promised to go up and see it lighted, and make it a kind of a party."

"What under the canopy did they want of a lamp, and where did they get the money to pay for it? If Abner was at home, I should think he'd been swappin' again," said Miss Miranda.

"The children got it as a prize for selling soap," replied Rebecca; "they've been working for a year, and you know I told you that Emma Jane and I helped them the Saturday afternoon you were in Portland."

"I didn't take notice, I s'pose, for it's the first time I ever heard the lamp mentioned. Well, you can for for an hour, and no more. Remember it's as dark at six as it is at midnight. Would you like to take along some Baldwin apples? What have you got in the

pocket of that new dress that makes it sag down so?"

"It's my nuts and raisins from dinner," replied Rebecca, who never succeeded in keeping the most innocent action a secret from her Aunt Miranda; "they're just what you gave me on my plate."

"Why didn't you eat them?"

"Because I'd had enough dinner, and I thought if I saved these, it would make the Simpsons' party better," stammered Rebecca, who hated to be scolded and examined before

company.

"They were your own, Rebecca," interposed Aunt Jane, "and if you chose to save them to give away, it is all right. We ought never to let this day pass without giving our neighbors something to be thankful for, instead of taking all the time to think of our own mercies."

The Burnham sisters nodded approvingly as Rebecca went out, and remarked that they had never seen a child grow and improve so fast in so short a time.

"There's plenty of room left for more improvement, as you'd know if she lived in the same house with you," answered Miranda. "She's into every namable thing in the neighborhood, an' not only into it, but generally at the head an' front of it, especially when it's mischief. Of all the foolishness I ever heard of, that lamp beats everything; it's just like those Simpsons, but I didn't suppose the children had brains enough to sell anything."

"One of them must have," said Miss Ellen Burnham, "for the girl that was selling soap at the Ladds' in North Riverboro was described by Adam Ladd as the most remarkable and winning child he ever saw."

"It must have been Clara Belle, and I should never call her remarkable," answered miss Miranda. "Has Adam been home again?"

"Yes, he's been staying a few days with his aunt. There's no limit to the money he's making, they say; and he always brings presents for all the neighbors. This time it was a full set of furs for Mrs. Ladd; and to think we can remember the time he was a barefoot boy without two shirts to his back! It is strange he hasn't married, with all his money, and him so fond of children that he always has a pack of them at his heels."

"There's hope for him still, though," said Miss Jane smilingly; "for I don't s'pose he's more than thirty."

"He could get a wife in Riverboro if he was a hundred and thirty," remarked Miss Miranda.

"Adam's aunt says he was so taken with the little girl that sold the soap (Clara Belle, did you say her name was?), that he declared he was going to bring her a Christmas present," continued Miss Ellen.

"Well, there's no accountin' for tastes," exclaimed Miss Miranda. "Clara Belle's got cross-eyes and red hair, but I'd be the last one to grudge her a Christmas present; the more Adam Ladd gives to her the less the town'll have to."

"Isn't there another Simpson girl?" asked Miss Lydia Burnham; "for this one couldn't have been cross-eyed; I remember Mrs. Ladd saying Adam remarked about this child's handsome eyes. He said it was her eyes that made him buy the three hundred cakes. Mrs. Ladd has it stacked up in the shed chamber."

"Three hundred cakes!" ejaculated Miranda. "Well, there's one crop that never fails in Riverboro!"

"What's that?" asked Miss Lydia politely.

"The fool crop," responded Miranda tersely, and changed the subject, much to Jane's gratitude, for she had been nervous and ill at ease for the last fifteen minutes. What child in Riverboro could be described as remarkable and winning, save Rebecca? What child had wonderful eyes, except the same Rebecca? And finally, was there ever a child in the world who could make a man buy soap by the hundred cakes, save Rebecca?

Meantime the "remarkable" child had flown up the road in the deepening dusk, but she had not gone far before she heard the sound of hurrying footsteps, and saw a well-known figure coming in her direction. In a moment she and Emma Jane met and exchanged a breathless embrace.

"Something awful has happened," panted Emma Jane.

"Don't tell me it's broken," exclaimed Rebecca.

"No! oh, no! not that! It was packed in straw, and every piece came out all right; and I was there, and I never said a single thing about your selling the three hundred cakes that got the lamp, so that we could be together when you told."

"*Our* selling the three hundred cakes," corrected Rebecca; "you did as much as I."

"No, I didn't, Rebecca Randall. I just sat at the gate and held the horse."

"Yes, but *whose* horse was it that took us to North Riverboro? And besides, it just happened to be my turn. If you had gone in and found Mr. Aladdin you would have had the wonderful lamp given to you; but what's the trouble?"

"The Simpsons have no kerosene and no wicks. I guess they thought a banquet lamp was something that lighted itself, and burned without any help. Seesaw has gone to the doctor's to try if he can borrow a wick, and mother let me have a pint of oil, but she says she won't give me any more. We never thought of the expense of keeping up the lamp, Rebecca."

"No, we didn't, but let's not worry about that till after the party. I have a handful of nuts and raisins and some apples."

"I have peppermints and maple sugar," said Emma Jane. "They had a real Thanksgiving dinner; the doctor gave them sweet potatoes and cranberries and turnips; father sent a sparerib, and Mrs. Cobb a chicken and a jar of mincemeat."

At half-past five one might have looked in at the Simpsons' windows, and seen the party at its height. Mrs. Simpson had let the kitchen fire die out, and had brought the baby to grace the festal scene. The lamp seemed to be having the party, and receiving the guests. The children had taken the one small table in the house, and it was placed in the far corner of the room to serve as a pedestal. On it stood the sacred, the adored, the long-desired object; almost as beautiful, and nearly half as large as the advertisement. The brass glistened like gold, and the crimson paper shade glowed like a giant ruby. In the wide splash of light that it flung upon the floor sat the Simpsons, in reverent and solemn silence, Emma Jane standing behind them, hand in hand with Rebecca. There seemed to be no desire for conversation; the occasion was too thrilling and serious for that. The lamp, it was tacitly felt by everybody, was dignifying the party, and providing sufficient entertainment simply by its presence; being fully as satisfactory in its way as a pianola or a string band.

"I wish father could see it," said Clara Belle loyally.

"If he onth thaw it he'd want to thwap it," murmured Susan sagaciously.

At the appointed hour Rebecca dragged herself reluctantly away from the enchanting scene.

"I'll turn the lamp out the minute I think you and Emma Jane are home," said Clara Belle. "And, oh! I'm so glad you both live where you can see it shine from our windows. I wonder how long it will burn without bein' filled if I only keep it lit one hour every night?"

"You needn't put it out for want o' kerosene," said Seesaw, coming in from the shed, "for there's a great keg of it settin' out there. Mr. Tubbs brought it over from North Riverboro and said somebody sent an order by mail for it."

Rebecca squeezed Emma Jane's arm, and Emma Jane gave a rapturous return squeeze. "It was Mr. Aladdin," whispered Rebecca, as they ran down the path to the gate. Seesaw followed them and handsomely offered to see them "a piece" down the road, but Rebecca declined his escort with such decision that he did not press the matter, but went to bed to dream of her instead. In his dreams flashes of lightning proceeded from both her eyes, and she held a flaming sword in either hand.

Rebecca entered the home dining room joyously. The Burnham sisters had gone and the two aunts were knitting.

"It was a heavenly party," she cried, taking off her hat and cape.

"Go back and see if you have shut the door tight, and then lock it," said Miss Miranda, in her usual austere manner.

"It was a heavenly party," reiterated Rebecca, coming in again, much too excited to be easily crushed, "and oh! Aunt Jane, Aunt Miranda, if you'll only come into the kitchen and look out of the sink window, you can see the banquet lamp shining all red, just as if the Simpsons' house was on fire."

"And probably it will be before long," observed Miranda. "I've got no patience with such foolish goin's-on."

Jane accompanied Rebecca into the kitchen. Although the feeble glimmer which she was able to see from that distance did not seem to her a dazzling exhibition, she tried to be as enthusiastic as possible.

"Rebecca, who was it that sold the three hundred cakes of soap to Mr. Ladd in North Riverboro?"

"Mr. *Who?*" exclaimed Rebecca.

"Mr. Ladd, in North Riverboro."

"Is that his real name?" queried Rebecca in astonishment. "I didn't make a bad guess." And she laughed softly to herself.

"I asked you who sold the soap to Adam Ladd?" resumed Miss Jane.

"Adam Ladd! Then he's A. Ladd, too; what fun!"

"Answer me, Rebecca."

"Oh! Excuse me, Aunt Jane, I was so busy thinking. Emma Jane and I sold the soap to Mr. Ladd."

"Did you tease him, or make him buy it?"

"Now, Aunt Jane, how could I make a big grown-up man buy anything if he didn't want to? He needed the soap dreadfully as a present for his aunt."

Miss Jane still looked a little unconvinced, though she only said, "I hope your Aunt Miranda won't mind, but you know how particular she is, Rebecca, and I really wish you wouldn't do anything out of the ordinary without asking her first, for your actions are very queer."

"There can't be anything wrong this time," Rebecca answered confidently. "Emma Jane sold her cakes to her own relations and to Uncle Jerry Cobb, and I went first to those new tenements near the lumber mill, and then to the Ladds'. Mr. Ladd bought all we had and made us promise to keep the secret until the premium came, and I've been going about ever since as if the banquet lamp was inside of me all lighted up and burning, for everybody to see."

Rebecca's hair was loosened and falling over her forehead in ruffled waves; her eyes were brilliant, her cheeks crimson; there was a hint of everything in the girl's face,—of sensitiveness and delicacy as well as of ardor; there was the sweetness of the mayflower and the strength of the young oak, but one could easily divine that she was one of

> The souls by nature pitched too high,
> By suffering plunged too low.

"That's just the way you look, for all the world as if you did have a lamp burning inside of you," sighed Aunt Jane. "Rebecca!

Rebecca! I wish you could take things easier, child; I am fearful for you sometimes."

13
SEASONS OF GROWTH

The days flew by; as summer had melted into autumn so autumn had given place to winter. Life in the brick house had gone on more placidly of late, for Rebecca was honestly trying to be more careful in the performance of her tasks and duties as well as more quiet in her plays, and she was slowly learning the power of the soft answer in turning away wrath.

Miranda had not had, perhaps, quite as many opportunities in which to lose her temper, but it is only just to say that she had not fully availed herself of all that had offered themselves.

There had been one outburst of righteous wrath occasioned by Rebecca's over-hospitable habits, which were later shown in a still more dramatic and unexpected fashion.

On a certain Friday afternoon she asked her Aunt Miranda if she might take half her bread and milk upstairs to a friend.

"What friend have you got up there, for pity's sake?" demanded Aunt Miranda.

"The Simpson baby, come to stay over Sunday; that is, if you're willing, Mrs. Simpson says she is. Shall I bring her down and show her? She's dressed in an old dress of Emma Jane's and she looks sweet."

"You can bring her down, but you can't show her to me! You can smuggle her out the way you smuggled her in and take her back to her mother. Where on earth do you get your notions, borrowing a baby for Sunday!"

"You're so used to a house without a baby you don't know how dull it is," sighed Rebecca resignedly, as she moved towards the door; "but at the farm there was always a nice fresh one to play with and cuddle. There were too many, but that's not half as bad as none at all. Well, I'll take her back. She'll be dreadfully disappointed and so will Mrs. Simpson. She was planning to go to Milltown."

"She can un-plan then," observed Miss Miranda.

"Perhaps I can go up there and take care of the baby?" suggested Rebecca. "I brought her home so 't I could do my Saturday work just the same."

"You've got enough to do right here, without any borrowed babies to make more steps. Now, no answering back, just give the child some supper and carry it home where it belongs."

"You don't want me to go down the front way; hadn't I better just come through this room and let you look at her? She has yellow hair and big blue eyes! Mrs. Simpson says she takes after her father."

Miss Miranda smiled acidly as she said she couldn't take after her father, for he'd take anything there was before she got there!

Aunt Jane was in the linen closet upstairs, sorting out the clean sheets and pillow cases for Saturday, and Rebecca sought comfort from her.

"I brought the Simpson baby home, Aunt Jane, thinking it would help us over a dull Sunday, but Aunt Miranda won't let her stay. Emma Jane has the promise of her next Sunday and Alice Robinson the next. Mrs. Simpson wanted I should have her first because I've had so much experience in babies. Come in and look at her sitting up in my bed, Aunt Jane! Isn't she lovely? She's the fat, gurgly kind, not thin and fussy like some babies, and I thought I was going to have her to undress and dress twice each day. Oh dear! I wish I could have a printed book with everything set down in it that I *could* do, and then I wouldn't get disappointed so often."

"No book could be printed that would fit you, Rebecca," answered Aunt Jane, "for nobody could imagine beforehand the things you'd want to do. Are you going to carry that heavy child home in your arms?"

"No, I'm going to drag her in the little soapwagon. Come, baby! Take your thumb out of your mouth and come to ride with Becky in your go-cart." She stretched out her strong young arms to the crowing baby, sat down in a chair with the child, turned her upside down unceremoniously, took from her waistband and scornfully flung away a crooked pin, walked with her (still in a highly reversed position) to the bureau, selected a large safety pin, and proceeded to attach her brief red flannel petticoat to a sort of shirt that she wore. Whether flat on her stomach, or head down, heels in the air, the Simpson baby knew she was in the hands of an expert, and continued gurgling placidly while Aunt Jane

regarded the pantomime with a kind of dazed awe.

"Bless my soul, Rebecca," she ejaculated, "it beats all how handy you are with babies!"

"I ought to be; I've brought up three and a half of 'em," Rebecca responded cheerfully, pulling up the infant Simpson's stockings.

"I should think you'd be fonder of dolls than you are," said Jane.

"I do like them, but there's never any change in a doll; it's always the same everlasting old doll, and you have to make believe it's cross or sick, or it loves you, or can't bear you. Babies are more trouble, but nicer."

Miss Jane stretched out a thin hand with a slender, worn band of gold on the finger, and the baby curled her dimpled fingers around it and held it fast.

"You wear a ring on your engagement finger, don't you, Aunt Jane? Did you ever think about getting married?"

"Yes, dear, long ago."

"What happened, Aunt Jane?"

"He died—just before."

"Oh!" And Rebecca's eyes grew misty.

"He was a soldier and he died of a gunshot wound, in a hospital, down South."

"Oh! Aunt Jane!" softly. "Away from you?"

"No, I was with him."

"Was he young?"

"Yes; young and brave and handsome, Rebecca; he was Mr. Carter's brother Tom."

"Oh! I'm so glad you were with him! Wasn't he glad, Aunt Jane?"

Jane looked back across the half-forgotten years, and the vision of Tom's gladness flashed upon her: his haggard smile, the tears in his tired eyes, his outstretched arms, his weak voice saying, "Oh, Jenny! Dear Jenny! I've wanted you so, Jenny!" It was too much! She had never breathed a word of it before to a human creature, for there was no one who would have understood. Now, in a shame-faced way, to hide her brimming eyes, she put her head down on the young shoulder beside her, saying, "It was hard, Rebecca!"

The Simpson baby had cuddled down sleepily in Rebecca's lap, leaning her head back and sucking her thumb contentedly. Rebecca put her cheek down until it touched her aunt's gray hair and softly patted her, as she said, "I'm sorry, Aunt Jane!"

The girl's eyes were soft and tender and the heart within her stretched a little and grew; grew in sweetness and intuition and depth of feeling. It had looked into another heart, felt it beat, and heard it sigh; and that is how all hearts grow.

Episodes like these enlivened the quiet course of everyday existence, made more quiet by the departure of Dick Carter, Living Perkins, and Huldah Meserve for Wareham, and the small attendance at the winter school, from which the younger children of the place stayed away during the cold weather.

Life, however, could never be thoroughly dull or lacking in adventure to a child of Rebecca's temperament. Her nature was full of adaptability, fluidity, receptivity. She made friends everywhere she went, and snatched up acquaintances in every corner.

It was she who ran to the shed door to take the dish to the "meat man" or "fish man"; she who knew the family histories of the itinerant fruit venders and tin peddlers; she who was asked to take supper or pass the night with children in neighboring villages—children of whose parents her aunts had never so much as heard. As to the nature of these friendships, which seemed so many to the eye of the superficial observer, they were of various kinds, and while the girl pursued them with enthusiasm and ardor, they left her unsatisfied and heart-hungry; they were never intimacies such as are so readily made by shallow natures. She loved Emma Jane, but it was a friendship born of propinquity and circumstance, not of true affinity. It was her neighbor's amiability, constancy, and devotion that she loved, and although she rated these qualities at their true value, she was always searching beyond them for intellectual treasures; searching and never finding, for although Emma Jane had the advantage in years she was still immature. Huldah Meserve had an instinctive love of fun which appealed to Rebecca; she also had a fascinating knowledge of the world, from having visited her married sisters in Milltown and Portland; but on the other hand there was a certain sharpness and lack of sympathy in Huldah which repelled rather than attracted. With Dick Carter she could at least talk intelligently about lessons. He was a very ambitious boy, full of plans for his future, which he discussed quite freely with Rebecca, but when she broached the subject of her future his interest sensibly lessened. Into the world of the ideal, Emma Jane, Huldah, and Dick alike never seemed to have peeped, and the consciousness of this was always a fixed gulf between them and Rebecca.

"Uncle Jerry" and "Aunt Sarah" Cobb were dear friends of quite another sort, a very satisfying and perhaps a somewhat dangerous one. A visit from Rebecca always sent them into a twitter of delight. Her merry conversation and quaint comments on life in general fairly dazzled the old couple, who hung on her lightest word as if it had been a prophet's utterance; and Rebecca, though she had had no previous experience, owned to herself a perilous pleasure in being dazzling, even to a couple of dear humdrum old people like Mr. and Mrs. Cobb. Aunt Sarah flew to the pantry and cellar whenever Rebecca's slim little shape first appeared on the crest of the hill, and a jelly tart or a frosted cake was sure to be forthcoming. The sight of old Uncle Jerry's spare figure in its clean white shirt sleeves, whatever the weather, always made Rebecca's heart warm when she saw him peer longingly from the kitchen window. Before the snow came, many was the time he had come out to sit on a pile of boards at the gate, to see if by any chance she was mounting the hill that led to their house. In the autumn Rebecca was often the old man's companion while he was digging potatoes or shelling beans, and now in the winter, when a younger man was driving the stage, she sometimes stayed with him while he did his evening milking. It is safe to say that he was the only creature in Riverboro who possessed Rebecca's entire confidence; the only being to whom she poured out her whole heart, with its wealth of hopes, and dreams, and vague ambitions. At the brick house she practiced scales and exercises, but at the Cobbs' cabinet organ she sang like a bird, improvising simple accompaniments that seemed to her ignorant auditors nothing short of marvelous. Here she was happy, here she was loved, here she was drawn out of herself and admired and made much of. But, she thought, if there were somebody who not only loved but understood; who spoke her language, comprehended her desires, and responded to her mysterious longings! Perhaps in the big world of Wareham there would be people who thought and dreamed and wondered as she did.

In reality Jane did not understand her niece very much better than Miranda; the difference between the sisters was, that while Jane was puzzled, she was also attracted, and when she was quite in the dark for an explanation of some quaint or unusual action she was sympathetic as to its possible motive and believed the best. A greater change had come over Jane than over any other person in the brick house, but it had been wrought so secretly, and concealed so religiously, that it scarcely appeared to the ordinary observer. Life had now a motive utterly lacking before. Breakfast was not eaten in the kitchen, because it seemed worth while, now that there were three persons, to lay the cloth in the dining-room; it was also a more bountiful meal than of yore, when there was no child to consider. The morning was made cheerful by Rebecca's start for school, the packing of the luncheon basket, the final word about umbrella, waterproof, or rubbers; the parting admonition and the unconscious waiting at the window for the last wave of the hand. She found herself taking pride in Rebecca's improved appearance, her rounded throat and cheeks, and her better color; she was wont to mention the length of Rebecca's hair and add a word as to its remarkable evenness and luster, at times when Mrs. Perkins grew too diffuse about Emma Jane's complexion. She threw herself wholeheartedly on her niece's side when it became a question between a crimson or a brown linsey-woolsey dress, and went through a memorable struggle with her sister concerning the purchase of a red bird for Rebecca's black felt hat. No one guessed the quiet pleasure that lay hidden in her heart when she watched the girl's dark head bent over her lessons at night, nor dreamed of her joy in certain quiet evenings when Miranda went to prayer meeting; evenings when Rebecca would read aloud "Hiawatha" or "Barbara Frietchie," "The Bugle

Song," or "The Brook." Her narrow, humdrum existence bloomed under the dews that fell from this fresh spirit; her dullness brightened under the kindling touch of the younger mind, took fire from the "vital spark of heavenly flame" that seemed always to radiate from Rebecca's presence.

Rebecca's idea of being a painter, like her friend Miss Ross was gradually receding, owing to the apparently insuperable difficulties in securing any instruction. Her Aunt Miranda saw no wisdom in cultivating such a talent, and could not conceive that any money could ever be earned by its exercise. "Hand-painted pictures" were held in little esteem in Riverboro, where the cheerful chromo or the dignified steel engraving were respected and valued. There was a slight, a very slight hope, that Rebecca might be allowed a few music lessons from Miss Morton, who played the church cabinet organ, but this depended entirely upon whether Mrs. Morton would decide to accept a hayrack in return for a year's instruction from her daughter. She had the matter under advisement, but a doubt as to whether or not she would sell or rent her hayfields kept her from coming to a conclusion. Music, in common with all other accomplishments, was viewed by Miss Miranda as a trivial, useless, and foolish amusement, but she allowed Rebecca an hour a day for practice on the old piano, and a little extra time for lessons, if Jane could secure them without payment of actual cash.

The news from Sunnybrook Farm was hopeful rather than otherwise. Cousin Ann's husband had died, and John, Rebecca's favorite brother, had gone to be the man of the house to the widowed cousin. He was to have good schooling in return for his care of the horse and cow and barn, and what was still more dazzling, the use of the old doctor's medical library of two or three dozen volumes. John's whole heart was set on becoming a country doctor, with Rebecca to keep house for him, and the vision seemed now so true, so near, that he could almost imagine his horse ploughing through snowdrifts on errands of mercy, or, less dramatic but none the less attractive, could see a physician's neat turnout trundling along the shady country roads, a medicine case between his, Dr. Randall's, feet, and Miss Rebecca Randall sitting in a black silk dress by his side.

Hannah now wore her hair in a coil and her dresses a trifle below her ankles, these concessions being due to her extreme height. Mark had broken his collar bone, but it was healing well. Little Mira was growing very pretty. There was even a rumor that the projected railroad from Temperance to Plumville might go near the Randall farm, in which case land would rise in value from nothing-at-all an acre to something at least resembling a price. Mrs. Randall refused to consider any improvement in their financial condition as a possibility. Content to work from sunrise to sunset to gain a mere subsistence for her children, she lived in their future, not in her own present, as a mother is wont to do when her own lot seems hard and cheerless.

14
GRAY DAYS AND GOLD

When Rebecca looked back upon the year or two that followed the Simpsons' Thanksgiving party, she could see only certain milestones rising in the quiet pathway of the months.

The first milestone was Christmas Day. It was a fresh, crystal morning, with icicles hanging like dazzling pendants from the trees and a glaze of pale blue on the surface of the snow. The Simpsons' red barn stood out, a glowing mass of color in the white landscape. Rebecca had been busy for weeks before, trying to make a present for each of the seven persons at Sunnybrook Farm, a somewhat difficult proceeding on an expenditure of fifty cents, hoarded by incredible exertion. Success had been achieved, however, and the precious packet had been sent by post two days previous. Miss Sawyer had bought her niece a nice gray squirrel muff and tippet, which was even more unbecoming, if possible, than Rebecca's other articles of wearing apparel; but Aunt Jane had made her the loveliest dress of green cashmere, a soft, soft green like that of a young leaf. It was very simply made, but the color delighted the eye. Then there was a beautiful "tatting" collar from her mother, some scarlet mittens from Mrs. Cobb, and a handkerchief from Emma Jane.

Rebecca herself had fashioned an elaborate tea-cozy with a letter "M" in outline stitch, and a pretty frilled pincushion marked with a "J," for her two aunts, so that taken all together the day would have been an unequivocal success had nothing else happened; but something else did.

There was a knock at the door at breakfast time, and Rebecca, answering it, was asked by a boy if Miss Rebecca Randall lived there. On being told that she did, he handed her a parcel bearing her name, a parcel which she took like one in a dream and bore into the dining-room.

"It's a present; it must be," she said, looking at it in a dazed sort of way; "but I can't

think who is could be from."

"A good way to find out would be to open it," remarked Miss Miranda.

The parcel being untied proved to have two smaller packages within, and Rebecca opened with trembling fingers the one addressed to her. Anybody's fingers would have trembled. There was a case which, when the cover was lifted, disclosed a long chain of delicate pink coral beads,—a chain ending in a cross made of coral rosebuds. A card with "Merry Christmas from Mr. Aladdin" lay under the cross.

"Of all things!" exclaimed the two old ladies, rising in their seats. "Who sent it?"

"Mr. Ladd," said Rebecca under her breath.

"Adam Ladd! Well, I never! Don't you remember Ellen Burnham said he was going to send Rebecca a Christmas present? But I never supposed he'd think of it again," said Jane. "What's the other package?"

It proved to be a silver chain with a blue enamel locket on it, marked for Emma Jane. That added the last touch—to have him remember them both! There was a letter also, which ran:—

DEAR MISS REBECCA ROWENA,—My idea of a Christmas present is something entirely unnecessary and useless. I have always noticed when I give this sort of thing that people love it, so I hope I have not chosen wrong for you and your friend. You must wear your chain this afternoon, please, and let me see it on your neck, for I am coming over in my new sleigh to take you both to drive. My aunt is delighted with the soap.
Sincerely your friend,
ADAM LADD.

"Well, well!" cried Miss Jane, "isn't that kind of him? He's very fond of children, Lyddy Burnham says. Now eat your breakfast, Rebecca, and after we've done the dishes you can run over to Emma's and give her her chain—What's the matter, child?"

Rebecca's emotions seemed always to be stored, as it were, in adjoining compartments, and to be continually getting mixed. At this moment, though her joy was too deep for words, her bread-and-butter almost choked her, and at intervals a tear stole furtively down her cheek.

Mr. Ladd called as he promised, and made the acquaintance of the aunts, understanding them both in five minutes as well as if he had known them for years. On a footstool near the open fire sat Rebecca, silent and shy, so conscious of her fine apparel and the presence of Aunt Miranda that she could not utter a word. It was one of her "beauty days." Happiness, excitement, the color of the green dress, and the touch of lovely pink in the coral necklace had transformed the little brown wren for the time into a bird of plumage, and Adam Ladd watched her with evident satisfaction. Then there was the sleigh ride, during which she found her tongue and chattered like any magpie, and so ended that glorious Christmas Day; and many and many a night thereafter did Rebecca go to sleep with the precious coral chain under her pillow, one hand always upon it to be certain that it was safe.

Another milestone was the departure of the Simpsons from Riverboro, bag and baggage, the banquet lamp being their most conspicuous possession. It was delightful to be rid of Seesaw's hateful presence; but otherwise the loss of several playmates at one fell swoop made rather a gap in Riverboro's "younger set," and Rebecca was obliged to make friends with the Robinson baby, he being the only long-clothes child in the village that winter. The faithful Seesaw had called at the side door of the brick house on the evening before his departure, and when Rebecca answered his knock, stammered solemnly, "Can I k-keep comp'ny with you when you g-g-row up?" "Certainly *not*," replied Rebecca, closing the door somewhat too speedily upon her precocious swain.

Mr. Simpson had come home in time to move his wife and children back to the town that had given them birth, a town by no means waiting with open arms to receive them. The Simpsons' moving was presided over by the village authorities and somewhat anxiously watched by the entire neighborhood, but in spite of all precautions a pulpit chair, several kerosene lamps, and a small stove disappeared from the church and were successfully swapped in the course of Mr. Simpson's driving tour from the old home to the new. It gave Rebecca and Emma Jane some hours of sorrow to learn that a certain village in the wake of Abner Simpson's line of progress had acquired, through the medium of an ambitious young minister, a magnificent lamp for its new church parlors. No money changed hands in the operation, for the minister succeeded in getting the lamp in return for an old bicycle. The only pleasant feature of the whole affair was that Mr. Simpson, wholly unable to console his offspring for the loss of the beloved object, mounted the bicycle and rode away on it, not to be seen or heard of again for many a long day.

The year was notable also as being the one in which Rebecca shot up like a young tree. She had seemingly never grown an inch since she was ten years old, but once started she attended to growing precisely as she did other things,—with such energy that Miss Jane did nothing for months but lengthen skirts, sleeves, and waists. In spite of all the arts known to a thrifty New England woman, the limit of letting down and piecing down was reached at last, and the dresses were sent to Sunnybrook Farm to be made over for Jenny.

There was another milestone, a sad one, marking a little grave under the willow tree at Sunnybrook Farm. Mira, the baby of the Randall family, died, and Rebecca went home for a fortnight's visit. The sight of the small still shape that had been Mira, the baby who had been her special charge ever since her birth, woke into being a host of new thoughts and wonderments; for it is sometimes the mystery of death that brings one to a consciousness of the still greater mystery of life.

It was a sorrowful home-coming for Rebecca. The death of Mira, the absence of John, who had been her special comrade, the sadness of her mother, the isolation of the little house, and the pinching economies that went on within it, all conspired to depress a child who was so sensitive to beauty and harmony as Rebecca.

Hannah seemed to have grown into a woman during Rebecca's absence. There had always been a strange unchildlike air about Hannah, but in certain ways she now appeared older than Aunt Jane—soberer, and more settled. She was pretty, though in a colorless fashion; pretty and capable.

Rebecca walked through all the old playgrounds and favorite haunts of her early childhood; all her familiar, her secret places; some of them known to John, some to herself alone. In the course of these lonely rambles she was ever thinking, thinking, of one subject. Hannah had never had a chance; never been freed from the daily care and work of the farm. She, Rebecca, had enjoyed all the privileges thus far. Life at the brick house had not been by any means a path of roses, but there had been comfort and the companionship of other children, as well as chances for study and reading. Riverboro had not been the world itself, but it had been a glimpse of it through a tiny peephole that was infinitely better than nothing. Rebecca shed more than one quiet tear before she could trust herself to offer up as a sacrifice that which she so much desired for herself. Then one morning as her visit neared its end she plunged into the subject boldly and said, "Hannah, after this term I'm going to stay at home and let you go away. Aunt Miranda has always wanted you, and it's only fair you should have your turn."

Hannah was darning stockings, and she threaded her needle and snipped off the yarn before she answered, "No, thank you, Becky. Mother couldn't do without me, and I hate going to school. I can read and write and cipher as well as anybody now, and that's enough for me. I'd die rather than teach school for a living. The winter'll go fast, for Will Melville is going to lend me his mother's sewing machine, and I'm going to make white petticoats out of the piece of muslin Aunt Jane sent, and have 'em just solid with tucks. Then there's going to be a singing-school and a social circle in Temperance after New Year's, and I shall have a real good time now I'm grown up. I'm not one to be lonesome, Becky," Hannah ended with a blush; "I love this place."

Rebecca saw that she was speaking the truth, but she did not understand the blush till a year or two later.

15
REBECCA REPRESENTS THE FAMILY

There was another milestone; it was more than that, it was an "event"; an event that made a deep impression in several quarters and left a wake of smaller events in its train. This was the coming to Riverboro of the Reverend Amos Burch and wife, returned missionaries from Syria.

The Aid Society had called its meeting for a certain Wednesday in March of the year in which Rebecca ended her Riverboro school days and began her studies in Wareham. It was a raw, blustering day, snow on the ground, and a look in the sky of more to follow. Both Miranda and Jane had taken cold and decided that they could not leave the house in such weather, and this deflection from the path of duty worried Miranda, since she was an officer of the society. After making the breakfast table sufficiently uncomfortable and wishing plaintively that Jane wouldn't always insist on being sick at the same time she was, she decided that Rebecca must go to the meeting in their stead. "You'll be better than nobody, Rebecca," she said flatteringly; "your Aunt Jane shall write an excuse from afternoon school for you; you can wear your rubber boots and come home by the way of the meetin'-house. This Mr. Burch, if I remember right, used to know your Grandfather Sawyer, and stayed here once when he was candidatin'. He'll mebbe look for us there, and you must just go and represent the family, an' give him our respects. Be careful how you behave. Bow your head in prayer; sing all the hymns, but not too loud and bold; ask after Mis' Strout's boy; tell everybody what awful colds we've got; if you see a good chance, take your pocket handkerchief and wipe the dust off the melodeon before the meetin' begins, and get twenty-five cents out of the sittin' room match-box in case there should be a collection."

Rebecca willingly assented. Anything interested her, even a village missionary meeting, and the idea of representing the family was rather intoxicating.

The service was held in the Sunday-School

room, and although the Reverend Mr. Burch was on the platform when Rebecca entered, there were only a dozen persons present. Feeling a little shy and considerably too young for this assemblage, Rebecca sought the shelter of a friendly face, and seeing Mrs. Robinson in one of the side seats near the front, she walked up the aisle and sat beside her.

"Both my aunts had bad colds," she said softly, "and sent me to represent the family."

"That's Mrs. Burch on the platform with her husband," whispered Mrs. Robinson. "She's awful tanned up, ain't she? If you're goin' to save souls seems like you hev' to part with your complexion. Eudoxy Morton ain't come yet; I hope to the land she will, or Mis' Deacon Milliken 'll pitch the tunes where we can't reach 'em with a ladder; can't you pitch, afore she gits her breath and clears her throat?"

Mrs. Burch was a slim, frail little woman with dark hair, a broad low forehead, and patient mouth. She was dressed in a well-worn black silk, and looked so tired that Rebecca's heart went out to her.

"They're poor as Job's turkey," whispered Mrs. Robinson; "but if you give 'em anything they'd turn right round and give it to the heathen. His congregation up to Parsonsfield clubbed together and give him that gold watch he carries; I s'pose he'd 'a' handed that over too, only heathens always tell time by the sun 'n' don't need watches. Eudoxy ain't comin'; now for massy's sake, Rebecca, do git ahead of Mis' Deacon Milliken and pitch real low."

The meeting began with prayer and then the Reverend Mr. Burch announced, to the tune of "Mendon":—

Church of our God! arise and shine,
Bright with the beams of truth divine:
Then shall thy radiance stream afar,
Wide as the heathen nations are.

Gentiles and kings thy light shall view,
And shall admire and love thee too;
They come, like clouds across the sky,
As doves that to their windows fly.

"Is there any one present who will assist us at the instrument?" he asked unexpectedly.

Everybody looked at everybody else, and nobody moved; then there came a voice out of a far corner saying informally "Rebecca, why don't you?" It was Mrs. Cobb. Rebecca could have played "Mendon" in the dark, so she went to the melodeon and did so without any ado, no member of her family being present to give her self-consciousness.

The talk that ensued was much the usual sort of thing. Mr. Burch made impassioned appeals for the spreading of the gospel, and added his entreaties that all who were prevented from visiting in person the peoples who sat in darkness should contribute liberally to the support of others who could. But he did more than this. He was a pleasant, earnest speaker, and he interwove his discourse with stories of life in a foreign land,— of the manners, the customs, the speech, the point of view; even giving glimpses of the daily round, the common task, of his own household, the work of his devoted helpmate and their little group of children, all born under Syrian skies.

Rebecca sat entranced, having been given the key of another world. Riverboro had faded; the Sunday-School room, with Mrs. Robinson's red plaid shawl, and Deacon Milliken's wig, on crooked, the bare benches and torn hymn-books, the hanging texts and maps, were no longer visible, and she saw blue skies and burning stars, white turbans and gay colors; Mr. Burch had not said so, but perhaps there were mosques and temples and minarets and date-palms. What stories they must know, those children born under Syrian skies! Then she was called upon to play "Jesus Shall Reign Where'er the Sun."

The contribution box was passed and Mr. Burch prayed. As he opened his eyes and gave out the last hymn he looked at the handful of people, at the scattered pennies and dimes in the contribution box, and reflected that his mission was not only to gather funds for the building of his church, but to keep alive, in all these remote and lonely neighborhoods, that love for the cause which was its only hope in the years to come.

"If any of the sisters will provide entertainment," he said, "Mrs. Burch and I will remain among you tonight and tomorrow. In that event we could hold a parlor meeting. My wife and one of my children would wear the native costume, we would display some specimens of Syrian handiwork, and give an account of our educational methods with the children. These informal parlor meetings, admitting of questions or conversation, are often the means of interesting those not commonly found at church services; so I repeat, if any member of the congregation desires it and offers her hospitality, we will gladly stay and tell you more of the Lord's work."

A pall of silence settled over the little assembly. There was some cogent reason why every "sister" there was disinclined for company. Some had no spare room, some had a larder less well stocked than usual, some had sickness in the family, some were "unequally yoked together with unbelievers" who disliked strange ministers. Mrs. Burch's thin hands fingered her black silk nervously. "Would no one speak!" thought Rebecca, her heart fluttering with sympathy. Mrs. Robinson leaned over and whispered significantly, "The missionaries always used to be entertained at the brick house; your grandfather never would let 'em sleep anywheres else when he was alive." She meant this for a stab at Miss Miranda's parsimony, remembering the four spare chambers, closed from January to December; but Rebecca thought it was intended as a suggestion. If it had been a former custom, perhaps her aunts would want her to do the right thing; for what else was she representing the family? So, delighted that duty lay in so pleasant a direction, she rose from her seat and said in a pretty voice and with the quaint manner that so separated her from all the other young people in the village, "My aunts, Miss Miranda and Miss Jane Sawyer, would be very happy to have you visit them at the brick house, as the ministers always used to do when their father was alive. They sent their respects by me." The "respects" might have been the freedom of the city, or an equestrian statue, when presented in this way, and the aunts would have shuddered could they have foreseen the manner of delivery; but it was vastly impressive to the audience, who concluded that Mirandy Sawyer must be making her way uncommonly fast to mansions in the skies, else what meant this abrupt change of heart?

Mr. Burch bowed courteously, accepted the invitation "in the same spirit in which it was offered," and asked Brother Milliken to lead in prayer.

If the Eternal Ear could ever tire it would have ceased long ere this to listen to Deacon Milliken, who had wafted to the throne of grace the same prayer, with very slight variations, for forty years. Mrs. Perkins followed; she had several petitions at her command, good sincere ones too, but a little cut and dried, made of Scripture texts laboriously woven together. Rebecca wondered why she always ended, at the most peaceful seasons, with the form, "Do Thou be with us, God of Battles, while we strive onward like Christian soldiers marching as to war." But everything sounded real to her today; she was in a devout mood, and many things Mr. Burch had said had moved her strangely. As she lifted her head the minister looked directly at her and said, "Will our young sister close the service by leading us in prayer?"

Every drop of blood in Rebecca's body seemed to stand still, and her heart almost stopped beating. Mrs. Cobb's excited breathing could be heard distinctly in the silence. There was nothing extraordinary in Mr. Burch's request. In his journeyings among country congregations he was constantly in the habit of meeting young members who had "experienced religion" and joined the church when nine or ten years old. Rebecca was now thirteen; she had played the melodeon, led the singing, delivered her aunts' invitation with an air of great worldly wisdom, and he, concluding that she must be a youthful pillar of the church, called upon her with the utmost simplicity.

Rebecca's plight was pathetic. How could she refuse; how could she explain she was not a "member"; how could she pray before all those elderly women! John Rogers at the stake hardly suffered more than this poor child for the moment as she rose to her feet, forgetting that ladies prayed sitting, while deacons stood in prayer. Her mind was a maze of pictures that the Reverend Mr. Burch had flung on the screen. She knew the conventional phrase-ology, of course; what New England child, accustomed to Wednesday evening meetings, does not? But her own secret prayers were different. However, she began slowly and tremulously:—

"Our Father who art in Heaven, . . . Thou art God in Syria just the same as in Maine; . . . over there today are blue skies and yellow stars and burning suns . . . the great trees are waving in the warm air, while here the snow lies thick under our feet, . . . but no distance it too far for God to travel and so He is with us here as He is with them there, . . . and our thoughts rise to Him 'as doves that to their windows fly.' . . .

"We cannot all be missionaries, teaching people to be good, . . . some of us have not learned yet how to be good ourselves, but if thy kingdom is to come and thy will is to be done on earth as it is in heaven, everybody must try and everybody must help, . . . those who are old and tired and those who are young and strong. . . . The little children of whom we have heard, those born under Syrian skies, have strange and interesting work to do for Thee, and some of us would like to travel in far lands and do wonderful brave things for the heathen and gently take away their idols of wood and stone. But perhaps we have to stay at home and do what is given us to do . . . sometimes even things we dislike, . . . but that must be what it means in the hymn we sang, when it talked about the sweet perfume that rises with every morning sacrifice. . . . This is the way that God teaches us to be meek and patient, and the thought that He has willed it so should rob us of our fears and help us bear the years. Amen."

The "Amen" said, she sat down, or presumed she sat down, on what she believed to be a bench, and there was a benediction. In a moment or two, when the room ceased spinning, she went up to Mrs. Burch, who kissed her affectionately and said, "My dear, how glad I am that we are going to stay with you. Will half-past five be too late for us to come? It is three now, and we have to go to the station for our valise and for our children. We left them there, being uncertain whether we should go back or stop here."

Rebecca said that half-past five was their

supper hour, and then accepted an invitation to drive home with Mrs. Cobb. Her face was flushed and her lip quivered in a way that Aunt Sarah had learned to know, so the homeward drive was taken almost in silence. The bleak wind and Aunt Sarah's quieting presence brought her back to herself, however, and she entered the brick house cheerily. Being too full of news to wait in the side entry to take off her rubber boots, she carefully lifted a braided rug into the sitting room and stood on that while she opened her budget.

"There are your shoes warming by the fire," said Aunt Jane. "Slip them right on while you talk."

16
DEACON ISRAEL'S SUCCESSOR

"It was a very small meeting, Aunt Miranda," began Rebecca, "and the missionary and his wife are lovely people, and they are coming here to stay all night and tomorrow with you. I hope you won't mind."

"Coming here!" exclaimed Miranda, letting her knitting fall in her lap, and taking her spectacles off, as she always did in moments of extreme excitement. "Did they invite themselves?"

"No," Rebecca answered. "I had to invite them for you; but I thought you'd like to have such interesting company. It was this way—"

"Stop your explainin', and tell me first when they'll be here. Right away?"

"No, not for two hours—about half-past five."

"Then you can explain, if you can, who gave you authority to invite a passel of strangers to stop here overnight, when you know we ain't had any company for twenty years, and don't intend to have any for another twenty,—or at any rate, while I'm the head of the house."

"Don't blame her, Miranda, till you've heard her story," said Jane. "It was in my mind right along, if we went to the meeting, some such thing might happen, on account of Mr. Burch knowing father."

"The meeting was a small one," began Rebecca. "I gave all your messages, and everybody was disappointed you couldn't come, for the president wasn't there, and Mrs. Matthews took the chair, which was a pity, for the seat wasn't nearly big enough for her, and she reminded me of a line in a hymn we sang, 'Wide as the heathen nations are,' and she wore that kind of a beaver garden-hat that always gets on one side. And Mr. Burch talked beautifully about the Syrian heathen, and the singing went real well, and there looked to be about forty cents in the basket that was passed on our side. And that wouldn't save even a heathen baby, would it? Then Mr. Burch said, if any sister would offer entertainment, they would pass the night, and have a parlor meeting in Riverboro tomorrow, with Mrs. Burch in Syrian costume, and lovely foreign things to show. Then he waited and waited, and nobody said a word. I was so mortified I didn't know what to do. And then he repeated what he said, and explained why he wanted to stay, and you could see he thought it was his duty. Just then Mrs. Robinson whispered to me and said the missionaries always used to go to the brick house when grandfather was alive, and that he never would let them sleep anywhere else. I didn't know you had stopped having them, because no traveling ministers have been here, except just for a Sunday morning, since I came to Riverboro. So I thought I ought to invite them as you weren't there to do it for yourself, and you told me to represent the family."

"What did you do—go up and introduce yourself as folks was goin' out?"

"No; I stood right up in meeting. I had to, for Mr. Burch's feelings were getting hurt at nobody's speaking. So I said, 'My aunts, Miss Miranda and Miss Jane Sawyer, would be happy to have you visit at the brick house, just as the missionaries always did when their father was alive, and they sent their respects by me.' Then I sat down; and Mr. Burch prayed for grandfather, and called him a man of God, and thanked our Heavenly Father that his spirit was still alive in his descendants (that was you), and that the good old house where so many of the brethren had been cheered and helped, and from which so many had gone out strengthened for the fight, was still hospitably open for the stranger and wayfarer."

Sometimes, when the heavenly bodies are in just the right conjunction, nature seems to be the most perfect art. The word or the deed coming straight from the heart, without any thought of effect, seems inspired.

A certain gateway in Miranda Sawyer's soul had been closed for years; not all at once had it been done, but gradually, and without her full knowledge. If Rebecca had plotted for days, and with the utmost cunning, she could not have effected an entrance into that forbidden country, and now, unknown to both of them, the gate swung on its stiff and rusty hinges, and the favoring wind of opportunity opened it wider and wider as time went on. All things had worked together amazingly for good. The memory of old days had been evoked, and the daily life of a pious and venerated father called to mind; the Sawyer name had been publicly dignified and praised; Rebecca had comported herself as the grand-daughter of Deacon Israel Sawyer should, and showed conclusively that she was not "all Randall," as had been supposed. Miranda was rather mollified by and pleased with the turn of events, although she did not intend to show it, or give anybody any reason to expect that this expression of hospitality was to serve for a precedent on any subsequent occasion.

"Well, I see you did only what you was obliged to do, Rebecca," she said, "and you worded your invitation as nice as anybody could have done. I wish your Aunt Jane and me wasn't both so worthless with these colds; but it only shows the good of havin' a clean house, with every room in order, whether open or shut, and enough victuals cooked so 't you can't be surprised and belittled by anybody, whatever happens. There was half a dozen there that might have entertained the Burches as easy as not, if they hadn't 'a' been too mean or lazy. Why didn't your missionaries come right along with you?"

"They had to go to the station for their valise and their children."

"Are there children?" groaned Miranda.

"Yes, Aunt Miranda, all born under Syrian skies."

"Syrian grandmother!" ejaculated Miranda (and it was not a fact). "How many?"

"I didn't think to ask; but I will get two rooms ready, and if there are any over I'll take 'em into my bed," said Rebecca, secretly hoping that this would be the case. "Now, as you're both half sick, couldn't you trust me just once to get ready for the company? You can come up when I call. Will you?"

"I believe I will," sighed Miranda reluctantly. "I'll lay down side o' Jane in our bedroom and see if I can get strength to cook supper. It's half-past three—don't you let me lay a minute past five. I kep' a good fire in the kitchen stove. I don't know, I'm sure, why I should have baked a pot o' beans in the middle of the week, but they'll come in handy. Father used to say there was nothing that went right to the spot with returned missionaries like pork 'n' beans 'n' brown bread. Fix up the two south chambers, Rebecca."

Rebecca, given a free hand for the only time in her life, dashed upstairs like a whirlwind. Every room in the brick house was as neat as wax, and she had only to pull up the shades, go over the floors with a whisk broom, and dust the furniture. The aunts could hear her scurrying to and fro, beating up pillows and feather beds, flapping towels, jingling crockery, singing meanwhile in her clear voice:—

In vain with lavish kindness
    The gifts of God are strown;
The heathen in his blindness
    Bows down to wood and stone.

She had grown to be a handy little creature, and tasks she was capable of doing at all she did like a flash, so that when she called her aunts at five o'clock to pass judgment, she had accomplished wonders. There were fresh towels on bureaus and washstands, the beds were fair and smooth, the pitchers were filled, and soap and matches were laid out; newspaper, kindling, and wood were in the boxes, and a large stick burned slowly in each airtight stove. "I thought I'd better just take the chill off," she explained, "as they're right from Syria; and that reminds me, I must look it up in the geography before they get here."

There was nothing to disapprove, so the two sisters went downstairs to make some slight changes in their dress. As they passed the parlor door Miranda thought she heard a crackle and looked in. The shades were up, there was a cheerful blaze in the open stove in the front parlor, and a fire laid on the hearth in the back room. Rebecca's own lamp, her second Christmas present from Mr. Aladdin, stood on a marble-topped table in the corner, the light that came softly through its rose-colored shade transforming the stiff and gloomy ugliness of the room into a place where one could sit and love one's neighbor.

"For massy's sake, Rebecca," called Miss Miranda up the stairs, "did you think we'd better open the parlor?"

Rebecca came out on the landing braiding her hair.

"We did on Thanksgiving and Christmas, and I thought this was about as great an occasion," she said. "I moved the wax flowers off the mantelpiece so they wouldn't melt, and

put the shells, the coral, and the green stuffed bird on top of the what-not, so the children wouldn't ask to play with them. Brother Milliken's coming over to see Mr. Burch about business, and I shouldn't wonder if Brother and Sister Cobb happened in. Don't go down cellar, I'll be there in a minute to do the running."

Miranda and Jane exchanged glances.

"Ain't she the beatin'est creetur that ever was born int' the world!" exclaimed Miranda; "but she can turn off work when she's got a mind to!"

At quarter-past five everything was ready, and the neighbors, those at least who were within sight of the brick house (a prominent object in the landscape when there were no leaves on the trees), were curious almost to desperation. Shades up in both parlors! Shades up in the two south bedrooms! And fires—if human vision was to be relied on—fires in about every room. If it had not been for the kind offices of a lady who had been at the meeting, and who charitably called in at one or two houses and explained the rea-

son of all this preparation, there would have been no sleep in many families.

The missionary party arrived promptly, and there were but two children, seven or eight having been left with the brethren in Portland, to diminish traveling expenses. Jane escorted them all upstairs, while Miranda watched the cooking of the supper; but Rebecca promptly took the two little girls away from their mother, divested them of their wraps, smoothed their hair, and brought them down to the kitchen to smell the beans.

There was a bountiful supper, and the presence of the young people robbed it of all possible stiffness. Aunt Jane helped clear the table and put away the food, while Miranda entertained in the parlor; but Rebecca and the infant Burches washed the dishes and held high carnival in the kitchen, doing only trifling damage—breaking a cup and plate that had been cracked before, emptying a silver spoon with some dishwater out of the back door (an act never permitted at the brick house), and putting coffee grounds in the sink. All evidences of crime having been removed by Rebecca, and damages repaired in all possible cases, the three entered the parlor, where Mr. and Mrs. Cobb and Deacon and Mrs. Milliken had already appeared.

It was such a pleasant evening! Occasionally they left the heathen in his blindness bowing down to wood and stone, not for long, but just to give themselves (and him) time enough to breathe, and then the Burches told strange, beautiful, marvelous things. The two smaller children sang together, and Rebecca, at the urgent request of Mrs. Burch, seated herself at the tinkling old piano and gave "Wild roved an Indian girl, bright Alfarata" with considerable spirit and style.

At eight o'clock she crossed the room, handed a palm-leaf fan to her Aunt Miranda, ostensibly that she might shade her eyes from the lamplight; but it was a piece of strategy that gave her an opportunity to whisper. "How about cookies?"

"Do you think it's worth while?" sibilated Miss Miranda in answer.

"The Perkinses always do."

"All right. You know where they be."

Rebecca moved quietly towards the door, and the young Burches cataracted after her as if they could not bear a second's separation. In five minutes they returned, the little ones bearing plates of thin caraway wafers,— hearts, diamonds, and circles daintily sugared, and flecked with caraway seed raised in the garden behind the house. These were a specialty of Miss Jane's, and Rebecca carried a tray with six tiny crystal glasses filled with dandelion wine, for which Miss Miranda had been famous in years gone by. Old Deacon Israel had always had it passed, and he had bought the glasses himself in Boston. Miranda admired them greatly, not only for their beauty but because they held so little. Before their advent the dandelion wine had been served in sherry glasses.

As soon as these refreshments—commonly called a "*co*lation" in Riverboro—had been genteelly partaken of, Rebecca looked at the clock, rose from her chair in the children's corner, and said cheerfully, "Come! Time for little missionaries to be in bed!"

Everybody laughed at this, the big missionaries most of all, as the young people shook hands and disappeared with Rebecca.

17

A CHANGE OF HEART

"That niece of yours is the most remarkable girl I have seen in years," said Mr. Burch when the door closed.

"She seems to be turnin' out smart enough lately, but she's consid'able heedless," answered Miranda, "an' most too lively."

"We must remember that it is deficient, not excessive vitality, that makes the greatest trouble in this world," returned Mr. Burch.

"She'd make a wonderful missionary," said Mrs. Burch; "with her voice, and her magnetism, and her gift of language."

"If I was to say which of the two she was best adapted for, I'd say she'd make a better heathen," remarked Miranda curtly.

"My sister don't believe in flattering children," hastily interpolated Jane, glancing toward Mrs. Burch, who seemed somewhat shocked, and was about to open her lips to ask if Rebecca was not a "professor."

Mrs. Cobb had been looking for this question all the evening and dreading some allusion to her favorite as gifted in prayer. She had taken an instantaneous and illogical dislike to the Reverend Mr. Burch in the afternoon because he called upon Rebecca to "lead." She had seen the pallor creep into the girl's face, the hunted look in her eyes, and the trembling of the lashes on her cheeks, and realized the ordeal through which she was passing. Her prejudice against the minister had relaxed under his genial talk and presence, but feeling that Mrs. Burch was about to tread on dangerous ground, she hastily asked her if one had to change cars many times going from Riverboro to Syria. She felt that it was not a particularly appropriate question, but it served her turn.

Deacon Milliken, meantime, said to Miss Sawyer, "Mirandy, do you know who Rebecky reminds me of?"

"I can guess pretty well," she replied.

"Then you've noticed it too! I thought at first, seein' she favored her father so on the outside, that she was the same all through; but she ain't; she's like your father, Israel Sawyer."

"I don't see how you make that out," said Miranda, thoroughly astonished.

"It struck me this afternoon when she got up to give your invitation in meetin'. It was kind o' cur'ous, but she set in the same seat he used to when he was leader o' the Sabbath-School. You know his old way of holding his chin up and throwin' his head back a leetle when he got up to say anything? Well, she done the very same thing; there was more'n one spoke of it."

The callers left before nine, and at that hour (an impossibly dissipated one for the brick house) the family retired for the night. As Rebecca carried Mrs. Burch's candle upstairs and found herself thus alone with her for a minute, she said shyly, "Will you please tell Mr. Burch that I'm not a member of the church? I didn't know what to do when he asked me to pray this afternoon. I hadn't the courage to say I had never done it out loud and didn't know how. I couldn't think; and I was so frightened I wanted to sink into the floor. It seemed bold and wicked for me to pray before all those old church members and make believe I was better than I really was; but then again, wouldn't God think I was wicked not to be willing to pray when a minister asked me to?"

The candlelight fell on Rebecca's flushed, sensitive face. Mrs. Burch bent and kissed her good-night. "Don't be troubled," she said. "I'll tell Mr. Burch, and I guess God will understand."

Rebecca waked before six the next morning, so full of household cares that sleep was impossible. She went to the window and looked out; it was still dark, and a blustering, boisterous day.

"Aunt Jane told me she would get up at half-past six and have breakfast at half-past seven," she thought; "but I dare say they are both sick with their colds, and Aunt Miranda will be fidgety with so many in the house. I believe I'll creep down and start things for a surprise."

She put on a wadded wrapper and slippers and stole quietly down the tabooed front stairs, carefully closed the kitchen door behind her so that no noise should waken the rest of the household, busied herself for a half-hour with the early morning routine she knew so well, and then went back to her room to dress before calling the children.

Contrary to expectation, Miss Jane, who the evening before felt better than Miranda, grew worse in the night, and was wholly unable to leave her bed in the morning. Miranda grumbled without ceasing during the progress of her hasty toilet, blaming everybody in the universe for the afflictions she had borne and was to bear during the day; she even castigated the Missionary Board that had sent the Burches to Syria, and gave it as her unbiased opinion that those who went to foreign lands for the purpose of saving heathen should stay there and save 'em, and not go gallivantin' all over the earth with a passel o' children, visitin' folks that didn't want 'em and never asked 'em.

Jane lay anxiously and restlessly in bed with a feverish headache, wondering how her sister could manage without her.

Miranda walked stiffly through the dining-room, tying a shawl over her head to keep the draughts away, intending to start the breakfast fire and then call Rebecca down, set her to work, and tell her, meanwhile, a few plain facts concerning the proper way of representing the family at a missionary meeting.

She opened the kitchen door and stared vaguely about her, wondering whether she had strayed into the wrong house by mistake.

The shades were up, and there was a roaring fire in the stove; the teakettle was singing and bubbling as it sent out a cloud of steam, and pushed over its capacious nose was a half-sheet of note paper with "Compliments of Rebecca" scrawled on it. The coffee pot was scalding, the coffee was measured out in a bowl, and broken eggshells for the settling process were standing near. The cold potatoes and corned beef were in the wooden tray, and "Regards of Rebecca" stuck on the chopping-knife. The brown loaf was out, the white loaf was out, the toast rack was out, the doughnuts were out, the milk was skimmed, the butter had been brought from the dairy.

Miranda removed the shawl from her head and sank into the kitchen rocker, ejaculating under her breath, "She is the beatin'est child! I declare she's all Sawyer!"

The day and the evening passed off with credit and honor to everybody concerned, even to Jane, who had the discretion to recover instead of growing worse and acting as a damper to the general enjoyment. The Burches left with lively regrets, and the little missionaries, bathed in tears, swore eternal friendship with Rebecca, who pressed into their hands at parting a poem composed before breakfast.

TO MARY AND MARTHA BURCH

Born under Syrian skies,
  'Neath hotter suns than ours;
The children grew and bloomed,
  Like little tropic flowers.

When they first saw the light,
  'T was in a heathen land.
Not Greenland's icy mountains,
  Nor India's coral strand,

But some mysterious country
  Where men are nearly black
And where of true religion,
  There is a painful lack.

Then let us haste in helping
  The Missionary Board
Seek dark-skinned unbelievers,
  And teach them of their Lord.
      REBECCA ROWENA RANDALL.

It can readily be seen that this visit of the returned missionaries to Riverboro was not without somewhat far-reaching results. Mr. and Mrs. Burch themselves looked back upon it as one of the rarest pleasures of their half year at home. The neighborhood extracted considerable eager conversation from it; argument, rebuttal, suspicion, certainty, retrospect, and prophecy. Deacon Milliken gave ten dollars towards the conversion of Syria to Congregationalism, and Mrs. Milliken had a spell of sickness over her husband's rash generosity.

It would be pleasant to state that Miranda Sawyer was an entirely changed woman afterwards, but that is not the fact. The tree that has been getting a twist for twenty years cannot be straightened in the twinkling of an eye. It is certain, however, that although the difference to the outward eye was very small, it nevertheless existed, and she was less censorious in her treatment of Rebecca, less harsh in her judgments, more hopeful of final salvation for her. This had come about largely from her sudden vision that Rebecca, after all, inherited something from the Sawyer side of the house instead of belonging, mind, body, and soul, to the despised Randall stock. Everything that was interesting in Rebecca, and every evidence of power, capability, or talent afterwards displayed by her, Miranda ascribed to the brick house training, and this gave her a feeling of honest pride, the pride of a master workman who has built success out of the most unpromising material; but never, to the very end, even when the waning of her bodily strength relaxed her iron grip and weakened her power of repression, never once did she show that pride or make a single demonstration of affection.

Poor misplaced, belittled Lorenzo de Medici Randall, thought ridiculous and good-for-naught by his associates, because he resembled them in nothing! If Riverboro could have been suddenly emptied into a larger community, with different and more flexible opinions, he was, perhaps, the only personage in the entire population who would have attracted the smallest attention. It was fortunate for his daughter that she had been dowered with a practical ability from her mother's family, but if Lorenzo had never done anything else in the world, he might have glorified himself that he had prevented Rebecca from being all Sawyer. Failure as he was, complete and entire, he had generously handed down to her all that was best in himself, and prudently retained all that was unworthy. Few fathers are capable of such delicate discrimination.

The brick house did not speedily become a sort of wayside inn, a place of innocent revelry and joyous welcome; but the missionary company was an entering wedge, and Miranda allowed one spare bed to be made up "in case anything should happen," while the crystal glasses were kept on the second from the top, instead of the top shelf, in the china closet. Rebecca had had to stand on a chair to reach them; now she could do it by stretching; and this is symbolic of the way in which she unconsciously scaled the walls of Miss Miranda's dogmatism and prejudice.

Miranda went so far as to say that she wouldn't mind if the Burches came every once in a while, but she was afraid he'd spread abroad the fact of his visit, and missionaries' families would be underfoot the whole continual time. As a case in point, she gracefully cited the fact that if a tramp got a good meal at anybody's back door, 't was said that he'd leave some kind of a sign so that all other tramps would know where they were likely to receive the same treatment.

It is to be feared that there is some truth in this homely illustration, and Miss Miranda's dread as to her future responsibilities had some foundation, though not of the precise

sort she had in mind. The soul grows into lovely habits as easily as into ugly ones, and the moment a life begins to blossom into beautiful words and deeds, that moment a new standard of conduct is established, and your eager neighbors look to you for a continuous manifestation of the good cheer, the sympathy, the ready wit, the comradeship, or the inspiration, you once showed yourself capable of. Bear figs for a season or two, and the world outside the orchard is very unwilling you should bear thistles.

The effect of the Burches' visit on Rebecca is not easily described. Nevertheless, as she looked back upon it from the vantage ground of after years, she felt that the moment when Mr. Burch asked her to "lead in prayer" marked an epoch in her life.

If you have ever observed how courteous and gracious and mannerly you feel when you don a beautiful new frock; if you have ever noticed the feeling of reverence stealing over you when you close your eyes, clasp your hands, and bow your head; if you have ever watched your sense of repulsion toward a fellow creature melt a little under the exercise of daily politeness, you may understand how the adoption of the outward and visible sign has some strange influence in developing the inward and spiritual state of which it is the expression.

It is only when one has grown old and dull that the soul is heavy and refuses to rise. The young soul is ever wingèd; a breath stirs it to an upward flight. Rebecca was asked to bear witness to a state of mind or feeling of whose existence she had only the vaguest consciousness. She obeyed, and as she uttered words they became true in the uttering; as she voiced aspirations they settled into realities.

As "dove that to its window flies," her spirit soared towards a great light, dimly discovered at first, but brighter as she came closer to it. To become sensible of oneness with the Divine heart before any sense of separation has been felt, this is surely the most beautiful way for the child to find God.

18

THE SKY-LINE WIDENS

The time so long and eagerly waited for had
come, and Rebecca was a student at Wareham. Persons who had enjoyed the social be-
wilderments and advantages of foreign courts,
or had mingled freely in the intellectual circles of great universities, might not have
looked upon Wareham as an extraordinary
experience; but it was as much of an advance
upon Riverboro as that village had been upon
Sunnybrook Farm. Rebecca's intention was
to complete the four years' course in three, as
it was felt by all the parties concerned that
when she had attained the ripe age of seventeen she must be ready to earn her own living and help in the education of the younger
children. While she was wondering how this
could be successfully accomplished, some of
the other girls were cogitating as to how they
could meander through the four years and
come out at the end knowing no more than
at the beginning. This would seem a difficult,
well-nigh an impossible task, but it can be
achieved, and has been, at other seats of
learning than modest little Wareham.

Rebecca was to go to and fro on the cars
daily from September to Christmas, and then
board in Wareham during the three coldest
months. Emma Jane's parents had always
thought that a year or two in the Edgewood
High School (three miles from Riverboro)
would serve every purpose for their daughter
and send her into the world with as fine an
intellectual polish as she could well sustain.
Emma Jane had hitherto heartily concurred
in this opinion, for if there was any one
thing that she detested it was the learning of
lessons. One book was as bad as another in
her eyes, and she could have seen the librar-
ies of the world sinking into ocean depths
and have eaten her dinner cheerfully the
while; but matters assumed a different complexion when she was sent to Edgewood and
Rebecca to Wareham. She bore it for a week
—seven endless days of absence from the beloved object, whom she could see only in the
evenings when both were busy with their
lessons. Sunday offered an opportunity to
put the matter before her father, who proved

obdurate. He didn't believe in education and thought she had full enough already. He never intended to keep up "blacksmithing" for good when he leased his farm and came into Riverboro, but proposed to go back to it presently, and by that time Emma Jane would have finished school and would be ready to help her mother with the dairy work.

Another week passed. Emma Jane pined visibly and audibly. Her color faded, and her appetite (at table) dwindled almost to nothing.

Her mother alluded plaintively to the fact that the Perkinses had a habit of going into declines; that she'd always feared that Emma Jane's complexion was too beautiful to be healthy; that some men would be proud of having an ambitious daughter, and be glad to give her the best advantages; that she feared the daily journeys to Edgewood were going to be too much for her own health, and Mr. Perkins would have to hire a boy to drive Emma Jane; and finally that when a girl had such a passion for learning as Emma Jane, it seemed almost like wickedness to cross her will.

Mr. Perkins bore this for several days until his temper, digestion, and appetite were all sensibly affected; then he bowed his head to the inevitable, and Emma Jane flew, like a captive set free, to the loved one's bower. Neither did her courage flag, although it was put to terrific tests when she entered the academic groves of Wareham. She passed in only two subjects, but went cheerfully into the preparatory department with her five "conditions," intending to let the stream of education play gently over her mental surfaces and not get any wetter than she could help. It is not possible to blink the truth that Emma Jane was dull; but a dogged, unswerving loyalty, and the gift of devoted, unselfish loving, these, after all, are talents of a sort, and may possibly be of as much value in the world as a sense of numbers or a faculty for languages.

Wareham was a pretty village with a broad main street shaded by great maples and elms. It had an apothecary, a blacksmith, a plumber, several shops of one sort and another, two churches, and many boarding-houses; but all its interests gathered about its seminary and its academy. These seats of learning were neither better nor worse than others of their kind, but differed much in efficiency, according as the principal who chanced to be at the head was a man of power and inspiration or the reverse. There were boys and girls gathered from all parts of the county and state, and they were of every kind and degree as to birth, position in the world, wealth or poverty. There was an opportunity for a deal of foolish and imprudent behavior, but on the whole surprisingly little advantage was taken of it. Among the third and fourth year students there was a certain amount of going to and from the trains in couples; some carrying of heavy books up the hill by the sterner sex for their feminine schoolmates, and occasional bursts of silliness on the part of heedless and precocious girls, among whom was Huldah Meserve. She was friendly enough with Emma Jane and Rebecca, but grew less and less intimate as time went on. She was extremely pretty, with a profusion of auburn hair, and a few very tiny freckles, to which she constantly alluded, as no one could possibly detect them without noting her porcelain skin and her curling lashes. She had merry eyes, a somewhat too plump figure for her years, and was popularly supposed to have a fascinating way with her. Riverboro being poorly furnished with beaux, she intended to have as good a time during her four years at Wareham as circumstances would permit. Her idea of pleasure was an ever-changing circle of admirers to fetch and carry for her, the more publicly the better; incessant chaff and laughter and vivacious conversation, made eloquent and effective by arch looks and telling glances. She had a habit of confiding her conquests to less fortunate girls and bewailing the incessant havoc and damage she was doing; a damage she avowed herself as innocent of, in intention, as any new-born lamb. It does not take much of this sort of thing to wreck an ordinary friendship, so before long Rebecca and Emma Jane sat in one end of the railway train in going to and from Riverboro, and Huldah occupied the other with her court. Sometimes this was brilliant beyond words, including a certain youthful Monte Cristo, who on Fridays expended thirty cents on a round-trip ticket and traveled from Wareham to Riverboro merely to be near Huldah; sometimes, too, the circle was reduced to the popcorn-and-peanut boy of the train, who seemed to serve every purpose in default of better game.

Rebecca was in the normally unconscious state that belonged to her years; boys were good comrades, but no more; she liked reciting in the same class with them, everything seemed to move better; but from vulgar and precocious flirtations she was protected by her ideals. There was little in the lads she had met thus far to awaken her fancy, for it habitually fed on better meat. Huldah's schoolgirl romances, with their wealth of commonplace detail, were not the stuff her dreams were made of, when dreams did flutter across the sensitive plate of her mind.

Among the teachers at Wareham was one who influenced Rebecca profoundly, Miss Emily Maxwell, with whom she studied English literature and composition. Miss Maxwell, as the niece of one of Maine's ex-governors and the daughter of one of Bowdoin's professors, was the most remarkable personality in Wareham, and that her few years of teaching happened to be in Rebecca's time was the happiest of all chances. There was no indecision or delay in the establishment of their relations; Rebecca's heart flew like an arrow to its mark, and her mind, meeting its superior, settled at once into an abiding attitude of respectful homage.

It was rumored that Miss Maxwell "wrote," which word, when uttered in a certain tone, was understood to mean not that a person had command of penmanship, Spencerian or otherwise, but that she had appeared in print.

"You'll like her; she writes," whispered Huldah to Rebecca the first morning at prayers, where the faculty sat in an imposing row on the front seats. "She writes; and I call her stuck up."

Nobody seemed possessed of exact information with which to satisfy the hungry mind, but there was believed to be at least one person in existence who had seen, with his own eyes, an essay by Miss Maxwell in a magazine. This height of achievement made Rebecca somewhat shy of her, but she looked her admiration; something that most of the class could never do with the unsatisfactory organs of vision given them by Mother Nature. Miss Maxwell's glance was always meeting a pair of eager dark eyes; when she said anything particularly good, she looked for approval to the corner of the second bench, where every shade of feeling she wished to evoke was reflected on a certain sensitive young face.

One day, when the first essay of the class was under discussion, she asked each new pupil to bring her some composition written during the year before, that she might judge the work, and know precisely with what material she had to deal. Rebecca lingered after the others, and approached the desk shyly.

"I haven't any compositions here, Miss Maxwell, but I can find one when I go home on Friday. They are packed away in a box in the attic."

"Carefully tied with pink and blue ribbons?" asked Miss Maxwell, with a whimsical smile.

"No," answered Rebecca, shaking her head decidedly; "I wanted to use ribbons,because all the other girls did, and they looked so pretty, but I used to tie my essays with twine strings on purpose; and the one on 'Solitude' I fastened with an old shoelacing just to show it what I thought of it!"

"'Solitude'!" laughed Miss Maxwell, raising her eyebrows. "Did you choose your own subject?"

"No; Miss Dearborn thought we were not old enough to find good ones."

"What were some of the others?"

"'Fireside Reveries,' 'Grant as a Soldier,' 'Reflections on the Life of P. T. Barnum,' 'Buried Cities'; I can't remember any more now. They were all bad, and I can't bear to show them; I can write poetry easier and better, Miss Maxwell."

"Poetry!" she exclaimed. "Did Miss Dearborn require you to do it?"

"Oh, no; I always did it even at the farm. Shall I bring all I have? It isn't much."

Rebecca took the blank book in which she kept copies of her effusions and left it at Miss Maxwell's door, hoping that she might be asked in and thus obtain a private interview; but a servant answered her ring, and she could only walk away, disappointed.

A few days afterward she saw the black-covered book on Miss Maxwell's desk and knew that the dreaded moment of criticism had come, so she was not surprised to be asked to remain after class.

The room was quiet; the red leaves rustled in the breeze and flew in at the open window, bearing the first compliments of the season. Miss Maxwell came and sat by Rebecca's side on the bench.

"Did you think these were good?" she asked, giving her the verses.

"Not so very," confessed Rebecca; "but it's hard to tell all by yourself. The Perkinses and the Cobbs always said they were wonderful, but when Mrs. Cobb told me she thought they were better than Mr. Longfellow's I was worried, because I knew that couldn't be true."

This ingenuous remark confirmed Miss Maxwell's opinion of Rebecca as a girl who could hear the truth and profit by it.

"Well, my child," she said smilingly, "your friends were wrong and you were right; judged by the proper tests, they are pretty bad."

"Then I must give up all hope of ever being a writer!" sighed Rebecca, who was tasting the bitterness of hemlock and wondering if she could keep the tears back until the interview was over.

"Don't go so fast," interrupted Miss Maxwell. "Though they don't amount to anything as poetry, they show a good deal of promise in certain directions. You almost never make a mistake in rhyme or meter, and this shows you have a natural sense of what is right; a 'sense of form,' poets would call it. When you grow older, have a little more experience,—in fact, when you have something to say, I think you may write very good verses. Poetry needs knowledge and vision, experience and imagination, Rebecca. You have not the first three yet, but I rather think you have a touch of the last."

"Must I never try any more poetry, not even to amuse myself?"

"Certainly you may; it will only help you to write better prose. Now for the first composi-

tion. I am going to ask all the new students to write a letter giving some description of the town and a hint of the school life."

"Shall I have to be myself?" asked Rebecca.

"What do you mean?"

"A letter from Rebecca Randall to her sister Hannah at Sunnybrook Farm, or to her Aunt Jane at the brick house, Riverboro, is so dull and stupid, if it is a real letter; but if I could make-believe I was a different girl altogether, and write to somebody who would be sure to understand everything I said, I could make it nicer."

"Very well; I think that's a delightful plan," said Miss Maxwell; "and who will you suppose yourself to be?"

"I like heiresses very much," replied Rebecca contemplatively. "Of course I never saw one, but interesting things are always happening to heiresses, especially to the golden-haired kind. My heiress wouldn't be vain and haughty like the wicked sisters in 'Cinderella'; she would be noble and generous. She would give up a grand school in Boston because she wanted to come here where her father lived when he was a boy, long before he made his fortune. The father is dead now, and she has a guardian, the best and kindest man in the world; he is rather old of course, and sometimes very quiet and grave, but sometimes when he is happy, he is full of fun, and then Evelyn is not afraid of him. Yes, the girl shall be called Evelyn Abercrombie, and her guardian's name shall be Mr. Adam Ladd."

"Do you know Mr. Ladd?" asked Miss Maxwell in surprise.

"Yes, he's my very best friend," cried Rebecca delightedly. "Do you know him too?"

"Oh, yes; he is a trustee of these schools, you know, and often comes here. But if I let you 'suppose' any more, you will tell me your whole letter and then I shall lose a pleasant surprise."

What Rebecca thought of Miss Maxwell we already know; how the teacher regarded the pupil may be gathered from the following letter written two or three months later:—

WAREHAM, December 1st.

MY DEAR FATHER,—As you well know, I have

136

not always been an enthusiast on the subject of teaching. The task of cramming knowledge into these self-sufficient, inefficient youngsters of both sexes discourages me at times. The more stupid they are, the less they are aware of it.

If my department were geography or mathematics, I believe I should feel that I was accomplishing something, for in those branches application and industry work wonders; but in English literature and composition one yearns for brains, for appreciation, for imagination! Month after month I toil on, opening oyster after oyster, but seldom finding a pearl.

Fancy my joy this term when, without any violent effort at shell-splitting, I came upon a rare pearl; a black one, but of satin skin and beautiful luster! Her name is Rebecca, and she looks not unlike Rebekah at the Well in our family Bible; her hair and eyes being so dark as to suggest a strain of Italian or Spanish blood. She is nobody in particular. Man has done nothing for her; she has no family to speak of, no money, no education worthy the name, has had no advantages of any sort; but Dame Nature flung herself into the breach and said:—

> This child I to myself will take;
> She shall be mine and I will make
> A Lady of my own.

Blessed Wordsworth! How he makes us understand! And the pearl never heard of him until now! Think of reading Lucy to a class, and when you finish, seeing a fourteen-year-old pair of lips quivering with delight, and a pair of eyes brimming with comprehending tears!

You poor darling! You, too, know the discouragement of sowing lovely seed in rocky earth, in sand, in water, and (it almost seems sometimes) in mud; knowing that if anything comes up at all it will be some poor starveling plant. Fancy the joy of finding a real mind; of dropping seed in a soil so warm, so fertile, that one knows there are sure to be foliage, blossoms, and fruit all in good time! I wish I were not so impatient and so greedy of results! I am not fit to be a teacher; no one is who is so scornful of stupidity as I am. . . .

The pearl writes quaint countrified little verses, doggerel they are; but somehow or other she always contrives to put in one line, one thought, one image, that shows you she is, quite unconsciously to herself, in possession of the secret. . . . Good-bye; I'll bring Rebecca home with me some Friday, and let you and mother see her for yourselves.

Your affectionate daughter,
EMILY.

19
CLOVER BLOSSOMS AND SUNFLOWERS

"How d' ye do, girls?" said Huldah Meserve, peeping in at the door. "Can you stop studying a minute and show me your room? Say, I've just been down to the store and bought me these gloves, for I was bound I wouldn't wear mittens this winter; they're simply too countrified. It's your first year here, and you're younger than I am, so I s'pose you don't mind, but I simply suffer if I don't keep up some kind of style. Say, your room is simply too cute for words! I don't believe any of the others can begin to compare with it! I don't know what gives it that simply gorgeous look, whether it's the full curtains, or that elegant screen, or Rebecca's lamp; but you certainly do have a faculty for fixing up. I like a pretty room too, but I never have a minute to attend to mine; I'm always so busy on my clothes that half the time I don't get my bed made up till noon; and after all, having no callers but the girls, it don't make much difference. When I graduate, I'm going to fix up our parlor at home so it'll be simply regal. I've learned decalcomania, and after I take up luster painting I shall have it simply stiff with drapes and tidies and plaques and sofa pillows, and make mother let me have a fire, and receive my friends there evenings. May I dry my feet at your register? I can't bear to wear rubbers unless the mud or the slush is simply knee-deep, they make your feet look so awfully big. I had such a fuss getting this pair of French-heeled boots that I don't intend to spoil the looks of them with rubbers any oftener than I can help. I believe boys notice feet quicker than anything. Elmer Webster stepped on one of mine yesterday when I accidentally had it out in the aisle, and when he apologized after class, he said he wasn't so much to blame, for the foot was so little he really couldn't see it! Isn't he perfectly great? Of course that's only his way of talking, for after all I only wear a number two, but these French heels and pointed toes do certainly make your foot look smaller, and it's always said a high instep helps, too. I used to think mine was almost a deformity, but they say it's a great beauty. Just put your feet beside mine, girls, and look at the difference; not that I care much, but just for fun."

"My feet are very comfortable where they are," responded Rebecca dryly. "I can't stop to measure insteps on algebra days; I've noticed your habit of keeping a foot in the aisle ever since you had those new shoes, so I don't wonder it was stepped on."

"Perhaps I am a little mite conscious of them, because they're not so very comfortable at first, till you get them broken in. Say, haven't you got a lot of new things?"

"Our Christmas presents, you mean," said Emma Jane. "The pillowcases are from Mrs. Cobb, the rug from cousin Mary in North Riverboro, the scrapbasket from Living and Dick. We gave each other the bureau and cushion covers, and the screen is mine from Mr. Ladd."

"Well, you were lucky when you met him! Gracious! I wish I could meet somebody like that. The way he keeps it up, too! It just hides your bed, doesn't it, and I always say that a bed takes the style off any room—specially when it's not made up; though you have an alcove, and it's the only one in the whole building. I don't see how you managed to get this good room when you're such new scholars," she finished discontentedly.

"We shouldn't have, except that Ruth Berry had to go away suddenly on account of her father's death. This room was empty, and Miss Maxwell asked if we might have it," returned Emma Jane.

"The great and only Max is more stiff and stand-offish than ever this year," said Huldah. "I've simply given up trying to please her, for there's no justice in her; she is good to her favorites, but she doesn't pay the least attention to anybody else, except to make sarcastic speeches about things that are none of her business. I wanted to tell her yesterday it was her place to teach me Latin, not manners."

"I wish you wouldn't talk against Miss Maxwell to me," said Rebecca hotly. "You know how I feel."

"I know; but I can't understand how you can abide her."

"I not only abide, I love her!" exclaimed Rebecca. "I wouldn't let the sun shine too hot on her, or the wind blow too cold. I'd like to put a marble platform in her classroom and have her sit in a velvet chair behind a golden table!"

"Well, don't have a fit!—because she can sit where she likes for all of me; I've got something better to think of." And Huldah tossed her head.

"Isn't this your study hour?" asked Emma Jane, to stop possible discussion.

"Yes, but I lost my Latin grammar yesterday; I left it in the hall half an hour while I was having a regular scene with Herbert Dunn. I haven't spoken to him for a week and gave him back his class pin. He was simply furious. Then when I came back to the hall, the book was gone. I had to go down town for my gloves and to the principal's office to see if the grammar had been handed in, and that's the reason I'm so fine."

Huldah was wearing a woolen dress that had once been gray, but had been dyed a brilliant blue. She had added three rows of white braid and large white pearl buttons to her gray jacket, in order to make it a little more "dressy." Her gray felt hat had a white feather on it, and a white tissue veil with large black dots made her delicate skin look brilliant. Rebecca thought how lovely the knot of red hair looked under the hat behind, and how the color of the front had been dulled by incessant frizzing with curling irons. Her open jacket disclosed a galaxy of souvenirs pinned to the background of bright blue, —a small American flag, a button of the Wareham Rowing Club, and one or two society pins. These decorations proved her popularity in very much the same way as do the cotillion favors hanging on the bedroom

138

walls of the fashionable belle. She had been pinning and unpinning, arranging and disarranging her veil ever since she entered the room, in the hope that the girls would ask her whose ring she was wearing this week; but although both had noticed the new ornament instantly, wild horses could not have drawn the question from them; her desire to be asked was too obvious. With her gay plumage, her "nods and becks and wreathèd smiles," and her cheerful cackle, Huldah closely resembled the parrot in Wordsworth's poem:—

> Arch, volatile, a sportive bird,
>   By social glee inspired;
> Ambitious to be seen or heard,
>   And pleased to be admired!

"Mr. Morrison thinks the grammar will be returned, and lent me another," Huldah continued. "He was rather snippy about my leaving a book in the hall. There was a perfectly elegant gentleman in the office, a stranger to me. I wish he was a new teacher, but there's no such luck. He was too young to be the father of any of the girls, and too old to be a brother, but he was handsome as a picture and had on an awful stylish suit of clothes. He looked at me about every minute I was in the room. It made me so embarrassed I couldn't hardly answer Mr. Morrison's questions straight."

"You'll have to wear a mask pretty soon, if you're going to have any comfort, Huldah," said Rebecca. "Did he offer to lend you his class pin, or has it been so long since he graduated that he's left off wearing it? And tell us now whether the principal asked for a lock of your hair to put in his watch?"

This was all said merrily and laughingly, but there were times when Huldah could scarcely make up her mind whether Rebecca was trying to be witty, or whether she was jealous; but she generally decided it was merely the latter feeling, rather natural in a girl who had little attention.

"He wore no jewelry but a cameo scarf pin and a perfectly gorgeous ring,—a queer kind of one that wound round and round his finger. Oh, dear, I must run! Where has the hour gone? There's the study bell!"

Rebecca had pricked up her ears at Huldah's speech. She remembered a certain strange ring, and it belonged to the only person in the world (save Miss Maxwell) who appealed to her imagination,—Mr. Aladdin. Her feeling for him, and that of Emma Jane, was a mixture of romantic and reverent admiration for the man himself and the liveliest gratitude for his beautiful gifts. Since they first met him not a Christmas had gone by without some remembrance for them both; remembrances chosen with the rarest taste and forethought. Emma Jane had seen him only twice, but he had called several times at the brick house, and Rebecca had learned to know him better. It was she, too, who always wrote the notes of acknowledgment and thanks, taking infinite pains to make Emma Jane's quite different from her own. Sometimes he had written from Boston and asked her the news of Riverboro, and she had sent him pages of quaint and childlike gossip, interspersed, on two occasions, with poetry, which he read and reread with infinite relish. If Huldah's stranger should be Mr. Aladdin, would he come to see her, and could she and Emma Jane show him their beautiful room with so many of his gifts in evidence?

When the girls had established themselves in Wareham as real boarding pupils, it seemed to them existence was as full of joy as it well could hold. This first winter was, in fact, the most tranquilly happy of Rebecca's school life,—a winter long to be looked back upon. She and Emma Jane were roommates, and had put their modest possessions together to make their surroundings pretty and homelike. The room had, to begin with, a cheerful red ingrain carpet and a set of maple furniture. As to the rest, Rebecca had furnished the ideas and Emma Jane the materials and labor, a method of dividing responsibilities that seemed to suit the circumstances admirably. Mrs. Perkins's father had been a storekeeper, and on his death had left the goods of which he was possessed to his married daughter. The molasses, vinegar, and kerosene had lasted the family for five years, and the Perkins attic was still a treasure-house of ginghams, cottons, and "Yankee notions." So at Rebecca's instigation Mrs. Perkins had made full curtains and lambrequins of unbleached muslin, which she had trimmed and looped back with bands of Turkey red cotton. There were two table covers to match, and each of the girls had her study corner. Rebecca, after much coaxing, had been allowed to bring over her precious lamp, which would have given a luxurious air to any apartment, and when Mr. Aladdin's last Christmas presents were added,— the Japanese screen for Emma Jane and the little shelf of English Poets for Rebecca,— they declared that it was all quite as much fun as being married and going into housekeeping.

The day of Huldah's call was Friday, and on Fridays from three to half-past four Rebecca was free to take a pleasure to which

she looked forward the entire week. She always ran down the snowy path through the pine woods at the back of the seminary, and coming out on a quiet village street, went directly to the large white house where Miss Maxwell lived. The maid-of-all-work answered her knock; she took off her hat and cape and hung them in the hall, put her rubber shoes and umbrella carefully in the corner, and then opened the door of paradise. Miss Maxwell's sitting room was lined on two sides with bookshelves, and Rebecca was allowed to sit before the fire and browse among the books to her heart's delight for an hour or more. Then Miss Maxwell would come back from her class, and there would be a precious half hour of chat before Rebecca had to meet Emma Jane at the station and take the train for Riverboro, where her Saturdays and Sundays were spent, and where she was washed, ironed, mended, and examined, approved and reproved, warned and advised in quite sufficient quantity to last her the succeeding week.

On this Friday she buried her face in the blooming geraniums on Miss Maxwell's plantstand, selected "Romola" from one of the bookcases, and sank into a seat by the window with a sigh of infinite content. She glanced at the clock now and then, remembering the day on which she had been so immersed in "David Copperfield" that the Riverboro train had no place in her mind. The distracted Emma Jane had refused to leave without her, and had run from the station to look for her at Miss Maxwell's. There was but one later train, and that went only to a place three miles the other side of Riverboro, so that the two girls appeared at their respective homes long after dark, having had a weary walk in the snow.

When she had read for half an hour she glanced out of the window and saw two figures issuing from the path through the woods. The knot of bright hair and the coquettish hat could belong to but one person; and her companion, as the couple approached, proved to be none other than Mr. Aladdin. Huldah was lifting her skirts daintily and picking safe stepping-places for the high-heeled shoes, her cheeks glowing, her eyes sparkling under the black and white veil.

Rebecca slipped from her post by the window to the rug before the bright fire and leaned her head on the seat of the great easy-chair. She was frightened at the storm in her heart; at the suddenness with which it had come on, as well as at the strangeness of an entirely new sensation. She felt all at once as if she could not bear to give up her share of Mr. Aladdin's friendship to Huldah: Huldah so bright, saucy, and pretty; so gay and ready, and such good company! She had always joyfully admitted Emma Jane into the precious partnership, but perhaps unconsciously to herself she had realized that Emma Jane had never held anything but a secondary place in Mr. Aladdin's regard; yet who was she herself, after all, that she could hope to be first?

Suddenly the door opened softly and somebody looked in, somebody who said: "Miss Maxwell told me I should find Miss Rebecca Randall here."

Rebecca started at the sound and sprang to her feet, saying joyfully, "Mr. Aladdin! Oh! I knew you were in Wareham, and I was afraid you wouldn't have time to come and see us."

"Who is 'us'? The aunts are not here, are they? Oh, you mean the rich blacksmith's daughter, whose name I can never remember. Is she here?"

"Yes, and my roommate," answered Rebecca, who thought her own knell of doom had sounded, if he had forgotten Emma Jane's name.

The light in the room grew softer, the fire crackled cheerily, and they talked of many things, until the old sweet sense of friendliness and familiarity crept back into Rebecca's heart. Adam had not seen her for several months, and there was much to be learned about school matters as viewed from her own standpoint; he had already inquired concerning her progress from Mr. Morrison.

"Well, little Miss Rebecca," he said, rousing himself at length, "I must be thinking of my drive to Portland. There is a meeting of railway directors there to-morrow, and I always take this opportunity of visiting the

142

school and giving my valuable advice concerning its affairs, educational and financial."

"It seems funny for you to be a school trustee," said Rebecca contemplatively. "I can't seem to make it fit."

"You are a remarkably wise young person and I quite agree with you," he answered; "the fact is," he added soberly, "I accepted the trusteeship in memory of my poor little mother, whose last happy years were spent here."

"That was a long time ago!"

"Let me see, I am thirty-two; only thirty-two, despite an occasional gray hair. My mother was married a month after she graduated, and she lived only until I was ten; yes, it is a long way back to my mother's time here, though the school was fifteen or twenty years old then, I believe. Would you like to see my mother, Miss Rebecca?"

The girl took the leather case gently and opened it to find an innocent, pink-and-white daisy of a face, so confiding, so sensitive, that it went straight to the heart. It made Rebecca feel old, experienced, and maternal. She longed on the instant to comfort and strengthen such a tender young thing.

"Oh, what a sweet, sweet, flowery face!" she whispered softly.

"The flower had to bear all sorts of storms," said Adam gravely. "The bitter weather of the world bent its slender stalk, bowed its head, and dragged it to the earth. I was only a child and could do nothing to protect and nourish it, and there was no one else to stand between it and trouble. Now I have success and money and power, all that would have kept her alive and happy, and it is too late. She died for lack of love and care, nursing and cherishing, and I can never forget it. All that has come to me seems now and then so useless, since I cannot share it with her!"

This was a new Mr. Aladdin, and Rebecca's heart gave a throb of sympathy and comprehension. This explained the tired look in his eyes, the look that peeped out now and then, under all his gay speech and laughter.

"I'm so glad I know," she said, "and so glad I could see her just as she was when she tied that white muslin hat under her chin and saw her yellow curls and her sky-blue eyes in the glass. Mustn't she have been happy! I wish she could have been kept so, and have lived to see you grow up strong and good. My mother is always sad and busy, but once when she looked at John I heard her say, 'He makes up for everything.' That's what your mother would have thought about you if she had lived,—and perhaps she does as it is."

"You are a comforting little person, Rebecca," said Adam, rising from his chair.

As Rebecca rose, the tears still trembling on her lashes, he looked at her suddenly as with new vision.

"Good-bye!" he said, taking her slim brown hands in his, adding, as if he saw her for the first time, "Why, little Rose-Red-Snow-White is making way for a new girl! Burning the midnight oil and doing four years' work in three is supposed to dull the eye and blanch the cheek, yet Rebecca's eyes are bright and she has a rosy color! Her long braids are looped one on the other so that they make a black letter U behind, and they are tied with grand bows at the top! She is so tall that she reaches almost to my shoulder. This will never do in the world! How will Mr. Aladdin get on without his comforting little friend! He doesn't like grown-up young ladies in long trains and wonderful fine clothes; they frighten and bore him!"

"Oh, Mr. Aladdin!" cried Rebecca eagerly, taking his jest quite seriously; "I am not fifteen yet, and it will be three years before I'm a young lady; please don't give me up until you have to!"

"I won't; I promise you that," said Adam. "Rebecca," he continued, after a moment's pause, "who is that young girl with a lot of pretty red hair and very citified manners? She escorted me down the hill; do you know whom I mean?"

"It must be Huldah Meserve; she is from Riverboro."

Adam put a finger under Rebecca's chin and looked into her eyes; eyes as soft, as clear, as unconscious, and childlike as they had been when she was ten. He remembered the other pair of challenging blue ones that had darted coquettish glances through half-dropped lids, shot arrowy beams from under archly lifted brows, and said gravely, "Don't form yourself on her, Rebecca; clover blossoms that grow in the fields beside Sunnybrook mustn't be tied in the same bouquet with gaudy sunflowers; they are too sweet and fragrant and wholesome."

20
THE HILL DIFFICULTY

The first happy year at Wareham, with its widened skyline, its larger vision, its greater opportunity, was over and gone. Rebecca had studied during the summer vacation, and had passed, on her return in the autumn, certain examinations which would enable her, if she carried out the same programme the next season, to complete the course in three instead of four years. She came off with no flying colors,—that would have been impossible in consideration of her inadequate training; but she did wonderfully well in some of the required subjects, and so brilliantly in others that the average was respectable. She would never have been a remarkable scholar under any circumstances, perhaps, and she was easily outstripped in mathematics and the natural sciences by a dozen girls, but in some inexplicable way she became, as the months went on, the foremost figure in the school. When she had entirely forgotten the facts which would enable her to answer a question fully and conclusively, she commonly had some original theory to expound; it was not always correct, but it was generally unique and sometimes amusing. She was only fair in Latin or French grammar, but when it came to translation, her freedom, her choice of words, and her sympathetic understanding of the spirit of the text made her the delight of her teachers and the despair of her rivals.

"She can be perfectly ignorant of a subject," said Miss Maxwell to Adam Ladd, "but entirely intelligent the moment she has a clue. Most of the other girls are full of information and as stupid as sheep."

Rebecca's gifts had not been discovered save by the few, during the first year, when she was adjusting herself quietly to the situation. She was distinctly one of the poorer girls; she had no fine dresses to attract attention, no visitors, no friends in the town. She had more study hours, and less time, therefore, for the companionship of other girls, gladly as she would have welcomed the gayety of that side of school life. Still, water will find its own level in some way, and by the spring of the second year she had naturally settled into the same sort of leadership which had been hers in the smaller community of Riverboro. She was unanimously elected assistant editor of the Wareham School "Pilot," being the first girl to assume that enviable, though somewhat arduous and thankless position, and when news of this reached the Cobbs, Uncle Jerry and Aunt Sarah could hardly eat or sleep for pride.

"She'll always get votes," said Huldah Meserve, when discussing the election, "for whether she knows anything or not, she looks as if she did, and whether she's capable of filling an office or not, she looks as if she was. I only wish I was tall and dark and had the gift of making people believe I was great things, like Rebecca Randall. There's one thing: though the boys call her handsome, you notice they don't trouble her with much attention."

It was a fact that Rebecca's attitude towards the opposite sex was still somewhat indifferent and oblivious, even for fifteen and a half! No one could look at her and doubt that she had potentialities of attraction latent within her somewhere, but that side of her nature was happily biding its time. A human being is capable only of a certain amount of activity at a given moment, and it will inevitably satisfy first its most pressing needs, its most ardent desires, its chief ambitions. Rebecca was full of small anxieties and fears, for matters were not going well at the brick house, and were anything but hopeful at the home farm. She was overbusy and overtaxed, and her thoughts were naturally drawn towards

the difficult problems of daily living.

It had seemed to her during the autumn and winter of that year as if her Aunt Miranda had never been, save at the very first, so censorious and so fault-finding. One Saturday Rebecca ran upstairs and, bursting into a flood of tears, exclaimed, "Aunt Jane, it seems as if I never could stand her continual scoldings. Nothing I can do suits Aunt Miranda; she's just said it will take me my whole life to get the Randall out of me, and I'm not convinced that I want it all out, so there we are!"

Aunt Jane, never demonstrative, cried with Rebecca as she attempted to soothe her.

"You must be patient," she said, wiping first her own eyes and then Rebecca's. I haven't told you, for it isn't fair you should be troubled when you're studying so hard, but your Aunt Miranda isn't well. One Monday morning about a month ago, she had a kind of faint spell; it wasn't bad but the doctor is afraid it was a shock, and if so, it's the beginning of the end. Seems to me she's failing right along, and that's what makes her so fretful and easily vexed. She has other troubles too, that you don't know anything about, and if you're not kind to your Aunt Miranda now, child, you'll be dreadful sorry some time."

All the temper faded from Rebecca's face, and she stopped crying to say penitently, "Oh! The poor dear thing! I won't mind a bit what she says now. She's just asked me for some milk toast and I was dreading to take it to her, but this will make everything different. Don't worry yet, Aunt Jane, for perhaps it won't be as bad as you think."

So when she carried the toast to her aunt a little later, it was in the best gilt-edged china bowl, with a fringed napkin on the tray and a sprig of geranium lying across the saltcellar.

"Now, Aunt Miranda," she said cheerily, "I expect you to smack your lips and say this is good; it's not Randall, but Sawyer milk toast."

"You've tried all kinds on me, one time an' another," Miranda answered. "This tastes real kind o' good; but I wish you hadn't wasted that nice geranium."

"You can't tell what's wasted," said Rebecca philosophically; "perhaps that geranium has been hoping this long time it could brighten somebody's supper, so don't disappoint it by making believe you don't like it. I've seen geraniums cry,—in the very early morning!"

The mysterious trouble to which Jane had alluded was a very real one, but it was held in profound secrecy. Twenty-five hundred dollars of the small Sawyer property had been invested in the business of a friend of their father's, and had returned them a regular annual income of a hundred dollars. The family friend had been dead for some five years, but his son had succeeded to his interests and all went on as formerly. Suddenly there came a letter saying that the firm had gone into bankruptcy, that the business had been completely wrecked, and that the Sawyer money had been swept away with everything else.

The loss of one hundred dollars a year is a very trifling matter, but it made all the difference between comfort and self-denial to the two old spinsters. Their manner of life had been so rigid and careful that it was difficult to economize any further, and the blow had fallen just when it was most inconvenient, for Rebecca's school and boarding expenses, small as they were, had to be paid promptly and in cash.

"Can we possibly go on doing it? Shan't we have to give up and tell her why?" asked Jane tearfully of the elder sister.

"We have put our hand to the plough, and we can't turn back," answered Miranda in her grimmest tone; "we've taken her away from her mother and offered her an education, and we've got to keep our word. She's Aurelia's only hope for years to come, to my way o' thinkin'. Hannah's beau takes all her time 'n' thought, and when she gits a husband her mother'll be out o' sight and out o' mind. John, instead of farmin', thinks he must be a doctor,—as if folks wasn't gettin' unhealthy enough these days, without turnin' out more young doctors to help 'em into their graves. No, Jane; we'll skimp 'n' do without, 'n' plan to git along on our interest money somehow, but we won't break into our principal, whatever happens."

"Breaking into the principal" was, in the minds of most thrifty New England women, a sin only second to arson, theft, or murder; and, though the rule was occasionally carried too far for common sense,—as in this case, where two elderly women of sixty might reasonably have drawn something from their little hoard in time of special need,—it doubtless wrought more of good than evil in the community.

Rebecca, who knew nothing of their business affairs, merely saw her aunts grow more and more saving, pinching here and there, cutting off this and that relentlessly. Less meat and fish were bought; the woman who had lately been coming two days a week for washing, ironing, and scrubbing was dismissed; the old bonnets of the season before were brushed up and retrimmed; there were no drives to Moderation or trips to Portland. Economy was carried to its very extreme; but though Miranda was well-nigh as gloomy and uncompromising in her manner and conversation as a woman could well be, she at least never twitted her niece of being a burden; so Rebecca's share of the Sawyers' misfortunes consisted only in wearing her old dresses, hats, and jackets, without any apparent hope of a change.

There was, however, no concealing the state of things at Sunnybrook, where chapters of accidents had unfolded themselves in a sort of serial story that had run through the year. The potato crop had failed; there were no apples to speak of; the hay had been poor; Aurelia had turns of dizziness in her head; Mark had broken his ankle. As this was his fourth offense, Miranda inquired how many bones there were in the human body, "so 't they'd know when Mark got through breakin' 'em." The time for paying the interest on the mortgage, that incubus that had crushed all the joy out of the Randall household, had come and gone, and there was no possibility, for the first time in fourteen years, of paying the required forty-eight dollars. The only bright spot in the horizon was Hannah's engagement to Will Melville, —a young farmer whose land joined Sunnybrook, who had a good house, was alone in

the world, and his own master. Hannah was so satisfied with her own unexpectedly radiant prospects that she hardly realized her mother's anxieties; for there are natures which flourish in adversity, and deteriorate when exposed to sudden prosperity. She had made a visit of a week at the brick house; and Miranda's impression, conveyed in privacy to Jane, was that Hannah was close as the bark of a tree, and consid'able selfish too; that when she'd clim' as fur as she could in the world, she'd kick the ladder out from under her, everlastin' quick; that, on being sounded as to her ability to be of use to the younger children in the future, she said she guessed she'd done her share a'ready, and she wa'nt goin' to burden Will with her poor relations. "She's Susan Randall through and through!" ejaculated Miranda. "I was glad to see her face turned towards Temperance. If that mortgage is ever cleared from the farm, 't won't be Hannah that'll do it; it'll be Rebecca or me!"

21
ALADDIN RUBS HIS LAMP

Your esteemed contribution entitled 'Wareham Wildflowers' has been accepted for 'The Pilot,' Miss Perkins," said Rebecca, entering the room where Emma Jane was darning the firm's stockings. "I stayed to tea with Miss Maxwell, but came home early to tell you."

"You are joking, Becky!" faltered Emma Jane, looking up from her work.

"Not a bit; the senior editor read it and thought it highly instructive; it appears in the next issue."

"Not in the same number with your poem about the golden gates that close behind us when we leave school?" And Emma Jane held her breath as she awaited the reply.

"Even so, Miss Perkins."

"Rebecca," said Emma Jane, with the nearest approach to tragedy that her nature would permit, "I don't know as I shall be able to bear it, and if anything happens to me, I ask you solemnly to bury that number of 'The Pilot' with me."

Rebecca did not seem to think this the expression of an exaggerated state of feeling, inasmuch as she replied, "I know; that's just the way it seemed to me at first, and even now, whenever I'm alone and take out the 'Pilot' back numbers to read over my contributions, I almost burst with pleasure; and it's not that they are good either, for they look worse to me every time I read them."

"If you would only live with me in some little house when we get older," mused Emma Jane, as with her darning needle poised in air she regarded the opposite wall dreamily, "I would do the housework and cooking, and copy all your poems and stories, and take them to the post office, and you needn't do anything but write. It would be perfectly elergant!"

"I'd like nothing better, if I hadn't promised to keep house for John," replied Rebecca.

"He won't have a house for a good many years, will he?"

"No," sighed Rebecca ruefully, flinging herself down by the table and resting her head on her hand. "Not unless we can contrive to pay off that detestable mortgage. The day grows farther off instead of nearer now that we haven't paid the interest this year."

She pulled a piece of paper towards her, and scribbling idly on it read aloud in a moment or two:—

"Will you pay a little faster?" said the mortgage to the farm;
"I confess I'm very tired of this place."
"The weariness is mutual," Rebecca Randall cried;
"I would I'd never gazed upon your face!"

"A note has a 'face,'" observed Emma Jane, who was gifted in arithmetic. "I didn't know that a mortgage had."

"Our mortgage has," said Rebecca revengefully. "I should know him if I met him in the dark. Wait and I'll draw him for you. It will be good for you to know how he looks, and then when you have a husband and seven children, you won't allow him to come anywhere within a mile of your farm."

The sketch when completed was of a sort to be shunned by a timid person on the verge of slumber. There was a tiny house on the right, and a weeping family gathered in front of it. The mortgage was depicted as a cross between a fiend and an ogre, and held an axe uplifted in his red right hand. A figure with streaming black locks was staying the blow, and this, Rebecca explained complacently, was intended as a likeness of herself, though she was rather vague as to the method she should use in attaining her end.

"He's terrible," said Emma Jane, "but awfully wizened and small."

"It's only a twelve-hundred-dollar mortgage," said Rebecca, "and that's called a small one. John saw a man once that was mortgaged for twelve thousand."

"Shall you be a writer or an editor?" asked Emma Jane presently, as if one had only to choose and the thing were done.

"I shall have to do what turns up first, I suppose."

"Why not go out as a missionary to Syria, as the Burches are always coaxing you to? The Board would pay your expenses."

"I can't make up my mind to be a missionary," Rebecca answered. "I'm not good enough in the first place, and I don't 'feel a call,' as Mr. Burch says you must. I would like to do something for somebody and make things move, somewhere, but I don't want to go thousands of miles away teaching people how to live when I haven't learned myself. It isn't as if the heathen really needed me; I'm sure they'll come out all right in the end."

"I can't see how; if all the people who ought to go out to save them stay at home as we do," argued Emma Jane.

"Why, whatever God is, and wherever He is, He must always be there, ready and waiting. He can't move about and miss people. It may take the heathen a little longer to find Him, but God will make allowances, of course. He knows if they live in such hot climates it must make them lazy and slow; and the parrots and tigers and snakes and breadfruit trees distract their minds; and having no books, they can't think as well; but they'll find God somehow, sometime."

"What if they die first?" asked Emma Jane.

"Oh, well, they can't be blamed for that; they don't die on purpose," said Rebecca, with a comfortable theology.

In these days Adam Ladd sometimes went to Temperance on business connected with the proposed branch of the railroad familiarly known as the "York and Yank 'em," and while there he gained an inkling of Sunnybrook affairs. The building of the new road was not yet a certainty, and there was a difference of opinion as to the best route from Temperance to Plumville. In one event the way would lead directly through Sunnybrook, from corner to corner, and Mrs. Randall would be compensated; in the other, her interests would not be affected, either for good or ill, save as all land in the immediate neighborhood might rise a little in value.

Coming from Temperance to Wareham one day, Adam had a long walk and talk with Rebecca, whom he thought looking pale and thin, though she was holding bravely to her self-imposed hours of work. She was wearing a black cashmere dress that had been her Aunt Jane's second best. We are familiar with the heroine of romance whose foot is so exquisitely shaped that the coarsest shoe cannot conceal its perfections, and one always cherishes a doubt of the statement; yet it is true that Rebecca's peculiar and individual charm seemed wholly independent of accessories. The lines of her figure, the rare coloring of skin and hair and eyes, triumphed over shabby clothing, though, had the advantage of artistic apparel been given her, the little world of Wareham would probably at once have dubbed her a beauty. The long black braids were now disposed after a quaint fashion of her own. They were crossed behind, carried up to the front, and crossed again, the tapering ends finally brought down and hidden in the thicker part at the neck. Then a purely feminine touch was given to the hair that waved back from the face,—a touch that rescued little crests and wavelets from bondage and set them free to take a new color in the sun.

Adam Ladd looked at her in a way that made her put her hands over her face and laugh through them shyly as she said: "I know what you are thinking, Mr. Aladdin,—that my dress is an inch longer than last year, and my hair different; but I'm not nearly a young lady yet; truly I'm not. Sixteen is a month off still, and you promised not to give me up till my dress trails. If you don't like me to grow old, why don't you grow young? Then we can meet in the halfway house and have nice times. Now that I think about it," she continued, "that's just what you've been doing all along. When you bought the soap, I though you were Grandfather Sawyer's age; when you danced with me at the flag-raising, you seemed like my father; but when you showed me your mother's picture, I felt as if you were my John, because I was so sorry for you."

"That will do very well," smiled Adam; "unless you go so swiftly that you become my grandmother before I really need one. You are studying too hard, Miss Rebecca Rowena!"

"Just a little," she confessed. "But vacation comes soon, you know."

"And are you going to have a good rest and try to recover your dimples? They are really worth preserving."

A shadow crept over Rebecca's face and her eyes suffused. "Don't be kind, Mr. Aladdin, I can't bear it;—it's—it's not one of my dimply days!" And she ran in at the seminary gate, and disappeared with a farewell wave of her hand.

Adam Ladd wended his way to the principal's office in a thoughtful mood. He had come to Wareham to unfold a plan that he had been considering for several days. This year was the fiftieth anniversary of the founding of the Wareham schools, and he meant to tell Mr. Morrison that in addition to his gift of a hundred volumes to the reference library, he intended to celebrate it by offering prizes in English composition, a subject in which he was much interested. He wished the boys and girls of the two upper classes to compete; the award to be made to the writers of the two best essays. As to the nature of the prizes he had not quite made up his mind, but they would be substantial ones, either of money or of books.

This interview accomplished, he called upon Miss Maxwell, thinking as he took the path through the woods, "Rose-Red-Snow-White needs the help, and since there is no way of my giving it to her without causing remark, she must earn it, poor little soul! I wonder if my money is always to be useless where most I wish to spend it!"

He had scarcely greeted his hostess when he said: "Miss Maxwell doesn't it strike you that our friend Rebecca looks wretchedly tired?"

"She does indeed, and I am considering whether I can take her away with me. I always go South for the spring vacation, traveling by sea to Old Point Comfort, and rusticating in some quiet spot near by. I should like nothing better than to have Rebecca for a companion."

"The very thing!" assented Adam heartily; "but why should you take the whole responsibility? Why not let me help? I am greatly interested in the child, and have been for some years."

"You needn't pretend you discovered her," interrupted Miss Maxwell warmly, "for I did that myself."

"She was an intimate friend of mine long before you ever came to Wareham," laughed Adam, and he told Miss Maxwell the circumstances of his first meeting with Rebecca. "From the beginning I've tried to think of a way I could be useful in her development, but no reasonable solution seemed to offer itself."

"Luckily she attends to her own development," answered Miss Maxwell. "In a sense she is independent of everything and everybody; she follows her saint without being conscious of it. But she needs a hundred practical things that money would buy for her, and alas! I have a slender purse."

"Take mine, I beg, and let me act through you," pleaded Adam. "I could not bear to see even a young tree trying its best to grow without light or air,—how much less a gifted child! I interviewed her aunts a year ago, hoping I might be permitted to give her a musical education. I assured them it was a most

150

ordinary occurrence, and that I was willing to be repaid later on if they insisted, but it was no use. The elder Miss Sawyer remarked that no member of her family ever had lived on charity, and she guessed they wouldn't begin at this late day."

"I rather like that uncompromising New England grit," exclaimed Miss Maxwell, "and so far, I don't regret one burden that Rebecca has borne or one sorrow that she has shared. Necessity has only made her brave; poverty has only made her daring and self-reliant. As to her present needs, there are certain things only a woman ought to do for a girl, and I should not like to have you do them for Rebecca; I should feel that I was wounding her pride and self-respect, even though she were ignorant; but there is no reason why I may not do them if necessary and let you pay her traveling expenses. I would accept those for her without the slightest embarrassment, but I agree that the matter would better be kept private between us."

"You are a real fairy godmother!" exclaimed Adam, shaking her hand warmly. "Would it be less trouble for you to invite her roommate too,—the pink-and-white inseparable?"

"No, thank you, I prefer to have Rebecca all to myself," said Miss Maxwell.

"I can understand that," replied Adam absent-mindedly; "I mean, of course, that one child is less trouble than two. There she is now."

Here Rebecca appeared in sight, walking down the quiet street with a lad of sixteen. They were in animated conversation, and were apparently reading something aloud to each other, for the black head and the curly brown one were both bent over a sheet of letter paper. Rebecca kept glancing up at her companion, her eyes sparkling with appreciation.

"Miss Maxwell," said Adam, "I am a trustee of this institution, but upon my word I don't believe in coeducation!"

"I have my own occasional hours of doubt," she answered, "but surely its disadvantages are reduced to a minimum with—children! That is a very impressive sight which you are privileged to witness, Mr.

Ladd. The folk in Cambridge often gloated on the spectacle of Longfellow and Lowell arm in arm. The little school world of Wareham palpitates with excitement when it sees the senior and the junior editors of 'The Pilot' walking together!"

22
"OVER THE TEACUPS"

The summer term at Wareham had ended, and Huldah Meserve, Dick Carter, and Living Perkins had finished school, leaving Rebecca and Emma Jane to represent Riverboro in the year to come. Delia Weeks was at home from Lewiston on a brief visit, and Mrs. Robinson was celebrating the occasion by a small and select party, the particular day having been set because strawberries were ripe and there was a rooster that wanted killing. Mrs. Robinson explained this to her husband, and requested that he eat his dinner on the carpenter's bench in the shed, as the party was to be a ladies' affair.

"All right; it won't be any loss to me," said Mr. Robinson. "Give me beans, that's all I ask. When a rooster wants to be killed, I want somebody else to eat him, not me!"

Mrs. Robinson had company only once or twice a year, and was generally much prostrated for several days afterward, the struggle between pride and parsimony being quite too great a strain upon her. It was necessary, in order to maintain her standing in the community, to furnish a good "set out," yet the extravagance of the proceeding goaded her from the first moment she began to stir the marble cake to the moment when the feast appeared upon the table.

The rooster had been boiling steadily over a slow fire since morning, but such was his power of resistance that his shape was as firm and handsome in the pot as on the first moment when he was lowered into it.

"He ain't goin' to give up!" said Alice,

151

peering nervously under the cover, "and he looks like a scarecrow."

"We'll see whether he gives up or not when I take a sharp knife to him," her mother answered; "and as to his looks, a platter full o' gravy makes a sight o' difference with old roosters, and I'll put dumplings round the aidge; they're turrible fillin', though they don't belong with boiled chicken."

The rooster did indeed make an impressive showing, lying in his border of dumplings, and the dish was much complimented when it was borne in by Alice. This was fortunate, as the chorus of admiration ceased abruptly when the ladies began to eat the fowl.

"I was glad you could git over to Huldy's graduation, Delia," said Mrs. Meserve, who sat at the foot of the table and served the chicken while Mrs. Robinson poured coffee at the other end. She was a fit mother for Huldah, being much the most stylish person in Riverboro; ill health and dress were, indeed, her two chief enjoyments in life.

"How'd you like Huldy's dress, Delia?" she asked, snapping the elastic in her black jet bracelets after an irritating fashion she had.

"I thought it was about the handsomest of any," answered Delia; "and her composition was first rate. It was the only real amusin' one there was, and she read it so loud and clear we didn't miss any of it; most o' the girls spoke as if they had hasty puddin' in their mouths."

"That was the composition she wrote for Adam Ladd's prize," explained Mrs. Meserve, "and they do say she'd 'a' come out first, 'stead o' fourth, if her subject had been dif'rent. There was three ministers and three deacons on the committee, and it was only natural they should choose a serious piece; hers was too lively to suit 'em."

Huldah's inspiring theme had been "Boys," and she certainly had a fund of knowledge and experience that fitted her to write most intelligently upon it. It was vastly popular with the audience, who enjoyed the rather cheap jokes and allusions with which it coruscated; but judged from a purely literary standpoint, it left much to be desired.

"Rebecca's piece wa'n't read out loud, but

the one that took the boy's prize was; why was that?" asked Mrs. Robinson.

"Because she wa'n't graduatin'," explained Mrs. Cobb, "and couldn't take part in the exercises; it'll be printed, with Herbert Dunn's, in the school paper."

"I'm glad o' that, for I'll never believe it was better'n Huldy's till I read it with my own eyes; it seems as if the prize ought to 'a' gone to one of the seniors."

"Well, no, Marthy, not if Ladd offered it to any of the two upper classes that wanted to try for it," argued Mrs. Robinson. "They say they asked him to give out the prizes, and he refused, up and down. It seems odd, his bein' so rich and travelin' about all over the country, that he was too modest to git up on that platform."

"My Huldy could 'a' done it, and not winked an eyelash," observed Mrs. Meserve complacently; a remark which there seemed no disposition on the part of any of the company to controvert.

"It was complete, though, the governor happening to be there to see his niece graduate," said Delia Weeks. "Land! he looked elegant! They say he's only six feet, but he might 'a' been sixteen, and he certainly did make a fine speech."

"Did you notice Rebecca, how white she was, and how she trembled when she and Herbert Dunn stood there while the governor was praisin' 'em? He'd read her composition, too, for he wrote the Sawyer girls a letter about it." This remark was from the sympathetic Mrs. Cobb.

"I thought 't was kind o' foolish, his makin' so much of her when it wa'n't her graduation," objected Mrs. Meserve; "layin' his hand on her head 'n' all that, as if he was a Pope pronouncin' benediction. But there! I'm glad the prize come to Riverboro 't any rate, and a han'somer one never was give out from the Wareham platform. I guess there ain't no end to Adam Ladd's money. The fifty dollars would 'a' been good enough, but he must needs go and put it into those elegant purses."

"I set so fur back I couldn't see 'em fairly," complained Delia, "and now Rebecca has taken hers home to show her mother."

"It was kind of a gold net bag with a

chain," said Mrs. Perkins, "and there was five ten-dollar gold pieces in it. Herbert Dunn's was put in a fine leather wallet."

"How long is Rebecca goin' to stay at the farm?" asked Delia.

"Till they get over Hannah's bein' married, and get the house to runnin' without her," answered Mrs. Perkins. "It seems as if Hannah might 'a' waited a little longer. Aurelia was set against her goin' away while Rebecca was at school, but she's obstinate as a mule, Hannah is, and she just took her own way in spite of her mother. She's been doin' her sewin' for a year; the awfulest coarse cotton cloth she had, but she's nearly blinded herself with fine stitchin' and rufflin' and tuckin'. Did you hear about the quilt she made?

"She'd better 'a' been takin' in sewin' and earnin' money, 'stead o' blindin' her eyes on such foolishness as quilted counterpanes," said Mrs. Cobb. "The next thing you know that mortgage will be foreclosed on Mis' Randall, and she and the children won't have a roof over their heads."

"Don't they say there's a good chance of the railroad goin' through her place?" asked Mrs. Robinson. "If it does, she'll git as much as the farm is worth and more. Adam Ladd's one of the stockholders, and everything is a success he takes holt of. They're fightin' it in Augusty, but I'd back Ladd agin any o' them legislaters if he thought he was in the right."

"Rebecca'll have some new clothes now," said Delia, "and the land knows she needs 'em. Seems to me the Sawyer girls are gittin' turrible near!"

"Rebecca won't have any new clothes out o' the prize money," remarked Mrs. Perkins, "for she sent it away the next day to pay the interest on that mortgage."

"Poor little girl!" exclaimed Delia Weeks.

"She might as well help along her folks as spend it on foolishness," affirmed Mrs. Robinson. "I think she was mighty lucky to git it to pay the interest with, but she's probably like all the Randalls; it was easy come, easy go, with them."

"That's more than can be said of the Sawyer stock," retorted Mrs. Perkins; "seems like they enjoyed savin' more'n anything in the world, and it's gainin' on Mirandy sence her shock."

"I don't believe it was a shock; it stands to reason she'd never 'a' got up after it and been so smart as she is now; we had three o' the worst shocks in our family that there ever was on this river, and I know every symptom of 'em better'n the doctors." And Mrs. Peter Meserve shook her head wisely.

"Mirandy's smart enough," said Mrs. Cobb, "but you notice she stays right to home, and she's more close-mouthed than ever she was; never took a mite o' pride in the prize, as I could see, though it pretty nigh drove Jeremiah out o' his senses. I thought I should 'a' died o' shame when he cried 'Hooray!' and swung his straw hat when the governor shook hands with Rebecca. It's lucky he couldn't get fur into the church and had to stand back by the door, for as it was, he made a spectacle of himself. My suspicion is"—and here every lady stopped eating and sat up straight—"that the Sawyer girls have lost money. They don't know a thing about business 'n' never did, and Mirandy's too secretive and contrary to ask advice."

"The most o' what they've got is in gov'-ment bonds, I always heard, and you can't lose money on them. Jane had the timber land left her, an' Mirandy had the brick house. She probably took it awful hard that Rebecca's fifty dollars had to be swallowed up in a mortgage, 'stead of goin' towards school expenses. The more I think of it, the more I think Adam Ladd intended Rebecca should have that prize when he gave it." The mind of Huldah's mother ran towards the idea that her daughter's rights had been assailed.

"Land, Marthy, what foolishness you talk!" exclaimed Mrs. Perkins; "you don't suppose he could tell what composition the committee was going to choose; and why should he offer another fifty dollars for a boy's prize, if he wa'n't interested in helpin' along the school? He's give Emma Jane about the same present as Rebecca every Christmas for five years; that's the way he does."

"Some time he'll forget one of 'em and give to the other, or drop 'em both and give to some new girl!" said Delia Weeks, with an experience born of fifty years of spinster-hood.

"Like as not," assented Mrs. Peter Meserve, "though it's easy to see he ain't the marryin' kind. There's men that would marry once a year if their wives would die fast enough, and there's men that seems to want to live alone."

"If Ladd was a Mormon, I guess he could have every woman in North Riverboro that's a suitable age, accordin' to what my cousins say," remarked Mrs. Perkins.

" 'T ain't likely he could be ketched by any North Riverboro girl," demurred Mrs. Robinson; "not when he prob'bly has had the pick o' Boston. I guess Marthy hit it when she said there's men that ain't the marryin' kind."

"I wouldn't trust any of 'em when Miss Right comes along!" laughed Mrs. Cobb genially. "You never can tell what 'n' who's goin' to please 'em. You know Jeremiah's contrary horse, Buster? He won't let anybody put the bit into his mouth if he can help it. He'll fight Jerry, and fight me, till he has to give in. Rebecca didn't know nothin' about his tricks, and the other day she went int' the barn to hitch up. I followed right along, knowing she'd have trouble with the headstall, and I declare if she wa'n't pattin' Buster's nose and talkin' to him, and when she put her little fingers into his mouth he opened it so fur I thought he'd swaller her, for sure. He jest smacked his lips over the bit as if 't was a lump o' sugar. 'Land, Rebecca,' I says, 'how'd you persuade him to take the bit?' 'I didn't,' she says, 'he seemed to want it; perhaps he's tired of his stall and wants to get out in the fresh air.' "

23

"THE VISION SPLENDID"

A year had elapsed since Adam Ladd's prize had been discussed over the teacups in Riverboro. The months had come and gone, and at

length the great day had dawned for Rebecca, —the day to which she had been looking forward for five years, as the first goal to be reached on her little journey through the world. School days were ended, and the mystic function known to the initiated as "graduation" was about to be celebrated; it was even now heralded by the sun dawning in the eastern sky. Rebecca stole softly out of bed, crept to the window, threw open the blinds, and welcomed the rosy light that meant a cloudless morning. Even the sun looked different somehow,—larger, redder, more important than usual; and if it were really so, there was no member of the graduating class who would have thought it strange or unbecoming, in view of all the circumstances. Emma Jane stirred on her pillow, woke, and seeing Rebecca at the window, came and knelt on the floor beside her. "It's going to be pleasant!" she sighed gratefully. "If it wasn't wicked, I could thank the Lord, I'm so relieved in mind! Did you sleep?"

"Not much; the words of my class poem kept running through my head, and the accompaniments of the songs; and worse than anything, Mary Queen of Scots' prayer in Latin; it seemed as if

Adoro, imploro,
Ut liberes me!

were burned into my brain."

No one who is unfamiliar with life in rural neighborhoods can imagine the gravity, the importance, the solemnity of this last day of school. In the matter of preparation, wealth of detail, and general excitement, it far surpasses a wedding. Wareham, then, was shaken to its very center on this day of days. Mothers and fathers of the scholars, as well as relatives to the remotest generation, had been coming on the train and driving into the town since breakfast time; old pupils, both married and single, with and without families, streamed back to the dear old village. The two livery stables were crowded with vehicles of all sorts, and lines of buggies and wagons were drawn up along the sides of the shady roads, the horses switching their tails in luxurious idleness. The streets were filled with people wearing their best clothes, and the fashions included not only "the latest thing," but the well-preserved relic of a bygone day. In the seminary building there was an excitement so deep and profound that it expressed itself in a kind of hushed silence, a transient suspension of life, as those most interested approached the crucial moment. The feminine graduates-to-be were seated in their own bedrooms, dressed with a completeness of detail to which all their past lives seemed to have been but a prelude. At least, this was the case with their bodies; but their heads, owing to the extreme heat of the day, were one and all ornamented with leads, or papers, or dozens of little braids, to issue later in every sort of curl known to the girl of that period. Rolling the hair on leads or papers was a favorite method of attaining the desired result, and though it often entailed a sleepless night, there were those who gladly paid the price. Others, in whose veins the blood of martyrs did not flow, substituted rags for leads and pretended that they made a more natural and less woolly curl. Heat, however, will melt the proudest head and reduce to fiddling strings the finest product of the waving-pin; so anxious mothers were stationed over their offspring, waving palm-leaf fans, it having been decided that the supreme instant when the town clock struck ten should be the one chosen for releasing the prisoners from their self-imposed tortures.

Dotted or plain Swiss muslin was the favorite garb, though there were those who were steaming in white cashmere or alpaca, because in some cases such frocks were thought more useful afterwards. Blue and pink waist ribbons were lying over the backs of chairs, and the girl who had a Roman sash was praying that she might be kept from vanity and pride.

The way to any graduating dress at all had not seemed clear to Rebecca until a month before. Then, in company with Emma Jane, she visited the Perkins attic, found piece after piece of white butter-muslin or cheesecloth, and decided that, at a pinch, it would do. The "rich blacksmith's daughter" cast the thought of dotted Swiss behind her, and elected to follow Rebecca in cheesecloth as she had in higher matters; straightway devising costumes that included such drawing of threads, such hem-stitching and pin-tucking, such insertions of fine thread tatting that, in order to be finished, Rebecca's dress was given out in sections,—the sash to Hannah, waist and sleeves to Mrs. Cobb, and skirt to Aunt Jane. The stitches that went into the despised material, worth only three or four pennies a yard, made the dresses altogether lovely, and as for the folds and lines into which they fell, they could have given points to satins and brocades.

The girls were waiting in their room alone, Emma Jane in rather a tearful state of mind. She kept thinking that it was the last day that they would be together in this altogether sweet and close intimacy. The beginning of the end seemed to have dawned, for two positions had been offered Rebecca by Mr. Morrison the day before: one in which she would play for singing and calisthenics, and superintend the piano practice of the younger girls in a boarding school; the other an assistant's place in the Edgewood High School. Both were very modest as to salary, but the former included educational advantages that Miss Maxwell thought might be valuable.

Rebecca's mood had passed from that of excitement into a sort of exaltation, and when the first bell rang through the corridors announcing that in five minutes the class would proceed in a body to the church for the exercises, she stood motionless and speechless at the window with her hand on her heart.

"It is coming, Emmie," she said presently; "do you remember in 'The Mill on the Floss,' when Maggie Tulliver closed the golden gates of childhood behind her? I can almost see them swing; almost hear them clang; and I can't tell whether I am glad or sorry."

"I shouldn't care how they swung or clanged," said Emma Jane, "if only you and I were on the same side of the gate; but we shan't be, I know we shan't!"

"Emmie, don't dare to cry, for I'm just on the brink myself! If only you were graduating with me; that's my only sorrow! There! I hear the rumble of the wheels! People will be seeing our grand surprise now! Hug me once for luck, dear Emmie; a careful hug, remembering our butter-muslin frailty!"

Ten minutes later, Adam Ladd, who had just arrived from Portland and was wending his way to the church, came suddenly into the main street and stopped short under a tree by the wayside, riveted to the spot by a scene of picturesque loveliness such as his eyes had seldom witnessed before. The class of which Rebecca was president was not likely to follow accepted customs. Instead of marching two by two from the seminary to the church, they had elected to proceed thither by royal chariot. A haycart had been decked with green vines and bunches of long-stemmed field daisies, those gay darlings of New England meadows. Every inch of the rail, the body, even the spokes, all were twined with yellow and green and white. There were two white horses, flower-trimmed reins, and in the floral bower, seated on maple boughs, were the twelve girls of the class, while the ten boys marched on either side of the vehicle, wearing buttonhole bouquets of daisies, the class flower.

Rebecca drove, seated on a green-covered bench that looked not unlike a throne. No girl clad in white muslin, no happy girl of seventen, is plain; and the twelve little country maids, from the vantage ground of their setting, looked beautiful, as the June sunlight filtered down on their uncovered heads, showing their bright eyes, their fresh cheeks, their smiles, and their dimples.

Rebecca, Adam thought, as he took off his hat and saluted the pretty panorama,—Rebecca, with her tall slenderness, her thoughtful brow, the fire of young joy in her face, her fillet of dark braided hair, might have been a young Muse or Sibyl; and the flowery hayrack, with its freight of blooming girlhood, might have been painted as an allegorical picture of "The Morning of Life." It all passed him, as he stood under the elms in the old village street where his mother had walked half a century ago, and he was turning with the crowd towards the church when he hard a little sob. Behind a hedge in the garden near where he was standing was a forlorn person in white, whose neat nose, chestnut hair, and blue eyes he seemed to know. He stepped inside the gate and said, "What's wrong, Miss

Emma?"

"Oh, is it you, Mr. Ladd? Rebecca wouldn't let me cry for fear of spoiling my looks, but I must have just one chance before I go in. I can be as homely as I like, after all, for I only have to sing with the school; I'm not graduating, I'm just leaving! Not that I mind that; it's only being separated from Rebecca that I never can stand!"

The two walked along together, Adam comforting the disconsolate Emma Jane, until they reached the old meeting house where the Commencement exercises were always held.

Rebecca saw Hannah and her husband in the audience; dear old John and Cousin Ann also, and felt a pang at the absence of her mother, though she had known there was no possibility of seeing her; for poor Aurelia was kept at Sunnybrook by cares of children and farm, and lack of money either for the journey or for suitable dress. The Cobbs she saw too but where was Aunt Jane, in her black silk made over especially for this occasion? Aunt Miranda had not intended to come, she knew, but where, on this day of days, was her beloved Aunt Jane? However, this thought, like all others, came and went in a flash, for the whole morning was like a series of magic-lantern pictures, crossing and recrossing her field of vision. She played, she sang, she recited Queen Mary's Latin prayer, like one in a dream, only brought to consciousness by meeting Mr. Aladdin's eyes as she spoke the last line. Then at the end of the program came her class poem, "Makers of Tomorrow"; and there, as on many a former occasion, her personality played so great a part that she seemed to be uttering Miltonic sentiments instead of schoolgirl verse. Her voice, her eyes, her body breathed conviction, earnestness, and emotion; and when she left the platform the audience felt that they had listened to a masterpiece. Most of her hearers knew little of Carlyle or Emerson, or they might have remembered that the one said, "We are all poets when we read a poem well," and the other, " 'Tis the good reader makes the good book."

It was over! The diplomas had been presented, and each girl, after giving furtive touches to her hair, sly tweaks to her muslin skirts, and caressing pats to her sash, had gone forward to receive the roll of parchment with a bow that had been the subject of anxious thought for weeks. Rounds of applause greeted each graduate at this thrilling moment, and Jeremiah Cobb's behavior, when Rebecca came forward, was the talk of Wareham and Riverboro for days. Old Mrs. Webb avowed that he, in the space of two hours, had worn out her pew more—the carpet, the cushions, and woodwork—than she had by sitting in it forty years. Yes, it was over, and after the crowd had thinned a little, Adam Ladd made his way to the platform.

Rebecca turned from speaking to some strangers and met him in the aisle. "Oh, Mr. Aladdin, I am so glad you could come! Tell me"—and she looked at him half shyly, for his approval was dearer to her, and more difficult to win, than that of the others—"tell me, Mr. Aladdin,—were you satisfied?"

"More than satisfied!" he said; "glad I met the child, proud I know the girl, longing to meet the woman!"

24

"TH' INEVITABLE YOKE"

Rebecca's heart beat high at this sweet praise from her hero's lips, but before she had found words to thank him, Mr. and Mrs. Cobb, who had been modestly biding their time in a corner, approached her and she introduced them to Mr. Ladd.

"Where, where is Aunt Jane?" she cried, holding Aunt Sarah's hand on one side and Uncle Jerry's on the other.

"I'm sorry, lovey, but we've got bad news for you."

"Is Aunt Miranda worse? She is; I can see it by your looks." And Rebecca's color faded.

"She had a second stroke yesterday morning jest when she was helpin' Jane lay out her things to come here today. Jane said you wa'n't to know anything about it till the exercises was all over, and we promised to keep it secret till then."

"I will go right home with you, Aunt Sarah. I must just run to tell Miss Maxwell, for after I had packed up tomorrow I was going to Brunswick with her. Poor Aunt Miranda! And I have been so gay and happy all day, except that I was longing for mother and Aunt Jane."

"There ain't no harm in bein' gay, lovey; that's what Jane wanted you to be. And Miranda's got her speech back, for your aunt has just sent a letter sayin' she's better; and I'm goin' to set up tonight, so you can stay here and have a good sleep, and get your things together comfortably tomorrow."

"I'll pack your trunk for you, Becky dear, and attend to all our room things," said Emma Jane, who had come towards the group and heard the sorrowful news from the brick house.

They moved into one of the quiet side pews, where Hannah and her husband and John joined them. From time to time some straggling acquaintance or old schoolmate would come up to congratulate Rebecca and ask why she had hidden herself in a corner. Then some member of the class would call to her excitedly, reminding her not to be late at the picnic luncheon, or begging her to be early at the class party in the evening. All this had an air of unreality to Rebecca. In the midst of the happy excitement of the last two days, when "blushing honors" had been falling thick upon her, and behind the delicious exaltation of the morning, had been the feeling that the condition was a transient one, and that the burden, the struggle, the anxiety, would soon loom again on the horizon. She longed to steal away into the woods with dear old John, grown so manly and handsome, and get some comfort from him.

Meantime Adam Ladd and Mr. Cobb had been having an animated conversation.

"I s'pose up to Boston, girls like that one are as thick as blackb'ries?" Uncle Jerry said, jerking his head interrogatively in Rebecca's direction.

"They may be," smiled Adam, taking in the old man's mood; "only I don't happen to know one."

"My eyesight bein' poor's the reason she looked han'somest of any girl on the platform, I s'pose?"

"There's no failure in my eyes," responded Adam, "but that was how the thing seemed to me!"

"What did you think of her voice? Anything extry about it?"

"Made the others sound poor and thin, I thought."

"Well, I'm glad to hear your opinion, you bein' a traveled man, for mother says I'm foolish 'bout Rebecky and hev been sence the fust. Mother scolds me for spoilin' her, but I notice mother ain't fur behind when it comes to spoilin'. Land! It made me sick, thinkin' o' them parents travelin' miles to see their young ones graduate, and then when they got here hevin' to compare 'em with Rebecky. Good-bye, Mr. Ladd, drop in some day when you come to Riverboro."

"I will," said Adam, shaking the old man's hand cordially; "perhaps tomorrow if I drive Rebecca home, as I shall offer to do. Do you think Miss Sawyer's condition is serious?"

"Well, the doctor don't seem to know; but anyhow she's paralyzed, and she'll never walk fur again, poor soul! She ain't lost her speech; that'll be a comfort to her."

Adam left the church, and in crossing the common came upon Miss Maxwell doing the honors of the institution, as she passed from group to group of strangers and guests. Knowing that she was deeply interested in all Rebecca's plans, he told her, as he drew her aside, that the girl would have to leave Wareham for Riverboro the next day.

"That is almost more than I can bear!" exclaimed Miss Maxwell, sitting down on a bench and stabbing the greensward with her parasol. "It seems to me Rebecca never has any respite. I had so many plans for her this next month in fitting her for her position, and now she will settle down to housework again, and to the nursing of that poor, sick, cross old aunt."

"If it had not been for the cross old aunt, Rebecca would still have been at Sunnybrook; and from the standpoint of educational advantages, or indeed advantages of any sort, she might as well have been in the backwoods," returned Adam.

"That is true; I was vexed when I spoke, for I thought an easier and happier day was dawning for my prodigy and pearl."

"*Our* prodigy and pearl," corrected Adam.

"Oh, yes!" she laughed. "I always forget that it pleases you to pretend you discovered Rebecca."

"I believe, though, that happier days are dawning for her," continued Adam. "It must be a secret for the present, but Mrs. Randall's farm will be bought by the new railroad. We must have right of way through the land, and the station will be built on her property. She will receive six thousand dollars, which, though not a fortune, will yield her three or four hundred dollars a year, if she will allow me to invest it for her. There is a mortgage on the land; that paid, and Rebecca self-supporting, the mother ought to push the education of the oldest boy, who is a fine, ambitious fellow. He should be taken away from farmwork and settled at his studies."

"We might form ourselves into a Randall Protective Agency, Limited," mused Miss Maxwell. "I confess I want Rebecca to have a career."

"I don't," said Adam promptly.

"Of course you don't. Men have no interest in the careers of women! But I know Rebecca better than you."

"You understand her mind better, but not necessarily her heart. You are considering her for the moment as prodigy; I am thinking of her more as pearl."

"Well," sighed Miss Maxwell whimsically, "prodigy or pearl, the Randall Protective Agency may pull Rebecca in opposite directions, but nevertheless she will follow her saint."

"That will content me," said Adam gravely.

"Particularly if the saint beckons your way." And Miss Maxwell looked up and smiled provokingly.

Rebecca did not see her Aunt Miranda till she had been at the brick house for several days. Miranda steadily refused to have any one but Jane in the room until her face had regained its natural look, but her door was always ajar, and Jane fancied she liked to hear Rebecca's quick, light step. Her mind was perfectly clear now, and, save that she could not move, she was most of the time quite free from pain, and alert in every nerve to all that was going on within or without the house. "Were the windfall apples being picked up for sauce; were the potatoes thick in the hills; was the corn tosselin' out; were they cuttin' the upper field; were they keepin' fly-paper laid out everywheres; were there any ants in the dairy; was the kindlin' wood holdin' out; had the bank sent the coupons?"

Poor Miranda Sawyer! Hovering on the verge of the great beyond—her body "struck" and no longer under control of her iron will, —no divine visions floated across her tired brain; nothing but petty cares and sordid anxieties. Not all at once can the soul talk with God, be He ever so near. If the heavenly language never has been learned, quick as is the spiritual sense in seizing the facts it needs, then the poor soul must use the words and phrases it has lived on and grown into day by day. Poor Miss Miranda!—held fast within the prison walls of her own nature, blind in the presence of revelation because she had never used the spiritual eye, deaf to angelic voices because she had not used the spiritual ear.

There came a morning when she asked for Rebecca. The door was opened into the dim sickroom, and Rebecca stood there with the sunlight behind her, her hands full of sweet peas. Miranda's pale, sharp face, framed in its nightcap, looked haggard on the pillow, and her body was pitifully still under the counterpane.

"Come in," she said; "I ain't dead yet. Don't mess up the bed with them flowers, will ye?"

"Oh, no! They're going in a glass pitcher," said Rebecca, turning to the washstand as she tried to control her voice and stop the tears that sprang to her eyes.

"Let me look at ye; come closer. What dress are ye wearin'?" said the old aunt in her cracked, weak voice.

"My blue calico."

"Is your cashmere holdin' its color?"

"Yes, Aunt Miranda."

"Do you keep it in a dark closet hung on the wrong side, as I told ye?"

"Always."

"Has your mother made her jelly?"

"She hasn't said."

"She always had the knack o' writin' letters with nothin' in 'em. What's Mark broke sence I've been sick?"

"Nothing at all, Aunt Miranda."

"Why, what's the matter with him? Gittin' lazy, ain't he? How's John turnin' out?"

"He's going to be the best of us all."

"I hope you don't slight things in the kitchen because I ain't there. Do you scald the coffee pot and turn it upside down on the windersill?"

"Yes, Aunt Miranda."

"It's always 'yes' with you, and 'yes' with Jane," groaned Miranda, trying to move her stiffened body; "but all the time I lay here knowin' there's things done the way I don't like 'em."

There was a long pause, during which Rebecca sat down by the bedside and timidly touched her aunt's hand, her heart swelling with tender pity at the gaunt face and closed eyes.

"I was dreadful ashamed to have you graduate in cheesecloth, Rebecca, but I couldn't help it nohow. You'll hear the reason some time, and know I tried to make it up to ye. I'm afraid you was a laughin' stock!"

"No," Rebecca answered. "Ever so many people said our dresses were the very prettiest; they looked like soft lace. You're not to be anxious about anything. Here I am all grown up and graduated,—number three in a class of twenty-two, Aunt Miranda,—and good positions offered me already. Look at me, big and strong and young, all ready to go into the world and show what you and Aunt Jane have done for me. If you want me near, I'll take the Edgewood School, so that I can be here nights and Sundays to help; and if you get better, then I'll go to Augusta,—for that's a hundred dollars more, with music lessons and other things beside."

"You listen to me," said Miranda quaveringly. "Take the best place, regardless o' my sickness. I'd like to live long enough to know you'd paid off that mortgage, but I guess I shan't."

Here she ceased abruptly, having talked more than she had for weeks; and Rebecca stole out of the room, to cry by herself and wonder if old age must be so grim, so hard, so unchastened and unsweetened, as it slipped into the valley of the shadow.

The days went on, and Miranda grew stronger and stronger; her will seemed unassailable, and before long she could be moved into a chair by the window, her dominant thought being to arrive at such a condition of improvement that the doctor need not call more than once a week, instead of daily; thereby diminishing the bill, that was mounting to such a terrifying sum that it haunted her thoughts by day and dreams by night.

Little by little hope stole back into Rebecca's young heart. Aunt Jane began to "clear-starch" her handkerchiefs and collars and purple muslin dress, so that she might be ready to go to Brunswick at any moment when the doctor pronounced Miranda well on the road to recovery. Everything beautiful was to happen in Brunswick if she could be there by August,—everything that heart could wish or imagination conceive, for she was to be Miss Emily's very own visitor, and sit at table with college professors and other great men.

At length the day dawned when the few clean, simple dresses were packed in the hair trunk, together with her beloved coral necklace, her cheesecloth graduating dress, her class pin, Aunt Jane's lace cape, and the one new hat, which she tried on every night before going to bed. It was of white chip with a wreath of cheap white roses and green leaves, and cost between two and three dollars, an unprecedented sum in Rebecca's experience. The effect of its glories when worn with her nightdress was dazzling enough, but if ever it appeared in conjunction with the cheesecloth gown, Rebecca felt that even reverend professors might regard it with respect. It is probable, indeed, that any professorial gaze lucky enough to meet a pair of dark eyes shining under that white-rose garland would never have stopped at respect!

Then, when all was ready and Abijah Flagg at the door, came a telegram from Hannah: "Come at once. Mother has had bad accident."

In less than an hour Rebecca was started on her way to Sunnybrook, her heart palpitating with fear as to what might be awaiting her at her journey's end.

Death, at all events, was not there to meet her; but something that looked at first only too much like it. Her mother had been standing on the haymow superintending some changes in the barn, had been seized with giddiness, they thought, and slipped. The right knee was fractured and the back strained and hurt, but she was conscious and in no immediate danger, so Rebecca wrote, when she had a moment to send Aunt Jane the particulars.

"I don' know how 't is," grumbled Miranda, who was not able to sit up that day; "but from a child I could never lay abed without Aurelia's gettin' sick too. I don' know's she could help fallin', though it ain't any place for a woman,—a haymow; but if it hadn't been that, 't would 'a' been somethin' else. Aurelia was born unfortunate. Now she'll probably be a cripple, and Rebecca'll have to nurse her instead of earning a good income somewheres else."

"Her first duty's to her mother," said Aunt Jane; "I hope she'll always remember that."

"Nobody remembers anything they'd ought to,—at seventeen," responded Miranda. "Now that I'm strong again, there's things I want to consider with you, Jane, things that are on my mind night and day. We've talked 'em over before; now we'll settle 'em. When I'm laid away, do you want to take Aurelia and the children down here to the brick house? There's an awful passel of 'em,—Aurelia, Jenny, and Fanny; but I won't have Mark. Hannah can take him; I won't have a great boy stompin' out the carpets and ruinin' the furniture, though I know when I'm dead I can't hinder ye, if you make up your mind to do anything."

"I shouldn't like to go against your feelings, especially in laying out your money, Miranda," said Jane.

"Don't tell Rebecca I've willed her the brick house. She won't git it till I'm gone, 162 and I want to take my time 'bout dyin' and not be hurried off by them that's goin' to profit by it; nor I don't want to be thanked, neither. I s'pose she'll use the front stairs as common as the back and like as not have water brought into the kitchen, but mebbe when I've been dead a few years I shan't mind. She sets such store by you, she'll want you to have your home here as long's you live, but, anyway, I've wrote it down that way; though Lawyer Burns's wills don't hold more'n half the time. He's cheaper, but I guess it comes out jest the same in the end. I wa'n't goin' to have the fust man Rebecca picks up for a husband turnin' you ou'doors."

There was a long pause, during which Jane knit silently, wiping the tears from her eyes from time to time, as she looked at the pitiful figure lying weakly on the pillows. Suddenly Miranda said slowly and feebly:—

"I don' know after all but you might as well take Mark; I s'pose there's tame boys as well as wild ones. There ain't a mite o' sense in havin' so many children, but it's a turrible risk splittin' up families and farmin' 'em out here 'n' there; they'd never come to no good, an' everybody would keep rememberin' their mother was a Sawyer. Now, if you'll draw down the curtain, I'll try to sleep."

25

MOTHER AND DAUGHTER

Two months had gone by,—two months of steady, fagging work; of cooking, washing, ironing; of mending and caring for the three children, although Jenny was fast becoming a notable little housewife, quick, ready, and capable. They were months in which there had been many a weary night of watching by Aurelia's bedside; of soothing and bandaging and rubbing; of reading and nursing, even of feeding and bathing. The ceaseless care was growing less now, and the family breathed more freely, for the mother's sigh of pain no

longer came from the stifling bedroom, where, during a hot and humid August, Aurelia had lain, suffering with every breath she drew. There would be no question of walking for many a month to come, but blessings seemed to multiply when the blinds could be opened and the bed drawn near the window; when mother, with pillows behind her, could at least sit and watch the work going on, could smile at the past agony and forget the weary hours that had led to her present comparative ease and comfort.

No girl of seventeen can pass through such an ordeal and come out unchanged; no girl of Rebecca's temperament could go through it without some inward repining and rebellion. She was doing tasks in which she could not be fully happy,—heavy and trying tasks, which perhaps she could never do with complete success or satisfaction; and like promise of nectar to thirsty lips was the vision of joys she had had to put aside for the performance of dull daily duty. How brief, how fleeting, had been those splendid visions when the universe seemed open for her young strength to battle and triumph in! How soon they had faded into the light of common day! At first, sympathy and grief were so keen she thought of nothing but her mother's pain. No consciousness of self interposed between her and her filial service; then, as the weeks passed, little blighted hopes began to stir and ache in her breast; defeated ambitions raised their heads as if to sting her; unattainable delights teased her by their very nearness; by the narrow line of separation that lay between her and their realization. It is easy, for the moment, to tread the narrow way, looking neither to the right nor left, upborne by the sense of right doing; but that first joy of self-denial, the joy that is like fire in the blood, dies away; the path seems drearier and the footsteps falter. Such a time came to Rebecca, and her bright spirit flagged when the letter was received saying that her position in Augusta had been filled. There was a mutinous leap of the heart then, a beating of the wings against the door of the cage, a longing for the freedom of the big world outside. It was the stirring of the powers within her, though she called it by no such grand name. She felt as if the wind

of destiny were blowing her flame hither and thither, burning, consuming her, but kindling nothing. All this meant one stormy night in her little room at Sunnybrook, but the clouds blew over, the sun shone again, a rainbow stretched across the sky, while "hope clad in April green" smiled into her upturned face and beckoned her on, saying:—

> Grow old along with me,
> The best is yet to be.

Threads of joy ran in and out of the gray tangled web of daily living. There was the attempt at odd moments to make the bare little house less bare by bringing in out-of-doors, taking a leaf from Nature's book and noting how she conceals ugliness wherever she finds it. Then there was the satisfaction of being mistress of the poor domain; of planning, governing, deciding; of bringing order out of chaos; of implanting gayety in the place of inert resignation to the inevitable. Another element of comfort was the children's love, for they turned to her as flowers to the sun, drawing confidently on her fund of stories, serene in the conviction that there was no limit to Rebecca's power of make-believe. In this, and in yet greater things, little as she realized it, the law of compensation was working in her behalf, for in those anxious days mother and daughter found and knew each other as never before. A new sense was born in Rebecca as she hung over her mother's bed of pain and unrest,—a sense that comes only of ministering, a sense that grows only when the strong bend toward the weak. As for Aurelia, words could never have expressed her dumb happiness when the real revelation of motherhood was vouchsafed her. In all the earlier years when her babies were young, carking cares and anxieties darkened the fireside with their brooding wings. Then Rebecca had gone away, and in the long months of absence her mind and soul had grown out of her mother's knowledge, so that now, when Aurelia had time and strength to study her child, she was like some enchanting changeling.

It was a marvelous morning. The sun had climbed into a world that held in remembrance only a succession of golden days and starlit nights. The air was fragrant with ripening fruit, and there was a mad little bird on a tree outside the door nearly bursting his throat with joy of living. He had forgotten that summer was over, that winter must ever come; and who could think of cold winds, bare boughs, or frozen streams on such a day? A painted moth came in at the open window and settled on the tuft of brilliant leaves. Aurelia heard the bird and looked from the beauty of the glowing bush to her tall, splendid daughter, standing like young Spring with golden Autumn in her arms.

Then suddenly she covered her eyes and cried, "I can't bear it! Here I lie chained to this bed, interfering with everything you want to do. It's all wasted! All my saving and doing without; all your hard study; all Mirandy's outlay; everything that we thought was going to be the making of you!"

"Mother, mother, don't talk so, don't think so!" exclaimed Rebecca, sitting down impetuously on the floor by the bed and dropping the goldenrod by her side. "Why, mother, I'm only a little past seventeen! This person in a purple calico apron with flour on her nose is only the beginnings of me!

"You can put a brave face on it," sobbed Aurelia, "but you can't deceive me. You've lost your place; you'll never see your friends here, and you're nothing but a drudge!"

"I look like a drudge," said Rebecca mysteriously, with laughing eyes, "but I really am a princess; you mustn't tell, but this is only a disguise; I wear it for reasons of state."

Aurelia smiled in spite of herself, and though not perhaps wholly deceived, she was comforted.

"I only hope you won't have to wait too long for your thrones and your kingdoms, Rebecca," she said, "and that I shall have a sight of them before I die; but life looks very hard and rough to me, what with your Aunt Miranda a cripple at the brick house, me another here at the farm, you tied hand and foot, first with one and then with the other, to say nothing of Jenny and Fanny and Mark! You've got something of your father's happy disposition, or it would weigh on you as it does on me."

"Why, mother!" cried Rebecca, clasping her knees with her hands; "why, mother, it's enough joy just to be here in the world on a day like this; to have the chance of seeing, feeling, doing, becoming! When you were seventeen, mother, wasn't it good just to be alive? You haven't forgotten?"

"No," said Aurelia, "but I wasn't so much alive as you are, never in the world."

"I often think," Rebecca continued, walking to the window and looking out at the trees, —"I often think how dreadful it would be if I were not here at all. If Hannah had come, and then, instead of me, John; John and Jenny and Fanny and the others, but no Rebecca; never any Rebecca! To be alive makes up for everything; there ought to be fears in my heart, but there aren't; something stronger sweeps them out something like a wind. Oh, see! There is Will driving up the lane, mother, and he ought to have a letter from the brick house."

26
GOOD-BYE, SUNNYBROOK

Will Melville drove up to the window and, tossing a letter into Rebecca's lap, went off to the barn on an errand.

"Sister's no worse, then," sighed Aurelia gratefully, "or Jane would have telegraphed. See what she says."

Rebecca opened the envelope and read in one flash of an eye the whole brief page:—

Your Aunt Miranda passed away an hour ago. Come at once, if your mother is out of danger. I shall not have the funeral till you are here. She died very suddenly and without any pain. Oh, Rebecca! I long for you so!

AUNT JANE.

The force of habit was too strong, and even in the hour of death Jane had remembered that a telegram was twenty-five cents, and that Aurelia would have to pay half a dollar for its delivery.

Rebecca burst into a passion of tears as she cried," Poor, poor Aunt Miranda! She is gone without taking a bit of comfort in life, and I couldn't say good-bye to her! Poor lonely Aunt Jane! What can I do, mother? I feel torn in two, between you and the brick house."

"You must go this very instant," said Aurelia, starting from her pillows. "If I was to die while you were away, I would say the very same thing. Your aunts have done everything in the world for you,—more than I've ever been able to do,—and it is your turn to pay back some o' their kindness and show your gratitude. The doctor says I've turned the corner and I feel I have. Jenny can make out somehow, if Hannah'll come over once a day."

"But, mother, I *can't* go! Who'll turn you in bed?" exclaimed Rebecca, walking the floor and wringing her hands distractedly.

"It don't make any difference if I don't get turned," replied Aurelia stoically. "If a woman of my age and the mother of a family hasn't got sense enough not to slip off hay-mows, she'd ought to suffer. Go put on your black dress and pack your bag. I'd give a good deal if I was able to go to my sister's funeral and prove that I've forgotten and forgiven all she said when I was married. Her acts were softer'n her words, Mirandy's were, and she's made up to you for all she ever sinned against me'n' your father! And oh, Rebecca," she continued with quivering voice, "I remember so well when we were little girls together and she took such pride in curling my hair: and another time, when we were grown up, she lent me her best blue muslin: it was when your father had asked me to lead the grand march with him at the Christmas dance, and I found out afterwards she thought he'd intended to ask her!"

Here Aurelia broke down and wept bitterly; for the recollection of the past had softened her heart and brought the comforting tears even more effectually than the news of her sister's death.

There was only an hour for preparation. Will would drive Rebecca to Temperance and send Jenny back from school. He volunteered also to engage a woman to sleep at the farm in case Mrs. Randall should be worse at any time in the night.

Rebecca flew down over the hill to get a last pail of spring water, and as she lifted the bucket from the crystal depths and looked out over the glowing beauty of the autumn landscape, she saw a company of surveyors with their instruments making calculations and laying lines that apparently crossed Sunnybrook at the favorite spot where Mirror Pool lay clear and placid, the yellow leaves on its surface no yellower than its sparkling sands.

She caught her breath. "The time has come!" she thought. "I am saying good-bye to Sunnybrook, and the golden gates that almost swung together that last day in Wareham will close forever now. Good-bye, dear brook and hills and meadows; you are going to see life too, so we must be hopeful and say to one another:—

'Grow old along with me,
The best is yet to be.' "

Will Melville had seen the surveyors too, and had heard in the Temperance post office that morning the probable sum that Mrs. Randall would receive from the railway company. He was in good spirits at his own improved prospects, for his farm was so placed that its value could be only increased by the new road; he was also relieved in mind that his wife's family would no longer be in dire poverty directly at his doorstep, so to speak. John could now be hurried forward and forced into the position of head of the family several years sooner than had been anticipated, so Hannah's husband was obliged to exercise great self-control or he would have whistled while he was driving Rebecca to the Temperance station. He could not understand her sad face or the tears that rolled silently down her cheeks from time to time; for Hannah had always represented her Aunt Miranda as an irascible, parsimonious old woman, who would be no loss to the world whenever she should elect to disappear from it.

"Cheer up, Becky!" he said, as he left her at the station. "You'll find your mother sitting up when you come back, and the next thing

you know the whole family'll be moving to some nice little house wherever your work is. Things will never be so bad again as they have been this last year; that's what Hannah and I think." And he drove away to tell his wife the news.

Adam Ladd was in the station and came up to Rebecca instantly, as she entered the door looking very unlike her bright self.

"The Princess is sad this morning," he said, taking her hand. "Aladdin must rub the magic lamp; then the slave will appear, and these tears be dried in a trice."

He spoke lightly, for he thought her trouble was something connected with affairs at Sunnybrook, and that he could soon bring the smiles by telling her that the farm was sold and that her mother was to receive a handsome price in return. He meant to remind her, too, that though she must leave the home of her youth, it was too remote a place to be a proper dwelling either for herself or for her lonely mother and the three younger children. He could hear her say as plainly as if it were yesterday, "I don't think one ever forgets the spot where one lived as a child." He could see the quaint little figure sitting on the piazza at North Riverboro and watch it disappear in the lilac bushes when he gave the memorable order for three hundred cakes of Rose-Red and Snow-White soap.

A word or two soon told him that her grief was of another sort, and her mood was so absent, so sensitive and tearful, that he could only assure her of his sympathy and beg that he might come soon to the brick house to see with his own eyes how she was faring.

Adam thought, when he had put her on the train and taken his leave, that Rebecca was, in her sad dignity and gravity, more beautiful than he had ever seen her,—all-beautiful and all-womanly. He turned from the little country station to walk in the woods by the wayside until his own train should be leaving, and from time to time he threw himself under a tree to think and dream and look at the glory of the foliage. He had brought a new copy of the "Arabian Nights" for Rebecca, wishing to replace the well-worn old one that had been the delight of her girlhood; but meeting her at such an inauspicious time, he had absently carried it away with him. He turned the pages idly until he came to the story of "Aladdin and the Wonderful Lamp," and presently, in spite of his thirty-four years, the old tale held him spellbound as it did in the days when he first read it as a boy. But there were certain paragraphs that especially caught his eye and arrested his attention,—paragraphs that he read and reread, finding in them he knew not what secret delight and significance.

27
AUNT MIRANDA'S APOLOGY

When Rebecca alighted from the train at Maplewood and hurried to the post office where the stage was standing, what was her joy to see Uncle Jerry Cobb holding the horses' heads.

"The reg'lar driver's sick," he explained, "and they sent for me. So here I be jest as I was more'n six years ago. Will you be a real lady passenger, or will ye sit up in front with me?"

Emotions of various sorts were all struggling together in the old man's face, and the two or three bystanders were astounded when they saw the handsome, stately girl fling herself on Mr. Cobb's dusty shoulder crying like a child.

"Oh, Uncle Jerry!" she sobbed; "dear Uncle Jerry! It's all so long ago, and so much has happened, and we've grown so old, and so much is going to happen that I'm fairly frightened."

"There, there, lovey," the old man whispered comfortingly, "we'll be all alone on the stage, and we'll talk things over's we go along the road an' mebbe they won't look so bad."

Every mile of the way was as familiar to Rebecca as to Uncle Jerry; every watering-trough, grindstone, red barn, weather-vane, duck-pond, and sandy brook. The drive was taken almost in silence, but it was a sweet, comforting silence both to Uncle Jerry and the girl.

Then came the sight of Abijah Flagg shelling beans in the barn, and then the Perkins attic windows with a white cloth fluttering from them. She could spell Emma Jane's loving thought and welcome in that little waving flag; a word and a message sent to her just at the first moment when Riverboro chimneys rose into view; something to warm her heart till they could meet.

The brick house came next, looking just as of yore; though it seemed to Rebecca as if death should have cast some mysterious spell over it. There were the rolling meadows, the stately elms, all yellow and brown now; the glowing maples, the garden beds bright with asters, and the hollyhocks, rising tall against the parlor windows; only in place of the cheerful pinks and reds of the nodding stalks, with their gay rosettes of bloom, was a crape scarf holding the blinds together, and another on the sitting room side, and another on the brass knocker of the brown-painted door.

"Stop, Uncle Jerry! Don't turn in at the side; hand me my satchel, please; drop me in the road and let me run up the path by myself. Then drive away quickly."

At the noise and rumble of the approaching stage the house door opened from within, just as Rebecca closed the gate behind her. Aunt Jane came down the stone steps, a changed woman, frail and broken and white. Rebecca held out her arms and the old aunt crept into them feebly. Warmth and strength and life flowed into the aged frame from the young one.

"Rebecca," she said, raising her head, "before you go in to look at her, do you feel any bitterness over anything she ever said to you?"

Rebecca's eyes blazed reproach, almost anger, as she said chokingly: "Oh, Aunt Jane. Could you believe it of me? I am going in with a heart brimful of gratitude!"

"She was a good woman, Rebecca; she had a quick temper and a sharp tongue, but she wanted to do right, and she did it as near as she could. She never said so, but I'm sure she was sorry for every hard word she spoke to you; she didn't take 'em back in life, but she acted so't you'd know her feeling when she was gone."

"I told her before I left that she'd been the making of me, just as mother says," sobbed Rebecca.

"She wasn't that," said Jane. "God made you in the first place, and you've done considerable yourself to help Him along; but she gave you the wherewithal to work with, and that ain't to be despised; specially when anybody gives up her own luxuries and pleasures to do it. Now let me tell you something, Rebecca. Your Aunt Mirandy's willed all this to you,—the brick house and buildings and furniture, and the land all round the house, as far's you can see."

Rebecca threw off her hat and put her hand to her heart, as she always did in moments of intense excitement. After a moment's silence she said: "Let me go in alone; I want to talk to her; I want to thank her; I feel as if I could make her hear and feel and understand!"

Ten minutes later Rebecca came out from the Great Presence looking white and spent, but chastened and glorified. She sat in the quiet doorway, shaded from the little Riverboro world by the overhanging elms. A wide sense of thankfulness and peace possessed her, as she looked at the autumn landscape, listened to the rumble of a wagon on the bridge, and heard the call of the river as it dashed to the sea. She put up her hand softly and touched first the shining brass knocker and then the red bricks, glowing in the October sun.

It was home; her roof, her garden, her green acres, her dear trees; it was shelter for the little family at Sunnybrook; her mother would have once more the companionship of her sister and the friends of her girlhood; the children would have teachers and playmates.

And she? Her own future was close-folded still; folded and hidden in beautiful mists; but she leaned her head against the sun-warmed door, and closing her eyes, whispered, just as if she had been a child saying her prayers: "God bless Aunt Miranda; God bless the brick house that was; God bless the brick house that is to be!"

CAPTAIN JANUARY

CHAPTER I

STAR BRIGHT

The Captain had sold all his lobsters. They had been particularly fine ones, and had gone off "like hot cakes," every one who passed by the wharf stopping to buy one or two. Now the red dory was empty, and the Captain had washed her out with his usual scrupulous care, and was making preparations for his homeward voyage, when he was hailed by a cheery voice from the street.

"Hillo, January!" said the voice. "Is that you? How goes it?" and the owner of the voice, a sturdy man in a blue coat with brass buttons, came down the wharf and greeted the Captain with a hearty shake of the hand.

"How goes it?" he repeated. "I haven't seen ye for a dog's age."

"I'm hearty, Cap'n Nazro!" replied Captain January. "Hearty, that's what I am, an' hopin' you're the same."

"That's right!" said the first speaker. "'Tain't often we set eyes on you, you stick so close to your light. And the little gal, she's well, I expect? She looks a picture, when I take a squint at her through the glass sometimes. Never misses running out and shaking her apron when we go by!"

"Cap'n Nazro," said January, speaking with emphasis, "if there is a pictur in this world, o' health, and pootiness, and goodness, it's that child. It's that little un, sir. Not to be beat in this country, nor yet any other, 'cordin' as I've voyaged."

"Nice little gal!" said Captain Nazro, assenting. "Mighty nice little gal! Ain't it time she was going to school, January? My wife and I were speaking about it only the other day. Seems as if she'd oughter be round with other children now, and learning what they do. Mis Nazro would be real pleased to have her stop with us a spell, and go to school with our gals. What do you say?" He spoke very heartily, but looked doubtfully at the old man, as if hardly expecting a favorable answer.

Captain January shook his head emphatically. "You're real kind, Cap'n Nazro!" he said; "real kind, you and Mis Nazro both are! And she makin' the little un's frocks and pinafores is a great help. But I can't feel to let her out o' my sight, nohow; and as for school, she ain't the kind to abear it, nor yet I couldn't for her. She's learnin'!" he added, proudly. "Learnin' well! I'll bet there ain't no gal in your school knows more nor that little un does. Won'erful, the way she walks ahead!"

"Get the school readers, hey! And teach her yourself, do you?" queried Captain Nazro.

"No, sir!" replied the old man; "I don't have no school readers. The child learns out o' the two best books in the world,—the Bible, and William Shakespeare's book; them's all the books she ever seed—*saw,* I should say."

"William Shak—" began Captain Nazro; and then he broke off in sheer amazement, and said, simply, "Well, I'm blowed!"

"The minister giv 'em to me," said Captain January. "I reckon he knows. There's a dictionary, too," he added, rather sadly; "but I can't make her take to that, nohow, though there's a power o' fine words in it."

Then, as the other man remained silent and open-mouthed, he said: "But I must be goin', Cap'n Nazro, sir! The little un'll be lookin' for me. Good day, sir, and thank ye kindly, all the same as if it was to be, which it ain't!" And with a friendly gesture, the old man stepped into his red dory, and rowed away with long, sturdy strokes.

Captain Nazro gazed after him meditatively, took out his pipe and looked at it, then gazed again. "January's cracked," he said;

"that's what's the matter with him. He's a good man, and a good lighthouse-keeper, and he's been an able seaman in his day, none better; but he's cracked!"

There is an island off a certain part of the coast of Maine,—a little rocky island, heaped and tumbled together as if Dame Nature had shaken down a heap of stones at random from her apron, when she had finished making the larger islands which lie between it and the mainland. At one end, the shoreward end, there is a tiny cove, and a bit of silver-sand beach, with a green meadow beyond it, and a single great pine; but all the rest is rocks, rocks. At the farther end the rocks are piled high, like a castle wall, making a brave barrier against the Atlantic waves; and on top of this cairn rises the lighthouse, rugged and sturdy as the rocks themselves, but painted white, and with its windows shining like great, smooth diamonds. This is Light Island; and it was in this direction that Captain January's red dory was headed when he took his leave of his brother captain, and rowed away from the wharf. It was a long pull; in fact, it took pretty nearly the whole afternoon, so that the evening shadows were lengthening when at length he laid down his oars, and he felt the boat's nose rub against the sand of the little home-cove. But rowing was no more effort than breathing to Captain January, and it was no fatigue, but only a trifle of stiffness from sitting so long, that troubled him a little in getting out of the boat. As he stepped slowly out upon the firm-grained silver of the little beach, he looked up and around with an expectant air, and seeing no one, a look of disappointment crossed his face. He opened his lips as if to call some one, but checking himself, "Happen she's gettin' supper!" he said. "It's later than I thought. I don't pull so spry as I used ter, 'pears ter me. Wal, thar! 'tain't to be expected. I sh'll be forty years old before I know it!"

Chuckling to himself, the Captain drew up the little boat and made her fast; then, taking sundry brown-paper parcels from under the thwart, he turned and made his way up towards the lighthouse. A picturesque figure he was, striding along among the heaped and tumbled rocks. His hair and beard, still thick and curly, were absolutely white, as white as

the foam that broke over the rocks at the cliff's foot. His face was tanned and weather-beaten to the color of mahogany, but the features were strong and sharply cut, while the piercing blue eyes which gleamed beneath his shaggy eyebrows showed all the fire of youth, and seemed to have no part in the seventy years which had bent the tall form, and rounded slightly the broad and massive shoulders. The Captain wore a rough pea-jacket and long boots, while his head was adorned with a nondescript covering which might have begun life either as a hat or a cap, but would now hardly be owned by either family.

Reaching the house, the old man mounted the rude steps which led to the door, and entered the room which was kitchen, dining, and drawing room at Storm Castle, as the lighthouse was called by its inhabitants. The room was light and cheerful, with a pleasant little fire crackling sociably on the hearth. The table was laid with a clean white cloth, the kettle was singing on the hob, and a little covered saucepan was simmering with an agreeable and suggestive sound; but no one was to be seen. Alarmed, he hardly knew why, at the silence and solitude, Captain January set his parcels down on the table, and going to the foot of the narrow stone staircase which wound upward beside the chimney, called, "Star! Star Bright, where are you? Is anything wrong?"

"No, Daddy Captain!" answered a clear, childish voice from above; "I'm coming in a minute. Be patient, Daddy dear!"

With a sigh of relief, Captain January retired to the fireplace, and sitting down in a huge high-backed armchair, began leisurely pulling off his great boots. One was already off and in his hand, when a slight noise made him look up. He started violently, and then, leaning back in his chair, gazed in silent amazement at the vision before him.

On the stone stairway, and slowly descending, with steps that were meant to be stately (and which might have been so, had not the stairs been so steep, and the little legs so short) was the figure of a child: a little girl about ten years old, with a face of almost startling beauty. Her hair floated like a cloud of pale gold about her shoulders; her

eyes were blue, not light and keen, like the old man's, but of that soft, deep, shadowy blue that poets love to call violet. Wonderful eyes, shaded by long, curved lashes of deepest black, which fell on the soft, rose-and-ivory tinted cheek, as the child carefully picked her way down, holding up her long dress from her little feet. It was the dress which so astonished Captain January. Instead of the pink calico frock and blue checked pinafore, to which his eyes were accustomed, the little figure was clad in a robe of dark green velvet with a long train, which spread out on the staircase behind her, very much like the train of a peacock. The body, made for a grown woman, hung back loosely from her shoulders, but she had tied a scarf of gold tissue under her arms and round her waist, while from the long hanging sleeves her arms shone round and white as sculptured ivory. A strange sight, this, for a lighthouse tower on the coast of Maine! But so fair a one, that the old mariner could not take his eyes from it.

"Might be Juliet!" he muttered to himself. "Juliet, when she was a little un. 'Her beauty hangs upon the cheek o' Night,'—only it ain't, so to say, exactly night,—'like a rich jewel in a nigger's ear.' No! That ain't right. 'Nigger' ain't right, 'Ethiop's ear,' that's it! Though I should judge they were much the same thing, and they more frekently wear 'em in their noses, them as I've seen in their own country."

As he thus soliloquized, the little maiden reached the bottom of the stairs in safety, and dropping the folds of the velvet about her, made a quaint little courtesy, and said, "Here I am, Daddy Captain! How do you like me, please?"

"Star Bright," replied Captain January, gazing fixedly at her, as he slowly drew his pipe from his pocket and lighted it. "I like you amazin'. A-mazin' I like you, my dear! But it is what you might call surprisin', to leave a little maid in a blue pinafore, and to come back and find a princess in gold and velvet. Yes, Pigeon Pie, you might call it surprisin', and yet not be stretchin' a p'int."

"Am I really like a princess?" said the child, clapping her hands, and laughing with pleasure. "Have you ever seen a princess, Daddy Captain, and did she look like me?"

"I seed—I *saw*—one, once," replied the Captain, gravely, puffing at his pipe. "In Africky it was, when I was fust mate to an Indiaman. And she wa'n't like you, Peach Blossom, no more than Hyperion to a Satyr, and that kind o' thing. She had on a short petticut, comin' half-way down to her knees, and a necklace, and a ring through her nose. And—"

"Where were her other clothes?" asked the child.

"Wal—maybe she kem off in a hurry and forgot 'em!" said the Captain, charitably. "Anyhow, not speakin' her language, I didn't ask her. And she was as black as the ace of spades, and shinin' all over with butter."

"Oh, *that* kind of princess!" said Star, loftily. "I didn't mean that kind, Daddy. I meant the kind who live in fretted palaces, with music in th' enamelled stones, you know, and wore clothes like these every day."

"Wal, Honey, I never saw one of that kind, till now!" said the Captain, meekly. "And I'm sorry I hain't—I mean I *ain't*—got no fretted palace for my princess to live in. This is a poor place for golden lasses and velvet trains."

"It *isn't!*" cried the child, her face flashing into sudden anger, and stamping her foot. "You sha'n't call it a poor place, Daddy! It's wicked of you. And I wouldn't live in a palace if there were *fifty* of them all set in a row. So there now!"

She folded her arms and looked defiantly at the old man, who returned her gaze placidly, and continued to puff at his pipe, until he was seized in a penitent embrace, hugged, and kissed, and scolded, and wept over, all at once.

The brief tempest over, the child seated herself comfortably on his knee, and said, "Now, Daddy, I want a story."

"Story before supper?" asked the Captain, meekly, looking at the saucepan, which was fairly lifting its lid in its eagerness to be attended to. A fresh access of remorseful hugging followed.

"You poor darling!" said Star; "I forgot all about supper. And it's stewed kidneys, too! But oh! my dress!" and she glanced down at

her velvet splendor. "I must go and take it off," she said, sadly.

"Not you, Honeysuckle," said the old man, rising and setting the child down carefully in the chair. "Sit you there, and be a real princess, and I will be your steward, and get supper this time. I like to see you in your fine clothes, and 'twould be a shame to take 'em off so soon."

She clapped her hands again, and settling herself cosily in the great chair, arranged her train with a graceful sweep, and pushed back her cloudy golden hair.

"Shall I really act princess!" she asked,— and without waiting for an answer, she began to give orders in lofty tones, holding her head high in the air, and pointing hither and thither with her tiny hands. "Take up the golden chafing dish, Grumio!" she cried. "The kidneys—I mean the capons—are quite ready now. And the milk—no! the sack—is in the silver flagon!" she pointed to an ancient blue jug which stood on the dresser.

The obedient Captain hastened to take up the saucepan, and soon the frugal supper was set out, and princess and steward were doing ample justice to it.

"You didn't say 'Anon! Anon! Madam' when I ordered you about," said the Princess, thoughtfully. "You ought to, you know. Servants always do in the book."

"Wal, I didn't think on't," the steward admitted. "I wa'n't brought up to the business, you see, Princess. It always seemed to me a foolish thing to say, anyhow: no disrespect to W. Shakespeare. The hull of the word's 'anonymous,' I believe, and the dictionary says *that* means 'wanting a name.' So, altogether, Star Bright, I haven't been able to make much sense out o' that answer."

"Oh, never mind!" said the Princess, tossing her head. "I don't like the dictionary. It's a wretch!"

"So 'tis, so 'tis," assented the Captain, with servile alacrity. "Have some more milk then, Sunshine."

"It isn't milk! It's sack," said the child, promptly, holding out her small yellow mug with a royal air. "Are the capons good, Grumio?"

"They are, my lamb, they are," replied the

Captain. "Oncommon good they are, to be sure, and me not knowin' to this day what capons was. A little more? Yes, Pigeon Pie, I *will* take a little more, thank ye kindly."

"I don't *think*, Grumio, that you ought to call me lambs and pigeon pies just now," remarked the Princess, judiciously. "Do you think it's respectful? They don't in Shakespeare, I'm sure."

"I won't do it again, Honey—I mean Madam," said the Captain, bowing with great humility. "I beg your honorable majesty's pardon, and I won't never presume to—"

"Yes, you will!" cried the Princess, flinging herself across the table at him, and nearly choking him with the sudden violence of her embrace. "You shall call me pigeon pie, and anything else you like. You shall call me rye porridge, though I hate it, and it's always full of lumps. And don't ever look that way again; it *kills* me!"

The Captain quietly removed the clinging arms, and kissed them, and set the half-weeping child back in her place. "There, there, there!" he said, soothingly. "What a little tempest it is!"

"Say 'delicate Ariel,' " sobbed Star. "You haven't said it to-day, and you always say it when you love me."

"Cream Cheese from the dairy of Heaven," replied the Captain; "if I always said it when I loved you, I should be sayin' it every minute of time, as well you know. But you *are* my delicate Ariel, so you are, and there ain't nothin' in the hull book as suits you better. So!" and his supper ended, the good man turned his chair again to the fire, and took the child, once more smiling, upon his knee.

"And now, Ariel, what have you been doin' all the time I was away? Tell Daddy all about it."

Star pondered a moment, with her head on one side, and a finger hooked confidentially through the Captain's buttonhole. "Well," she said, "I've had a *very* interesting time, Daddy Captain. First I cleaned the lamps, of course, and filled and trimmed them. And then I played Samson a good while; and—"

"And how might you play Samson?" inquired the Captain.

"With flies!" replied Star, promptly. "Heaps

upon heaps, you know; 'With the jawbone of an ass have I slain a thousand men.' The flies were the Philistines, and I took a clam shell for the jawbone; it did just as well. And I made a song out of it, to one of the tunes you whistle: 'With the jawbone! with the jawbone! with the jawbone of an ass!' It was very exciting."

"Must ha' been," said the Captain, dryly. "Well, Honeysuckle, what did you do then?"

"Oh, that took some time!" said the child. "And afterward I fished a little, but I didn't catch anything, 'cept an old flounder, and he winked at me so, I put him back. And then I thought a long time—oh! a very long time, sitting like Patience on the doorstep. And *suddenly,* Daddy Captain, I thought about those boxes of clothes, and how you said they would be mine when I was big. And I measured myself against the doorpost, and found that I *was very* big. I thought I must be almost as big as you, but I s'pose I'd forgotten how big you were. So I went up, and opened one box, and I was just putting the dress on when you came in. You knew where it came from, of course, Daddy, the moment you saw it."

The Captain nodded gravely, and pulled his long moustaches.

"Do you suppose my poor mamma wore it often?" the child went on, eagerly. "Do you think she looked like me when she wore it? Do I look as she did when you saw her?"

"Wal," began the Captain, meditatively; but Star ran on without waiting for an answer.

"Of course, though, she looked very different, because she was dead. You are quite very positively sure my poor mamma was dead, Daddy Captain?"

"She were," replied the Captain, with emphasis. "She were that, Pigeon Pie! You couldn't find nobody deader, not if you'd sarched for a week. Why, door nails, and Julius Caesar, and things o' that description, would ha' been *lively* compared with your poor ma when I see her. Lively! That's what they'd ha' been."

The child nodded with an air of familiar interest, wholly untinged with sadness. "I think," she said, laying her head against the old man's shoulder, and curling one arm about his neck, "I think I should like to hear about it again, please, Daddy. It's a long, long time since you told me the whole of it."

"Much as a month, I should think it must be," assented the Captain. "Why, Snowdrop, you know the story by heart, better'n I do, I believe. 'Pears to me I've told it reg'lar, once a month or so, ever since you were old enough to understand it."

"Never mind!" said the Princess, with an imperious gesture. "That makes no difference. I *want* it now!"

"Wal, wal!" said the Captain, smoothing back the golden hair. "If you *want* it, why of course you must have it, Blossom! But first I must light up, ye know. One star inside the old house, and the other atop of it: that's what makes Light Island the lightest spot in the natural world. Sit ye here, Star Bright, and play Princess till Daddy comes back!"

CHAPTER II

THE STORY

The lamps were lighted, and the long, level rays flashed their golden warning over the murmuring darkness of the summer sea, giving cheer to many hearts on inbound barque or schooner. Bright indeed was the star on the top of the old lighthouse; but no less radiant was the face of little Star, as she turned it eagerly towards Captain January, and waited for the beginning of the well-known and well-loved story.

"Wal," said the Captain, when his pipe was refilled and drawing bravely. "Let me see now! where shall I begin?"

"At the beginning!" said Star, promptly.

"Jes' so!" assented the old man. "Ten year ago this—"

"No! No!!" cried the child. "*That* isn't the beginning, Daddy! That's almost halfway to the middle. 'When I was a young lad.' That's the beginning."

"Bound to have it all, are ye, Honeysuckle?" said the obedient Captain. "Wal' wal! When I were a young lad, I was a wild un, ye see, Treasure. My father, he 'prenticed me to a blacksmith, being big and strong for my years; but I hadn't no heart for the work. All I cared about was the sea, and boats, and sailors, and sea talk. I ran away down to the wharf whenever I could get a chance, and left my work. Why, even when I went to meetin', 'stead o' listenin' to the minister, I was lookin' out the places about them as go down to the sea in ships, ye know, and 'that leviathan whom Thou hast made,' and all that. And there was Hiram, King of Tyre, and his ships! Lord! How I used to think about them ships, and wonder how they was rigged, and how many tons they were, and all about it. Yes! I was a wild un, and no mistake; and after awhile I got so roused up—after my mother died, it was, and my father married again—that I just run away, and shipped aboard of a whaler, bound for the north seas. Wal, Honey, 'twould take me a week to tell ye about all my voyages. Long and short of it, 'twas the life I was meant for, and I done well in it. Had tumbles and toss-ups, here and there, same as everybody has in any kind o' life; but I done well, and by the time I was forty year old I was captain of the *Bonito,* East Indiaman, sailin' from New York to Calcutta."

The Captain paused, and puffed gravely at his pipe for a few minutes.

"Well, Rosebud," he continued, presently, "you know what comes next. The *Bonito* was cast away, in a cyclone, on a desert island, and all hands lost, except me and one other."

"Dear Daddy! Poor Daddy!" cried the child, putting her little hands up to the weather-beaten face, and drawing it down to hers. "Don't talk about that dreadful part. Go on to the next!"

"No, I won't talk about it, Star Bright!" said the old man, very gravely. "Fust place I can't, and second place it ain't fit for little maids to hear of. But I lived on that island fifteen year,—five year with my good mate Job Hotham, and ten year alone, after Job died. When a ship kem by, after that, and took me off, I'd forgot most everything, and was partly like the beasts that perish; but it kem back to me. Slow, like, and by fits, as you may say; but it kem back, all there was before, and maybe a good bit more!"

"Poor Daddy!" murmured the child again, pressing her soft cheek against the white

beard. "It's all over now! Don't think of it! I am here, Daddy, loving you: loving you *all to pieces,* you know!"

The old man was silent for a few minutes, caressing the little white hands which lay like twin snowflakes in his broad, brown palm. Then he resumed, cheerfully:

"And so, Cream Cheese from the dairy of Heaven, I kem home. Your old Daddy kem home, and landed on the same wharf he'd sailed from twenty-five years before. Not direct, you understand, but takin' steamer from New York, and so on. Wal, there wa'n't nobody that knew me, or cared for me. Father was dead, and his wife; and their children, as weren't born when I sailed from home, were growed up and gone away. No, there wa'n't nobody. Wal, I tried for a spell to settle down and live like other folks, but 'twa'n't no use. I wasn't used to the life, and I couldn't stand it. For ten years I hadn't heard the sound of a human voice, and now they was buzz, buzzin' all the time; it seemed as if there was a swarm of wasps round my ears the everlastin' day. Buzz! buzz! and then clack! clack! like an everlasting mill-clapper; and folks starin' at my brown face and white hair, and askin' me foolish questions. I couldn't stand it, that was all. I heard that a light-keeper was wanted here, and I asked for the place, and got it. And that's all of the fust part, Peach Blossom."

The child drew a long breath, and her face glowed with eager anticipation. "And *now,* Daddy Captain," she said, "*now* you may say, 'Ten year ago this fall!'"

"Ten year ago this fall," said the Captain, meekly acquiescing, "on the fourteenth day of September, as ever was, I looks out from the tower, bein' a-fillin' of the lamps, and says I, 'There's a storm comin'!' So I made all taut above and below, and fastened the door, and took my glass and went out on the rocks, to see how things looked. Wal, they looked pooty bad. There had been a heavy sea on for a couple o' days, and the clouds that was comin' up didn't look as if they was goin' to smooth it down any. There was a kind o' brassy look over everythin', and when the wind began to rise, it warn't with no nat'ral sound, but a kind of screech to it, on'arthly like. Wal, thar! The wind did rise, and it riz to stay. In half an

hour it was blowin' half a gale; in an hour it blew a gale, and as tough a one (barrin' cyclones) as ever I see. 'T had like to ha' blow me off my pins, half a dozen times. Then nat'rally the sea kem up; and 'twas all creation on them rocks, now I tell ye. 'The sea, mountin' to the welkin's cheek;' ye remember, Pigeon Pie?"

The child nodded eagerly. "Tempest!" she said, "Act I., Scene 2: 'Enter Prospero and Miranda.' Go on, Daddy!"

"Wal, my Lily Flower," continued the old man. "And the storm went on. It roared, it bellowed, and it screeched: it thumped and it kerwhalloped. The great seas would come bunt up agin the rocks, as if they was bound to go right through to Jersey City, which they used to say was the end of the world. Then they'd go scoopin' back, as if they was callin' all their friends and neighbors to help; and then, bang! they'd come at it agin. The spray was flyin' in great white sheets, and whiles, it seemed as if the hull island was goin' to be swallowed up then and thar. 'Tain't nothin' but a little heap o' rocks, anyhow, to face the hull Atlantic Ocean gone mad: and on that heap o' rocks was Januarius Judkins, holdin' on for dear life, and feelin' like a hoppergrass that had got lost in Niag'ry Falls."

"Don't say that name, Daddy!" interrupted the child. "You know I don't like it. Say 'Captain January'!"

"I tell ye, Honeysuckle," said the old man, "I felt more like a sea-cook than a cap'n *that* night. A cap'n on a quarter-deck's a good thing; but a cap'n on a p'int o' rock, out to sea in a northeast gale, might just as well be a fo'c'sle hand and done with it. Wal, as I was holdin' on thar, I seed a flash to windward, as wasn't lightning; and next minute kem a sound as wasn't thunder nor yet wind nor sea."

"The guns! The guns!" cried the child, in great excitement. "The guns of my poor mamma's ship. And then you heard them again, Daddy?"

"Then I heard them agin!" the old man assented. "And agin! A flash, and a boom! and then in a minute agin, a flash and a boom! 'Oh, Lord!' says I. 'Take her by to the mainland, and put her ashore there!' I says; 'cause there's life-saving station thar, ye know, Blossom, and there might be some chance for them as were in her. But the Lord had His views, my dear, the Lord had His views! Amen! So be it! In another minute there kem a break in the clouds, and thar she was, comin' full head on, straight for Light Island. Oh! my little Star, that was an awful thing to see. And I couldn't do nothin', you understand. Not a livin' a'rthly thing could I do, 'cept hide my face agin the rock I was clingin' to, and say, 'Dear Lord, take 'em easy! It's Thy will as they should be took,' I says, 'and there ain't no one to hender, if so be as they could. But take 'em easy, good Lord, and take 'em suddin!'"

"And He did!" cried the child. "The good Lord did take 'em sudden, didn't He, Daddy Captain?"

"He did, my child!" said the old man, solemnly. "They was all home, them that was goin', in ten minutes from the time I saw the ship. You know the Roarin' Bull, as sticks his horns out o' water just to windward of us? The cruelest rock on the coast, he is, and the treacherousest: and the ship struck him full and fair on the starboard quarter, and in ten minutes she was kindlin' wood, as ye may say. The Lord rest their souls as went down in her! Amen!"

"Amen!" said little Star, softly. But she added in an eager tone, "And now, Daddy, you are coming to me!"

"Pooty soon, Jewel Bright!" said the old man, stroking the gold hair tenderly. "I'm a-comin' to you pooty soon. 'Twas along about eight bells when she struck, and none so dark, for the moon had risen. After the ship had gone down, I strained my eyes through the driving spray, to see whether anything was comin' ashore. Presently I seed somethin' black, driftin' towards the rocks: and lo' ye, 'twas a boat, bottom side up, and all hands gone down. Wal' wal! The Lord knew what was right: but it's wuss by a deal to *see* them things than to be in 'em yourself, to my thinkin'. Wal, after a spell I looked agin, and there was somethin' else a-driftin' looked like a spar, it did: and somethin' was lashed to it. My heart! 'twas tossed about like a eggshell, up and down, and here and thar! 'Twas

white, whatever was lashed to it, and I couldn't take my eyes off'n it. 'It can't be alive!' I says, 'whatever it is!' I says. 'But I'll get it, if it takes a leg!' I says. For down in my heart, Jewel, I knew they wouldn't ha' taken such care of anythin' *but* what was alive, and they perishin', but I didn't think it could live in such a sea long enough to get ashore. Wal, I kep' my eyes on that spar, and I see that 'twas comin' along by the south side. Then I ran, or crawled, 'cordin' as the wind allowed me, back to the shed, and got a boat-hook and a coil o' rope; and then I clumb down as far as I dared, on the south rocks. I scooched down under the lee of a p'int o' rock, and made the rope fast round my waist, and the other end round the rock, and then I waited for the spar to come along. 'Twas hard to make out anythin', for the water was all a white, bilin' churn, and the spray flyin' fit to blind you; but bimeby I co't sight of her comin' swashin' along, now up on top of a big roarer, and then scootin' down into the holler, and then up agin. I crep' out on the rocks, grippin' 'em for all I was wuth, with the boat-hook under my arm. The wind screeched and clawed at me like a wildcat in a caniption fit, but I hadn't been through those cyclones for nothin.' I lay down flat and wriggled myself out to the edge, and thar I waited."

"And the big waves were breaking over you all the time?" cried the child, with eager inquiry.

"Wal, they was that, Honeysuckle!" said the Captain. "Bless ye, I sh'd ha' been washed off like a log if 't hadn't ben for the rope. But that held; 'twas a good one, and tied with a bowline, and it held. Wal, I lay thar, and all to wunst I see her comin' by like a flash, close to me. '*Now!*' says I, 'ef ther's any stuff in you, J. Judkins, let's see it!' says I. And I chucks myself over the side o' the rock and grabs her with the boat-hook, and hauls her in. 'All together,' I says. '*Now,* my hearties! Yo heave *ho!*' and I hed her up, and hauled her over the rocks and round under the lèe of the p'int, before I stopped to breathe. How did I do it? Don't ask me, Jewel Bright! *I* don't know how I did it. There's times when a man has strength given to him, seemin'ly, over and above human strength. 'Twas like as if the Lord ketched holt and helped me: maybe He did, seein' what 'twas I was doing. Maybe He did!" He paused a moment in thought, but Star was impatient.

"Well, Daddy!" she cried. "And then you looked and found it was—go on, Daddy dear!"

"I looked," continued the old man, "and I found it was a sail, that had showed so white against the spar; a sail, wrapped tight round somethin'. I cut the ropes, and pulled away the canvas and a tarpaulin that was inside that; and thar I seed—"

"My poor mamma and me!" cried the child, joyously, clapping her hands. "Oh, Daddy Captain, it *is* so delightful when you come to this part! And my poor mamma was dead? You are quite positively sure that she was dead, Daddy?"

"She were, my lamb!" replied the Captain, gravely. "You needn't never have no doubt about it. She had had a blow on the head, your poor ma had, from one o' the bull's horns, likely; and I'll warrant she never knowed anythin' after it, poor lady! She was wrapped in a great fur cloak, the same as you have on your bed in winter, Blossom: and lyin' all clost and warm in her cold arms, that held on still, though the life was gone out of 'em, was"—the old man faltered, and brushed his rough hand across his eyes—"was a—a little baby. Asleep, it seemed to be, all curled up like a rose on its mother's breast, and its pooty eyes tight shut. I loosed the poor arms—they was like a stattoo's, so round and white and cold; and I took the child up in my arms; and lo' ye! it opened its eyes and looked straight at me and laughed."

"And it said, Daddy?" cried the delighted child, clapping her hands. "Tell what it said!"

"It said ' 'Tar,' " the old man continued, in a hushed voice. " ' 'Tar,' it said as plain as I say it to you. 'And "Star" it is!' says I; for 'if ever a star shone on a dark night, it's you, my pooty,' I says. 'Praise the Lord,' I says. 'Amen, so be it.' Then I laid your poor ma in a corner, under the lee of the big rock, where the spray wouldn't fly over her, and I covered her with the sail; and then I took the fur cloak, seein' the baby needed it and she didn't, and wrapped it round the little un, and clumb back over the rocks, up to the house. And so, Honeysuckle—"

"And so," cried the child, taking his two great hands and putting them softly together, "so I came to be your little Star!"

"To be my little Star!" assented the old man, stooping to kiss the golden head.

"Your light and your joy!" exclaimed the child, laughing with pleasure.

"My light and my joy!" said the old man, solemnly. "A light from heaven to shine in a dark place, and the Lord's message to a sinful man."

He was silent for a little, looking earnestly into the child's radiant face. Presently, "You've been happy, Star Bright?" he asked. "You haven't missed nothin'?"

Star opened wide eyes of surprise at him. "Of course I've been happy!" she said. "Why shouldn't I be?"

"You ain't—I mean you haven't mourned for your poor ma, have ye, Jewel?" He was still looking curiously at her, and his look puzzled her.

"No," she said, after a pause. "Of course not. I never knew my poor mamma. Why should I mourn for her? She is in heaven, and I am very glad. You say heaven is much nicer than here, so it must be pleasanter for my poor mamma; and I don't need her, because I have you, Daddy. But go on, now, please, Daddy dear. 'Next day'—"

"Next day," resumed the obedient Captain, "the sky was bright and clear, and only the heavy sea, and your poor ma, and you, Peach Blossom, to tell what had happened, so far as I seed at fust. Bimeby, when I went out to look, I found other things."

"My poor papa!" said Star, with an air of great satisfaction.

The Captain nodded. "Yer poor pa," he said, "and two others with him. How did I know he was your poor pa? Along of his havin' your poor ma's pictur hung round his neck. And a fine-lookin' man he was, to be sure!"

"And his name was 'H. M.'!" cried the child, eagerly.

"Them was the letters of it!" assented the Captain. "Worked on his shirt and hank'cher, so fine as ever was. Well, Jewel Bright, when I seed all this, I says, 'January,' says I, 'here's Christian corpses, and they must have Christian burial!' I says. So I brought 'em all up to the house, and laid 'em comfortable; and then I gave you a good drink of warm milk (you'd been sleepin' like a little angil, and only waked up to smile and crow and say ' 'Tar'), and gave you a bright spoon to play with; and then I rowed over to shore to fetch the minister and the crowner, and everybody else as was proper. You don't care about this part, Honeysuckle, and you ain't no need to, but everything was done decent and Christian, and your parents and the other two laid peaceful under the big pine tree. Then the minister, when 'twas all done, he says to me, 'And now, my friend,' he says, 'I'll relieve you of the child, as would be a care to you, and I can find some one to take charge of it!' he says. 'Meanin' no disrespect, Minister,' I says, 'don't think it! The Lord has His views, you'll allow, most times, and He had 'em when He sent the child here. He could have sent her ashore by the station jest as easy,' I says, 'if so be't had seemed best; but He sent her to me,' I says, 'and I'll keep her.' 'But how can you bring up a child?' he says, 'alone, here on a rock in the ocean?' he says. 'I've been

thinking that over, Minister,' I says, 'ever since I holt that little un in my arms, takin' her from her dead mother's breast,' I says; 'and I can't see that there's more than three things needed to bring up a child,—the Lord's help, common sense, and a cow. The last two I hev, and the fust is likely to be round when a man asks for it!' I says. So then we shakes hands, and he doesn't say nothin' more, 'cept to pray a blessin' for me and for the child. And the blessin' kem, and the blessin' stayed, Star Bright; and there's the end of the story, my maid.

"And now it's time these two eyes were shut, and only the top star shinin' in the old tower. Good night, Jewel! Good night, and God bless you!"

CHAPTER III

INTRODUCING IMOGEN AND BOB

"Imogen!" said Star, looking up from her book, "I don't believe you have been listening!"

Imogen looked up meekly, but made no attempt to deny the charge.

"You *must* listen!" said the child, sternly. "First place, it's beautiful: and besides, it's very rude not to listen when people read. And you ought *not* to be rude, Imogen!" After which short lecture, Star turned to her book again,—a great book it was, lying open on the little pink calico lap,—and went on reading, in her clear childish voice:

    " 'Over hill, over dale,
        Thorough bush, thorough brier,
    Over park, over pale,
        Thorough flood, thorough fire,
    I do wander everywhere,
    Swifter than the moony sphere;
    And I serve the fairy queen,
    To dew her orbs upon the green:'

Do you know what a fairy is, Imogen?" asked Star, looking up again suddenly.

But this time it was very evident that Imogen (who was, in truth, a large white cow, with a bell round her neck) was paying no at-

tention whatever to the reading; for she had fairly turned her back, and was leisurely cropping the short grass, swaying her tail in a comfortable and reflective manner the while.

Star sprang to her feet, and seizing the delinquent's horns, shook them with all her might.

"How dare you turn your back when I am reading?" she cried. "I'm just ashamed of you! You're a disgrace to me, Imogen. Why, you are as ignorant as a—as—as a lobster! And you a great cow with four whole legs. A—a—ah! shame on you!"

Imogen rubbed her head deprecatingly against the small pink shoulder, and uttered a soft and apologetic "moo;" but Star was not ready to be mollified yet.

"And you know it's my *own* book, too!" she continued, reproachfully. "My own Willum Shakespeare, that I love more—well, no! not *more* than I love you, Imogen, but just as much, and almost nearly half as much as I love Daddy Captain.

"But after all," she added, with a smile flitting over her frowning little face, "after all, you poor dear, you *are* only a cow, and I don't suppose you know." And then she hugged Imogen, and blew a little into one of her ears, to make her wink it, and the two were very friendly again.

"Perhaps you would like to know, Imogen," said Star, confidentially, seating herself once more on the ground, "*why* I am so fond of Willum Shakespeare. So I will tell you. It is really part of *my* story, but Daddy Captain didn't get as far as that last night, so I think I will tell it to you. Well!" she drew a long breath of enjoyment, and, clasping her hands round her knees, settled herself for a "good talk."

"Well, Imogen: you see, at first I was a little baby, and didn't know anything at all. But by and by I began to grow big, and then Daddy Captain said to himself, 'Here's a child,' he says, 'and a child of gentlefolks, and she mustn't grow up in ignorance, and me doing my duty by her poor pa and ma,' he says. So he rows over to the town, and he goes to the minister (the same minister who came over here before), and he says, 'Good morning, Minister!' and the minister shakes him by the hand hearty, and says, 'Why, Captain January!' he says, 'I'm amazing glad to see you. And how is the child?' And Daddy says, 'The child is a-growing with the flowers,' he says; 'and she's a-growing like the flowers. Show me a rose that's as sweet and as well growed as that child,' he says, 'and I'll give you my head, Minister.' That's the way Daddy talks, you know, Imogen. And then he told the minister how he didn't want the child (that was me, of course) to grow up in ignorance, and how he wanted to teach me. And the minister asked him was he qualified to teach. 'Not yet, I ain't!' says Daddy Captain, 'but I'm a-going to be. I want a book, or maybe a couple of books, that'll edicate me in a manner all round!' he says. 'I couldn't do with a lot of 'em,' he says, ''cause I ain't used to it, and it makes things go round inside my head. But I think I could tackle two if they was fustrate,' he says. The minister laughed, and told Daddy he wanted a good deal. Then he asked him if he had the Good Book. That's the Bible, you know, Imogen. Daddy Captain won't let me read that to you, because you are a beast that perish. Poor dear!" she leaned forward and kissed Imogen's pink nose. "And Daddy said *of course* he had that, only the letters weren't so clear as they used to be, somehow, perhaps along of getting wet in his weskit pocket, being he carried it along always. So the minister gave him a *new big* BEAUTIFUL Bible, Imogen! It isn't so new *now,* but it's just as big and beautiful, and I love it. And then he thought for a long time, the minister did, walking about the room and looking at all the books. The whole room was full of books, Daddy says, all on shelves, 'cept some on the floor and the table and the chairs. It made his head go round dreadful to see them all, Daddy says (I mean Daddy's head), and think of anybody reading them. He says he doesn't see how in creation the minister manages to keep his bearings, and look out for a change in the wind, and things that *have* to be done, and read all those books too. *Well!*" she kissed Imogen's nose again, from sheer enjoyment, and threw her head back with a laugh of delight. "I'm coming to it now, Imogen!" she cried. "At last the minister took down a big book—OH! you precious old

thing, how I love you!" (this apostrophe was addressed to the quarto volume which she was now hugging rapturously), "and said, 'Well, Captain January, here's the best book in the world, *next* to the Good Book!' he says. 'You'll take this,' he says, 'as my gift to you and the child; and with these two books to guide you, the child's education won't go far wrong!' he says; and then he gave Daddy the dictionary, too, Imogen; but I sha'n't tell you about that, because it's a brute, and I hate and 'spise it. But—well! *so,* you see, *that* was the way I got my Willum Shakespeare, my joy and my pride, my—"

At this moment a shadow fell upon the grass, and a deep, gruff voice was heard, saying, "Star, ahoy!" The child started up, and turned to meet the newcomer with a joyous smile. "Why, Bob!" she cried, seizing one of his hands in both of hers, and dancing round and round him. "Where did you come from? Why aren't you on the boat?"

"Boat's aground!" replied the person addressed as Bob. He spoke in short, jerky sentences. He was dressed as a seafaring man; had wide, helpless-looking brown eyes, an apologetic smile, and a bass voice of appalling depth and power. "Boat's aground," he repeated, seating himself on the grass and looking about for a stem of grass long enough to put in his mouth. "Hard and fast. Waiting for tide to turn; thought I'd come, pass time o' day."

"And how came you to run her aground?" inquired the child, severely. "A pretty pilot you are! Why, I could steer her myself better than that."

"Fog!" replied the man, in a meek and muffled roar. Then finding a bit of sorrel, he fell upon it with avidity, and seemed to think he had said enough.

"H'm!" said Star, with a disdainful little sniff. "You'd better get Daddy to steer your boat. *He* doesn't mind fog. Are there many people on board?" she added, with an air of interest.

"Heaps!" replied Bob, succinctly. Then, after a pause of meditative chewing: "Like to go aboard? Take ye—boat—Cap'n willin'."

"No, I don't want to go aboard, thank you!" said Star. "I don't like people. But you might just row me round her once, Bob," she added. "I think I should like *that*. But we must wait till Daddy comes, of course."

"Cap'n round?" inquired Bob.

"He's setting the lobster-pots," replied the child. "He'll be back soon. Bob," she added, irrelevantly, a moment after, "I never noticed before that you looked like Imogen. Why, you are the very image of her, Bob! Your eyes and your expression are *exactly* the same."

Bob raised his eyes and surveyed Imogen with a critical air. "Fine cow!" he said at last. "D'no's I mind—'f she doesn't."

"*Isn't* she a fine cow?" cried little Star, patting the meek and graceful head of her favorite. "I don't believe there's another such cow in the world. I *know* there isn't! I think," she added, "I will take a little ride on her, while we are waiting for Daddy Captain. Will you put me up, please, Bob?"

The obedient Bob lifted her as if she were a ball of thistledown, and set her on the broad back of the good cow, who straightway began to pace sedately along the bit of meadow, following the guidance of the small hands which clasped her horns. Ah! Who will paint me that picture, as my mind's eye sees it? The blue of sky and sea, the ripples breaking in silver on silver sand, the jewelled green, where the late dandelions flecked the grass with gold; and in the midst the lovely, laughing child, mounted on the white cow, tossing her cloudy golden hair, and looking back with eyes of delight towards her companion.

The beauty of it all filled the eyes and the heart of Captain January, as he came up among the rocks. He paused, and stood for some time in silence, watching the little well-beloved figure. "Wal!" he said, "if that ain't one of the young-eyed cherubims, then I never seed one, that's all."

At this moment Star caught sight of him. "O Daddy," she cried. "My Daddy Captain, I'm having such a fine ride! It isn't *quite* as high as a heaven-kissing hill, but it's a heaven-kissing cow, for Imogen is really *very* high. Dear Daddy, won't you come and try it? there's plenty of room!"

"Thanky, Peach Blossom!" said the Captain, advancing, and greeting the apologetic Bob with a hearty shake of the hand.

"Thanky kindly, but I don't believe I will try it. Ridin' was never, so as to say, in my line. I'm stiddy enough on my own pins, but defend me from tryin' to git about on another critter's. And how's all with you, Bob? And why ain't you aboard the *Huntress?*"

Bob in the fewest possible words related the mishap which had befallen the boat, and asked if he might take Missy out to see her.

"To be sure! To be sure!" said Captain January. "That'll be a nice trip for ye, Honeysuckle. Put on your bunnit and go with Bob. He'll take good care of ye, Bob will."

And so, by what seemed the merest chance, that lovely afternoon, little Star went with Bob Peet, in his old black boat, to see the steamer *Huntress* aground on a sand-bank off the main shore.

The sea lay all shining and dimpling in the afternoon light, and not a cloud was to be seen overhead. Here and there a white gull was slowly waving his wings through the clear air, and little fish came popping their heads out of the water, just for the pleasure of popping them back again. Star dipped her hands in the blue crystal below, and sang little snatches of song, being light of heart and without a care in the world. They were no nursery songs that she sang, for she considered herself to have outgrown the very few Mother Goose ditties which Captain January had treasured in his mind and heart ever since his mother sang them to him, all the many years ago. She was tired of

"Jacky Barber's coming to town:
  Clear away, gentlemen! clear away, gentlemen!
  One foot up and t'other foot down,
  Jacky Barber's coming to town."

But she loved the scraps of sea-song that the old Captain still hummed over his work: "Baltimore," and "Blow a Man Down," and half a dozen other salt-water ditties: and it might have been strange to less accustomed ears than Bob Peet's to hear the sweet child-voice carolling merrily:

"Boney was a warrior,
    Weigh! heigh! oh!
  Boney was a warrior,

John François!
Boney whipped the Rooshians,
Weigh! heigh! oh!
Boney whipped the Prooshians,
John François!
Boney went to Elba,
Weigh! heigh! oh!" etc.

Bob's oars kept time with the song, and his portentous voice thundered out the refrain with an energy which shook the little skiff from stem to stern. By the time that "Boney" was safely consigned to his grave in sunny France, they were nearing the flats on which the steamer *Huntress* lay, quietly awaiting the turn of the tide.

Star knew the great white boat well, for twice a day she went thundering past Light Island, churning the quiet blue water into foam with her huge paddles, on her way to and from the gay summer city which all the world came to visit. Nearly every day the child would run out on the south rocks to wave a greeting to some of her acquaintances among the crew; for she knew them all, from the black-bearded captain down to the tiniest cabin boy; and they, for their part, were always eager—good souls!—for a smile or a nod from the "Star of Light Island." Not a man of them but envied Bob Peet his privilege of going when he pleased to the lighthouse rock. For Captain January was not fond of visitors, and gave them no encouragement to come, Bob Peet being the single exception to the rule. The Captain liked Bob because he was not "given to clatter," and "knew how to belay his jaw."

"I do love to see a man belay his jaw!" said Captain January, unconsciously quoting the words of another and a more famous captain, the beloved David Dodd. So Bob was free to come and go as he liked, and to smoke his pipe in sociable silence for hours at a time, within the walls of Storm Castle.

"Stop here, Bob!" said Star, with an imperious motion of her hand. "I don't want to go any nearer." The obedient Bob lay on his oars, and both looked up at the great boat, now only a few yards away. The decks were crowded with passengers, who leaned over the railings, idly chatting, or watching the water to see if the tide had turned.

"Sight o' folks," said Bob Peet, nodding towards the afterdeck, which seemed a solid mass of human beings.

"Yes," said the child, speaking half to herself, in a low tone. "It's just like the Tower of Babel, isn't it? I should think they would be afraid. 'And the Lord scattered them abroad from thence upon the face of all the earth.' And it's so *stupid*!" she added, after a moment's pause. "Why don't they stay at home? Haven't they any homes to stay at? Who takes care of their homes while they go sailing about like loons?"

"Folks likes to v'yage," said Bob Peet, with mild toleration. "Heaps—nothin' t' do—hot spells—v'yages." He added, with an approach to a twinkle in his meek and cow-like eyes, "Try it—some day—git tired of ol' Cap'n—ol' rock—pooty soon—take ye—v'yage—"

His speech was interrupted by a sudden and violent dash of water in his face.

"Take that!" cried Star, panting with fury, and flinging the water at him with all her small might. "I wish it was sharp stones, instead of just water. I wish it was needles, and jagged rocks, and quills upon the fretful porkypine,

so I do! How dare you say such things to me, Bob Peet? How dare you?" She paused, breathless, but with flashing eyes and burning cheeks; while Bob meekly mopped his face and head with a red cotton handkerchief, and shook the water from his ears, eyeing her the while with humble and deprecatory looks.

"No offense," he muttered, in apologetic thunder-rumble. "Poor ol' Bob—eh, Missy? Sorry, beg pardon! Never no more. Didn't mean it—nohow!"

The tempest subsided as suddenly as it rose, and Star, with a forgiving nod, took out her own little handkerchief and daintily wiped a few drops from her victim's forehead.

"You're so stupid, Bob," she said, frankly, "that I suppose I ought not to get angry with you, any more than I would with Imogen, though even she provokes me sometimes. So I forgive you, Bob. But if you ever say such a thing again as my getting tired of Daddy, I'll kill you. So now you know!"

"Jes' so!" assented Bob. "Nat'rally! *To b'* sure!"

The sudden splashing of the water had caught many eyes on the deck of the *Huntress,* and people admired the "playfulness" of the pretty child in the little boat. One pair of eyes, however, was sharper than the rest.

"Just look at that child, Isabel!" said a tall, bronzed gentleman who was leaning over the taffrail. "She is a perfect little fury! I never saw a pair of eyes flash so. Very fine eyes they are, too. A very beautiful child. Isabel! Why, my dear, what is the matter? You are ill—faint! Let me—"

But the lady at his side pushed his arm away, and leaned forward, her eyes fixed upon Star's face.

"George," she said, in a low, trembling voice, "I want to know who that child is. I *must* know, George! Find out for me, dear, please!"

As she spoke, she made a sign towards the boat, so earnest, so imperative, that it caught Star's wondering gaze. Their eyes met, and the little child in the pink calico frock, and the stately lady in the India shawl, gazed at each other as if they saw nothing else in the world. The gentleman looked from one to the other in amazement.

"Isabel!" he whispered," the child looks like you. What can this mean?"

But little Star, in the old black boat, cried, "Take me away, Bob! Take me home to my Daddy Captain! *Quick!* Do you hear?"

"Jes' so!" said Bob Peet. "Nat'rally!"

CHAPTER IV

THE VISIT

A gray day! Soft gray sky, like the breast of a dove; sheeny gray sea, with gleams of steel running across; trailing skirts of mist shutting off the mainland, leaving Light Island alone with the ocean; the white tower gleaming spectral among the folding mists; the dark pine tree pointing a sombre finger to heaven; the wet, black rocks, from which the tide had gone down, huddling together in fantastic groups as if to hide their nakedness.

On the little beach two men were slowly pacing up and down, up and down, one silent, the other talking earnestly. Old men, both, with white, reverend hair: one slender and small, the other a son of Anak, big and brawny,—Captain January and the minister.

It was the minister who had been speaking. But now he had done, and they took a few turns in silence before the Captain spoke in reply.

"Minister," he said,—and his voice was strangely altered from the gruff, hearty tone which had greeted his guest fifteen minutes before. "Minister, I ain't a man that's used to hearin' much talk, and it confuses my mind a bit. There's things inside my head that seems to go round and round, sometimes, and put me out. Now, if it isn't askin' too much, I'll git you to go over them p'ints again. Slow, like! Slow, Minister, bearin' in mind that I'm a slow man, and not used to it. This—this lady, she come to your house yisterday, as ever was?"

"Yesterday," assented the minster; and his voice had a tender, almost compassionate tone, as if he were speaking to a child.

"And a fine day it were!" said Captain January. "Wind steady, sou'west by sou'. Fog in the mornin', and Bob Peet run the *Huntress* aground on the bank. I never liked fog, Minister! 'Give me a gale,' I'd say, 'or anythin' short of a cyclone,' I'd say, 'but don't give me fog!' and see now, how it's come about! But it lifted, soon as the harm were done. It lifted, and as fine a day as ever you see."

The minister looked at him in some alarm, but the old man's keen blue eyes were clear and intelligent, and met his gaze openly.

"You're thinkin' I'm crazy, Minister, or maybe drunk," he said, quietly; "but I ain't neither one. I'm on'y takin' it by and large. When a man has been fifteen year on a desert island, ye see, he learns to take things by and large. But I never see good come of a fog yet. Amen! So be it! And so Cap'n Nazro brought the lady to your house, Minister?"

"Captain Nazro came with her," said the minister, "and also her husband, Mr. Morton, and Robert Peet, the pilot. Mrs. Morton had seen little Star in Peet's boat, and was greatly and painfully struck by the child's likeness to a beloved sister of hers, who had, it was supposed, perished at sea, with her husband and infant child, some ten years ago."

"Ten year ago," repeated Captain January, passing his hand across his weather-beaten face, which looked older, somehow, than it was wont to do. "Ten year ago this September. 'He holdeth the waters in the hollow of His hand.' Go on, Minister. The lady thought my little Star, as the Lord dropped out of the hollow of His hand into my arms ten year ago, had a look of her sister."

"She was so strongly impressed by it," the minister continued, quietly, "that, failing to attract Peet's attention as he rowed away, she sent for the captain, and begged him to give her all the information he could about the child. What she heard moved her so deeply that she became convinced of the child's identity with her sister's lost infant. As soon as Peet returned after putting Star ashore, she questioned him even more closely. He, good fellow, refused to commit himself to anything which he fancied you might not like, but he told her of my having performed the last rites over the mortal remains of the child's parents, and Mr. Morton wisely counselled her to go 190

at once to me, instead of coming here, as she at first wished to do. After my interview with her, I am bound to say—"

"Easy now, Minister!" interrupted Captain January. "I'm an old man, though I never knowed it till this day. Easy with this part!"

"I am bound to say," continued the minister, laying his hand kindly on his companion's arm, "that I think there is little doubt of Star's being Mrs. Morton's niece."

"And what if she be?" exclaimed the old sailor, turning with a sudden violence which made the gentle minister start back in alarm. "What if she be? What have the lady done for her niece? Did she take her out o' the sea, as raged like all the devils let loose, and death itself a-hangin' round and fairly howlin' for that child? did she stand on that rock, blind and deef and e'en a'most mazed with the beatin' and roarin' and on'arthly screechin' all round, and take that child from its dead mother's breast, and vow to the Lord, as helped in savin' it, to do as should be done by it? Has she prayed, and worked, and sweat, and laid awake nights, for fear that child's fingers should ache, this ten years past? Has she—" the old man's voice, which had been ringing out like a trumpet, broke off suddenly. The angry fire died out of his blue eyes, and he bowed his head humbly. "I ask yer pardon, Minister!" he said, quietly, after a pause. "I humbly ask yer pardon. I had forgotten the Lord, ye see, for all I was talkin' about Him so glib. I was takin' my view, and forgettin' that the Lord had His. *He* takes things by and large, and nat'rally He takes 'em larger than mortal man kin do. Amen! So be it!" He took off his battered hat, and stood motionless for a few moments, with bent head: nor was his the only silent prayer that went up from the little gray beach to the gray heaven above.

"Well, Minister," he said, presently, in a calm and even cheerful voice, "and so that bein' all clear to your mind, the lady have sent you to take my—to take her niece—the little lady (and a lady she were from her cradle) back to her. Is that the way it stands?"

"Oh, no! No indeed!" cried the kind old minister. "Mrs. Morton would do nothing so cruel as that, Captain January. She is very kind-hearted, and fully appreciates all that you have done for the little girl. But she naturally wants to see the child, and to do whatever is for her best advantage."

"For the child's advantage. That's it!" repeated Captain January. "That's somethin' to hold on by. Go on, Minister!"

"So she begged me to come over alone," continued the minister, "to—to prepare your mind, and give you time to think the matter well over. And she and Mr. Morton were to follow in the course of an hour, in Robert Peet's boat. He is a very singular fellow, that Peet!" added the good man, shaking his head. "Do you think he is quite in his right mind? He has taken the most inveterate dislike to Mr. and Mrs. Morton, and positively refuses to speak to either of them. I could hardly prevail upon him to bring them over here, and yet he fell into a strange fury when I spoke of getting some one else to bring them. He— he is quite safe, I suppose?"

"Wal, yes!" replied Captain January, with a half smile. "Bob's safe, if any one is. Old Bob! So he doesn't like them, eh?"

At that moment his eye caught something, and he said, in an altered voice, "Here's Bob's boat coming now, Minister, and the lady and gentleman in her."

"They must have come much more rapidly than I did," said the minister, "and yet my boy rows well enough. Compose yourself, January! This is a heavy blow for you, my good friend. Compose yourself! Things are strangely ordered in this world. 'We see through a glass darkly'!"

"Not meanin' to set my betters right, Minister," said Captain January, "I never seed as it made any difference whether a man seed or not, darkly or howsumdever, so long as the Lord made *His* views clear. And He's makin' 'em!" he added. "He's makin' 'em, Minister! Amen! So be it!" And quietly and courteously, ten minutes later, he was bidding his visitors welcome to Light Island, as if it were a kingdom, and he the crownless monarch of it. "It's a poor place, Lady!" he said, with a certain stately humility, as he helped Mrs. Morton out of the boat. "Good anchorage for a shipwrecked mariner like me, but no place for ladies or—or them as belongs to ladies."

"O Captain January!" cried Mrs. Morton,

who was a tall, fair woman, with eyes like Star's own. "What shall I say to you? I must seem to you so cruel, so heartless, to come and ask for the child whom you have loved and cared for so long. For that is what I have come for! I must speak frankly, now that I see your kind, honest face. I have come to take my sister's child, for it is my duty to do so." She laid both hands on the old man's arm, and looked up in his face with pleading, tearful eyes.

But Captain January's face did not move as he answered, quietly, "It is your duty, Lady. No question o' that, to my mind or any. But," he added, with a wistful look, "I'll ask ye to do it easy, Lady. It'll be sudden like for the—for the young lady. And—she ain't used to bein' took sudden, my ways bein' in a manner slow. You'll happen find her a little quick, Lady, in her ways, she bein' used to a person as was in a manner slow, and havin' to be quick for two, so to say. But it's the sparkle o' gold, Lady, and a glint o' diamonds."

But the lady was weeping, and could not answer; so Captain January turned to her husband, who met him with a warm grasp of the hand, and a few hearty and kindly words.

"And now I'll leave ye with the minister for a minute, Lady and Gentleman," the Captain said; "for Bob Peet is a-signallin' me as if he'd sprung a leak below the water line, and all hands goin' to the bottom."

Bob, who had withdrawn a few paces after beaching his boat, was indeed making frantic demonstrations to attract the Captain's attention, dancing and snapping his fingers, and contorting his features in strange and hideous fashion.

"Well, Bob," said the old man, walking up to him, "what's up with you, and why are ye h'istin' and lowerin' your jib in that on'arthly fashion?"

Bob Peet seized him by the arm, and led him away up the beach. "Cap'n," he said, looking round to make sure that they were out of hearing of the others, "I can't touch a lady—not seamanly! But 'f you say the word—knock gen'l'm'n feller—middle o' next week. Say the word, Cap'n! Good's a meal o' vittles t' me—h'ist him over cliff!"

CHAPTER V

CAPTAIN JANUARY'S STAR

And where was little Star, while all this was going on down on the beach? Oh, she had been having a delightful afternoon. It was cloudy, and Daddy was going to be busy, so she had determined to spend an hour or so in her own room, and enjoy all the delights of "dressing up." For the great chest that had been washed ashore from the wreck, the day after she herself had come to the island, was full of clothes belonging to her "poor mamma"; and as we have seen, the little woman was fully inclined to make use of them.

Beautiful clothes they were; rich silks and velvets, with here and there cloudy laces and strange webs of Eastern gauze. For she had been a beautiful woman, this poor mamma, and it had been the delight of Hugh Maynard, her proud and fond husband, to deck his lovely wife in all rare and precious stuffs. Some of them were stained with sea-water, and many of the softer stuffs were crumpled and matted hopelessly, but that mattered little to Star. Her eyes delighted in soft, rich colors, and she was never weary of turning them over and over, trying them on, and "playing s'pose" with them.

"S'pose," she would say, "my poor mamma was going to a banquet, like the Capulet one, or Macbeth's. Oh, no! 'cause that would have been horrid, with ghosts and daggers and things. S'pose it was the Capulets! Then she would put on this pink silk. Isn't it pretty, and soft, and creamy? Just like the wild roses on the south side of the meadow, that I made a wreath of for Imogen on her birthday. Dear Imogen! It was so becoming to her. Well, so my poor mamma put it on—so! and then she paced through the hall, and all the lords turned round and said, 'Mark'st thou yon lady?' 'Cause she was so beautiful, you know. This is the way she paced!" and then the little creature would fall to pacing up and down the room, dragging the voluminous pink folds behind her, her head thrown back, and a look of delighted pride lighting up her small face.

It was the funniest little place, this room of Star's, the queerest, quaintest little elfin bower! It was built out from the south side of the tower, almost like a swallow's nest, only a swallow's nest has no window looking out on the blue sea. There was a little white bed in a corner, and a neat chest of drawers, and a washstand, all made by Captain January's skilful hands, and all shining and spotless. The bare floor was shining too, and so was the little looking glass which hung upon the wall. And beside the looking glass, and above it, and in fact all over the walls, were trophies and wonders of all kinds and descriptions. There was the starfish with ten legs, pinned up in sprawling scarlet; and there, beside him, the king of all the sea urchins, resplendent with green and purple horns. And here were ropes of shells, and branches of coral, and over the bed a great shining star, made of the delicate gold shells. That was Daddy's present to her on her last birthday. Dear Daddy! There, sitting in the corner, was Mrs. Neptune, the doll which Captain January had carved out of a piece of fine wood that had drifted ashore after a storm. Her eyes were tiny black snail shells, her hair was of brown sea-moss, very thick and soft ("though as for combing it," said Star, "it is im-*possible!*"), and a smooth pink shell was set in either cheek, "to make a blush." Mrs. Neptune was somewhat battered, as Star was in the habit of knocking her head against the wall when she was in a passion; but she maintained her gravity of demeanor, and always sat with her back perfectly straight, and with an air of protest against everything in general.

In the window stood the great chest, at once a treasure-chamber and a seat; and over it hung one of the most precious things of Star's little world. It was a string of cocoanut shells. Fifteen of them there were, and each one was covered with curious and delicate carving, and each one meant a whole year of a man's life. "For the nuts was ripe when we kem ashore, my good mate Job Hotham and me, on that island. So when the nuts was ripe agin, ye see, Jewel Bright, we knowed 'twas a year since we kem. So I took my jackknife and carved this first shell, as a kind o' token, ye know, and not thinkin' there'd be so many to carve." So the first shell was all covered

with ships: fair vessels, with sails all set, and smooth seas rippling beneath them,—the ships that were even then on their way to rescue the two castaways. And the second was carved with anchors, the sign of hope, and with coils of rope, and nautical instruments, and things familiar to seamen's eyes. But the third was carved with stars, and sickle-curved moons, and broad-rayed suns, "Because, ye see, Peach Blossom, 'arthly hope bein' as ye might say foundered, them things, and what was above 'em, stayed where they was; and it stiddied a man's mind to think on 'em, and to make a note on 'em as fur as might be." And then came one covered with flowers and berries, and another with fruits, and another with shells, and so on through the whole fifteen. They hung now in little Star's window, a strange and piteous record; and every night before the child said her prayers, she kissed the first and last shell, and then prayed that Daddy Captain might forget the "dreadful time," and never, never think about it again.

So, on this gray day, when other things were going on out-of-doors, Star was having a "good time" in her room. She had found in the treasure-chest a short mantle of gold-colored velvet, which made "a just exactly skirt" for her, the two ends trailing behind enough to give her a sense of dignity, but not enough to impede her movements. "For I am not a princess today!" she said; "I am delicate Ariel, and the long ones get round my feet so I can't run." Then came a long web of what she called "sunshine," and really it might have been woven of sunbeams, so airy-light was the silken gauze of the fabric. This my lady had wound round and round her small person with considerable art, the fringed ends hanging from either shoulder, and making, to her mind, a fair substitute for wings. "See!" she cried, running to and fro, and glancing backward as she ran. "They wave! They really do wave! Look, Mrs. Neptune! Aren't they lovely? But you are envious, and that is why you look so cross. 'Merrily, merrily, shall I live now, under the blossom that hangs on the bough.'" She leaped and danced about the room, light and radiant as a creature of another world: then stopped, to survey with frowning brows her little blue

stockings and stout laced boots. "Ariel *never* wore such things as those!" she declared; "if you say she did, Mrs. Neptune, you show your ignorance, and that is all I have to say to you." Off came the shoes and stockings, and the little white feet were certainly much prettier to look at. "Now," cried Star, "I will go downstairs and wait for Daddy Captain, and perhaps he will think I am a real fairy. Oh, wouldn't that be fun? I am *sure* I look like one!" and down the stairs she flitted like a golden butterfly. Once in the kitchen, the housewife in her triumphed for a moment over the fairy: she raked up the fire, put on more wood, and swept the hearth daintily. "But Ariel did such things for Prospero," she said. "I'm Ariel just the same, so I may as well fill the kettle and put some apples down to roast." This was soon done, and clapping her hands with delight the "tricksy spirit" began to dance and frolic anew.

" 'Come unto these yellow sands,
And then take hands!' "

she sang, holding out her hands to invisible companions.

" 'Courtesied when ye have, and kissed
(The wild waves whist!)
Foot it featly here and there.'

"Oh! foot it featly, and feat it footly, and dance and sing, and tootle-ty ting!" cried the child, as she flitted like a golden cloud about the room. Then, as she whirled round and faced the door, she stopped short. Her arms fell by her side, and she stood as if spellbound, looking at the lady who stood in the doorway.

The lady made no motion at first, but only gazed at her with loving and tender eyes. She was a beautiful lady, and her eyes were soft and blue, with a look of tears in them. But there was no answering softness in the starry eyes of the child: only a wide, wild look of wonder, of anger, perhaps of fear. Presently the lady, still silent, raised both hands, and kissed them tenderly to the child; then laid them on her breast, and then held them out to her with a gesture of loving appeal.

"I don't know whether you are a spirit of

health or a goblin damned," said Star; "but anyhow it isn't polite to come into people's houses without knocking, I think. I knowed you were a spirit when you looked at me yesterday, if you did have a red shawl on."

"How did you know that I was a spirit?" asked the lady softly. "Oh, little Star, how did you know?"

" 'Cause you looked like my poor mamma's picture," replied the child, "that my poor papa had round his neck. Are you my mamma's spirit?"

The lady shook her head. "No, darling," she said, "I am no spirit. But I have come to see you, little Star, to tell you something. Will you not let me come in, Sweetheart?"

Star blushed, and hung her head for a moment, remembering Captain January's lessons on politeness and "quarter-deck manners." She brought a chair at once, and in a more gracious tone said (mindful of William Shakespeare's lords and ladies), "I pray you sit!"

The lady sat down, and taking the child's hand, drew her gently towards her. "Were you playing fairy, dear?" she asked, smoothing back the golden hair with loving touch.

Star nodded. "I was delicate Ariel," she said. "I was footing it featly, you know, on these yellow sands. Sometimes I am Puck, and sometimes Titania; but Daddy likes Ariel best, and so do I. Did you ever play it?" she asked, looking up into the kindly face that bent over her.

The lady smiled and shook her head. "No, dear child," she said, still with that motherly touch of the hand on the fair head. "I never thought of such a pretty play as that, but I was very happy as a child playing with my— with my sister. I had a dear, dear sister, Star. Would you like to hear about her?"

"Yes," said Star, with wondering eyes. "Was she a little girl?"

"Such a lovely little girl!" said the lady. "Her hair was dark, but her eyes were like yours, Star, blue and soft. We played together always as children, and we grew up together, two loving, happy girls. Then my sister married: and by and by, dear, she had a little baby. A sweet little girl baby, and she named it Isabel, after me."

"I was a little girl baby, too," said Star, "but I wasn't named anything; I came so: just Star."

"Little Isabel had another name," said the lady. "Her other name was Maynard, because that was her father's name. Her father was Hugh Maynard. Have you ever seen or heard that name, my child?"

Star shook her head. "No!" she said; "my poor papa's name was H. M. It was marked on his shirt and han'k'chief, Daddy says. And my poor mamma's name was Helena, just like Helena in 'Midsummer Night's Dream.' " The motherly hand trembled, and the lady's voice faltered as she said, "Star, my dear sister's name was Helena, too. Is not that strange, my little one?"

The child looked curiously at her. "Where is your dear sister?" she asked. "Why do you cry when you say her name? Is she naughty?"

"Listen, Star," said the lady, wiping the tears from her eyes, and striving to speak composedly.

"My sister made a voyage to Europe, with her husband and her little baby. They spent the summer travelling in beautiful countries; and in the autumn, in September, Star, ten years ago this very year,—think of it, my dear!—they sailed for home. They came in a sailing vessel, because the sea voyage was thought good for your—for my sister. And— and—the vessel was never heard from. There was a terrible storm and many vessels were lost in it."

"Just like my poor mamma's ship," said the child. "Perhaps it was the same storm. Do you think—why do you look at me so?" she cried, breaking off suddenly.

But the lady put both arms round her and drew her close, close, while her tears fell fast on the golden hair. "My darling!" she cried, "my dear, dear little one! It was the same storm; the same storm and the same ship. Your poor mamma was my own sweet sister Helena, and you are my niece, my little Isabel, my own, own little namesake. Will you love me, darling? will you love your Aunt Isabel, and let her care for you and cherish you as your sweet mother would have done?"

Star stood very still, neither returning nor repelling the lady's caresses. She was pale, and her breath came short and quick, but otherwise she showed no sign of agitation. Presently she put up her hand and stroked the lady's cheek gently. "Why do you cry?" she asked, quietly. "My poor mamma is in heaven. Don't you like her to be in heaven? Daddy says it is much nicer than here, and he knows."

Mrs. Morton checked her tears, and smiled tenderly in the little wondering face. "Dear child!" she said, "I do like to have her in heaven, and I will not cry any more. But you have not told me whether you will love me, Star. Will you try, dear? And will you let me call you my little Isabel?"

"I will love you," replied the child, "if Daddy Captain loves you; I will love you very much. But you must not call me that name, 'cause I'm not *it*. I am just Star. *Does* Daddy love you?" she asked; and then, with a sudden note of anxiety in her voice, she exclaimed, "Where is Daddy? Where is my Daddy Captain? Did you see him when you came in?"

Her question was answered by the sound of voices outside; and the next moment the minister appeared, followed by Mr. Morton and Captain January. The old Captain hastened to place a chair for each of the gentlemen by the fireside, and then took his stand against the wall on the further side of the room. He held his weather-beaten cap in his hand, and turned it slowly round and round, considering it attentively. It might have been observed by one quick to notice trifles, that he did not look at the child, though no slightest motion of hers was lost upon him.

"George," said Mrs. Morton, joyously, to her husband, "here is our little niece, dearest Helena's child. She is going to love me, she says, and she will love you, too. Star, my darling, this is your Uncle George. Will you not give him a kiss, and be his little girl as well as mine? We have two little girls at home, and you shall be the third."

Star went obediently to Mr. Morton, who kissed her warmly, and tried to take her on his knee. "You are taller than our Grace," he said, "but I don't believe you are as heavy, my dear. Grace is just your age, and I am sure you will be great friends."

But Star slipped quietly from his arms, and, running to the Captain, took one of his hands in both of hers and kissed it. "I am Daddy Captain's little girl!" she said, looking round bravely at the others. "Why do you talk as if I belonged to you?" Then seeing the trouble in Mrs. Morton's face, she added, "I *will* love you, truly I will, and I will call you Aunt Isabel; but I cannot belong to different people, 'cause I'm only just one. Just Captain January's Star."

She looked up in the old man's face with shining eyes, but no tender, confident look returned her glance. The brown hand trembled between her two little white palms; the keen blue eyes were still bent fixedly upon the old woollen cap, as if studying its texture; but it was in a quiet and soothing tone that the Captain murmured:

"Easy, Jewel Bright! Easy, now! Helm steady, and stand by!"

There was a moment of troubled silence; and then the old minister, clearing his throat, spoke in his gentle, tranquil voice. "My dear child," he said, "a very strange thing has come to pass; but what seems strange to us is doubtless clear and simple to the Infinite Wisdom above us. You have been a faithful and loving child, little Star, to your beloved guardian and friend here, and no father could have cared for you more tenderly than he has done. But the tie of blood is a strong one, my dear, and should not be lightly set aside. This lady is your own near relation, the sister of your dear dead mother. Through the merciful providence of God, she has been led to you, and she feels it her duty to claim you, in the name of your parents. We have considered the matter carefully, and we all feel that it is right that you should hereafter make your home with her and your uncle. This may be painful to you, my dear; but you are a good and intelligent child, and you will understand that if we give you pain now, it is to secure your future good and happiness."

He paused; and all eyes, save those keen blue ones which were studying so carefully the texture of the battered woollen cap, turned anxiously on the child. A deep flush passed over Star's face; then vanished, leaving it deadly pale, a mask of ivory with eyes of flame. When she spoke, it was in a low, suppressed voice, wholly unlike her own.

"You may kill me," said the child, "and take my body away, if you like. I will not go while I am alive."

She turned her eyes from one to the other, as if watching for the slightest motion to approach her.

Mrs. Morton, in great distress, spoke next. "My darling, it grieves me to the heart to take you from your dear, kind Daddy. But think, my Star; you are a child now, but you will soon be a woman. You cannot grow up to womanhood in a place like this. You must be with your own people, and have companions of your own age. My children will be like your own sisters and brothers. My dear, if you could only know how they will love you, how we shall all cherish and care for you!"

"When I am dead?" asked Star. "It will make no difference to me, your love, for I shall be dead. I will not go alive."

"Oh, Captain January!" cried Mrs. Morton, turning to the old man with clasped hands. "Speak to her! She will listen to you. Tell her—tell her what you said to me. Tell her that it is right for her to go; that you wish her to go!"

The old man's breathing was heavy and la-

bored, and for a moment it seemed as if he strove in vain for utterance; but when he spoke, his voice was still soothing and cheerful, though his whole great frame was trembling like a withered leaf. "Star Bright," he said (and between almost every word he paused to draw the short, heavy breath), "I always told ye, ye 'member, that ye was the child of gentlefolks. So bein', 'tis but right that you should have gentle raisin' by them as is yer own flesh and blood. You've done your duty, and more than your duty, by me. Now 'tis time ye did your duty by them as the Lord has sent to ye. You'll have—my—my respeckful love and duty wherever you go, my dear, and you growin' up to be a beautiful lady, as has been a little wild lass. And you'll not forget the old Cap'n, well I know, as will be very comf'table here—"

But here the child broke out with a wild, loud cry, which made all the others start to their feet. "Do you want me to go?" she cried. "Look at me, Daddy Captain! You *shall* look at me!" She snatched the cap from his hands and flung it into the fire, then faced him with blazing eyes and quivering lip. "Do you want me to go? Are you tired of me?"

Heavier and heavier grew that weight on Captain January's chest: shorter and harder came his breath. His eyes met the child's for a moment, then wavered and fell. "Why—honey—" he said, slowly, "I—I'm an old man now—a very old man. And—and—an old man likes quiet, ye see: and—I'd be quieter by myself, like; and—and so, honey—I—I'd like ye to go."

"*You lie!*" cried the child; and her voice rang like a silver trumpet in the startled ears of the listeners. "You lie to me, and you lie to God: and you *know* you lie!"

The next moment she had sprung on to the low windowsill, then turned for an instant, with her little hands clenched in menace, and her great eyes flashing fire that fell like a burning touch on every heart. Her fantastic dress gleamed like a fiery cloud against the gray outside: her hair fell like a glory about her vivid, shining face. A moment she stood there, a vision, a flying star, trailing angry light, never to be forgotten by those who saw; then, like a flash, she vanished.

Captain January tottered to his old chair and sat down in it. "The child is right, Lady and Gentleman!" he said. "I lied! I lied to my God, and to the little child who loved me. May God and the child forgive me!" And he hid his face in his hands, and silence fell for a moment.

Then Mr. Morton, who had walked hastily to the window, and was doing something with his handkerchief, beckoned to his wife. "Isabel," he said, in a low tone, "I will not be a party to this. It's an atrocious and vindictive outrage. I—I—you are not the woman I took you for, if you say another word to that old angel. Let him have the child, and send him one or two of your own into the bar—" but Isabel Morton, laughing through her tears, laid her hand over her husband's lips for a moment. Then going to the old man's chair, she knelt down by it, and took his two hands in hers.

"Captain January!" she said, tenderly. "Dear, dear Captain January! The lie is forgiven: I am very, very sure it is forgiven in heaven, as it will be forgiven in the child's loving heart. And may God never pardon me, if ever word or look of mine come again between you and the child whom God gave you!"

The gray evening was closing in around the lighthouse tower. The guests were gone, and Captain January sat alone beside the fire in his old armchair. The window was still open, for the air was soft and mild. The old man's hands were clasped upon his knee; his heart was lifted as high as heaven, in silent prayer and praise.

Suddenly, at the window, there was a gleam of yellow, a flitting shape, a look, a pause; then a great glad cry, and Star flitted like a ray of moonlight through the window, and fell on Captain January's breast.

"Daddy," she said, breaking the long, unhappy silence, "dear Daddy, I am sorry I burned your horrid old cap!"

CHAPTER VI

THE SIGNAL

Quietly passed the days, the weeks, the months, in the lonely tower on the rock fronting the Atlantic surge. Winter came, and folded it in a white mantle, and decked it with frost-jewels. Like a pillar of ice, the tower shone in the keen brilliance of the northern sun; but within was always summer, the summer of perfect peace and contentment. To the child Star, winter was always a season of great delight; for Captain January had little to occupy him out-of-doors, and could devote much of his time to her. So there were long, delightful "jackknife times," as Star called them, when the Captain sat fashioning all sorts of wonderful trifles with his magic knife, the child sitting at his elbow and watching him with happy eyes. There were "story times," instituted years before, as soon as Star had learned to sew on patchwork; for as for sewing *without* a story to listen to, *"that,"* said Star, "is against my nature, Daddy. And you don't want me to do things that are against my nature, do you?" So whenever the squares of gay calico came out, and the golden head bent to and fro over them, like a paradise bird hovering over a bed of gaudy flowers, the story came out, too, between puffs of the pipe, while the fire crackled a cheery accompaniment, sputtering defiance to the wind that whistled outside. Some tale of the southern seas, and the wild tropic islands, of coral reefs and pearl-fisheries, sharks and devilfish; or else a whaling story, fresh and breezy as the north, full of icebergs, and seal-hunts over the cracking floes, polar bears, and all the wild delights of whale-fishing.

Then, on fine days (and oh, but the days are fine, in these glorious northern winters!) there was much joy to be had out-of-doors. For there was a spot in the little meadow,—once of gold-flecked emerald, now of spotless pearl, —a spot where the ground "tilted," to use Star's expression, suddenly down to a tiny hollow, where a fairy spring bubbled out of the rock into a fairy lake. In summer, Star rather despised this lake, which was, truth to tell, only twenty feet long and ten feet wide. It was very nice for Imogen to drink from and to stand in on hot days, and it did many lovely things in the way of reflecting blue skies and fleecy clouds and delicate traceries of leaf and bough; but as water, it seemed a very trifling thing to a child who had the whole sweep of the Atlantic to fill her eyes, and who had the breakers for her playfellows and gossips.

But in winter, matters were different. All the laughing lips of ripples, all the white tossing crests of waves, must content themselves with the ice-bound rocks, till spring should bring them their child-comrade again; and the little sheet of dark crystal in the hollow of the meadow had things all its own way, and mirrored back her bright face every day. The little red sled, launched at the top of the "tilt," came skimming down the slope, and shot like an arrow over the smooth ice, kept always clear of snow by the Captain's ever-busy hands; or else, when tired of coasting, the child would plant her small feet wide apart, and slide, and run, and slide again, till the pond could have cracked with pleasure, if such a thing had been in accordance with its principles.

But of all the joyous hours, none was more welcome to the child than that after the simple supper was cleared away and the room "redded up." Then, while fire and lamplight made their merriest cheer, the table was drawn up to the warmest spot; Star took her place upon Captain January's knee, and the two heads, the silver one and the golden, bent in absorbed interest over "Willum Shakespeare" or the Good Book.

Generally the Captain read aloud, but sometimes they read the parts in turn; and again sometimes the child would break off, and recite whole passages alone, with a fire and pathos which might have been that of Maid Marjorie, swaying at her childish will the heart of Sir Walter and his friends.

So quietly, in the unbroken peace which love brightened into joy, the winter passed.

At Christmas, they had, as usual, a visit from the faithful Bob, who brought all his many pockets full of candy and oranges and all manner of "truck," as he called it, for Missy Star. Also he brought a letter and a box directed only to "Captain January's Star."

201

The letter, which the child opened with wondering eagerness, being the first she had ever received, was from Mrs. Morton. It was full of tender and loving words, wishes for Christmas cheer and New Year blessing, and with it was a photograph of the beautiful face, its soft and tender eyes, which Star remembered so well. On the back was written, "For Little Star, from Aunt Isabel." And the box? Why, that was quite as wonderful in its way. For it contained a most beautiful pipe for the Captain, of sweet brierwood, mounted in silver; and oh! oh! such a doll! Other children have seen such dools, but Star never had; a blue-eyed waxen beauty, with fringed lashes that opened and shut, rose-leaf cheeks, and fabulous wealth of silky flaxen curls. Also it had a blue velvet frock, and its underclothing was a wonder to behold; and the box was full of other frocks and garments.

Star took the doll in her arms with delighted awe, and seemed for a few moments absorbed in her new treasure. Presently, however, a shadow crossed her bright face. She glanced at Bob and the Captain, and seeing that they were both engaged in busy talk, she quietly went up to her own room, carrying the doll with her. Here she did a strange thing. She crossed the room to the corner where Mrs. Neptune sat, with her back rigid, protesting against circumstances, and set the radiant stranger down beside her; then, with her hands clasped behind her, and brows bent, she considered the pair long and attentively. Truly they were a strange contrast: the delicate, glowing, velvet-clad doll, and the battered old wooden image, with eyes of snail-shells and hair of brown sea-moss. But when Star had finished her scrutiny, she took the beautiful doll, and buried it deep under velvets and satins at the very bottom of the great chest. This done, she kissed Mrs. Neptune solemnly, and proceeded to adorn her with a gorgeous Eastern scarf, the very gayest her treasure-house could afford.

Meanwhile, in the room below, the talk went on, grave and earnest. Troubled it was, too, on one side; for though the Captain sat quietly in his chair, and spoke in his usual cheerful voice, Bob Peet's rough tones were harsh and broken, and he rose from his place once or twice and moved uneasily about the room.

"Cap'n," he said, " 'tain't so. Don't tell me! Strong man—hearty—live twenty years yet—like's not thirty! Uncle o' mine—Punksquid—hundred and three—peart's chicken."

Captain January puffed at his pipe in silence for some minutes. "Bob," he said, presently, "it ain't always as it's given to a man to know his time. I've allers thought I should take it particular kind if it 'corded with the Lord's views to let me know when He was ready for me. And now that He *has* let me know, and moreover has set my mind that easy about the child that it's a pleasure to think of, why, it ain't likely I shall take it anyway *but* kind. Thankin' you all the same, Bob, as have been a good mate to me, and as I sha'n't forget wherever I am. But see now!" he added, hastily, hearing a sound in the room above. "You understand, Bob; I h'ist that signal, as it might be tomorrow, and I keep her flyin' night and day. And so long as you see her flyin', you says, 'Cap'n's all right so far!' you says. But you keep a sharp lookout; and if some mornin' you don't see her, you says, 'Sailin' orders!' you says, and then you calls Cap'n Nazro, as never failed in a kindness yet, nor ain't likely to, to take the wheel, and you put for this island. And Cap'n Nazro he takes the *Huntress* in, and then goes straightway and sends a telegraft to the lady and gentleman, sayin' as Cap'n January has sailin' orders, and they please to come and take the child, as lawfully to them belongs. And you, Bob,—" the old man's steady voice faltered a little, as he laid his hand on the other's arm, —"you'll do all you can, well I know. For she'll take it hard, ye see. She has that depth o' love in her little heart, and never nobody *to* love 'cept me since she were a baby, that she'll take it cruel hard. But the Lord'll have her in mind! He'll have her in mind! And you'll stand by, Bob, and bear a hand till the lady and gentleman come."

Bob Peet held out his honest brown hand, and the two men shook hands with a certain solemnity; but before either of them could speak again, Star came singing down the stairs, and summoned them both to play at ball with oranges.

And so it came to pass that a little blue signal was hoisted at the top of the white tower, and fluttered there bravely in sun and wind. And every time the *Huntress* went thundering by (which was twice a week at this season instead of every day), Bob Peet looked out anxiously from the wheel-house window, and seeing the little banner, took cheer, and rubbed his hands and said, "Cap'n's all right so far!"

Spring came, and the little meadow was green again. Robins and bluebirds fluttered above the great pine tree, and swallows built their nests under the eaves of the tower itself. The child Star sang with the birds, and danced with the dancing leaves, all unconscious of what was coming; but the old Captain's steps grew slower and heavier, day by day, and the cheery voice grew feeble, and lost its hearty ring, though never its cheeriness. "I'll set here in the porch, Jewel Bright," he would say, when the child begged him to come for a scramble on the rocks. "I think I'll jest set here, where I can see ye an' hear to ye. I'm gittin' lazy, Star Light; that's the truth. Yer old Daddy's gittin' lazy, and it's comf'tabler settin' here in the sun, than scramblin' round the rocks.

And Star would fling herself on his neck, and scold and caress him, and then go off with a half-sense of disappointment to her play. Very, very careful Captain January had to be, lest the child should suspect that which he was determined to keep from her to the last. Sometimes he half thought she must suspect, so tender was she in these days; so thoughtful, so mindful of his lightest wish. But " 'tis only the woman growin' up in her," he decided; and looking back, he remembered that she had not once broken his pipe (as she had been used to do every three or four weeks, in her sudden rages) since last September.

At last there came a day when the Captain did not even go out to the porch. It was a lovely May morning, bright and soft, with wreaths of silvery fog floating up from the blue water, and much sweet sound of singing birds and lapping waves in the air. Making some pretense of work at his carpenter's bench, the old man sent Star out to loose the cow and lead her to the water; and when she was gone, he tottered to his old chair and sat

down heavily. There was no pain now, only a strange numbness, a creeping coldness, a ringing in the ears. If it might "seem right" to let him wait till the *Huntress* came by! "It's nearly time," he said, half aloud. "Nearly time, and 'twould be easier for the child."

At this moment, through the open doorway, came the silver sound of Star's voice. "But I don't think there can be any harm in my just telling you a little about it, Imogen. And the floor is the paved work of a sapphire: sapphire is a stone, just like the water over there, in the bluest place, and oh! so clear and bright, Daddy says. He saw one once. And there will be most beautiful music, Imogen. Oh! You can't think what lovely music Daddy Captain will play on a harp. I know he will, 'cause he will be a spirit of just men made perfect: and that will be a *great* thing, Imogen; for he has never known how to play on anything before: and—" Ah! The sweet, childish prattle! But already it was growing faint upon the old man's ears.

"Star Bright!" he called; and the dancing shape came flying, and stood on tiptoe in the doorway. Steady, now, January! Keep your

voice steady, if there is any will left in you. Keep your head turned a little away, lest there be any change in your face, yet not turned enough to make her wonder. "Star Bright," said Captain January, "it's about—time—for the *Huntress*—to be along, isn't it?"

"Yes, Daddy," said the child; "she's just in sight now. Shall I go down and wave to Bob as he goes by?"

"Yes, Honeysuckle," said the old man. "And—and wait to see if he comes ashore. I think—likely—Bob'll come ashore to-day. He was goin' to bring—somethin'—for me. Is ther a squall comin' up, Jewel Bright?"

"A squall, Daddy?" said the child wondering. "Why, there isn't a cloud in the sky."

"Jes' so!" said Captain January. "I—only jist asked. Good-bye, Star Bright."

"Dear Daddy! Good-bye!" cried the child, and she sped away over the rocks.

So dark! And not a cloud in the sky. If he might have looked once more, with those fast-darkening eyes, at the little blessed face which held all the world in it! If he could call her back now, and kiss her once more, and hold her little hand.

Quite dark now. But that does not matter. Slowly the old man raises himself; feels for the wall, creeps along beside it. Here is the line. Is there any strength left in that be-numbed arm? Yes! "For the child, dear Lord, and Thou helpin' me, as ever has been!"

Down comes the signal, and the old man creeps back to his chair again, and composes himself decently, with reverent, folded hands, and head bowed in waiting. "'He holdeth the waters in the hollow of His hand. Behold, He taketh up the isles as a very little thing,' Amen! So be it!"

Wave, little Star! wave your little blue apron from the rocks, and laugh and clap your hands for pleasure, as the ripples from the steamer's bow break in snowy foam at your feet. Bend to your oar, Bob Peet, and send your little black boat flying over the water as she never flew before! And press on, friendly *Huntress,* to your port, whence the winged message may speed on its way to the stately lady with the tender eyes, who waits for tidings in her distant home.

Captain January's last voyage is over and he is already in the haven where he would be.